DOUBLEDAY
CELEBRATES
100 YEARS OF
EXCELLENCE

The New York Public Library Collector's Editions are illustrated with original art and handwritten letters, diaries, and manuscripts from the collections of the Library. They are designed to evoke the world of the writer and the book, and to enhance the pleasure of reading the great works of literature.

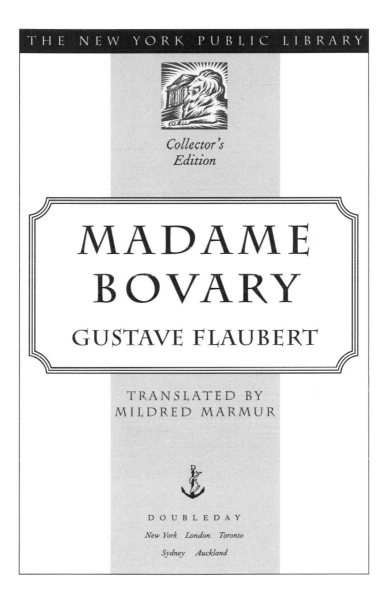

Collector's
Edition

MADAME BOVARY

GUSTAVE FLAUBERT

TRANSLATED BY
MILDRED MARMUR

DOUBLEDAY

New York   London   Toronto

Sydney   Auckland

FRONTISPIECE: *Wood engraving after the 1864 photograph of Gustave Flaubert by Nadar.*

PUBLISHED BY DOUBLEDAY
a division of Bantam Doubleday Dell Publishing Group, Inc.
1540 Broadway, New York, New York 10036

DOUBLEDAY and the portrayal of an anchor with a dolphin
are trademarks of Doubleday, a division of
Bantam Doubleday Dell Publishing Group, Inc.

Book design by Marysarah Quinn

Library of Congress Cataloging-in-Publication Data
Flaubert, Gustave, 1821–1880.
[Madame Bovary.   English]
Madame Bovary / Gustave Flaubert.
p.   cm. — (New York Public Library collector's edition)
Includes bibliographical references.
I. Title.   II. Series.
PQ2246.M2E5   1997
843'.8—DC20   96-36797
                                                                 CIP

ISBN 0-385-48719-3

Printed in the United States of America
May 1997
First New York Public Library Collector's Edition

1   3   5   7   9   10   8   6   4   2

ACKNOWLEDGMENTS

This volume was created with the participation of many people throughout The New York Public Library. For their help in developing this edition of *Madame Bovary*, we are grateful for the contributions of the curators and staffs of the Henry W. and Albert A. Berg Collection of English and American Literature and the Miriam and Ira D. Wallach Division of Art, Prints and Photographs. Special recognition and thanks go to researcher and writer Kenneth Benson; Anne Skillion, Series Editor; and Karen Van Westering, Manager of Publications.

The New York Public Library wishes to extend thanks to its trustees Catherine Marron and Marshall Rose, as well as to Morton Janklow, for their early support and help in initiating this project.

Paul LeClerc, President

Michael Zavelle, Senior Vice President

Marie Salerno, Vice President for Public Affairs

CONTENTS

Madame Bovary, from the Ferroud edition of Flaubert's great novel, with etchings by C. Chessa after the original drawings by Alfred de Richemont, printed in Paris in 1905. A selection of de Richemont's elegant illustrations are reproduced in this Collector's Edition.

ABOUT GUSTAVE FLAUBERT

A romantic who swoons at the thought of a beautiful sunset by the sea, Emma, the heroine of Gustave Flaubert's great novel *Madame Bovary*, is convinced that love should strike with the blinding intensity of a thunderbolt. Unfortunately, she is married to the numbingly dull Charles Bovary, the medical officer of a small town in the French provinces, whose very kindness, patience, and dogged, unquestioning devotion soon become loathsome to his young wife, who longs for the fireworks, delirium, and ecstasy of a grand passion.

She rebels, fleeing from the maddening sameness of her day-to-day existence to an adulterous and ill-fated love affair. The story of her recklessness and audacity, told in a detached, impersonal manner, was to shock many readers when *Madame Bovary* was first published in 1856. But Flaubert went on to become the most influential French novelist of the century, and his heroine has never ceased to intrigue readers and critics alike. The great French poet Charles Baudelaire wrote of her when the book first appeared, "[T]his woman is truly great, but, above all, worthy of pity . . . all women with intellectual pretensions will be grateful to [Flaubert] for having developed the feminine potential to such a degree of power . . ." And, more recently, the Latin American novelist Mario Vargas Llosa wrote an

(27)

I should like you to ponder most carefully
the following fact : ~~Even the~~ a master
of Flaubert's ~~poetical~~ artistic power manages to
transform what he has conceived as
a sordid world inhabitated by frauds
and philistines and mediocrities and
brutes and ~~the~~ wayward ladies, into
~~one~~ one of the most perfect pieces of
poetical fiction known and this
he achieves by bringing all the parts
into harmony, by ~~and~~ the inner
force of style, by all such devices
of form as those we have discussed
when speaking of the counterpoint, or
of the transitions from one theme to another
~~part~~ of foreshadowing and echoes.)

Спокойно ноль ночь.

A page from the autograph manuscript of Vladimir Nabokov's lectures on Madame
Bovary. *According to Nabokov, Flaubert has transformed a world of "frauds and
philistines and mediocrities and brutes" into "one of the most perfect pieces of
poetical fiction known."*

entire book of homage to Emma, with whom he fell helplessly in love for wanting life "to be wholly and completely fulfilled here and now." Today *Madame Bovary* is generally considered one of the greatest novels ever written. For Ernest Hemingway, the author of *Madame Bovary* was, as he told William Faulkner, "our most respected, honored master."

Flaubert was born on December 12, 1821, in Rouen, a bustling provincial capital on the Seine about sixty miles from Paris. His father was the eminent Dr. Achille-Cléophas Flaubert, director and chief surgeon of the Hôtel-Dieu, the municipal hospital. He had an older brother, Achille, who became a doctor, and a greatly beloved younger sister, Caroline. The family lived in a residential wing attached to the Hôtel-Dieu. "The dissecting room of the hospital," he later recalled, "gave on our garden. How many times my sister and I used to climb the trellis, cling to the vines, and peer curiously at the cadavers on their slabs! The sun shone on them, and the same flies that were flitting about us and about the flowers would light on them and come buzzing back to us . . ." He began writing at an early age.

After attending the local *lycée*, Flaubert found himself in Paris, studying—with great repugnance—the "pretty science" of the law. In the summer of 1842, he complained to a friend: "I am so harassed by it all that the other night I dreamed of the law! I felt ashamed at having so dishonored dreaming." Late in January 1844, on the road from Deauville to Honfleur, Flaubert collapsed and was "carried away in a sea of flame." He had suffered a severe seizure, probably some form of epilepsy.

He now abandoned, without regret, the "flatly bourgeois . . . wooden benches of the Law School," and retired to a small eighteenth-century château at Croisset, a village on the Seine a few miles below Rouen. With a commitment almost monastic in its purity, he now devoted his life to writing. Twenty-five years later Flaubert would write George Sand from Croisset: "I see no one, I know nothing about anything, I live like a stuffed bear."

Charles Bovary

Now what about the husband. He is a dull, heavy,
plodding fellow, with no charm, no brains, no
culture, and with a complete set of conventional
notions and habits. He is a philistine, but he also a pathetic human being.

The two following points are of the utmost importance:
what seduces him in Emma and what he finds in her is exactly what
Emma herself is looking for and not finding in
her romantic day-dreams. The iridescent loveliness,
luxury, a dreamy remoteness, poetry, romance —
all this emanates from her personality, all this
is dimly but deeply perceived by Charles. This is one point and I shall share with you some samples
in a moment.) Now the second point is that the
love Charles develops for Emma, almost unwittingly, is a
real feeling, a deep and true, in absolute contrast
to the brutal or frivolous emotions experienced by her
smug and vulgar lovers. So here is the pleasing paradox of the Flaubert
fairytale (remember that all great novels are fairytales):
the dullest and most inept person in his book
is the only one who is redeemed by something,
by a divine something in the all-powerful,
forgiving and unswerving love that he
bears Emma, alive or dead. You will
note that there is yet a fourth character in the book
who is in love with Emma, but that ... I recommend him to your sympathetic attention.

*Nabokov's discussion of Charles Bovary, from the autograph manuscript of his
lectures on* Madame Bovary. *While acknowledging that Emma's hapless husband is
a "dull, heavy, plodding fellow, with no charm, no brains, no culture," Nabokov
here identifies the "pleasing paradox" of Flaubert's masterpiece: that "the dullest
and most inept person in his book is the only one who is redeemed by a divine
something in the all-powerful, forgiving, and unswerving love that he bears Emma,
alive or dead."*

Dr. Flaubert died in January 1846, and within nine weeks, Caroline had succumbed to an infection she had developed after giving birth to her first child. In April, Flaubert wrote to a friend: ". . . my recent bereavements have saddened me but not surprised me. Without feeling them any the less acutely, I have analyzed them as an artist. This task has revived my grief in a melancholy way. Had I expected better things of life, I should have cursed it. That is just what I have not done." A sculptor was commissioned to execute a portrait bust of Caroline, and on a day in late July, Flaubert arrived at the artist's studio in Paris with his sister's death mask. It was a fateful day for the young writer. Louise Colet, a well-known poet and a great beauty, happened to be posing for the sculptor that day, and Flaubert was soon plunged into a tumultuous, ill-starred affair that is now one of the most celebrated in literary history. Colet was to be the recipient of some of Flaubert's most important letters, and they form a particularly fascinating record of his tortuous struggles with *Madame Bovary*, on which he labored for five years.

He worked on this masterpiece with such incredible intensity that his mother was alarmed. "Your mania for sentences," she told him, "has dried up your heart." Flaubert revised the novel incessantly and obsessively. "Writing this book," he told Colet, "I am like a man playing the piano with lead balls attached to his knuckles." But the style which he perfected in *Madame Bovary*—rhythmic, meticulously shaped, sonorous, impersonal—revolutionized the novel. He chose a subject—adultery—worthy of a potboiler, and a cast of characters who are exceptional only because they are entirely unexceptional. Flaubert believed that poetry was as precise a science as geometry, and his gaze was dispassionate. In this, his artistic sensibility seems strikingly modern.

Madame Bovary first appeared serially in the *Revue de France* from October 1 to December 15, 1856. Even though the novel was published—against Flaubert's objections—with some cuts, Flaubert, the printer, and the editor of the *Revue de France* were all charged by the government with having "outraged public morals and religion."

Flaubert's signature.

Flaubert wrote ruefully to his brother that for the "crime of writing in French" he would soon be sitting "on the bench usually occupied by pickpockets and prostitutes." The prosecution presented its case vigorously, but Flaubert and his co-defendants were acquitted. He was now famous, and *Madame Bovary* a *succès de scandale*.

Charles-Augustin Sainte-Beuve, the preeminent French literary critic of the day, recognized that Flaubert was in the vanguard of a new generation of writers. While acknowledging the novel's remarkable power and its author's commanding style, Sainte-Beuve worried that *Madame Bovary* seemed to implicitly deny the importance of the moral and the comforting in a work of art. Flaubert the artist asked himself but one thing: "Is it true?" A celebrated caricature of the day showed Flaubert in an operating room, holding aloft the dissected heart of Emma Bovary, nicely skewered on a very large knife. "Son and brother of eminent doctors," Sainte-Beuve had written, "M. Gustave Flaubert wields the pen as others wield the scalpel."

Although his later novels *Salammbô* (1862) and *Sentimental Education* (1869) were either misunderstood or dismissed by most critics, Flaubert was revered by other writers. Henry James called him a

The book is concerned with adultery and contains situations and allusions that shocked the prude government of Napoleon the Third. *[handwritten manuscript facsimile]*

The second page of the autograph manuscript of Nabokov's lectures on Madame Bovary. *Here, the author of* Lolita (1955)—*itself banned in France and described as "repulsive" by the* New York Times—*explains why* Madame Bovary *ruffled the feathers of so many respectable citizens when it was first published in 1856.*

"novelist's novelist," and his impact on the literary culture which followed him was profound. Nabokov stated the case categorically: "Without Flaubert there would have been no Marcel Proust in France, no James Joyce in Ireland. Chekhov in Russia would not have been quite Chekhov. So much for Flaubert's literary influence."

Flaubert maintained many close friendships with the leading lights of the Parisian literary world, and his correspondence with such distinguished writers as George Sand and Ivan Turgenev ranks him indisputably as one of the world's great letter writers. He died suddenly on May 8, 1880, at Croisset. A press clipping found on his writing table described him as "one of the uncontested masters of the contemporary novel, perhaps the only one who owes nothing to anyone, and whom everyone else has more or less imitated."

ABOUT THIS EDITION

Madame Bovary, c'est moi, d'après moi!: "Madame Bovary is myself—drawn from life!" Thus Flaubert on the real-life model for one of the most compelling characters in world literature. And this to Louise Colet in 1853: "It is a delicious thing to write, to be no longer yourself but to move in an entire universe of your own creating. Today . . . as man and woman, both lover and mistress, I rode in a forest on an autumn afternoon under the yellow leaves, and I was also the horses, the leaves, the wind, the words my people uttered, even the red sun that made them almost close their love-drowned eyes."

With treasure drawn from The New York Public Library's Vladimir Nabokov Archive and its Spencer Collection of fine illustrated books, this edition evokes Flaubert's incomparable heroine by looking at her through the eyes of artists who have been inspired by his wizardry. In the handwritten draft of Nabokov's brilliantly insightful lectures on *Madame Bovary*, one master of enchantment analyzes the "world of fancy" conjured up by another. And in drawings executed for a turn-of-the-century deluxe French edition of the novel, Alfred de Richemont renders Flaubert's imagined world in a manner which ironically might have infuriated the author, for during his lifetime Flaubert forbade illustrations in any of his books.

Emma Bovary made her sensational *début* almost 150 years ago. In this Collector's Edition of Flaubert's masterwork, she continues to captivate.

ORIGINAL HANDWRITTEN MATERIALS

Vladimir Nabokov's Lectures on Madame Bovary. The great Russian-born American novelist and lepidopterist Vladimir Nabokov taught for nearly twenty years at various colleges in the United States before the success of *Lolita* in 1958 allowed him to abandon the lecture halls of Cornell for a life devoted solely to writing. According to his biographer Brian Boyd, the course at Cornell in which Nabokov lectured on a small selection of "supreme masterpieces"—Literature 311–312: Masters of European Fiction—was the most popular academic offering on campus, "eclipsed in student number only by Pete Seeger's folk-song class." As John Updike wrote in his introduction to the published lectures, lucky the students at Cornell who found themselves subject to the "admonitions and intoxications" of Nabokov's "irresistibly artistic sensibility."

The pages reproduced in this edition allow us to look over Nabokov's shoulder as he works out his plan of attack on *Madame Bovary*. They are but four of the fifty-six heavily corrected and annotated hand- and typewritten sheets of his now famous lectures on Flaubert's masterpiece. His estimation of the novel is very high: "Stylistically it is prose doing what poetry is supposed to do." And clearly, he was a dryly witty as well as an iconoclastic guide.

In one characteristic passage Nabokov comments, ". . . I am opposed to those who insist upon the influence of objective social conditions upon the heroine Emma Bovary. Flaubert's novel deals with the delicate calculus of human fate, not the arithmetic of social conditioning." And elsewhere: "We are told that most of the charac-

Introduction.

12 minut[es]

Madame Bovary

Flaub. 1821-1880
Dickens 1812-1870
1

To day —

We start to enjoy our next / yet another masterpiece. yet
another fairytale. Of all the fairy tales we shall enjoy
in this course, the one man Flaubert's story, Mme Bovary
is most romantic fairytale — It is prose doing
what poetry is supposed to do.

A child to whom you read a story may ask you
is the story true — and, if not, demand a true one.
Let us not preserve in this juvenile attitude towards
the books we read.

Of course, if somebody tells you that Mr Smith
has seen a blue man with a green operator whizz by
you do ask: is it true? — because in one way
or another the fact of it is true would affect your whole life, would
be infinite practical consequence to you. But I didn't
ask whether a poem or a novel is true. Let us
remember that literature is of no immense practical
value whatsoever — except in the very special case
of somebody's wishing to become a professor of
literature. Madame Bovary never existed. The
book Bovary shall exist for ever and ever. A book
longer than a girl.

The first page of the autograph manuscript of Vladimir Nabokov's lectures on
Madame Bovary. *At the very beginning of this lecture, Nabokov urges his students
at Cornell not to waste their time asking "whether a poem or a novel is true." And
he goes on: "Let us not kid ourselves; let us remember that literature is of no
practical value whatsoever, except in the very special case of somebody's wishing to
become, of all things, a professor of literature."*

ters in *Madame Bovary* are bourgeois. But one thing that we should clear up once and for all is the meaning that Flaubert gives to the term *bourgeois*. Unless it simply means *townsman,* as it often does in French, the term *bourgeois* as used by Flaubert means 'philistine,' people preoccupied with the material side of life and believing only in conventional values."

The *specifics* of a novel's style and structure were of the utmost interest to Nabokov, and he urged his students to "notice and fondle details" when reading. "We should always remember that the work of art is invariably the creation of a new world, so that the first thing we should do is to study that new world as closely as possible." He drew maps, worked out detailed chronologies, sketched out floor plans, and concocted elaborate diagrams—all in an effort to bring the author's imaginative world to life with as much sensual force as possible.

Nabokov was also passionate about the precise sense of a word and, by extension, its correct translation into another language. A lifetime's immersion in languages other than his native Russian made him extremely sensitive to the nuances of a great stylist like Flaubert. In the first chapter of *Madame Bovary,* poor Charles Bovary is made a laughingstock of at school because he arrives on his first day sporting a completely ridiculous piece of headgear. When Nabokov lectured on this passage, he read aloud Flaubert's description of Charles's cap (the translation greatly revised, of course); and the page from which he read was embellished with a precise and fetching rendering, in carbon pencil with red highlights, of the "pathetic thing" which brought Charles so much grief.

Even Nabokov's instructions for the dreaded blue book examination possessed a bias for precision (and a brio) seldom encountered in the groves of academe:

Clear hand. One blue book. Ink. Think. Abbreviate obvious names (e.g. MB). Do not pad ignorance with eloquence. Un-ning to lawyers, to the judge, remembering when notes fell due and obtaining renewals; and at home she was forever ironing, sewing, washing, keeping an eye on the hired men, figuring their wages. Monsieur, meanwhile, never lifted a finger. He sat smoking in the chimney corner and spitting into the ashes, continually falling into a grumpy doze and waking to utter uncomplimentary remarks.

When she had a child it had to be placed out with a wet nurse. And then later, when the little boy was back with its parents, he was pampered like a prince. His mother stuffed him with jams and jellies; his father let him run barefoot, and fancied himself a disciple of Rousseau to the point of saying he'd be quite willing to have the boy go naked like a young animal. To counter his wife's maternal tendencies he tried to form his son according to a certain virile ideal of childhood and to harden his constitution by subjecting him to strict discipline, Spartan-style. He sent him to bed without a fire, taught him to take great swigs of rum and to ridicule religious processions. But the child was pacific by nature, and such training had little effect. His mother kept him tied to her apron-strings: she made him paper cutouts, told him stories, and conversed with him in endless bitter-sweet monologues full of coaxing chatter. In the isolation of her life she transferred to her baby all her own poor frustrated ambitions. She dreamed of glamorous careers: she saw him tall, handsome, witty, successful—a bridge builder or a judge. She taught him to read, and even, on an old piano she had, to sing two or three sentimental little songs. But from Monsieur Bovary, who cared little for culture, all this brought merely the comment that it was "useless." Could they ever afford to give him an education, to buy him a practice or a business? Besides, "with enough nerve a man could always get ahead in the world." Madame Bovary pursed her lips, and the boy ran wild in the village.

Vladimir Nabokov's teaching copy of the Francis Steegmuller translation of Madame Bovary *(New York, 1957), with Nabokov's annotations.*

less medical advice is produced, nobody will be permitted to retire to the WC.

EDITIONS

Vladimir Nabokov's copy, with his annotations, of the Francis Steegmuller translation of Madame Bovary *(New York: Random House, 1957).* Nabokov was frequently driven to distraction by the infelicities and downright inaccuracies that plagued many of the standard translations which he was forced to assign to his students at Cornell. The first lecture on *Madame Bovary* would usually begin with a sort of housecleaning of the most egregious errors in the translation being used that semester. From the lectern, Nabokov took the offensive: "So before placing in your innocent hands this book, let me give you a list of the worst mistranslations to be corrected in the first sixty or so pages . . ." And a typical examination question might be: "All translations of *Madame Bovary* are full of blunders; you have corrected some of them. Describe Emma's eyes, hands, sunshade, hairdo, dress, shoes."

For several years, Nabokov used the Eleanor Marx Aveling translation of *Madame Bovary* but not without warning his students that it was "full of boners and couched in a style that is in the nature of an insult to Flaubert by its lack of artistic quality." Aveling was, interestingly enough, the daughter of Karl Marx (in his attitude toward the arts, the philistine *par excellence* for Nabokov).

While rather gentle with Steegmuller's translation, Nabokov shows his exasperation, perhaps, with such renderings as "fancied himself a disciple of Rousseau" from the original *"pour faire le philosophe"* by noting the original French in the margin. In one place he circles the title "bridge builder" and notes the more literal and precise translation, "civil engineer." On such details, he always insisted, rests our ability to enter the very particular and painstakingly created "new world" of a great work of the imagination like *Madame Bovary*.

Alfred de Richemont's illustrations for a limited edition of Madame Bovary, *printed in Paris by F. Ferroud in 1905* (p. x and throughout the novel). This sumptuously bound edition of Flaubert's masterwork was once part of the great private collection of French illustrated books assembled by William Augustus Spencer, a New Yorker who lived in Paris around the turn of the century. Spencer also collected contemporary French art, but his great passions were book illustration and bookbinding. He was especially fond of this very beautiful edition of *Madame Bovary*, which he had bound in dark blue crushed morocco with ornaments inlaid in leather of seven different colors. Only 200 copies were printed by Ferroud (the Library's, initialed by Ferroud, is no. 72).

The edition's illustrations—by the Vicomte Alfred Paul Marie Panon Desbassyns de Richemont—have a panache that is unmistakably French, and are characteristic of the sort of elegant illustration that Spencer most admired. The Paris-born de Richemont (1857–1911) was a painter and illustrator who exhibited his work widely, including at the 1893 World's Columbian Exposition in Chicago.

Tragically, Spencer lost his life in the *Titanic* disaster in April 1912. Eight years later, his collection of some 232 illustrated books and a large endowment came to the Library. Now holding more than 10,000 rare books and manuscripts, the Spencer Collection has evolved into one of the world's most important showcases for the art of the book.

"Emma Bovary at the Hotel de Boulogne"—An illustration by Albert-Auguste Fourié from an edition of Madame Bovary *printed in Paris by A. Quantin in 1885* (p. 282). For Flaubert, there were "no noble subjects or ignoble subjects"—style was nothing more or less than "an absolute manner of seeing things." The government censors who objected to *Madame Bovary* saw things differently: "Art without

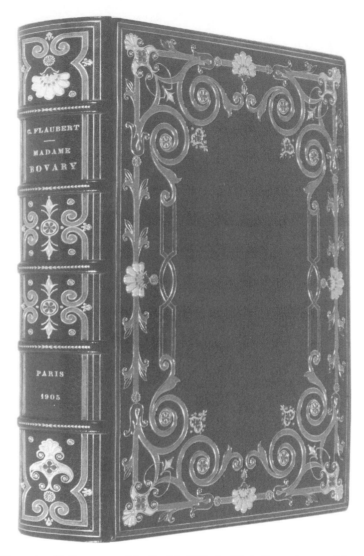

The opulent binding, executed by Gruel in 1907, for W. A. Spencer's copy of the Ferroud edition of Madame Bovary.

rules is no longer art; it is like a woman who throws off all garments. To impose upon art the single rule of public decency is not to enslave but to honor it." One of the "lascivious paintings" to which attention was particularly drawn at the obscenity trial of *Madame Bovary* was Flaubert's famous description of Emma disrobing before Léon in "their" room at the Hôtel de Boulogne in Rouen: "She would undress savagely, tearing at the thin lacing of her corset, which fell down around her hips like a gliding snake . . ." For the prosecution, this was the "poetry of adultery," and Fourié's sensuous drawing has caught the moment perfectly.

PORTRAIT

Portrait of Gustave Flaubert (wood engraving from an early twentieth-century German calendar, after the photograph by Nadar) (frontispiece). Born in Lyon, Gaspar-Felix Tournachon (1820–1910) arrived in Paris in 1848 looking for work as a journalist. He rechristened himself Nadar and was quickly established as the foremost satirical cartoonist of the day. With the intention of producing a kind of backup for his cartoons, Nadar began to photograph his subjects around 1850. Inadvertently, he produced a new kind of collective portrait of the most important writers and artists of his generation, including Flaubert, Baudelaire, Sand, Manet, Delacroix, Rossini, and Verdi. As the biographer Richard Holmes has written:

> Here was the next literary and artistic generation after Shelley and Byron, suddenly brought back to life—their hairstyles, their wrinkles, their buttoned jackets, their scuffed shoes, their watch-chains or necklaces, their pince-nez, their frayed shirt-cuffs, the smile-lines round their eyes, the worry-lines over the brow, their mouths turned up with hope or turned down with disappointment—in a way that made them almost com-

pletely contemporary . . . Here they were, alive, like us, flesh and blood, and touched by the marks of life.

Nadar was the first aerial photographer, and he made numerous flights over Paris in his celebrated balloon *Le Géant* ("The Giant"). In a letter to George Sand, Flaubert told of his delight when he chanced upon a paragraph in Nadar's *Mémoires du Géant* (1864) about himself and his fellow Rouennais which, as he put it, was "utterly exact." Nadar had written:

> . . . I still remember a nice young man, something of a dandy, in Rouen, whom I congratulated on the very great, very deserved, and at that time recent success of his fellow-citizen, the author of *Madame Bovary*. "You find it a good book?" that young Rouennais of good family replied, with a tone of superiority utterly crushing towards Flaubert. "Not I! The author is a kind of eccentric—something we don't at all care for in Rouen. He was always trying to attract attention to himself. He didn't want to belong to the National Guard. And then, *without saying a word*, he left for Africa! We don't like that sort, in Rouen."

Flaubert did indeed devote eighteen months (1849–51) to travels in Egypt, Lebanon, Turkey, and Greece. Upon his return to Croisset, he immediately began work on *Madame Bovary*.

GUSTAVE FLAUBERT

MADAME BOVARY

COMPOSITIONS DE ALFRED DE RICHEMONT

GRAVÉES A L'EAU-FORTE

PAR

C. CHESSA

PRÉFACE PAR LÉON HENNIQUE

PARIS

LIBRAIRIE DES AMATEURS

A. FERROUD — F. FERROUD, SUCCESSEUR

127, BOULEVARD SAINT-GERMAIN, 127

1905

Facsimile of title page from 1905 Ferroud edition.

The room was calm again. Heads were bent over notebooks, and the new boy sat still for two hours . . .

PART ONE

I

We were studying when the headmaster came in, followed by a new boy, not yet wearing a school uniform, and a monitor carrying a large desk. Those of us who had been sleeping awoke, and we all stood up as if we had been interrupted in our work.

The headmaster motioned to us to sit down again; then, turning toward the teacher, he said in a low voice, "Monsieur Roger, here is a student I'm placing in your charge. He is starting in the fifth. If he does well, he will advance into the upper school, where he belongs at his age."

Keeping himself in the corner behind the door so that you could hardly see him, the new arrival was a country boy, about fifteen years old and taller than any of us. His hair was cut straight across his forehead like a village choirboy's; he looked sensible and very shy. Although he was not broad shouldered, his black-buttoned green suit seemed tight under the arms, and it revealed through the slits in his cuffs a pair of red wrists accustomed to going bare. His blue-stockinged legs emerged from yellowish trousers held up by suspenders. He wore heavy hobnail shoes, badly polished.

We began to recite our lessons. He concentrated with all his might, as attentive as if he were listening to a sermon, not even daring to cross his legs or lean on his elbow; and at two o'clock, when the bell rang, the teacher had to tell him to line up with us.

We were in the habit of throwing our caps to the floor on entering the classroom in order to free our hands. From the doorway you had to throw them under the bench as soon as you entered so that you would hit the wall and raise a lot of dust. This was "the thing to do."

But either the new boy had not noticed this game or he didn't dare attempt it; he was still holding his cap on his knees when the prayer was over. It was one of those hybrid hats, in which you could find elements of a busby, a lancer cap, a bowler, an otterskin cap, and a nightcap, one of those poor concoctions whose mute ugliness contains depths of expression like the face of an imbecile. Egg shaped and stiffened with whalebone, it began with three circular sausage-like twists, then alternate diamonds of velvet and rabbit fur, separated by red bands; then came a sort of bag ending in a cardboard-lined polygon covered with complicated braiding from which a small crosspiece of gold threads dangled like a tassel at the end of a long, too thin cord. It was a new hat: the visor gleamed.

"Stand up," said the teacher.

He stood up; the cap fell. The entire class began to laugh.

He stooped down and picked it up. His neighbor made it fall again by poking it with his elbow. He picked it up a second time.

"Get rid of your helmet," said the teacher, who was a witty man.

There was a burst of laughter from the students. It rattled the poor boy so much that he didn't know if he should keep the cap in his hand, leave it on the floor, or put it on his head. He sat down and placed it on his lap.

"Stand up," said the teacher, "and tell me your name."

The new boy stammered some unintelligible name.

"Once more!"

The same garbled syllables were heard, drowned by the hoots from the class.

"Louder," shouted the teacher, "louder!"

The new boy, now mustering up all his courage, opened an

abnormally large mouth and, as if he were calling someone, shouted at the top of his voice the word: *Charbovari.*

Pandemonium broke loose, rose to a roar punctuated by piercing shrieks (they shouted, howled, stamped their feet, and kept repeating *Charbovari! Charbovari!*), then subsided to isolated sounds, died down with great difficulty, and flared up again suddenly on one bench along which there were still some muffled giggles, sputtering like a badly extinguished firecracker.

However, by dint of a shower of threats, order was slowly restored in class, and the teacher, who had managed to grasp the name of Charles Bovary by having it dictated, spelled out, and read over, immediately ordered the poor devil to sit in the dunce chair at the foot of the lecture desk. He started toward it, then hesitated.

"What are you looking for?" asked the teacher.

"My ca-a-p," the new boy said timidly, looking anxiously around.

"Five hundred lines for the whole class!" shouted in a furious voice, like Neptune's *"Quos ego,"* stopped a new outburst. "Quiet!" continued the angry teacher, wiping his forehead with a handkerchief that he had pulled from under his cap. "As for you, new boy, you will write the verb *ridiculus sum* twenty times."

Then, in gentler tones: "You'll find that cap of yours. No one's stolen it."

The room was calm again. Heads were bent over notebooks, and the new boy sat still for two hours, behaving in exemplary fashion despite the fact that from time to time a wad of paper launched with a penholder would hit him square in the face. He would merely wipe it off with his hand and remain motionless, his eyes lowered.

In the evening, during the study period, he pulled his cuff guards from his desk, arranged his meager possessions, and ruled his paper carefully. We noticed that he was working very diligently, looking all the words up in the dictionary and taking a lot of pains. The even temper he displayed was undoubtedly what kept him from being sent down to the lower class, for while he knew the rules passably, he had absolutely no grace in his style. The priest of his village had started him on his Latin, his parents having kept him out of school until the last possible moment in order to save money.

His father, Monsieur Charles-Denis-Bartholomé Bovary, ex-aide to a surgeon major, had been implicated about 1812 in some conscription scandal and had been forced to leave the service. He then exploited his personable appearance to acquire a dowry of sixty thousand francs offered by a hosier for his daughter, a girl who had fallen in love with his good looks. A handsome, boastful fellow, jingling his spurs, with sideburns trimmed to meet his mustache, fingers always adorned with rings, and clothes in lively colors, he seemed to combine the looks of a warrior with the easygoing ways of a traveling salesman. After the marriage he lived on his wife's fortune for two or three years, eating well, sleeping late in the morning, smoking huge porcelain pipes, never coming home in the evening until after the theater, and frequenting cafés. His father-in-law died, leaving very little. He was furious about it, took a fling at manufacturing, lost a bit of money, and then retired to the country, where he hoped to make the land pay off. But since he understood as little about farming as he did about calico, since he rode his horses instead of working them, drank his cider in bottles instead of selling it in barrels, ate the choicest poultry in his barnyard and greased his hunting boots with his pigs' lard, he soon realized that it was better to give up any hope of profit from that quarter.

He managed to rent, for two hundred francs a year, a sort of lodging, half farm, half country home, in a village on the border between Picardy and Caux. Unhappy, consumed with regrets, filled with resentment against fate and envy of his fellow men, he shut himself away at the age of forty-five, disgusted with mankind, he claimed, and determined to live in peace.

His wife loved him madly at first; she showed her love with a thousand gestures of servility, which estranged him even further from her. Once lively, expansive, and generous, she had become difficult, shrill voiced, and nervous as she grew older, like uncorked wine which turns to vinegar. At first she suffered in silence when he spent evenings running after all the village trollops, only to be brought back to her late at night, dead drunk, from various places of ill repute. Then her pride asserted itself. But she still said nothing, stifling her rage with a mute stoicism that she was to maintain until her death. She kept herself busy with various things, mainly business matters. She consulted the lawyers, or the magistrate, remembered when bills fell due, obtained postponements. At home she ironed, sewed, washed, kept an eye on the workers, and settled their accounts, while the master of the house, without a worry in the world, perpetually sunk in a sullen torpor from which he roused himself only to make insulting remarks, remained by the fireside smoking and spitting into the ashes.

When she gave birth to a child, she had to send him out to nurse. After he was brought back home, he was spoiled like a prince. His mother stuffed him with candies; his father let him run around without shoes and, aping the philosophers, even claimed it was all right for him to run around nude, like a young animal. In opposition to her maternal instincts, he conceived the notion of a manly childhood, which he tried to impose on his son; he wanted the boy brought up austerely, Spartan fashion, in order to develop a strong constitution. He sent him to bed in an unheated room and taught him to gulp down large amounts of rum and shout insults at church processions. But the child, mild tempered by nature, responded badly to his efforts. His mother was always dragging him around with her; she would cut out paper dolls for him, tell him stories; and involve herself in endless monologues full of melancholy humor and baby talk. In the loneliness of her life she lavished all her thwarted ambitions on this childish head. She dreamed about important positions, could already see him grown up, handsome, witty, a successful civil engineer or magistrate. She taught him to read and even to sing two or three little ballads, accompanying him on her old piano. But

Monsieur Bovary, caring little about education, kept saying that none of this was worth the trouble. Would they ever have the money to support him in the government schools, buy him a post, or set him up in business? Besides, "If a man has enough nerve, he'll always succeed in the world." Madame Bovary bit her lips, and the child wandered about the village.

He would follow the farmhands and scare off the crows by throwing clumps of earth at them. He ate the blackberries growing along the ditches, minded the turkeys with a stick, pitched hay during harvesttime, and ran through the woods. He played hopscotch under the church porch on rainy days and begged the sexton to let him ring the bells on holidays so that he could pull on the heavy cord with all his might and swing along as the bell clanged.

And so he grew like an oak. His hands developed strength, his complexion a healthy color.

When he was twelve, his mother arranged for him to begin his studies. The parish priest was given the assignment. But the lessons were so short and so badly organized that they did no real good. They were given in haste at odd moments in the vestry, while he remained standing, between a baptism and a burial; or sometimes the priest would send for his pupil after the Angelus, when he didn't have to go out. They would go up to his room and settle down; the gnats and moths would fly around the candle. It would be warm, and the child would doze off; and the good priest, folding his hands over his belly, would soon start snoring with his mouth agape. Other times, when the curé, returning from administering the sacrament to some ailing soul, chanced on Charles running wild through the countryside, he would call him, lecture him for a quarter of an hour, and take advantage of the occasion to make him conjugate his verbs at the foot of a tree. The rain or some passerby would interrupt them. In general he was rather pleased with the boy, even saying that the "young lad" had a good memory.

Charles's education could not stop there. His mother was firm about it. Ashamed, or rather, worn out, his father gave in without a fight, and they waited one more year until the boy had made his first Communion.

Six months more went by; the next year Charles was finally sent off to school in Rouen toward the end of October, at about the time of the Saint-Romain fair. His father even accompanied him.

None of us now can remember anything about him. He was a mild-tempered boy who played during recess, worked in study periods, listened in class, slept soundly in the dormitory, and ate heartily in the dining hall. His local guardian was a man who had a wholesale hardware business on the Rue Ganterie. The guardian took him out one Sunday a month, after the store was closed, sent him for a walk down to the quay to look at the boats, then took him back to school by seven, before supper. Every Thursday evening he wrote a long letter to his mother in red ink and sealed it with three wafers; then he skimmed his history notebooks or read an old volume of the philosopher Anacharsis that happened to be in the study hall. When he went out walking, he would chat with the servant who, like himself, came from the country.

He managed to stay in the middle of his class by working very hard; once he even won an "honorable mention" in natural history. But at the end of his third year his parents took him out of school to study medicine, convinced that he could win his school degree by studying on his own.

His mother chose a room for him on the fourth floor of a house that belonged to a dyer she knew. It overlooked the Eau-de-Robec. She made arrangements for his room and board, bought furniture—a table and two chairs—and sent him an old cherrywood bedstead from home. She also purchased a small cast-iron stove and enough wood to keep her poor child warm. She left after a week, having given him a thousand lectures about being on his best behavior now that he was going to be left to his own devices.

The courses that were listed on the bulletin board terrified him: anatomy, pathology, physiology, pharmacology, chemistry, botany, clinical medicine, and therapy, not to mention hygiene and materia medica, all names of whose etymology he was ignorant and that loomed like majestic shadows in temple doors.

He understood nothing. No matter how hard he listened, he just couldn't grasp the subject. Yet he worked hard, he acquired bound notebooks, went to all his lectures, did not miss one single class. He managed his daily assignment of work like a millhorse who trots around in blinkers, unaware of what he is grinding.

To save him money, his mother would send some baked veal by the carrier each week. He would lunch on it in the morning when he came back from the hospital, stamping his feet against the wall as he ate. Then he had to run off to his lessons in the lecture hall or at the hospital and would return home later through the maze of streets. After the meager evening meal his landlord gave him, he would climb back up to his room and start working again, his damp clothes steaming on his body before the glowing stove.

During the lovely summer evenings, at the hour when the warm streets are empty and the maids play shuttlecock on the doorsteps, he would open his window and look out, leaning on his elbow. The river, which makes this section of Rouen a poor version of Venice, flowed below him, yellow, violet, or blue beneath its bridges and its railings. Workmen leaning over the edge would wash their arms in the water. Skeins of cotton dried in the air; they were suspended on poles projecting from the lofts above. Opposite, above the rooftops, the red sun was setting in the unclouded expanse of sky. How good it must be back home under the beeches! And he would open his nostrils wide, trying to breathe in the good country air that did not reach him.

He grew thin and tall, and his face acquired a sort of mournful expression that made it almost interesting.

Gradually, out of indifference, he managed to forget all his resolutions. Once he missed his hospital round, the next day a class. Enjoying his idleness, he did not go back.

He formed the habit of going to the café and acquired a passion for dominoes. To be cooped up each evening in a filthy public room in order to click small sheep bones marked with black dots on the marble tables seemed to him a precious act of liberty that heightened his self-esteem.

It was an initiation into the world, an access to forbidden pleasures. When he entered he would place his hand on the doorknob with an almost sensual joy. So many of his repressed feelings expanded; he learned songs by heart and sang them to entertain the women present, developed a taste for Béranger, learned how to make punch, and finally how to make love.

Having neglected his studies, he completely failed the test for health officer. And he was expected home that very evening to celebrate his success!

He set out on foot and stopped at the village outskirts, where he asked someone to summon his mother; he told her the whole story. She made excuses for him, blamed the failure on the unfairness of the examiners, and cheered him up a bit, taking it on herself to arrange matters. Only five years later did Monsieur Bovary learn the truth; by then he accepted it as ancient history. Moreover, he was unable to accept the fact that a son of his might be a fool.

So Charles went back to work and prepared unceasingly for his examination. He memorized all the questions beforehand and passed with a decent grade. It was a happy day for his mother. They celebrated with a big dinner party.

Where would he practice? In Tostes. There was only one old doctor there. Madame Bovary had been watching out for his death for a long time, and the good soul had barely expired when Charles moved in across the street as his successor.

But it was not enough to have raised her son, arranged for him to study medicine, and discovered Tostes for him to practice in. He needed a wife. She found him one: the widow of a Dieppe bailiff, who was forty-five years old and had an income of twelve hundred pounds.

Although she was ugly, thin as a rail, and had as many pimples as the springtime has buds, Madame Dubuc was not lacking in suitors.

In order to achieve her goal Mother Bovary had to overcome them all, and she even frustrated quite cleverly the intrigues of a pork butcher whose suit was being supported by the priests.

Charles had hoped for better days following his marriage. He assumed he would be freer to choose his own actions and spend his money as he pleased. But his wife was the ruler; he had to watch what he said and didn't say in public, eat fish on Friday, dress as she prescribed, and harass the patients who didn't pay. She would open his letters, spy on his whereabouts, and listen behind the partition when there were women in his consulting room.

She had to have her chocolate every morning and constantly demanded various services. She complained incessantly about her nerves, her chest, her moods. She couldn't stand the sound of footsteps; if he went away she couldn't bear solitude; if he hovered near her it was surely in order to see her die. When Charles came home in the evening, she would extend her long thin arms out from under the sheets, twine them around his neck, and make him sit down on the edge of the bed in order to begin telling him her worries; he was forgetting her, he was in love with someone else! She had been rightly forewarned that she would be unhappy; and she would end by asking him for some medicine for her health and a bit more love.

I I

One night at about eleven, they were awakened by the sound of a horse stopping right at their door. The maid opened the attic window and spoke for some time with a man below. He had come for the doctor; he had a letter. Nastasie shivered as she went down the stairs; she unlocked the door and drew all the bolts. The man left his horse and walked into the house, following right behind the maid. He pulled a letter, wrapped in a piece of fabric, from his gray-tasseled woolen cap and gingerly presented it to Charles, who propped his elbow on the pillow to read it. Nastasie held the lamp near the bed. Madame remained facing the wall out of modesty and showed only her back.

The letter, sealed with a dab of blue wax, begged Monsieur Bovary to come immediately to Les Bertaux to set a broken leg. Now, it is a good fourteen miles from Tostes to Les Bertaux by way of Longueville and Saint-Victor. The night was dark. Madame Bovary was afraid some accident might befall her husband. Therefore it was decided that the stableboy would go ahead of him. Charles would leave three hours later, when the moon would be visible. They would send a boy to meet him, show him the road to the farm, and open the fence gates for him.

About four A.M. Charles, well wrapped in his cloak, set out for Les Bertaux. Still drowsy from the warmth of sleep, he let himself be rocked by the gentle trot of his horse. When she stopped of her own accord before the holes surrounded by thornbush that are dug at the ends of the furrows, Charles would awake with a start and, quickly remembering the broken leg, try to recall all the fractures he knew. The rain had stopped. Daylight was starting to appear. Birds virtually motionless on the branches of the leafless apple trees were ruffling their tiny feathers in the cold morning wind. The flat countryside stretched out as far as the eye could see, and the clusters of trees surrounding the farms made regular patches of dark purple against the large gray surface that blended at the horizon into the dull tone of the sky. Charles would open his eyes from time to time; then, his mind tiring, and falling asleep against his will, he soon entered into a sort of drowsy state in which his recent sensations mingled with memories. He saw himself as two people at one and the same time, student and husband, lying in his bed as he just had been, and crossing an operating room as in the old days. The warm smell of poultices blended in his head with the fresh odor of dew; he heard the iron rings tinkling on the curtain rods of the ward beds and saw his wife sleeping. As he passed through Vassonville, he noticed a boy sitting on the grass at the edge of a ditch.

"Are you the doctor?" the child asked. And, at Charles's answer, he picked up his wooden shoes in his hand and began to run ahead of him.

As he rode along, the doctor gathered from his guide's talk that Monsieur Rouault must be a very prosperous farmer. He had broken his leg the evening before, coming home from a Twelfth Night celebration at a neighbor's. His wife had died two years ago. There was no one with him but his daughter, who helped him keep house.

The ruts were becoming deeper. They were approaching Les Bertaux. The little boy slipped through a space in the hedge and disappeared, then came back to the edge of a courtyard to open the gate. The horse skidded on the wet grass. Charles bent his head to pass under the branches. The watchdogs in the kennel barked and pulled at their chains. As he entered Les Bertaux, his horse became frightened and stumbled.

It was an impressive farm. In the stables, over the open doors, big workhorses could be seen feeding leisurely at their new mangers. A large dunghill extended along the buildings; liquid manure oozed from it and, among the hens and turkeys, five or six peacocks, considered luxuries in Caux farmyards, were foraging on top. The sheepfold was long, the barn high ceilinged, with walls smooth as a woman's hand. In the shed there were two large carts and four plows complete with their whips, shafts, and harnesses. The blue wool fleeces were becoming soiled from the fine dust falling from the lofts. The yard, its trees planted equidistant from one another, sloped upward, and the gay cackle of a flock of geese came from the pond.

A young woman in a blue wool dress trimmed with three flounces came out to the threshold of the door to receive Monsieur Bovary, and she invited him into the kitchen, where a large fire was blazing. The farmhands' dinner was boiling around it, in small pots of varying sizes. Some damp garments were drying inside the fireplace. The shovel, tongs, and the nozzle of the bellows, all huge, shone like polished steel, and an abundant supply of kitchen utensils hung along the walls, reflecting here and there the clear flame of the hearth, mingled with the first rays of the sun that were piercing through the windowpanes.

Charles went up to the second floor to see the patient. He found him in his bed, perspiring under the covers, his cotton nightcap thrown far from the bed. He was a short, heavy man of fifty, with white skin and blue eyes; he was bald on the forepart of his head and wore earrings. On a chair at his side he had a large decanter of brandy, from which he kept pouring himself drinks to keep his spirits up, but as soon as he saw the doctor, his excitement subsided, and instead of swearing as he had been doing for the last twelve hours, he began to moan feebly.

It was an extremely simple fracture, with no complications whatsoever. Charles couldn't have wished for an easier one. Then, remembering the bedside manners of his teachers, he comforted the patient with all sorts of kind words—medical caresses like the oil used on scalpels. A bundle of laths to be used for splints was brought up from the cart shed. Charles selected one from the pack, cut it in pieces, and planed it with a piece of broken glass while the maid was ripping sheets to make bandages. Mademoiselle Emma, the daughter, was about to sew some pads. Her father became impatient when it took her too long to find her workbox. She made no comment. But as she sewed she pricked her fingers and then put them into her mouth to suck them.

Charles was surprised at the whiteness of her nails. They gleamed, were finely tapered, cleaner than Dieppe ivories, and almond shaped. Her hand was not attractive, however, perhaps not white enough and slightly dry at the knuckles; also, it was too long and lacked softness in its outlines. Her real beauty was in her eyes; although they were brown, they seemed black because of the lashes, and she would look at you frankly, with bold candor.

The bandages in place, the doctor was invited by Monsieur Rouault himself to "have a bite" before leaving.

Charles went downstairs to the dining room on the ground floor. Two settings, with silver goblets, had been laid on a small table at the foot of a large bed with Turkish figures printed on its cotton canopy. An odor of iris and damp sheets emanated from the tall oak cupboard facing the window. On the floor, in the corners, were sacks of grain stacked upright. This was the surplus from the nearby granary, connected by three stone steps. A charcoal portrait of Minerva in a gilt frame, on the bottom of which was written in Gothic lettering, "To my darling Papa," served as decoration for the room. It hung on a nail in the middle of a green wall whose paint was scaling off from the effects of saltpeter.

At first they discussed the patient, then the weather, the cold spells, the wolves roaming the fields at night. Mademoiselle Rouault did not like the country at all, especially now that she was almost solely responsible for the care of the farm. As the room was chilly, she shivered a little while eating. This caused her full lips to part slightly. She had a habit of biting them when she wasn't talking.

She wore a white, turned-down collar. Her black hair was parted down the middle. The two sections, so smooth that each seemed to be one solid mass, were separated by a thin part that curved downward slightly along with the curve of the head. Barely revealing the tip of the ear, the hair was gathered behind in a thick bun with waves at the temples, which the country doctor was seeing for the first time in his life. Her cheeks were rosy. She wore a mannish-style tortoise-shell lorgnon tucked in between two buttons of her bodice.

When Charles, after going upstairs to say good-bye to Monsieur Rouault, came back into the room before leaving, he found her standing up, forehead pressed against the window, looking into the garden, where the bean props had been knocked down by the wind. She turned around.

"Are you looking for something?" she asked.

"My riding crop, please," he answered.

He began rummaging on the bed, behind the doors, under the chairs. It had fallen to the ground between the sacks and the wall. Mademoiselle Emma saw it and leaned over the sacks of wheat. Charles dashed over out of courtesy, and as he extended his hand in the same gesture, he sensed his chest brush against the back of the girl bending beneath him. She stood up with a blush and looked at him over her shoulder as she gave him his crop.

Instead of returning to Les Bertaux three days later, as he had promised, he appeared the very next day, then regularly twice a week, not counting the unscheduled visits that he paid from time to time as if by accident.

Everything was going well. The injury was healing properly, and when, at the end of forty-six days, old man Rouault was seen trying to walk by himself in his room, people began to consider Monsieur Bovary a very talented man. Old Rouault said that he wouldn't have been treated better by the most prominent doctors of Yvetot or even of Rouen.

As for Charles, he didn't try to ask himself why he came to Les Bertaux with pleasure. Had he thought about it he would no doubt have attributed his zeal to the seriousness of the case or perhaps to the fee he anticipated from it. Was that the reason, however, why his visits to the farm came as a delightful change to the dull occupations of his life? On those days he arose early in the morning and left at a gallop, urging his horse on; then he would alight to wipe his feet on the grass and pull on his black gloves before going in. He liked to see himself arrive in the courtyard, to feel the gate giving way against his shoulder and the rooster crowing on the wall, the farmhands coming to meet him. He loved the barn and the stables; he liked old Rouault, who would keep patting his hand while calling him his savior; he loved the sound of Mademoiselle Emma's small wooden shoes against the scrubbed kitchen tiles; their high heels increased her height a little, and when she walked in front of him, the wooden soles, lifting up rapidly, would make a sharp clack against the leather of the boot.

She would always walk him back to the first step of the porch. If his horse had not yet been brought around, she would remain there. They had said good-bye to each other and were no longer chatting; the fresh air would envelop her, blowing the little wisps of hair on her nape in all directions or moving over her hips the strings of her apron, which were twisting like streamers. One time during a thaw, moisture was trickling from the tree bark in the yard; the snow on the roofs of the buildings was melting. She stood on the threshold, then went to fetch her parasol and opened it. The sun came through the dove-colored silk parasol, its rays moving over the white skin of her face. She smiled beneath it at the mild warmth of the season, and you could hear drops of water, one by one, falling on the taut-stretched silk.

During the first weeks that Charles frequented Les Bertaux, his wife did not fail to keep herself informed about the patient. She had even chosen a lovely white page for Monsieur Rouault in the double-entry account book. But when she heard that he had a daughter, she sought information; and she learned that Mademoiselle Rouault, brought up in a convent of the Ursuline order, had received, as they say, a good education—as a result, she knew dancing, geography, drawing, tapestry weaving, and piano playing. It was just too much!

"So that's the reason he looks so radiant when he goes to see her," she told herself; "that's why he puts on his new waistcoat, at the risk of soiling it in the rain. Oh, that woman! That woman!"

And she hated her instinctively. At first she contented herself with allusions. Charles didn't understand them. Then, by casual comments that he let pass for fear of a storm; finally, by point-blank insults, to which he did not know how to reply. Why did he keep going back to Les Bertaux if Monsieur Rouault was well and those people hadn't even paid yet? Aha! It was because there was someone there, someone who knew the art of conversation, an embroideress, a person of wit. That was what he liked; he needed city girls! And she resumed her attack: "Rouault's daughter, a city girl! Come now! Their grandfather was a shepherd and they have a cousin who barely escaped being haled into court for some misdeed he committed during an argument. It's not necessary to show off so much or appear in church on Sunday with a silk dress like a countess. Besides, that poor man who would have found it quite hard to pay his bills without last year's rapeseed crop!"

Charles stopped going to Les Bertaux, out of inertia. Heloise had made him swear, his hand on his prayer book, that he would no longer go there—after many sobs and kisses and a great explosion of love. So he obeyed; but the boldness of his desire protested against the servility of his conduct, and with a sort of naïve hypocrisy, he concluded that his being forbidden to see her gave him the right to love her. And besides, the widow was skinny; her teeth were elongated; she wore in season and out a small black shawl the ends of which reached down between her shoulder blades; her angular body was encased in straight, narrow dresses, too short, that revealed her ankles with the ribbons of her big shoes crossed over gray stockings.

Charles's mother came to see them from time to time, but at the end of a few days the daughter-in-law seemed to infect her with her own sharpness. Then, like two scissors, they would cut into him with their comments and their observations. He was wrong to eat so much! Why always offer a drink to the first comer? How stubborn not to wear flannel!

At the beginning of spring, a notary of Ingouville, the holder of the Widow Dubuc's money, ran off one fine day, taking along with him all the funds in his custody. Heloise still had, it is true, her house on the Rue Saint-François plus a share in a boat valued at six thousand francs; and yet, out of all that fortune, about which so much noise had been made, nothing but a bit of furniture and some old clothes had turned up in the Bovary household. It was necessary to look into the matter. The Dieppe house turned out to be mortgaged down to its foundations; God alone knew what she had deposited with the notary, and the share in the boat did not exceed three thousand francs. So the good lady had lied. In his exasperation, Monsieur Bovary senior smashed a chair against the paving stones and accused his wife of having caused their son's unhappiness by harnessing him to such an old workhorse, whose harness wasn't worth its skin. They went to Tostes. There were explanations, scenes. Heloise, in tears, threw herself into her husband's arms and begged him to defend her against his parents. Charles tried to speak on her behalf. They became angry and left.

But the damage was done. Eight days later, as she was hanging out the wash in the yard, she began to spit up blood. The next day, while Charles had turned his back to her in order to draw the curtain, she said "Oh God!" sighed, and passed away. She was dead! How strange!

When services at the cemetery were over, Charles came back home. He found no one downstairs; he went up to the first floor, into her room, and saw her dress still hanging at the foot of the alcove. Then, leaning against the writing desk, he remained lost in a sad reverie until evening. She had loved him, after all.

III

One morning old Rouault came to pay Charles for setting his leg: seventy-five francs in forty-sou pieces plus a turkey. He had heard about his misfortune and consoled him as best he could.

"I know what it is," he said, patting him on the shoulder; "I was also like you. When I lost my poor wife, I would go into the woods to be all alone, I would sink down at the foot of a tree and cry or call out to God to tell him all sorts of foolish things. I wanted to be like the moles I saw in the branches, with worms crawling in their bellies. In a word, dead. And when I remembered that others at that very moment were holding their beloved wives in their arms, I would beat my stick into the ground with fury. I was half crazy. I stopped eating. The mere idea of going to the café repelled me. You wouldn't believe it. And then, slowly, as one day followed another, springtime replaced winter, and autumn summer, it dwindled away bit by bit, crumb by crumb. It went away, and disappeared. It went inside, I mean, because you always retain something deep down, a sort of heaviness here, in the chest. But since we all share that fate, we mustn't let ourselves waste away hoping to die because others are dead. You must cheer up, Monsieur Bovary; it will pass! Come visit us. My daughter thinks about you quite often, you know. She says that you're forgetting her. Spring is almost here. You can shoot a rabbit in the warren. It will distract you a bit."

Charles heeded his advice and returned to Les Bertaux. He found everything exactly as it had been five months before. The pear trees were already blossoming, and good-natured Rouault, back on his feet now, was all over the place, making the farm that much livelier.

He believed it his duty to lavish all possible attention on the doctor because of his recent bereavement: he told him not to take his hat off, spoke to him in a low voice as if he had been ill, and even pretended to become angry that the food prepared for him wasn't a bit lighter than that for the others—such as small pots of cream or stewed pears. He would tell him stories. To Charles's surprise, he would hear himself laugh, but the sudden thought of his wife would make him gloomy. Then they would serve coffee and he would no longer think about her.

He thought less about her as he became accustomed to living alone. The new pleasure of independence soon made solitude more bearable. He could change his eating hours now, come or go without explanations, and stretch out over the entire bed when he was very tired. So he coddled and pampered himself and accepted the consolations that were offered him. Besides, his wife's death had not served him badly in his profession, since people had repeated for a month, "The poor young man. How sad." His reputation had spread, his clientele increased. And he went to Les Bertaux whenever he felt like it. He felt an undefined hope, a vague happiness. As he brushed his sideburns in front of the mirror, he found his face more pleasing.

One day he arrived there about three o'clock. They were all out in the field. He entered the kitchen but didn't see Emma at first. The shutters were closed. The sun's rays, coming through the wooden slats, became long thin stripes that shattered upon contact with the furniture and quivered on the ceiling. Flies were climbing up the glasses that had been set out on the table. They buzzed as they drowned in the leftover cider. The daylight coming in through the fireplace made the soot on the hearth look like velvet and turned the cold ashes slightly blue. Emma sat sewing between the window and the fireplace. She wasn't wearing a shawl and he could see tiny drops of perspiration on her bare shoulders.

As was the custom in the country, she asked him if he would like a drink. He refused. She insisted and finally suggested with a laugh, that he take a glass of liqueur with her. She went to look for a bottle of curaçao in the cupboard, reached for two small glasses, filled one to the top, poured just a bit in the other, and brought it to her mouth after they had touched glasses. Since it was almost empty, she leaned back to drink, and with her head tilted, lips pouting in readiness and neck extended, she laughed because she wasn't tasting anything, and the tip of her tongue, passing between her finely formed teeth, licked the bottom of the glass daintily.

She sat down again and picked up her work, a white cotton stocking she was mending. She sewed with her forehead lowered and said nothing. Charles was also silent. A gust of air blew in under the door and scattered a little dust over the tiles. As he watched it float along, he could only hear the pounding inside his head and the far-off cry of a hen laying an egg in the barnyard. Emma would occasionally cool her cheeks by placing her palms against them, then she would cool the palms against the metal knobs of the big andirons.

She complained that she had been suffering from dizzy spells since the beginning of the season and asked if ocean bathing would help her. She started chatting about the convent, Charles about his school. It seemed easy to talk. They went up to her room. She showed him her old music notebooks, the small books she had received as prizes, and the oak-leaf wreaths lying forgotten at the bottom of the wardrobe. She spoke to him again about her mother, and about the cemetery, and even showed him the flower bed in the garden from which she picked flowers the first Friday of every month for her grave. But their gardener didn't understand a thing about his job. You just couldn't get good servants! She would adore living in the city even if only in the winter, although the country was possibly even more boring in the summer because of the long days. Her voice reflected her various topics of conversation; it would be clear and sharp or, suddenly becoming listless, would drag out its inflections until it ended almost in murmurs, and she would be talking to herself. Sometimes the voice would be joyous, and naïvely she would open wide her eyes; then the eyelids would droop, she would look terribly bored, and her thoughts would wander.

On the way home in the evening Charles analyzed everything she had said, trying to remember it all, to complete the meaning, to become acquainted with that portion of her life she had spent before he met her. But he could never imagine her differently from the way he had seen her the first time, or as the girl he had just left. Then he wondered what would become of her if she got married. And to whom? Alas! Her father was quite rich and she was so lovely! But Emma's face kept coming back before his eyes, and something monotonous, like the sound of a spinning top, hummed in his ears: "Suppose you did get married! Suppose you did!" He couldn't sleep that night. His throat was constricted, dry. He arose to take a drink from his water jug and opened the window. The sky was filled with stars. There was a warm wind blowing. Dogs were barking in the distance. He turned his head in the direction of Les Bertaux.

Thinking that, after all, he wasn't risking anything, Charles made up his mind to propose when the occasion presented itself; but each time that it did, the fear of not finding any of the right words kept his lips sealed.

Old man Rouault would not have been sorry to be rid of his daughter, who was of little help to him in the house. Inwardly he forgave her, feeling that she was too intelligent for farming—an accursed occupation in which one never found a millionaire. Far from having made a fortune at it, Rouault kept losing money each year. Although he excelled in the marketplace, where the wily bargaining amused him, he was not at all suited for actual farming and the running of the household. He was not generous with his money but spared no expense for anything having to do with his personal life: he wanted to be well fed, sufficiently warm, and comfortably bedded down. He liked his cider full bodied, his legs of lamb rare, and his coffee well mixed with brandy. He ate his meals alone in the kitchen, facing the fire, on a small table that was brought to him preset, as in the theater.

Also, having noticed Charles blushing in his daughter's presence—which meant that one of these days he would be asked for her hand in marriage—he thought about the matter in advance. He found Charles rather puny and not the sort of son-in-law he had hoped for; but he was reputed to be of steady character, thrifty and well educated, and he would surely not haggle too much about the dowry. And so, since old man Rouault was going to be forced to sell twenty-two acres of his property, since he was heavily in debt to the mason and to the harnessmaker, since the winepress shaft had to be repaired, he told himself, "If he asks me for her, I'll consent."

At Michaelmas, Charles came to spend three days at Les Bertaux. The last day passed like the preceding ones. He kept putting the matter off from one quarter of an hour to the next. Monsieur Rouault set him on his way. They were walking along an empty road and were about to say good-bye. It was the moment. Charles gave himself until they reached the hedge and finally, after they had passed it, murmured, "Sir, I would like very much to tell you something."

They stopped walking. Charles said no more.

"Tell me your story! Don't I know it all?" Rouault said, laughing affectionately.

"Father Rouault—Father Rouault," Charles stammered.

"I couldn't ask for anything better," the farmer continued. "And although the little one no doubt agrees, we have to ask her anyway. You go along. I'll go home now. Now listen carefully; if it's yes, you won't have to return, because people might notice, and besides, she'll be too excited. But so that you won't worry, I'll open the window shutter all the way. You'll be able to see it if you turn around and lean over the hedge." And he went off.

Charles tied his horse to a tree. He stationed himself in the path and waited. A half hour went by, then he counted nineteen minutes on his watch. Suddenly there was a noise against the wall: the shutter had been turned out; the catch was still rattling.

He was at the farm at nine the next morning. Emma blushed when he entered, but tried to smile a little to hide her confusion. Old man Rouault kissed his future son-in-law. They postponed discussing financial arrangements. They had time enough, since the marriage couldn't with any decency take place before Charles's mourning period was over, and that was around springtime of the following year.

So they waited for the winter to pass. Mademoiselle Rouault busied herself with her trousseau. Part of it was ordered in Rouen, and she herself made some shifts and nightcaps, copying them from borrowed fashion patterns. During Charles's visits to the farm, they would talk about the preparations for the wedding, wonder what room to prepare the dinner in, dream about the number of dishes they would need and what they would serve.

Emma wanted to get married by torchlight at the unusual hour of midnight, but old man Rouault could not understand this notion at all. And so a wedding took place, to which forty-three people came and sat at the table for sixteen hours. It began again the next day and continued to a lesser extent the following days.

I V

The guests arrived early in their vehicles: one-horse carts, two-wheeled charabancs, old cabriolets lacking hoods, and delivery vans with leather curtains. The young people from the nearest villages came in wagons in which they were standing in rows, holding on to the rails to keep from falling, moving at a trot and jolted about. They came from twenty-five miles off, from Goderville, Normanville, and Cany. All the relatives from each side had been invited; they had made up with estranged friends; they had written to long-lost acquaintances.

From time to time, whiplashes could be heard from behind the hedge. Soon the gate would open and a cart would come in. Galloping up to the foot of the steps, it would stop short and pour out its passengers, who would exit from each side rubbing their knees and stretching their arms. The ladies, in bonnets, wore city-style dresses, gold watch chains, capes with the ends tucked into their belts, or small colored scarves attached in back with a pin and revealing the napes of their necks. The boys, dressed like their fathers, seemed uncomfortable in their new suits (many of them were wearing boots for the first time in their lives). At their sides you could see, not breathing a word, in the white dress of her first Communion lengthened for the occasion, some cousin or older sister, ruddy faced, bewildered, hair greased with rose pomade, and terribly frightened of soiling her gloves. Since there weren't enough stableboys to unhitch all the horses, the gentlemen rolled up their sleeves and attended to it themselves. They wore, according to their social position, suits, frock coats, jackets, or waistcoats; good suits, which received all the care of the family and left the closet only for solemn occasions; frock coats with large tails floating in the wind, cylindrical collars, and pockets as big as sacks; jackets of coarse cloth, usually worn with caps that had copper rims on the visors; very short waistcoats, with two buttons in the back as close together as eyes and tails that looked as if they were carved from one piece of wood by the carpenter's ax. Still others (but these people, obviously, would be eating at the lower end of the table) wore holiday blouses, with collars turned down over the shoulders, backs gathered in tiny pleats, and a very low waistline marked with a sewn-on belt.

And the shirts bulged over the chests like breastplates. Everyone was freshly shorn, ear sticking out of heads. All were close shaven;

some, having risen before dawn, and not seeing clearly how to shave, had diagonal gashes under their noses or, along the jaws, skinned-off areas the size of three-franc pieces, which had been inflamed by the open air on the way and which, with their pink patches, gave a marbled effect to all those fat, white, shiny faces.

The mayor's chambers being a mile or so from the farm, they went there on foot and came back the same way after the ceremony at the church. The procession, at first holding together like a colored scarf waving in the countryside, all along the narrow path winding through the fields of unripe corn, soon grew longer and separated into different groups, many lagging behind to chat. The fiddler led the way with his violin decorated with ribbon rosettes; the bride and groom followed, then relatives and friends in no special order, and the children stayed in the rear, enjoying themselves by plucking the ears of young oat shoots or by playing games and hiding. Emma's dress, too long, was dragging a little at the bottom; she would stop once in a while to pick it up, and then, delicately, with her gloved fingers, she would pull off the blades of wild grass and thistle burrs while Charles would wait with empty hands until she had finished. Old Rouault, a new silk hat on his head and the cuffs of his black suit covering his hands up to his fingernails, offered his arm to Madame Bovary senior. As for Monsieur Bovary senior, feeling contempt for all these people, he had come dressed simply in a single-breasted frock coat of a military cut and was telling off-color jokes to a fair-haired young farm girl. She curtseyed and blushed and didn't know what to answer. The other wedding guests talked about business matters or played little pranks on one another, anticipating the gaiety in advance. By listening carefully one could still hear the fiddler scraping away as he continued to play along the road. When he noticed that they were far behind him, he stopped to catch his breath, waxed his bow thoroughly with resin so that the strings would respond better, and then began to walk again, raising and lowering the neck of his fiddle in order to keep good time for himself. The noise of the instrument frightened the little birds away.

The table was set in the cart shed. On it there were four sirloins, six chicken fricassees, some stewed veal, three legs of lamb, and, in the middle, a fine roast suckling pig, flanked by four pork sausages and cooked with sorrel. In the corners there were decanters filled with brandy. The bottled sweet cider was frothing thickly around the corks, and all the glasses had already been filled to the brim with wine. Huge platters of yellow custard that quivered at the slightest movement of the table had the initials of the new couple traced on their smooth surface in arabesques of sugared almonds. They had gone to Yvetot to find a baker for the pastry and the nougats. As he was a newcomer to the area, he had taken special pains; and he brought for dessert with his own hands a layered cake that elicited loud hurrahs. The base was a square of blue cardboard representing a temple with porticos and colonnades, and there were stucco statuettes all around it in niches papered with gilded stars; then, on the second tier there was a turret of Savoy cake, surrounded by tiny fortifications in angelica, almonds, raisins, and orange segments; and finally, on the top layer, which was a green meadow on which there were rocks with candied lakes and boats of hazelnut shells, you could see a small Cupid, poised on a chocolate swing whose two posts ended in two real rosebuds, representing finials, at the summit.

They ate until evening. When they grew too tired of sitting, they went for walks in the yard or played a game of quoits in the barn, then came back to the table. Toward the end, a few fell asleep and snored. But everyone revived during coffee; they sang, performed feats of strength, lifted weights, played a game called "went under your thumbs," tried to lift carts on their shoulders, made coarse jokes, kissed the women. The horses, gorged to the nostrils with oats, could barely be squeezed into their shafts when it was time to leave late in the evening; they kicked and reared and broke their harnesses, while their masters swore or laughed; and all night long in the moonlight there were runaway carriages galloping along the roads, plunging into ditches, jolting over tall piles of stones, and bumping

The table was set in the cart shed. On it there were four sirloins, six chicken fricassees, some stewed veal, three legs of lamb . . .

into the embankments, with women leaning out of the doors to grasp the reins.

Those who remained at Les Bertaux spent the night drinking in the kitchen. The children had fallen asleep under the benches.

The bride begged her father to be spared the customary wedding-night jokes. Nevertheless, a fishmonger cousin of theirs (the same who had brought a pair of soles as a wedding gift) was about to spit water through the keyhole when old Rouault arrived just in time to stop him, and explained to him that his son-in-law's dignified position did not permit such impertinences. The cousin gave in only reluctantly to these arguments. Inwardly he accused Rouault of being conceited, and he went to join in a corner four or five other guests who, having by chance received the end cuts of meat several times in a row while at the table, had also decided that they had been badly treated and were whispering guardedly against their host and wishing him evil.

Madame Bovary senior had not unclenched her teeth all day long. She had not been consulted about her daughter-in-law's dress, nor about the wedding arrangements. She went to bed early. Her husband, instead of following her, sent off to Saint-Victor for some cigars and smoked until daybreak, all the while drinking grogs of kirsch, a mixture unknown to the company, which raised him even higher in their esteem.

Charles was humorless; he did not shine during the evening. He replied stolidly to the witty remarks, puns, double-entendre jokes, compliments, and broad remarks that they seemed to feel called upon to direct at him from the soup course on.

The next day, however, he seemed to be a new man. It was he who could have been taken for the virgin of the night before, rather than the bride, whose self-control gave no opportunity for conjecture. Even the most daring jokesters were silenced, and they looked at her with bewilderment when she passed near them.

But Charles hid nothing. He called her "my wife," spoke to her in familiar terms, asked everyone where she was, sought her everywhere, and frequently drew her into the yard, where he could be seen from afar, between the trees, putting his arm around her waist, leaning toward her as he walked, and burying his face in the tucker of her bodice.

Two days after the wedding the couple left: Charles could not stay any longer because of his patients. Old Rouault sent them home in his trap and accompanied them himself as far as Vassonville. There he kissed his daughter one last time, stepped down from the wagon, and headed home. When he had gone about a hundred steps he stopped, and as he saw the trap moving off into the distance, its wheels in the dust, he gave a mighty sigh. Then he remembered his own marriage, his youthful days, his wife's first pregnancy. He too had been very happy the day that he brought her home from her father's house, when she rode behind him on the horse, trotting over the snow; for it was Christmastime and the country was all white. She held him with one arm; the other carried her basket. The wind was blowing the long lace ribbons of her Norman bonnet. They occasionally flew into her mouth, and when he turned his head he would see near him, on his shoulder, her little pink face smiling at him silently beneath the gold disk of her headdress. She put her fingers next to his chest from time to time to warm them. How far away all that was! Their son would now be thirty! Then he looked behind him and saw nothing on the road. He felt sad, like an abandoned house. In his head, which was still in a fog from the effects of the feast, tender memories mingled with sad thoughts; for a moment he felt like taking a walk near the church. As he was afraid, however, that this would make him even sadder, he went straight home.

Monsieur and Madame Charles arrived at Tostes at about six o'clock. The neighbors stationed themselves at the windows to see their doctor's new wife.

The old servant introduced herself, greeted Emma, apologized that dinner was not yet ready, and invited Madame to become acquainted with her home while waiting.

V

The brick front was flush with the street, or rather the highway. Behind the door hung a narrow-collared coat, a bridle, and a black leather cap; in a corner on the ground was a pair of leggings still covered with dry mud. To the right was the parlor, that is, the room where they ate and sat. Canary-yellow wallpaper, set off along the upper edge by a garland of pale flowers, quivered all over on its badly hung canvas underlayer; white calico curtains, red bordered, were crossed along the windows; and on the narrow mantelpiece a clock with a head of Hippocrates shone resplendent between two silver-plated candlesticks with oval-shaped globes. Charles's consulting room was on the other side of the hall, a small room about six feet wide, with a table, three regular chairs, and an office chair. The volumes of the *Dictionary of Medical Sciences,* uncut but with bindings that had suffered in the successive hands through which they had passed, adorned almost by themselves the six shelves of a pine bookcase. The smell of browned butter penetrated the wall during examinations, just as in the kitchen one could hear the patients coughing in the consulting room and pouring out their life stories. Next, overlooking the stable yard, came a large ramshackle room that had an oven and now served as woodshed, wine cellar, and storeroom; it was full of scrap iron, empty barrels, discarded farm tools, and a quantity of other dusty objects the purpose of which was impossible to guess.

The garden, long and narrow, was laid out between two clay walls lined with apricot trees, as far as a thorny hedge which separated it from the fields. In the middle there was a slate sundial on a stone pedestal; four flower beds planted with scrawny rosebushes were set symmetrically around the more utilitarian vegetable patch.

Under the spruce trees at the very back was a plaster cast of a priest reading his breviary.

Emma went up to the bedrooms. The first was completely unfurnished, but the second, which was the nuptial chamber, had a mahogany bed in a red-curtained alcove. A box trimmed with shells adorned the chest of drawers; on the secretary, near the window, there was a bouquet of orange blossoms tied with white satin ribbons in a water bottle. It was a marriage bouquet, the other one's bouquet! She looked at it. Charles noticed her glance, picked it up, and took it to the attic, while Emma, seated in an armchair (her things meanwhile were being set down around her), thought of her wedding bouquet, which was packed away in a box, and drowsily wondered what would happen to it if by chance she died.

She kept herself busy the first days, thinking about changes in the house. She took off the candlestick globes, had new wallpaper hung, the staircase painted, and benches built in the garden all around the sundial; she even asked how she could obtain a fountain stocked with fish. Finally her husband, knowing that she liked to go out for drives, found a second-hand carriage that, when it was fitted with new lanterns and mudguards in padded leather, almost resembled a tilbury.

So they were happy and without a care in the world. A meal together, a walk in the evening along the highway, a movement of her hand over her hair, the sight of her straw hat hung on the window latch, and many other things as well that Charles never suspected could be pleasurable, now constituted the continuity of his happiness. In bed in the morning and side by side on the pillow, he looked at the sunlight on the blond down of her cheeks, which were half covered by the scalloped edges of her nightcap. Seen so near, her eyes seemed to him to have grown larger, especially when she blinked her eyelids several times in a row while waking up; black at night and dark blue in the daylight, they seemed to have successive layers of color, which, darkest at their deepest, became lighter as they approached the surface. His own eye became lost in their depths and he saw himself reflected in miniature as far as his shoulders, with his scarf tied around his head and the top of his opened nightshirt. He would get up. She would place herself at the window to see him go off and remain with her elbow on the ledge, between two geranium pots, dressed in her robe, which floated loosely around her. In the street, Charles would buckle his spurs on at the mounting block, and she would continue to talk to him, all the while plucking with her mouth some morsel of a flower or greenery, which she blew toward him and which, fluttering and floating, making semicircles in the air like a bird, would, before falling, become caught in the badly groomed mane of the old white mare standing motionless at the door. Charles, on horseback, would throw her a kiss; she would answer with a wave and shut the window. He would go off. Then, along the highway, stretching out like an endlessly long ribbon of dust, along the empty roads over which the tree branches bent low, in the paths whose corn reached as high as his knees, with the sun on his shoulders and the morning air in his nostrils, his heart filled with the joys of the previous night, his spirit calm, flesh content, he went off pondering his happiness like those who after dinner still savor the taste of the truffles they are digesting.

What good things had happened to him until now? Were his school days good, when he remained locked between those tall walls, alone in the midst of schoolmates richer or smarter than he, whom he amused by his accent, who made fun of his clothes, and whose mothers came to the visitors' parlor with cakes in their muffs? Was it good later on, when he was studying medicine and never had a purse full enough to pay for a dance with some little working girl who might have become his mistress? Or still later, when he lived fourteen months with the widow whose feet in bed were as cold as ice? But now he possessed for life this lovely woman whom he adored. For him the universe was bounded by the circumference of her silk petticoat; and he reproached himself for not loving her enough. He wished he could see her again; he would return in a hurry, climb the staircase, his heart pounding. Emma would be getting dressed in her room; he would arrive silently, kiss her on the back, she would give a startled cry.

He could not keep himself from constantly touching her comb, her rings, her shawl; sometimes he would give her big smacking kisses on her cheeks or a row of little kisses all along her bare arm from the tips of her fingers up to the shoulder; and she would push him away, half smiling, half annoyed, as one treats a bothersome child.

Before she had married she thought she was in love. But the happiness that should have resulted from this love had not come; she must have deceived herself, she thought. Emma sought to learn what was really meant in life by the words "happiness," "passion," and "intoxication"—words that had seemed so beautiful to her in books.

V I

She had read *Paul and Virginia* and dreamed about the bamboo cottage, the Negro Domingo, and the dog Fidèle, but most of all about the sweet friendship of some dear little brother who gathers ripe fruit for you in huge trees taller than steeples or who runs barefoot over the sand, bringing you a bird's nest.

When she was thirteen, her father took her to the city to enter her in the convent. They stopped at an inn in the Saint-Gervais section, where they were served their supper on painted dishes depicting Mademoiselle de La Vallière's story. The explanatory legends, interrupted in several places by knife scratches, accorded equal glory to religion, the delicacy of the heart, and courtly pomp.

Far from being bored in the convent, she was happy at first in the company of the kind sisters who, to amuse her, would take her into the chapel, which was connected to the refectory by a long corridor. She played very little during recess periods and understood the catechism well; and it was she who always answered the vicar's difficult questions. Living thus, without ever leaving the drowsy atmosphere of the classroom and among these white-faced women wearing rosaries with copper crosses, she succumbed peacefully to the mystic languor emanating from the fragrances of the altar, from the freshness of the font and the glow of the candles. Instead of following the Mass, she looked at the pious vignettes edged in azure in her book, and she loved the sick lamb, the Sacred Heart pierced with sharp arrows, and poor Jesus stumbling as He walked under His cross. She tried to fast one entire day to mortify her soul. She attempted to think of some vow to fulfill.

When she went to confession, she would invent trivial sins in order to prolong her stay there, on her knees in the shadow, hands clasped, her face at the grill as the priest whispered above her. The references to fiancé, husband, heavenly lover, and eternal marriage that recur in sermons awakened unexpected joys within her.

In the evening, before prayers, some religious selection would be read at study. During the week it was a summary of Abbé Frayssinous's religious-history lectures and on Sunday, for relaxation, passages from *le Génie du Christianisme*. How she listened, those first times, to the sonorous lamentation of romantic melancholy being echoed throughout the world and unto eternity! Had her childhood been spent in an apartment behind a store in some business district, she might have been receptive to nature's lyric effusions that ordinarily reach us only via the interpretations of writers. But she knew the countryside too well; she knew the lowing of the flocks, the milking, and the plowing. Accustomed to the calm life, she turned away from it toward excitement. She loved the sea only for its storms, and greenery only when it was scattered among ruins. She needed to derive immediate gratification from things and rejected as useless everything that did not supply this satisfaction. Her temperament was more sentimental than artistic. She sought emotions and not landscapes.

There was an old maid who came to the convent for one week every month to work in the laundry. Protected by the archbishop because she belonged to an old aristocratic family ruined during the Revolution, she ate in the refectory at the good sisters' table and would chat with them for a while after dinner before returning to her work. The girls would often steal out of class to visit her. She knew the romantic songs of the past century by heart and would sing them softly as she plied her needle. She told stories, brought in news of the outside world, ran errands in the city, and would secretly lend the older girls some novel that she always kept in the pocket of her apron, of which the good creature herself devoured long chapters between tasks. It was always love, lovers, mistresses, persecuted women fainting in solitary little houses, postilions expiring at every relay, horses killed on every page, gloomy forests, romantic woes, oaths, sobs, tears and kisses, small boats in the moonlight, nightingales in the groves, gentlemen brave as lions, gentle as lambs, impossibly virtuous, always well dressed, who wept copiously. For six months, at the age of fifteen, Emma soiled her hands with these dusty remains of old reading rooms. Later, with Walter Scott, she grew enamored of historic events, dreamed of traveling chests, guardrooms, and minstrels. She wished that she had lived in some old manor, like those long-waisted ladies of the manor who spent their days under the trefoil of pointed arches, elbows on the rampart and chin in hand, watching a cavalier with a white feather emerge from the horizon on a galloping black charger. During that period she had a passion for Mary Stuart and adored unfortunate or celebrated women. Joan of Arc, Héloïse, Agnès Sorel, La Belle Ferronnière, and Clémence Isaure blazed for her like comets over the murky immensity of history, on which, still standing out in relief, but more lost in the shadow and with no relationship to each other, were Saint Louis with his oak, the dying Bayard, a few vicious crimes of Louis XI, a bit of the Saint Bartholomew Massacre, Henri IV's plume, and the continuing memory of the painted plates praising Louis XIV.

In the ballads she sang in music class there were only tiny angels with golden wings, madonnas, lagoons, gondoliers—gentle compositions that enabled her to perceive, through the foolishness of the style and the weaknesses of the music, the attractive fantasy of sentimental realities. Several of her friends brought to the convent keepsake books they had received as gifts. They made a great to-do about hiding them. They would read them in the dormitory. Handling their lovely satin bindings delicately, Emma would focus her dazzled eyes on the names of the unknown authors, who usually signed their pieces "count" or "viscount." She would tremble as she breathed gently on the tissue paper covering the illustrations. It would lift in a double fold and then fall back gently against the page. Behind a balcony balustrade there would be a young man in a short coat holding tight in his arms a girl in a white dress with an alms purse on her sash, or anonymous portraits of English ladies with blond curls who looked at you with bright eyes from under their round straw hats. Some were relaxing in their carriages, gliding through parks while a greyhound jumped in front of the team being led at a trot by two small postilions in white breeches. Others, dreaming on sofas near an opened letter, were gazing at the moon through an open window half draped by a black curtain. The naïve ones were revealed with a tear on their cheek, feeding a turtledove through the bars of a Gothic cage or smiling, head to one side, and pulling daisy leaves with their tapered fingers, which curved like pointed slippers. And you were also there, you sultans with long pipes, swooning with delight in bowers in the arms of dancing girls! You giaours, Turkish sabers, fezzes! And you especially, pale landscapes of fabulous lands, which often show us at one and the same time palm trees and evergreens, tigers to the right, a lion to the left, Tartar minarets against the horizon, Roman ruins in the foreground, and camels crouching; the whole framed by a well-kept virgin forest with a large ray of perpendicular sunshine shimmering on the water upon which, like white gashes on a steel-gray background, swans are swimming into the distance.

And the lampshade, attached to the wall above Emma's head, shed light on all these tableaux of the world that passed before her one after the other in the silence of the dormitory to the sound of rumbles in the distance of some late fiacre still rolling down the boulevards.

She cried a great deal the first days after her mother's death. She had a memorial picture made with the dead woman's hair, and in a letter that she sent to Les Bertaux, all filled with sad reflections about life, she asked to be buried in the same tomb when she died. Her father thought she must be ill and came to see her. Emma was inwardly pleased to feel that she had achieved at her first attempt this rare ideal of pallid existences that mediocre hearts never achieve. She let herself glide into Lamartinian meanderings, listened to all the harps on the lake, to the songs of the dying swans, to all the falling leaves, the pure virgins rising to heaven, and the voice of the Eternal reverberating in the valleys. She tired of this, didn't want to admit it, continued first out of habit, then out of vanity, and was finally surprised to find herself soothed and with as little sadness in her heart as wrinkles on her forehead.

The good sisters, who had been so sure about her vocation, realized with great astonishment that Mademoiselle Rouault seemed to be eluding their influence. They had, in fact, lavished on her so many prayers, retreats, novenas, and sermons, had so well preached the veneration that is owed to saints and martyrs, and given so much good advice about bodily modesty and the salvation of her soul that she responded as do tightly reined horses; she stopped short and the bit slipped from her teeth. This temperament, positive in the midst of its enthusiasms, which had loved the church for its flowers, the music for the romantic lyrics, and literature for its passion-inspiring stimulation, rebelled before the mysteries of faith in proportion to her growing irritation against the discipline, which was antipathetic to her nature. When her father came to take her from the convent, they were not sorry to see her go. The Mother Superior even found that toward the end Emma had become quite irreverent toward the community.

Back home Emma amused herself at first by taking charge of the servants, then she began disliking the country and missed the convent. When Charles came to Les Bertaux for the first time, she felt quite disillusioned, having nothing more to learn, nothing more to feel.

But the uneasiness at a new role or perhaps the disturbance caused by the presence of this man, had been sufficient to make her believe that she finally felt that marvelous passion that until now had been like a huge pink-winged bird soaring through the splendor of poetic skies. She could not believe that the calm in which she was now living was the happiness of which she had dreamed.

VII

Yet sometimes she thought that these were the most beautiful days of her life—the honeymoon, as it was called. To savor its sweetness, it would have doubtless been necessary to go off to one of those sonorous-sounding countries where the first days of married life are languorously spent. Behind the blue silk shades of the mail coaches they would slowly climb up steep roads, listening to the song of the postilion being echoed through the mountain together with the sound of goat bells and the muffled roar of a waterfall. At sunset they would inhale the scent of the lemon trees by the shores of the gulfs; then, in the evening, on the terraces of the villas, alone, fingers intertwined, they would gaze at the stars and dream. She felt that certain places on the earth must produce happiness, just as a plant that languishes everywhere else thrives only in special soil. Why couldn't she be leaning her elbow on the balcony of a Swiss chalet or indulging her moods in a Scottish cottage with a husband dressed in a black velvet suit with long coattails, soft boots, a pointed hat, and elegant cuffs!

She might have wanted to confide all these things to someone. But how do you describe an intangible uneasiness that changes shape like a cloud and blows about like the wind? Words failed her—as well as the opportunity and the courage.

If Charles only suspected, if his gaze had even once penetrated her thought, it seemed to her that a sudden abundance would have broken away from her heart, as the fruit falls from a tree when you shake it. But as their life together brought increased physical intimacy, she built up an inner emotional detachment that separated her from him.

Charles's conversation was as flat as a sidewalk, with everyone's ideas walking through it in ordinary dress, arousing neither emotion, nor laughter, nor dreams. He had never been curious, he said, the whole time he was living in Rouen to go see a touring company of Paris actors at the theater. He couldn't swim, or fence, or shoot, and once he couldn't even explain to Emma a term about horseback riding she had come across in a novel.

But a man should know everything, shouldn't he? Excel in many activities, initiate you into the excitements of passion, into life's refinements, into all its mysteries? Yet this man taught nothing, knew nothing, hoped for nothing. He thought she was happy, and she was angry at him for this placid stolidity, for this leaden serenity, for the very happiness she gave to him.

Sometimes she would draw. Charles was always happy watching her lean over her drawing board, squinting in order to see her work better, or rolling little bread pellets between her fingers. As for the piano, the faster her fingers flew over it, the more he marveled. She struck the keys with aplomb and ran from one end of the keyboard to the other without a stop. The old instrument, with its frayed strings, could then be heard at the other end of the village if the window were open; and often the bailiff's clerk passing over the highway, bare-headed and in moccasins, would stop to listen to her, his sheet of paper in his hand.

On the other hand, Emma did know how to run the house. She sent patients statements of their visits in well-written letters that didn't look like bills. When some neighbor came to dine on Sundays, she managed to offer some tasty dish, would arrange handsome pyramids of greengages on vine leaves, serve fruit preserves on a dish, and even spoke of buying finger bowls for dessert. All this reflected favorably on Bovary.

Charles ended up by thinking all the more highly of himself for possessing such a wife. In the living room he pointed with pride to her two small pencil sketches that he had mounted in very large frames and hung against the wallpaper on long green cords. People returning from Mass would see him at his door wearing handsome needlepoint slippers.

He would come home late, at ten o'clock, sometimes at midnight. Then he would want something to eat, and Emma would serve him because the maid was asleep. He would remove his coat in order to eat more comfortably. He would report on all the people he had met one after the other, the villages he had been to, the prescriptions he had written, and, content with himself, would eat the remainder of the stew, peel his cheese, bite into an apple, empty the decanter, then go to sleep, lying on his back and snoring.

Since he had been accustomed for a long time to wearing a nightcap, his scarf would not stay put around his ears, and in the morning his hair was all disheveled about his face and whitened by the down from his pillow, the ties of which would become undone during the night. He always wore heavy boots, which had at the instep two thick folds slanting obliquely toward the ankles whereas the rest of the upper continued in a straight line, as taut as if stretched on a wooden leg. He said that it was "good enough for the country."

His mother approved his economy. She came to visit him as before, after some violent battle at her home. Yet, she seemed rather prejudiced against her daughter-in-law. She found her "a bit too haughty for their station in life"; wood, sugar, and candles were consumed "as if it were a great mansion" and the amount of charcoal that was burned in the kitchen would have sufficed for twenty-five meals! She arranged Emma's linens in the cupboards and taught her to keep an eye on the butcher when he delivered the meat. Emma accepted the lessons; Madame Bovary lavished them. And the words "daughter" and "mother" were exchanged all day long, accompanied by a tiny quivering of the lips, each of them offering gentle phrases in a voice trembling with anger.

During Madame Dubuc's day, the old woman still felt herself the favorite. But now Charles's love for Emma seemed to her desertion, an encroachment on that which belonged to her; and she observed her son's happiness with a sad silence like a ruined person who watches, through the windowpanes, people sitting around the table of his former home. She would recall her exertions and her sacrifices to him in the form of reminiscences, and comparing them to Emma's neglectful habits, would conclude that it was not reasonable for him to adore her in such an exclusive way.

Charles didn't know what to say. He respected his mother, and he loved his wife boundlessly. He considered the former's judgment infallible but found the other irreproachable. When his mother had left he would try timidly, and in the same terms, one or two of the milder observations he had heard her make. Emma would show him in but few words that he was mistaken and send him off to his patients.

And yet, in line with the theories she admired, she wanted to give herself up to love. In the moonlight of the garden she would recite all the passionate poetry she knew by heart and would sing melancholy adagios to him with sighs, but she found herself as calm afterward as before and Charles didn't appear more amorous or moved because of it.

After she had several times struck the flint on her heart without eliciting a single spark, incapable as she was of understanding that which she did not feel or of believing things that didn't manifest themselves in conventional forms, she convinced herself without difficulty that Charles's passion no longer offered anything extravagant. His effusions had become routine; he embraced her at certain hours. It was one habit among others, like the established custom of eating dessert after the monotony of dinner.

A gamekeeper, having been cured by Charles of a chest inflammation, had given Emma a small Italian greyhound; she would take it out to walk since she went out occasionally in order to escape for a moment and not have the eternal garden with the dusty road constantly before her eyes.

She would go as far as the Banneville beech grove, near the abandoned pavilion that forms an angle of the wall at the side of the fields. Sharp-edged leaves from the reeds would be scattered through the vegetation in the ditch.

First she would look all around to see if anything had changed since her last visit. She would find again, in the same places, foxglove and wallflowers, beds of nettles surrounding the huge stones, and patches of lichen along the three windows whose perpetually closed shutters were rattling away on their rusty iron bars. Her thoughts, at first unfocused, wandered at random like her greyhound, who ran around in circles through the countryside, yapping at yellow butterflies, chasing shrewmice, and nibbling the poppies on the edge of a wheat field. Then her thoughts would start to crystallize. She would sit on the grass into which she would dig the tip of her parasol with brief thrusts and would ask herself: "My God, why did I get married?"

She would ask herself if there might not be a way, by other combinations of fate, to meet some other man, and she tried to imagine what these unrealized events, this different life, this husband she did not know, would be like. None of them resembled her present husband. He might have been handsome, witty, distinguished, attractive, as, doubtless, were all the men her old friends from the convent had married. What were they doing now? In the city, with the street noises, the hum of the theaters, and the lights of the ballroom, they were living lives in which the heart expands, in which the senses blossom. But her life was as cold as an attic with northern exposure, and boredom, that silent spider, was spinning its web in all the dark corners of her heart. She remembered the days on which prizes were distributed, when she climbed to the platform to receive her small wreaths. With her braided hair, white dress, and openwork shoes, she had a gentle manner, and when she was back in her seat the gentlemen leaned over to compliment her. The courtyard was filled with carriages; the people said good-bye to her through the windows; the music master greeted her as he passed by with his violin case. How far it all was! How far!

She signaled to her greyhound, Djali, took her between her knees, passed her fingers along the long delicate head, and said: "Come kiss your mistress; you have no worries."

Then as she looked at the melancholy expression of the graceful animal, who was slowly yawning, she softened and spoke aloud to her, as to someone in need of consolation.

Sometimes there were gusts of wind, breezes from the sea, that, rolling over the entire plateau of the Caux country all the way into the fields, carried with them a salty freshness. Close to the ground the rushes whistled and the beech leaves rustled, while their tops, continually swaying, kept up their deep murmuring. Emma tightened her shawl around her shoulders and arose.

In the avenue between the trees a green light filtered by the foliage lit up the moss that was gently crackling under her feet. The sun was setting; the sky was red between the branches, and the uniform trunks of trees planted in a straight line seemed a dark colonnade standing out against a golden background. Fear came over her, she called to Djali, went rapidly back to Tostes by the highway, collapsed into an armchair, and did not say one word the entire evening.

But toward the end of September something extraordinary happened in her life; she was invited to Vaubyessard, to the home of the Marquis d'Andervilliers.

The marquis, secretary of state during the Restoration, seeking to reenter political life, was preparing his candidacy for the office of deputy well in advance. He distributed a great deal of wood during the winter and was always eloquently demanding new roads for his district in the General Council. During the hot weather he had an abscess in his mouth that Charles had miraculously cured with a touch of the lancet. The clerk he sent to Tostes to pay for the operation reported that evening that he had seen some superb cherries in the doctor's little garden. Now, cherry trees did not grow well in Vaubyessard; the marquis asked Bovary for a few slips, made it a point to thank him in person, noticed Emma, thought she had a pretty figure and a manner not at all like a peasant's, so much so that he did not feel he was going beyond the bounds of condescension nor on the other hand that he was making a mistake by inviting the young couple to the château.

One Wednesday at three o'clock, Monsieur and Madame Bovary set off in their buggy for Vaubyessard with a large trunk attached in the rear and a hatbox set in front on the dashboard. Charles also had a bandbox between his knees.

They arrived at nightfall, just as the lamps in the park were being lit to illuminate the way for the carriages.

VIII

The château, of modern construction, in the Italian style, had two projecting wings and three front entrances. It was spread out at the back of an immense lawn on which several cows were grazing between clumps of large, evenly spaced trees while groups of shrubs, rhododendron, syringa, and snowballs projected their unequal tufts of foliage along the winding sandy road. A stream passed under a bridge. Through the haze could be seen the thatch-roofed buildings scattered across the meadow. This latter was set in between the gentle slopes of two tree-covered hills. In the groves behind the house, set on two parallel lines, were the coach houses and stables, sole remains of the old, demolished château.

Charles's carriage arrived at the middle flight of steps; servants appeared; the marquis came forward, and offering his arm to the doctor's wife, he led her into the foyer.

It was high ceilinged and paved with marble tiles, and the combined noise of steps and voices echoed in it as in a church. A staircase faced it, and to the left a gallery overlooking the garden led to a billiard room, from which you could hear the ivory balls clicking as soon as you approached the door.

As she was crossing it to get to the drawing room, Emma noticed the serious-faced men, chins set over cravats folded high and all wearing decorations, standing around the table. They would smile silently as they hit with their cues. On the dark wood panels were large gilded frames with names written in black letters on their lower borders. She read: "Jean-Antoine d'Andervilliers d'Yverbonville, Count de la Vaubyessard, and Baron de la Fresnaye, killed in the battle of Coutras, October 20, 1587." And on another: "Jean-Antoine-Henri-Guy d'Andervilliers de la Vaubyessard, Admiral of France and Knight of the Order of St. Michael, wounded in the battle of La Hougue-Saint-Vaast, May 29, 1692, died at La Vaubyessard, January 23, 1693." Those that followed could barely be made out because the light from the lamps, directed on the green cloth of the billiard table, left the rest of the room in shadow. It turned the hanging canvases brown and highlighted only the cracks in the varnish; and from all the large gilt-edged black squares only some lighter part of the painting would emerge here and there—a pale forehead, two eyes staring at you, wigs unfurling over the powdered shoulders, red suits, or perhaps the buckle of a garter at the top of a fleshy calf.

The marquis opened the drawing-room door; one of the women arose (the marquise herself), came forward to meet Emma, and sat her down beside her on a small settee, where she began to chat amiably, as if she had known her a long time. She was a woman of about forty, with handsome shoulders, an aquiline nose, and a drawling voice; she wore a simple lace shawl that fell back in a point over her chestnut hair. A fair-haired young woman was sitting beside her in a high-backed chair, and gentlemen with tiny flowers in their lapels were talking to the ladies gathered around the fireplace.

Dinner was served at seven. The men, who outnumbered the ladies, sat down at the first table, in the hall, and the women were placed at the second, in the dining room with the marquis and the marquise.

As she entered, Emma felt herself enveloped in a warm atmosphere, a mixture of flower scent and the aroma of fine linens, of well-seasoned meat and truffles. The candles in the candelabra played their elongated flames over the silver platter covers; crystal pieces misted over reflected each other with pale glimmers. There were bunches of flowers set in a line along the entire table, and in the wide-bordered dishes napkins folded in the shape of bishop's miters held small oval-shaped rolls.

The red claws of the lobsters hung over the dishes; huge pieces of fruit were piled on each other in openwork baskets; the quails still bore their plumage; clouds of steam kept rising; and the butler, in silk stockings, knee breeches, white cravat, and frilled shirt, solemn as a judge, passing the already carved platters between the guests' shoulders, would make the piece you selected jump with one flick of the knife. On the large porcelain stove with its copper fittings, a statue of a woman draped to the chin stared steadily at the roomful of people.

Madame Bovary noticed that several of the women had not put their gloves in their wineglasses.

At the upper end of the table, alone among all the women, there was one old man eating, bending over his well-filled platter with his napkin knotted in back like a child, drops of sauce dribbling from his mouth. His eyes were bloodshot and he wore a small pigtail tied with a black ribbon. It was the marquis' father-in-law, the old Duke of Laverdière, once favorite of the Count d'Artois in the days of the Marquis de Conflans's hunting parties in Vaudreuil; it was said he had been Marie-Antoinette's lover between Messieurs de Coigny and de Lauzun. He had led a thoroughly debauched life, filled with duels, wagers, and abductions, had run through his fortune and been the terror of his entire family. A servant behind his chair was shouting into his ear the names of dishes that the old man would point to with his finger, mumbling. Emma could not keep herself from staring at the slack-mouthed old man as on someone extraordinary and august. He had lived at Court and slept in the bed of queens!

Iced champagne was served. Emma shivered all over at the prickly sensation in her mouth. She had never seen pomegranates before nor eaten pineapple. Even the granulated sugar seemed to her whiter and finer than elsewhere.

After dinner the ladies went up to their rooms to get ready for the ball.

Emma dressed with the meticulous care of an actress making her debut. She arranged her hair as the hairdresser had suggested and pulled on the *barège* dress that had been spread out on the bed. Charles's pants were too tight around the stomach.

"The shoe straps are going to be in my way when I dance," he said.

"Dance?" she asked.

"Yes."

"You're out of your mind! They'll laugh at you. Stay in your place. Besides, it's more suitable for a doctor," she added.

Charles said no more. He paced up and down the room waiting for Emma to finish dressing.

Her back was turned to him, and he looked at her reflection in the mirror between the two candles. Her black eyes seemed even blacker. Her hair, gently puffed toward the ears, gleamed with a bluish luster; a rose in her chignon was trembling on its fragile stem. It had artificial dewdrops at the tips of its leaves. She wore a pale saffron-colored dress, set off by three bunches of pompon roses mingled with greenery.

Charles went over to kiss her on the shoulder.

"Let go of me!" she said. "You'll wrinkle my dress!"

A violin flourish and the sounds of a horn could be heard. She descended the staircase, restraining herself from running.

The quadrilles had begun. More people were arriving, jostling each other. She stationed herself on a settee near the door.

When the quadrille was over, the floor remained free. Groups of men stood and chatted while the liveried servants brought in large trays. Along the row of seated women, painted fans were fluttering, bouquets half concealed smiling faces, and gold-stoppered perfume bottles were being turned in half-opened hands whose tight white gloves revealed the shape of the fingernails and hugged the wrists. Lace trimmings, diamond brooches, and bracelets with lockets trembled on bodices, sparkled on breasts, jingled on bare arms. The hairdos, securely arranged and twisted at the napes, were crowned with clusters or bunches of forget-me-nots, jasmine, pomegranate blossoms, wheat ears, or cornflowers. The mothers, sitting quietly in their places, wore red turbans and frowning expressions.

Emma's heart was beating a bit faster when, her partner holding her by the tips of his fingers, she took her place in line and awaited the fiddler's stroke to begin. But the emotion soon disappeared, and swaying to the rhythm of the orchestra, she glided forward, moving her neck lightly. A smile came to her lips at certain delicate strains of the violin during its solo moments; you could hear the clinking of gold coins dropping onto the card tables in the next room; then everything began at once, the cornet emitted a loud blast, feet fell in measure, skirts swirled out and rustled against each other, hands joined, then separated; the same eyes that lowered before you looked up again at yours.

Several men (about fifteen) between twenty-five and forty years of age, scattered among the dancers or chatting at the entrances, distinguished themselves from the crowd by their family resemblance despite the differences in their ages, dress, and facial features.

Their clothes, better made, seemed of a finer cloth, and their hair, made to gleam by more refined pomades, was brought forward in curls toward the temples. They had the complexion of wealth, that

Emma's heart was beating a bit faster when, her partner holding her by the tips of his fingers . . .

whiteness that is accentuated by the pallor of porcelain, the sheen of watered satin, the varnish of fine furniture, and that is nurtured by a diet of exquisitely prepared food. Their necks turned in relaxed manner over low-folded cravats, their long sideburns fell over turned-down collars; they wiped their lips with elegantly scented handkerchiefs embroidered with large monograms. Those who were beginning to age looked young, and a certain maturity lay over the faces of the young ones. The calm of daily satisfied passions showed in their indifferent glances, but their gentle manners did not completely mask that special brutality that stems from their relatively easy conquests, the handling of thoroughbred horses and the company of fallen women, in which the muscles are flexed and vanity sated.

A few feet from Emma a gentleman in a blue coat was talking about Italy with a pale young woman wearing a pearl necklace. They were praising the size of the pillars at St. Peter's, Tivoli, Vesuvius, Castellamare, and the Cascine; the roses of Genoa; the Colosseum in the moonlight. Emma listened with her other ear to a conversation full of words she did not understand. In the center of a group was a very young man who had beaten Miss Arabelle and Romulus the week before and won two thousand louis by jumping a ditch in England. One man was complaining that his racers were getting fat; another, about the way a printing error had garbled his horse's name.

The air in the ballroom grew heavy; the lights were fading. People began moving toward the billiard room. A servant climbing on a chair broke two windowpanes; at the noise of the shattered glass, Madame Bovary looked round and saw some peasants, their faces pressed to the window, staring at her from the garden. Then the memory of Les Bertaux came back to her. She saw the farm again, the muddy pond, her father in a smock under the apple trees, and she saw once more herself in the dairy skimming the cream from the milk cans with her finger. But in the splendor of the present hour, her past life, so clear until now, was disappearing completely, and she almost doubted that she had lived it. She was here, and outside the ballroom there was merely shadow cast over all the rest. She ate a maraschino-flavored ice, which she held in her left hand in a silvergilt shell, and half closed her eyes, the spoon between her teeth.

A woman near her dropped her fan as a man danced by. "Would you be so kind, Monsieur," the woman said, "and pick my fan up from under the sofa?"

The gentleman kneeled down, and as he reached out, Emma saw the young woman's hand throw something white, folded into a triangle, into his hat. The gentleman picked up the fan and held it out to the woman respectfully; she thanked him with a nod and began to sniff her bouquet.

After supper, at which many Spanish and Rhine wines were served, along with bisque and cream-of-almond soups, Trafalgar puddings, and all sorts of cold meats, surrounded by jellied molds, quivering on the plates, the carriages began going off, one after the other. By pulling the muslin curtain away from the corner one could see the light of their lanterns gliding through the night. The settees began to empty; there were still some card players; the musicians moistened the tips of their fingers on their tongues; Charles was leaning against a door, half asleep.

The cotillion began at three in the morning. Emma did not know how to waltz. Everyone was waltzing, even Mademoiselle d'Andervilliers and the marquise; there remained now only the château guests, about a dozen people.

One of the dancers, familiarly addressed as viscount, whose extremely low-cut waistcoat seemed molded on his chest, came a second time to invite Madame Bovary, assuring her that he would lead her and that she would manage well.

They began slowly, then moved more rapidly. Everything was turning around them, the lights, furniture, paneling, and the floor, like a disk on a pivot. Passing near the doors, the hem of Emma's dress flared out against her partner's trousers; their legs intertwined; he looked down at her, she raised her eyes to him; a numbness overcame her, she stopped. They started again and the viscount, with a more rapid movement, swept her away, disappeared with her to the end of the gallery, where, out of breath, she almost fell and for one moment leaned her head on his chest. And then, still turning, but more gently now, he led her back to her place; she leaned back against the wall and put her hand before her eyes.

When she opened them again, there was a woman seated on a stool in the middle of the floor with three dancers on their knees before her. She chose the viscount and the violin struck up again.

They were stared at. Up and down they went, she with her body held rigid, chin down, and he always in the same pose, holding himself erect, elbow rounded, face jutting forward. How she could waltz! They continued for a long time and tired out the others.

People chatted a while and after the "good nights," or rather "good mornings," the house guests went to sleep.

Charles dragged himself upstairs, clinging to the banister; his legs "couldn't stand up another minute." He had spent five solid hours standing near the tables watching the whist games without understanding a thing about them. And so he heaved a great sigh of relief when his boots were finally removed.

Emma wrapped a shawl around her shoulders, opened the window, and leaned out.

The night was black. A few drops of rain were falling. She breathed in the humid breeze that was refreshing her eyelids. With the ball music still humming in her ears, she was trying to stay awake in order to prolong the illusion of this luxurious life that she would have to abandon in a short while.

Day broke. She looked at the château windows for a long time, trying to guess which were the bedrooms of the various people she had noticed the night before. She would have liked to know about their lives, to enter into them, to become involved with them.

But she was shivering with cold. She undressed and snuggled between the sheets against Charles, who was asleep.

There were a lot of people at breakfast; the doctor was amazed that no liquor was served. Later Mademoiselle d'Andervilliers picked up what was left of the rolls in a basket to carry them to the swans on the lake, and they went for a walk in the hothouses, where exotic plants bristling with hairy leaves rose in pyramids beneath hanging vases, which, like over-crowded serpents' nests, dropped long, twisted green tendrils over their edges. The orangery at the far end led via a covered passage to the outhouses. The marquis took Emma to the stable to amuse her. Above the basket-shaped racks, porcelain plaques bore the horses' names in black. When they passed by, each animal stirred in its stall and clicked its tongue. The floor of the saddle room glistened like a drawing-room floor. Coach harnesses were set in the middle on two revolving columns and the bits, whips, stirrups, and curbs were all lined up along the wall.

Meanwhile, Charles went to ask a servant to ready his buggy. They brought it around to the front, and when all their luggage had been packed in, the Bovarys took leave of the marquis and marquise and headed back to Tostes.

Emma said nothing and watched the wheels turn. Charles, seated on the edge of the seat, was driving with his arms outstretched, and the small horse ambled along between its oversized shafts. The slack reins hitting its crupper grew moist with its lather, and the box roped on behind kept making loud, steady thuds against the body.

They were on the heights of Thibourville when suddenly some horsemen passed before them, laughing, with cigars in their mouths. Emma thought she recognized the viscount; she turned around and saw nothing on the horizon but heads moving up and down in rhythm with the uneven cadence of the trot and gallop.

Half a mile later they had to stop to tie a cord around the breech band, which had broken. As Charles took one last look at the harness, he saw something on the ground between the horse's legs; and he picked up a cigar case edged with green silk and emblazoned with a coat of arms in the center as on a coach door.

"There are still two cigars inside," he said. "They'll be for tonight after dinner."

"You smoke?" she asked.

"Sometimes, when I have the chance."

He put his find in his pocket and whipped the horse.

Dinner was not ready when they arrived home. Madame became furious. Nastasie answered with insolence.

"Get out!" Emma said. "You brazen creature! I'm sending you away!"

For dinner there was onion soup with a bit of veal cooked in sorrel. Facing Emma, Charles said, rubbing his hands together with a contented look: "It feels good to be home again!"

They could hear Nastasie crying. He was rather fond of the poor girl. In the old days when he had been a widower, she had kept him company on many an empty evening. She was his first patient, his oldest acquaintance in the district.

"Have you sent her away for good?" he said finally.

"Yes. Who's stopping me?" she answered.

They warmed themselves in the kitchen while their bedroom was being readied. Charles began to smoke. He smoked with his lips puckered, spitting every minute, recoiling at each puff.

"You'll make yourself sick," she said disdainfully.

He put his cigar down and ran off to gulp down a glass of cold water from the pump. Emma, seizing the cigar case, threw it hastily into the bottom of the cupboard.

The next day was long. She walked about in her garden, passing back and forth over the same paths, stopping in front of the flower beds, the fruit-tree trellises, the plaster curé, staring with bewilderment at all these once familiar things. How far away the ball already seemed! Why should there be such a distance between yesterday morning and tonight? Her trip to Vaubyessard had made a gap in her life like one of those great crevices that a storm sometimes carves out in the mountains in a single night. She resigned herself, however; reverently she packed away in the chest of drawers her lovely dress and even her satin slippers, whose soles had yellowed from the floor wax. Her heart was like them; the wealth had rubbed off on her, something that would never be erased.

And so the memory of the ball became a preoccupation for Emma. Every Wednesday she would say to herself on awaking: "Ah! A week ago today—two weeks ago—three weeks ago, I was there." Little by little the faces blurred in her memory; she forgot the quadrille tunes; she no longer saw the livery and the rooms so clearly; some of the details faded away, but the regret remained.

I X

Often, when Charles had gone out, she would take the green silk cigar case out of the cupboard from between the piles of linen where she had left it.

She would look at it, open it, and even sniff the lining. A blend of verbena and tobacco. To whom did it belong? To the viscount. Perhaps it was a gift from his mistress. It had been embroidered on some rosewood frame, a delicate item hidden from all eyes. Presumably it had taken up many hours, during which the soft curls of the pensive worker had fallen over it. A breath of love had passed through the meshes of the canvas; each stitch of the needle had fixed a hope or a memory, and all these threads of intertwined silk were but the continuation of the same silent passion. And then the viscount had borne it off with him one morning. What had they spoken about while he was standing near the fireplace with the large mantelpiece between the vases of flowers and the Pompadour clocks? She was in Tostes. He, he was in Paris now—Paris!

What was it like, that city? What a marvelous name! She would repeat it under her breath to make herself feel good; it resounded in her ears like a cathedral bell; it blazed before her eyes on the labels of her cosmetics jars.

At night, when the fishmongers in their carts passed in front of her windows singing the *Marjolaine*, she would awake and tell herself, as she listened to the noise of the iron-rimmed wheels dying away rapidly as they left the area. "They'll be there tomorrow!"

And she would follow them in her thoughts, climbing hills and descending them, crossing villages, moving over the highway by the light of the stars. And away off in the distance there was always some obscure spot where her dream expired.

She bought a plan of Paris, and moving the tip of her finger on the map, she would wander about the capital. She would go up boulevards, stop at each corner between the street lines, in front of the white squares that signified houses. Toward the end she would shut her tired eyes and see in the shadows the gas jets of carriages flickering in the wind, with the lowered tailboards unloading their passengers amid great tumult in front of the theaters.

She subscribed to *The Workbasket*, a woman's magazine, and to *The Sylph of the Salons*. She devoured all the reviews of opening nights, races, and soirees, without missing a single one; she would become interested in a singer's debut, in the opening of a store. She knew the latest fashions, the addresses of good tailors, the days for the Bois or the opera. She studied descriptions of furniture in Eugène Sue's books; she read Balzac and George Sand, searching in their writings for vicarious satisfaction of her own desires. She would even bring her book to the table and turn the pages while Charles spoke to her as he ate. The thought of the viscount came back to her continually as she read. She would create liaisons between him and the fictitious characters. But the circle of which he was the focal point gradually widened out, and the halo emanating from his face spread further out to illuminate other dreams.

Paris, more vast than the ocean, glistened in Emma's eyes in a silver-gold atmosphere. The crowded life that bustled in this tumult was nevertheless divided into parts, acted out in distinct tableaux. Emma saw only two or three, which obscured all the others and that alone represented all humanity. The world of ambassadors trod over gleaming parquet floors, in salons paneled with mirrors, around oval tables covered with gold-fringed velvet cloths. There were dresses with bustles there, vast intrigues, anguish dissimulated under smiles. Then came the society of duchesses. There you were pale, arose at four in the afternoon; the women, poor darlings, wore English lace at the bottom of their petticoats, and the men, with unrecognized talents beneath futile exteriors, rode their horses to death at every outing, went to Baden for the summer season, and married heiresses when they had finally reached their fortieth year. In the private rooms of restaurants where you dine after midnight, the motley crowd of men of letters and actresses laughed in the candlelight. That world was as prodigal as kings, full of ideals, ambitions, and fantastic dreams. It was an existence above the others, between heaven and earth, in the midst of the elements, something sublime. As for the rest of the world, it was lost, shadowy, and ill-defined, as if it did not exist. Besides, the closer things were, the more she turned her thoughts from them. Everything that immediately surrounded her, the dull countryside, imbecilic petty-bourgeois people, the mediocrity of existence, seemed to her an exception in the world, an unusual accident in which she found herself trapped, while beyond it the immense world of happiness and passion extended itself as far as the eye could see. In her yearnings she confused the sensualities of luxury with the joys of the heart, the elegance of convention with delicacy of sentiment. Didn't love, like the Indian plants, need cultivated land, a special temperature? Sighs in the moonlight, long embraces, tears flowing over forlorn hands, all the fevers of the flesh and languors of tenderness, did not separate themselves from the balcony of the great castle which was full of leisure, of boudoirs with silken shades, thick rugs, filled flower stands, and a bed mounted on a platform, nor from the glistening of precious stones and the lace ornaments of livery.

The postboy who came to groom the mare every morning crossed the corridor in his sockless feet in thick wooden shoes. His smock was filled with holes. This was the groom in knee breeches with whom she had to content herself! Once his work was done, he would not come the rest of the day because Charles would put the horse into the stable himself when he came home, unsaddle her, and adjust the halter while the maid brought a bucket of straw and threw it, as best she could, into the manger.

To replace Nastasie (who had finally left Tostes in tears) Emma took into her employ a young girl of fourteen, an orphan with a sweet face. She forbade her to wear cotton bonnets, taught her it was necessary to address people in the third person, to bring a glass of water on a saucer, to knock on doors before entering, and to iron, to starch, and to dress her. She wanted to make her into a lady's maid. The new girl obeyed without a murmur in order not to be sent away, and since Emma usually left the key in the buffet, Félicité would take a small supply of sugar each evening, which she would eat in bed all by herself after having said her prayers.

Sometimes during the afternoon she would go off to chat with the postilions across the way. Emma would stay upstairs in her chambers.

She would wear a dressing gown, entirely open, which revealed a pleated chemisette with three gold buttons between the challis lapels of the bodice. Her belt was a large-tasseled rope, and her tiny garnet-colored slippers had a cluster of wide ribbons that spilled all over the instep. She had bought herself a blotter, a writing case, a penholder, and envelopes, even though she had no one to write to. She would dust her shelves, look at herself in the mirror, take a book, and then let it fall onto her knees while she dreamed between the lines. She wanted to go traveling or return to live in her convent. At one and the same time she wanted to die and to live in Paris.

When it rained or snowed, Charles would direct his horse over the shortcuts. He would eat omelets at farm tables, put his hand into humid beds, receive full in the face the tepid spurt of bloodletting, listen to death rattles, examine the bedpans, and tuck in a great deal of dirty linens; but every night he would come home to a glowing fire, the table set, the furniture arranged comfortably, and a charming woman, neatly dressed, smelling so fresh you wondered where the fragrance came from and whether it wasn't her skin lending the scent to her petticoat.

She charmed him by a number of elegant gestures. Sometimes it was a new way of cutting paper sconces for the candles, a flounce that she changed on her dress, or the extraordinary name of some quite simple dish that the maid had spoiled, but that Charles swallowed with pleasure down to the bitter end. In Rouen she saw some women wearing charms on their watches; she bought charms. She wanted two large vases of blue glass on her fireplace, and a while later, an ivory workbox with a vermeil thimble. The less Charles understood those elegant touches, the more he responded to their attraction. They added something to his sensual pleasures and to the sweetness of his home. It was as if gold dust were being spread all along the narrow path of his life.

He was in good health and looked well. His reputation was quite established. The country people adored him because he wasn't conceited. He would pat the children, never entered a café, and otherwise inspired confidence by his good morals. He was especially successful with catarrhs and chest diseases. Being quite afraid of killing his patients, Charles hardly prescribed anything but sedatives, occasionally an emetic, a foot bath, or leeches. It wasn't that he was afraid of surgery. He bled people frequently, like horses, and he had "one hell of a fist" for extracting teeth.

Finally, "to keep up to date" he subscribed to the *Medical News,* a new journal whose prospectus he had received. He would read a little from it after dinner, but the warmth of the room, combined with his digestion, made him fall asleep within five minutes, and he would stay there, his chin propped up on both his hands and his hair falling in fringes down to the lamp base. Emma would look at him and shrug her shoulders. Why wasn't she at least married to one of those silent, impassioned men who work at their books all night and who, finally, at the age of sixty, when rheumatism sets in, wear a string of decorations on their badly made black suits? She would have liked the Bovary name, which was hers, to be famous, to see it displayed in the bookstores, repeated in newspapers, known by all of France. But Charles had no ambition whatsoever! A doctor from Yvetot, with whom he had recently found himself in consultation, had insulted him slightly, at the very bed of the patient, in front of the assembled relatives. When Charles told this to her that evening, Emma became furious at the other doctor. Charles was touched. He kissed her on the forehead with a tear in his eye. But she was exasperated with shame and felt like hitting him. She went into the hallway to open the window and breathe in some fresh air to calm herself.

"What a sad creature! What a sad creature!" she said to herself in a low voice, biting her lips.

She was beginning to feel more irritated with him in general. As he grew older he acquired some crude habits: during dessert he would whittle the corks of empty bottles, pass his tongue over his teeth after eating; he made a gulping noise at every mouthful as he swallowed his soup; and as he began putting on weight, his eyes, already small, seemed to sink in toward his temples because of his puffy cheeks.

Emma would sometimes tuck the red border of his undershirt into his waistcoat, straighten his cravat, or throw away worn gloves that he was about to put on. This was not, as he assumed, for him; it was for herself, for her own ego, out of nervous irritation. Sometimes, too, she told him about things she had read, a passage from a novel, for example, a new play or an anecdote about high society that was being reported in the paper. Charles was someone after all—an ever-available ear, an everready source of approval. She confided enough in her greyhound! She would even have confided in the fireplace logs and in the clock pendulum.

Deep down within her she was waiting for something to happen. Like sailors in distress, she gazed at the solitude of her life with despairing eyes, seeking some white sail in the far-off haze of the horizon. She didn't know what this change would be, what wind would bring it to her, toward what shore it would take her, whether it was a launch or a triple-deck ship, laden with anxiety or filled to the portholes with joy. But each morning when she awoke she hoped for it that day, and she would listen to every noise, leap out of bed, be amazed that it hadn't come; then, at sunset, growing continually sadder, she would look forward to the next day.

Spring returned. She felt stifled at the first warm spells, when the pear trees blossomed.

From the beginning of July she counted on her fingers how many weeks remained before October, thinking that the Marquis d'Andervilliers would perhaps give another ball at Vaubyessard. But September passed by without one letter or visit.

After the distress of this disappointment, her heart once more remained empty and the succession of identical days began again.

Now they were going to succeed each other one after the other, always the same, innumerable, and bringing nothing! Other people's existences, as dull as they were, at least had the chance of something happening. Some occurrence would occasionally bring about a series of ups and downs or a change of scene. But it was God's will that nothing should happen to her. The future was a totally dark corridor with a solidly locked door at its end.

She gave up her music. Why play? Who would listen to her? Since she would never be able to play in a concert on an Érard piano, in a velvet gown with short sleeves, tapping the ivory keys with her light fingers, feeling an ecstatic murmur, like a breeze, waft around her, it was not worth it to be bored studying. She left her drawing portfolios and tapestry in the cupboard. What for? For what reason? Sewing irritated her.

"I've read everything," she told herself.

And she would sit heating the tongs or watching the rain fall.

How sad she was when they rang Vespers on Sunday. She would listen in an attentive stupor to each cracked chime of the bell. A cat, walking slowly across the rooftops, would arch its back against the pale rays of the sun. The wind was blowing clouds of dust along the highway. Once in a while a dog would howl in the distance and the bell would continue its monotonous, evenly spaced ringing, which faded off into the countryside.

Then people would emerge from the church. The women in polished clogs, the farmers in new smocks, the little children skipping bareheaded in front of them—all were going back to their homes. And until nighttime five or six men, always the same ones, would remain playing quoits in front of the main entrance of the inn.

It was a cold winter. The windowpanes were covered with frost each morning and the milky white light coming through them sometimes did not change all day long. They had to light the lamp by four o'clock.

In good weather she would go down to the garden. The dew on the cabbages formed a silvery lace with long transparent filaments stretching from one to the other. There were no birds singing, everything seemed asleep, even the strawcovered espalier and the vine beneath the wall coping looked like some large, ailing serpent. As you neared it, you could see wood lice with many feelers crawling about. Under the spruce trees near the hedge the sculptured curé in the three-cornered hat reading his breviary had lost his right foot, and the plaster on his face peeling off from the frost had left white patches.

Then she would go back, shut the door, stoke the fire, and wilting in its warmth, feel even more heavily the boredom that was overcoming her again. She would have gone to chat with the maid, but was held back by a sense of propriety.

Every day, at the same time, the schoolmaster in a black silk cap would fold back the shutters of his house and the village policemen would pass by, wearing his saber strapped over his shirt. Morning and evening the mail horses, three at a time, would cross the street to water themselves at the pond. Occasionally the bell of a tavern door would tinkle; and when there was a wind, you could hear creaking on their two rods the wigmaker's small copper basins, which served as a sign for his store. The store was decorated with an old-fashioned print of women's fashions glued to a pane and a wax bust of a yellow-haired woman. The wigmaker also lamented his unfulfilled talent, his lost future, and dreamed of a shop in a big city, Rouen for example, on the quay, near the theater. He would walk back and forth all day long, from the church to the city hall, waiting for customers. Whenever Madame Bovary would look up, she would see him there, like a guard on sentry duty, with his cap pulled over one ear and his heavy woolen jacket.

Sometimes in the afternoon a man's head would appear at the living-room window: bronzed face, black sideburns, and a slow, gentle, gleaming, open smile. Then a waltz would begin on an organ; in a miniature drawing room, dancers as tall as a finger (women in pink turbans, Tyrolean peasants in jackets, monkeys in black coats, gentlemen in knee breeches) would turn repeatedly around the arm-chairs, sofas and end tables, and be reflected in the bits of mirror held together at their corners by strips of gold paper. The man would turn the handle, look to the right, to the left, and toward the windows. From time to time, while directing a long jet of dark saliva toward the curbstone, he would lift the instrument, its heavy strap tiring his arm, with his knee; and sometimes languid and slow, sometimes joyous and fast, the music from the box would grind out across a pink taffeta curtain held by a copper clasp shaped like an arabesque. The tunes were those that were being played in the theaters, sung in drawing rooms, danced to in the evening beneath lighted chande-liers—echoes from the world that reached as far as Emma. Never-ending sarabands whirled in her head, and like a dancing girl on a flowered carpet, her thoughts leaped with the notes, swinging from dream to dream, from sadness to sadness. When the man had received a little money in his cap, he would pull an old blue wool cover down, slip his organ onto his back, and go off with a heavy step. She would watch him until he disappeared.

Mealtime was the worst of all in that tiny room on the ground floor, with the smoking oven, the creaking door, the damp walls, and the moist flagstones; all the bitterness of her existence seemed to be

Mealtime was the worst of all in that tiny room on the ground floor . . .

served up to her on her plate, and the steam from the boiled beef brought up waves of nausea from the depths of her soul. It took Charles a long time to eat; she would nibble a few hazelnuts, or leaning on her elbow, would amuse herself by drawing lines on the oilcloth with the tip of her knife.

She was neglecting everything in the household now, and her mother-in-law, when she came to spend part of Lent in Tostes, was amazed at the change. She who had been so fastidious and delicate before now spent entire days without dressing, wearing gray cotton stockings, using candle ends for light. She kept saying that it was necessary to economize since they were not rich, adding that she was quite content, very happy, that she liked Tostes very much, and making other similar statements that silenced her mother-in-law's objections. She seemed as disinclined as ever to follow the older woman's advice, and once when Madame Bovary senior took it into her head to claim that masters should watch over their servants' religion, Emma answered her with such an angry look and cold smile that the good woman did not meddle any more.

Emma was becoming difficult and capricious. She would order certain dishes for herself and not touch a thing. One day she would drink only fresh milk, and the next, dozens of cups of tea. Often she would refuse to go out, then she would feel stifled, fling open the windows, dress in light garments. After she had roundly scolded her maid she would give her presents or send her to the neighbors', just as she would sometimes throw all the coins in her purse to the poor, although she was far from softhearted or especially responsive to others' feelings, like most people of country stock, who always retain something of the callousness of their fathers in their souls.

Toward the end of February old man Rouault, in gratitude for his recovery, brought with his own hands a superb turkey to his son-in-law. He remained in Tostes three days. Since Charles was with his patients, Emma kept him company. He smoked in his bedroom, spat on the andirons, spoke of farming, calves, cows, poultry, and the town council, so much so that she closed the door when he left with a feeling of relief that surprised even her. Moreover, she was no longer hiding her distaste for everything and everyone; and she began to express very odd opinions sometimes, condemning things that were generally approved and approving perverse and immoral things. This often caused her husband to stare at her.

Would this misery last forever? Would she never be out of it? She certainly deserved as much as all those women who were living happily. She had seen duchesses at Vaubyessard who had clumsier figures and more common manners than she, and she cursed God's injustice; she would lean her head against the wall and cry; she envied tumultuous lives, masked balls, and insolent pleasures with all the mad distractions they probably offered and that she had never known.

She became pale and suffered heart palpitations. Charles gave her valerian and camphor baths. Everything he tried seemed to irritate her more.

Some days she would talk with feverish abandon. These moments of exultation were suddenly succeeded by sullen moods in which she remained silent and motionless. Then she would revive herself by splashing the contents of a flask of eau de cologne over her arms.

Since she was constantly complaining about Tostes, Charles assumed that her illness was due to some local cause, and the idea taking hold, he thought seriously about setting up his practice elsewhere.

Then she started drinking vinegar in order to lose weight, contracted a small dry cough, and lost her appetite completely.

It meant a lot to Charles to abandon Tostes after four years' residence and at the moment "when he was beginning to take root." But if it was necessary! He took her to Rouen to his old professor. It was a nervous disorder; she needed a change of air.

After looking in every direction, Charles heard that there was a substantial market town named Yonville-l'Abbaye, in the Neufchâtel district, whose doctor, a Polish refugee, had run off the week before. So he wrote to the local pharmacist inquiring about the population, the distance from the nearest doctor, how much his predecessor had earned per year, etc. The answers were satisfactory and he decided to move toward spring if Emma's health did not improve.

One day, as she was straightening up a drawer in preparation for moving, she pricked her fingers on something. It was an iron wire from her wedding bouquet. The orange blossoms were yellow with dust and the silver-bordered satin ribbons were fraying at the edge. She threw it into the fire. It flared up faster than a dry straw. Then it looked like a red bush on the ashes, slowly disintegrating. She watched it burn. The little cardboard berries burst, the brass wires twisted, the braiding melted; and the shriveled paper petals fluttered on the grate like black butterflies, then flew up the chimney.

When they left Tostes in the month of March, Madame Bovary was pregnant.

PART TWO

I

Yonville-l'Abbaye (so named because of an old Capuchin abbey even the ruins of which no longer exist) is a small town about twenty-five miles from Rouen, between the Abbeville and Beauvais roads, at the bottom of a valley watered by the Rieule. This is a small stream that empties into the Andelle after working three mills near its mouth. It contains a few trout that boys enjoy fishing for on Sundays.

You leave the highway at La Boissière and continue straight on until you reach the summit of Leux Hill, at which point the valley appears. The river crossing it divides it into two distinct regions; everything on the left is pasture, everything on the right is farmland. The meadow stretches out beneath several rolling hills and joins, behind them, the Bray pasturelands, while on the east the plain climbs slowly, becoming wider, spreading its gold-colored grainfields as far as the eye can see. The water flowing at the edge of the grass divides the colors of the meadows and the fields with a streak of white and makes the countryside resemble a large spread-out cloak with a velvet collar edged with silver braid.

At the end of the valley appear the oaks of the Argueil forest and the steep slopes of Saint-Jean Hill, streaked from top to bottom by long, uneven, red tracks. These are traces of rain, and their brick-red tones, cutting finely over the gray color of the mountain, come from the iron particles contained in the springs that flow in the surrounding area.

This is the border area of Normandy, Picardy, and the Île-de-France, a bastard section where the language is without accent as the scenery is without character. It is here that the worst Neufchâtel cheeses of the entire district are made. Here, too, farming is expensive because a lot of manure is needed to enrich the crumbly soil filled with sand and pebbles.

Until 1835 there was no proper road to Yonville; but about that time the local government built a byroad connecting Abbeville and Amiens that sometimes is used by wagoners going from Rouen to Flanders.

Nevertheless, Yonville-l'Abbaye has remained stagnant despite its new outlets. Instead of improving its cultivable land, the farmers cling stubbornly to pasture despite the decrease in value, and the lazy little town turning away from the plain has continued its automatic growth toward the river. You can see it from afar, sprawling out along the bank like a cowherd taking a siesta at the edge of the water.

At the foot of the hill, past the bridge, is a road planted with young aspens that leads in a straight line to the first houses of the area. These are enclosed by hedges and set in the center of yards filled with scattered buildings, winepresses, cart sheds, and distilleries placed under thick trees whose branches support ladders, poles, and scythes. The thatched roofs, like fur hats pulled down over the eyes, cover nearly one third of the low windows (which have bulging panes adorned with a knot in the center, like the base of bottles). An occasional scrawny pear sapling leans on the plaster wall diagonally crossed by black joists. In the ground floor doorways a small revolving gate keeps out the chicks who come to peck at the brown bread crumbs dipped in cider. As you walk on, the yards become narrower, the houses are closer together, the hedges disappear; a bundle of ferns swings from a window at the end of a broomstick. There is a blacksmith's forge and then a wheelwright's shop with two or three new carts outside obstructing the road. Then, through an opening in the wall, you can see a new house in the middle of a circular lawn on which rests a Cupid with a finger in his mouth. Two cast-iron urns are set at each side of the front steps and a coat of arms gleams on the door. This is the notary's home, the finest in the area.

The church is across the street, twenty feet farther down, on one side of the square. The small cemetery around it, enclosed by a wall waist high, is so filled with graves that the old stones sunk into the ground form a continual pavement marked off in equal squares by the grass pushing up in between. The church was rebuilt in the last years of the reign of Charles X. The roof's wooden arch is starting to rot on top and there are occasional black holes in the blue color. Above the door, where the organ would be, is a loft for the men, reached by a spiral staircase that creaks under their wooden shoes.

Daylight coming through the plain glass windows slants across the benches lined up perpendicular to the walls; the occasional straw mats nailed to them have large lettered signs below them: "Monsieur So-and-So's Bench." Further down, where the nave narrows, the confessional box is balanced by a statuette of the Virgin, dressed in satin, with a tulle veil sown with silver stars on her head, and her cheeks a deep purple like some Sandwich Islands idol. Finally at the back there is a replica of the Holy Family, sent by the minister of the interior, which dominates the high altar between four candlesticks. The pine choir stalls have remained unpainted.

The marketplace, which consists of a tiled roof supported by about twenty pillars, takes up about half of the Yonville square. The town hall, on the corner next to the pharmacist's house, was built "to the plans of a Paris architect" and is a sort of Greek temple. It has three Ionic columns on the ground floor and a semicircular gallery above that ends with a pediment occupied by a Gallic cock leaning with one foot on the constitution and holding in the other the scales of justice.

But it is Monsieur Homais's pharmacy, facing the Golden Lion Inn, that most attracts the eye. Especially in the evening when his lamp is lit and the red and green apothecary jars in his window send their colors across the sidewalk. Then through them, as in Bengal lights, the pharmacist's shadow can be seen as he leans on his desk. From top to bottom his house is papered with signs written in script, round hand and in block letters: "Vichy, Seltzer, and Barèges Waters; Purifying Agents; Raspail Medicine; Arabian Racahout; Darcet's Lozenges; Rengault's Salve; Bandages; Bath Preparations; Medicinal Chocolate; etc." And the sign that stretches the entire width of the store announces in gilded letters: "Homais, Pharmacist." At the rear of the shop, behind the large scales on the counter, the "Laboratory" can be seen above a glass door in the middle of which the name "Homais" appears once more in gilded letters against a black background.

There is nothing else to see in Yonville. The street, the only one, is as long as a rifle bullet's range and has a few stores on either side; it stops short at the road bend. If you leave it on the right and follow along the foot of Saint-Jean Hill, you will soon reach the cemetery.

In order to enlarge it during the cholera epidemic, they removed part of the wall and bought three acres of land adjoining it; but this new portion is virtually uninhabited, the graves as before continuing to crowd together near the gate. The watchman, who is also the gravedigger and the church sexton (thus deriving a double profit from the parish corpses) has utilized the vacant land to plant potatoes there. From year to year, however, his little field narrows, and when an epidemic strikes, he doesn't know if he should be happy about the deaths or miserable about the burials.

"You feed on the dead, Lestiboudois!" the parish priest finally said to him one day.

This morbid remark made him ponder; it bothered him for some time. But he still continues to farm his crop and even maintains coolly that his vegetables come up without cultivation.

Since the events about to be recorded here, nothing has changed in Yonville. The tinplate tricolor flag still revolves above the church steeple; the two calico streamers outside the store of the dry-goods man still flap in the wind; the pharmacist's fetuses, like packets of white tinder, grow progressively more rotten in their muddy alcohol; and above the main entrance of the inn, the old golden lion, its gilt worn off by the rains, still displays its poodlelike mane to passersby.

The evening on which the Bovarys were to arrive at Yonville, the Widow Lefrançois, mistress of the inn, was so busy that the perspiration poured off in droplets as she busied herself with her pots. The next day was market day in the town, and meat had to be cut in advance, pullets cleaned, soup and coffee prepared. Besides, she had to feed her boarders, as well as the doctor, his wife, and their maid. The billiard room rang with bursts of laughter. Three millers in the small parlor were calling for brandy. The wood blazed, the coal crackled, and piles of dishes on the long kitchen tables, set down among quarters of raw lamb, trembled at the jolts caused by the spinach chopper. The chickens could be heard squawking as the kitchen maid chased them in order to cut off their heads.

A pockmarked man in green leather slippers, with a gold-tasseled velvet cap on his head, was warming his back against the fireplace. His face expressed nothing but self-satisfaction, and he seemed as much at peace as the goldfinch hanging above his head in a wicker cage; this was the pharmacist.

"Artémise!" shouted the landlady; "chop some firewood! Fill the pitchers! Bring some brandy! Hurry! If I only knew what dessert to serve the people you're waiting for. Good heavens, the moving men are starting their racket in the billiard room again. And their cart is standing right in front of the door! The Hirondelle may smash into it when it gets here! Call 'Polyte to move it away. Just think, they must have played fifteen games since this morning, Monsieur Homais, and drunk eight jugs of cider! They'll tear my cloth," she continued, looking at them from afar with a skimmer in her hand.

"They won't do so much damage," Monsieur Homais answered; "you can buy another."

"Another billiard cloth!" the widow exclaimed.

"This one's falling apart, Madame Lefrançois. I keep telling you,

you're making a mistake! A mistake! The players want narrow pockets and heavy cues today. They've stopped playing billiards the way they used to; everything's changed! One must move with the times! Now take Tellier—"

The landlady's face flushed with anger. The pharmacist added: "No matter what you say, his billiard table is nicer than yours. And suppose they thought of sponsoring a match to aid Poland or for the victims of the Lyons flood—"

"Good-for-nothings like him don't frighten me!" the landlady interrupted, shrugging her immense shoulders. "Come on now, Monsieur Homais, as long as the Golden Lion exists, people will come here. My nest is nicely feathered, thank you. You'll see the Café Français closed instead, one of these mornings, and with a pretty sign on the shutters! Change my billiard table," she continued, talking to herself, "that's so convenient for sorting laundry! Why, I've bedded down six travelers at a time on it during hunting season! Where is that slowpoke Hivert!"

"Are you waiting for him to get here before you serve your guests' dinner?" the pharmacist asked.

"Wait for him? What about Monsieur Binet? At six o'clock sharp you'll see him come in. There's no one in the world like him when it comes to being on time. He always has to have his place in the small parlor. Sooner die than eat somewhere else, and he's so fussy! And so choosy about cider! Not at all like Monsieur Léon. Now, he comes sometimes at seven, sometimes even seven-thirty. And he doesn't just stare at his food. Such a nice young man! Never a loud word."

"That's the difference between someone who's received an education and an old cavalryman turned tax collector."

The clock struck six. Binet entered.

He wore a blue frock coat hanging straight down his thin body. His leather cap with the ear flaps tied on top of his head revealed, under the turned-up visor, a bald forehead pressed flat by the helmet worn so many years. He wore a black waistcoat, a horsehair collar, gray trousers, and, in all seasons, carefully polished boots with two parallel swellings where his toes turned up. Not one hair was out of place in the light-colored beard that encircled his jawline like the border of a flower bed, framing his uninteresting face with its small eyes and aquiline nose. He was an able card player, a skilled hunter, and an excellent penman. He kept a lathe at home and made napkin rings with which he littered up his house, with the jealousy of an artist and the selfishness of a bourgeois.

He headed toward the small parlor; but the three millers had to be ejected first; and while they were setting his table, Binet remained silent in his place near the stove. Then as usual, he closed the door and took off his hat.

"His tongue won't wear out from being polite!" said the pharmacist as soon as he was alone with the landlady.

"He never talks much," she answered. "Last week there were two traveling salesmen here, boys full of fun. They told such jokes one evening that I laughed till I cried. And he sat there all clammed up, not saying a word."

"Yes," said the pharmacist, "no imagination, no humor, no social talents."

"But he's supposed to be clever," the landlady objected.

"Clever!" Monsieur Homais retorted. "He clever? Maybe in his own field," he added in a calmer tone.

He continued: "Should an active businessman, a doctor, or a pharmacist be so absorbed in his affairs that he becomes odd and even ill-tempered, I can understand it. Such instances have been recorded. But at least they think about something. Take me, for instance, how many times have I searched for my pen on my desk to write a label, only to end up finding it behind my ear where I had stuck it!"

As he spoke, Madame Lefrançois went out to the doorstep to see if the Hirondelle were in sight. She started as a man dressed in black suddenly came into the kitchen. In the dying glimmers of twilight one could see that he had a ruddy complexion and an athletic body.

"May I help you, Monsieur le Curé?" the landlady asked,

reaching for one of the brass candlesticks lined up along the mantelpiece. "Would you like something? A drop of cassis, a glass of wine?"

The priest refused quite politely. He had come for his umbrella: he had forgotten it the other day at the Ernemont convent. After asking Madame Lefrançois to send it to him at the parish house in the evening, he headed back to the church, where the Angelus was ringing.

When the pharmacist could no longer hear the sound of his shoes in the square, he began criticizing the curé's recent conduct. The refusal of a drink seemed to him the most detestable hypocrisy. All priests tippled in secret and were trying to bring back the days of the tithe.

The landlady came to the curé's defense.

"And anyway, he could bend four of you over his knee. Last year he helped our people bring in the hay. He carried six bales at a time, that's how strong he is!"

"Bravo!" said the pharmacist. "So send your daughters to confess to such healthy brutes. Now, if I were the government, I would want the priests bled once a month. Yes, Madame Lefrançois, an extensive bloodletting every month for the sake of law and order."

"Oh, stop talking, Monsieur Homais. You're blaspheming. You have no religion."

The pharmacist answered, "I do have a religion—my religion; and it's even deeper than all of theirs with their mummery and their tricks! On the contrary, I worship God, I believe in a Supreme Being, in a Creator whoever He is, it doesn't matter, who placed us here below to fulfill our duties to family and state, but I don't need to go into a church to kiss silver plates and fatten up a bunch of fakers who eat better than we do! You can worship Him just as well in the woods or in a field or even by studying the heavens, like the ancients. God, for me, is the God of Socrates, Franklin, Voltaire, and Béranger! I am for the *Savoyard Vicar's Profession of Faith* and for the immortal principles of eighty-nine! So I cannot accept a doddering deity who parades around in his garden with a cane in his hand, sends his friend up a whale's belly, dies with a shriek, and is resurrected three days later. These things are obviously absurd, and besides, they're completely opposed to the laws of physics; which incidentally shows us that the priests have always wallowed in a shameful ignorance in which they try to engulf their entire flock!"

He stopped talking and looked around for an audience. In his fervor the pharmacist had believed himself for a moment in a Town Council plenary session. But the mistress of the inn had stopped listening to him. She was straining her ears to hear a distant rumble. The sound of a carriage mingled with a clicking of loose chains hitting the ground, and the Hirondelle finally stopped at the door.

It had a yellow body supported by two large wheels that, reaching to the level of the tilt, prevented the passengers from seeing the road and soiled their shoulders with mud. The small panes of its narrow transoms rattled in their frames when the carriage was closed, and there were mud spots scattered through the old layers of dust that even the rainstorms did not quite wash off. It was drawn by three horses, one leading and two in the shafts, and when it went downhill its bottom portion would bump into the ground.

A group of Yonville residents arrived in the square, all talking at once, asking for news, information, and food baskets. Hivert did not know which one to answer first. It was he who did all the village purchasing in the city. He went to the shops, brought rolls of leather to the shoemaker, iron to the blacksmith, a barrel of herring for the inn, bonnets from the milliner, and wigs from the hairdresser. As he drove back he distributed his packages along the road, throwing them over garden walls from his seat and shouting at the top of his lungs while the horses trotted along by themselves.

He had been delayed by an accident; Madame Bovary's greyhound had run off across the fields. They whistled for it a good fifteen minutes. Hivert even retraced his steps for about a mile, hoping to catch a glimpse of it any minute; but they finally had to move on. Emma burst into tears and lost her temper. She accused

Charles of causing the tragedy. Monsieur Lheureux, the dry-goods merchant, who happened to be with her in the carriage, tried to console her with many stories about lost dogs recognizing their masters after many years. There was one such case, he said, of a dog who came back to Paris from Constantinople. Another had done a hundred and twenty miles in a straight line, swimming four rivers. And his own father had owned a poodle that after being lost for twelve years had suddenly jumped on his back in the street one evening as he was going out to dinner.

I I

Emma alighted first, followed by Félicité, Monsieur Lheureux, and a nurse. They had to awaken Charles, who had fallen into a deep sleep in his corner as soon as night fell.

Homais introduced himself. He offered his respects to Madame, his compliments to Monsieur, said that he was delighted to have the opportunity to be of some service to them, and added with a cordial air that he had presumed to invite himself along in his wife's absence.

Madame Bovary entered the kitchen and walked over to the fireplace. She took hold of her dress at the knees with the tips of two fingers, and having lifted it in this fashion to the ankles, held out to the flame a foot encased in a black boot, above the leg of lamb turning on a spit. The fire cast a glow over her entire body, its harsh glare penetrating the cloth of her dress, the even pores of her white skin, and the eyelids that she blinked from time to time. The wind coming in through the half-open door intensified the reflection.

On the other side of the fireplace a fair-haired young man looked at her in silence.

Since he was very bored in Yonville, where he was a clerk at Maître Guillaumin's, Monsieur Léon Dupuis (it was he who was the second of the regular visitors to the Golden Lion) kept postponing his dinner in the hope that some traveler with whom he could talk would come to the inn. On the days when he finished his work early, he arrived exactly on time for want of knowing what else to do and had to endure Binet's company from soup to cheese. Therefore he accepted with joy the landlady's suggestion that he dine with the new arrivals, and they filed into the large room when Madame Lefrançois had ostentatiously set four places.

Homais asked for permission to keep his skullcap on his head for fear of catching cold.

Then, turning toward his neighbor: "You are doubtless a bit tired? We're so frightfully jolted about in our Hirondelle!"

"I am," Emma answered, "but moving around always amuses me. I love a change of scene."

"It's so dull to live nailed to the same spot," the clerk said, sighing.

"If you were like me," Charles said, "continually forced to be on horseback—"

"But," Léon went on, addressing Madame Bovary, "nothing should be more agreeable, it seems to me. When one has the choice," he added.

"Besides," the apothecary said, "practicing medicine isn't too strenuous in these parts because the condition of our roads permits the use of a trap, and generally, the fees are pretty good since the farmers are well off. From the medical point of view, we have few serious illnesses apart from ordinary cases of enteritis, bronchitis, liver ailments, etc., and occasionally some intermittent fevers at harvesttime. Nothing of special note except for many cases of scrofula, caused no doubt by the deplorable sanitary conditions in the farmhands' lodgings. Ah! You'll find a lot of prejudices to combat, Monsieur Bovary, much stubbornness in defense of traditional methods, with which all your scientific efforts are going to clash daily. For we still have recourse here to novenas, relics, and the priest, instead of going naturally to the doctor or the pharmacist. The climate, however, is not at all bad, and we even count several ninety-year-olds in the district. The thermometer (I've made some observations) goes down in winter to four degrees and in the hot season touches twenty-five, thirty degrees Centigrade at the most, which gives us a maximum of twenty-four Réaumur or fifty-four degrees Fahrenheit, to use the English measure—no more! You see, we are sheltered from the north wind by the Argueil forest on one side and from the west wind by the Saint-Jean Hill on the other. That warmth, however, which arises from the steam given off by the river and the presence of considerable cattle in the meadows, cattle that exhale as you know a great deal of ammonia, that is to say, nitrogen, hydrogen, and oxygen (no, nitrogen and hydrogen only) and which, sucking up the earth's humus and blending all these different emanations, unites them in one bundle, so to speak, and combining with whatever electricity there is in the atmosphere, could in the long run, as in tropical countries, engender unhealthy air; that heat, I say, finds itself tempered in the very place it comes from—from which it should come, I should say, from the south—by the southeastern winds, which, having refreshed themselves passing over the Seine, sometimes reach us all at once, like the winds from Russia!"

"Are there any pleasant places to walk around here?" Madame Bovary continued, speaking to the young man.

"Very few," he answered. "There's one spot called the Pasture on top of the hill, at the edge of the forest. Sometimes on Sunday I go there with a book and watch the sunset."

"I find nothing as inspiring as sunsets," she said, "but especially at the seashore."

"Oh, I adore the sea," Monsieur Léon said.

"And don't you agree," Madame Bovary continued, "that your spirit soars more freely over that limitless expanse? That just looking at it elevates your soul and inspires thoughts about the infinite and the ideal?"

"Mountain landscapes do the same," Léon said. "I have a cousin who traveled through Switzerland last year, and he told me that you can't imagine the poetry of the lakes, the charm of the waterfalls, the gigantic effect of the glaciers. You see evergreens of an unbelievable size spanning the torrents, cabins jutting out over precipices, and there are entire valleys a thousand feet below you, when the clouds part. Sights such as these overwhelm you, dispose you toward prayer and ecstasy! I'm no longer surprised about that famous musician who used to play the piano in front of some imposing sight in order to stimulate his imagination."

"Are you a musician?" she asked.

"No, but I like music very much," he answered.

"Ah, don't listen to him, Madame Bovary," Homais interrupted, leaning over his plate. "It's pure modesty. Why, dear boy, just the other day in your room you were singing *The Guardian Angel* magnificently. I could hear you from my laboratory. You were sending it out like an actor."

Léon happened to lodge at the pharmacist's house, where he had a small room on the second floor facing the square. He blushed at this compliment from his landlord, who had already turned toward the doctor and was enumerating to him the principal inhabitants of Yonville. He was telling stories and supplying information. The notary's exact fortune was not known. As for the Tuvache business firm, they were making a lot of trouble.

Emma went on: "What kind of music do you prefer?"

"German, the sort that sets you dreaming."

"Do you know Italian music?"

"Not yet, but I'll hear some next year when I go to Paris to finish my law studies."

"I've just had the honor," said the pharmacist, "of telling your husband about poor Yanoda, who ran off. Thanks to the idiotic mistakes he made, you will find yourselves enjoying one of the most comfortable houses in Yonville. It's especially convenient for a doctor because it has a door to the lane so that people can enter and leave without being seen. Besides, it's furnished with all sorts of conveniences; it has a laundry, kitchen and pantry, sitting room, storeroom for fruit, etc. He was a bit of a spendthrift. He had an arbor built at the end of the garden beside the river just to have a place to drink beer in summer, and if Madame likes gardening, she'll be able—"

"My wife doesn't care much about it," Charles said. "She prefers to stay in her room all the time and read, even though she's been told to exercise."

"Like myself," Léon said. "What better occupation, really, than to spend the evening at the fireside with a book, with the wind beating on the windows and the lamp burning bright?"

"You're right," she said, fixing her large black eyes on him.

"Nothing disturbs your thoughts," he continued. "The hours pass. Without moving, you walk through the countries you see in your mind's eye; and your thoughts, caught up in the story, stop at the details or rush through for the plot. You pretend you're the characters and feel it's your own heart beating beneath their costumes."

"I know exactly what you mean!" she said.

"Have you ever happened to come across in a book some vague notion that you've had," Léon went on, "some obscure idea that returns from afar and that seems to express completely your most subtle feelings?"

"Oh, yes!" she answered.

"That's why I love the poets above all," he said. "I find verse more tender than prose and much more moving."

"Yet poets are tiring in the long run," Emma said. "Now, I adore stories that you can read in one gulp, stories that frighten you. I hate everyday heroes and restrained emotions like the ones in real life."

"Of course," the clerk said, "those works that don't affect the emotions miss the real goal of art, I think. With all the disillusionments of life, it is good to be able to identify oneself mentally with noble characters, pure affections, and portrayals of happiness. As for myself, living here far from the world, it's my one distraction. Yonville has so little to offer!"

"Like Tostes, no doubt," said Emma. "I always subscribed to the circulating library there."

"If Madame will do me the honor of using it," said the pharmacist, who had heard these last words, "I myself place at your disposal a library composed of the best authors: Voltaire, Rousseau, Delille, Walter Scott, *The Literary Echo*, etc. Moreover, I receive various periodicals, among them the daily *Rouen Beacon*, since I have the advantage of being its correspondent for the area of Buchy, Forges, Neufchâtel, Yonville, and the surroundings."

They had been at the table for the last two and a half hours because Artémise, the servant girl, dragging her old slippers over the flagstones with great indifference, had brought the dishes in separately, forgotten some things, misunderstood other things, and left open the door to the billiard room so that the latch banged against the wall.

Without being aware of it, Léon had placed his foot on one of the crossbars of Madame Bovary's chair as he spoke. She was wearing a small blue silk scarf that kept her frilled cambric ruff in place, and her chin would gently dip into or emerge from the material as she moved her head. Sitting side by side as Charles and the pharmacist chatted, they entered into one of those vague conversations in which chance remarks inevitably lead to the discovery of common tastes. They discussed everything during dinner: Paris plays, titles of novels, new quadrilles, and the world they didn't know, Tostes where she had lived, Yonville where they were.

After coffee was served, Félicité went off to prepare the bedroom in the new house, and soon after, the diners arose. Madame Lefrançois was sleeping near the embers, and the ostler, with a lantern in his hand, was waiting to lead Monsieur and Madame Bovary to their new home. Wisps of straw were stuck in his red hair, and he limped with his left leg. He took the curé's umbrella in his other hand and they started off.

The town was fast asleep. The marketplace pillars cast long shadows. The ground was all gray, as on a summer night.

The doctor's house being but fifty feet from the inn, it was necessary to say good night almost immediately, and the company parted.

From the moment she entered the hall, Emma felt the cold of the plaster falling over her shoulders like a damp cloth. The walls were freshly painted and the wooden steps creaked. In the first-floor bedroom a whitish light passed through the curtainless windows. Through it one could see treetops, and farther away, the meadow, half drowned in the mist that wreathed around the river's edge like smoke in the moonlight. Helter-skelter in the middle of the room there were chest drawers, bottles, curtain rods, gilt poles, mattresses over the chairs, and basins on the floor—the two men who had brought the furniture had dumped everything there without a care.

It was the fourth time she was sleeping in an unknown place. The first had been the day she entered the convent, the second her arrival at Tostes, the third at Vaubyessard, the fourth here; and each of them had turned out to mark a new phase in her life. She did not believe that things could turn out the same in different places, and since her life so far had been bad, maybe that which was to come would be better.

I I I

As she got up the next morning, she noticed the clerk in the square. She was in her dressing gown. He glanced up and greeted her. She nodded rapidly and closed the window.

Léon waited all day for six o'clock to come; but when he entered the inn, he found only Monsieur Binet at the table.

The dinner of the previous evening had been a considerable event for him; never until now had he spoken for two consecutive hours with a "lady." How then had he been able to express to her so eloquently so many things he wouldn't have said so well before? He was shy by nature, with the sort of reserve made up of both modesty and dissimulation. In Yonville it was found that he had "very elegant" manners. He listened to older people's opinions and showed no extreme political views, a remarkable thing for a young man. Then too he possessed talents: he painted in watercolors, could read the key of G, and liked to discuss literature after dinner when he wasn't playing cards. Monsieur Homais valued him for his education, and Madame Homais was fond of him for his friendliness since he often took the children to the garden. The Homais brood was a grubby lot, very badly brought up and slightly sluggish, like the mother. Besides the maid, they were looked after by Justin, the pharmacist's apprentice, a distant cousin of Monsieur Homais who had been taken into the house out of charity and who also performed domestic duties.

The apothecary turned out to be the best of neighbors. He gave Madame Bovary information about the tradesmen, had his cider merchant call on her, tasted the brew himself, and supervised the proper installation of the cask in the cellar; furthermore, he showed her how to obtain butter at a cheap price and made an arrangement with Lestiboudois, the sexton, who, in addition to his ecclesiastical and mortuary functions, took care of the principal gardens of Yonville by the hour or the year—as was preferred.

It was not sheer altruism that prompted the pharmacist to so much obsequious cordiality. There was a plan beneath it.

He had violated Article 1 of the law of 19th Ventôse, year XI, which prohibits the practice of medicine to anyone not holding a diploma. On the basis of some obscure denunciations against him, Homais had been summoned to Rouen to the private office of the royal prosecutor. The magistrate, with his ermine robe on his shoulders and wearing the official headpiece, had received him standing up. It was in the morning before the court sat. The policemen's heavy boots could be heard in the corridor, and in the distance the faint noise of huge locks being turned. The pharmacist's ears rang so intensely he thought he was going to have a stroke. He could see himself in the lowest depths of a dungeon, his family in tears, the pharmacy sold, all his display bottles dispersed. He had to go into the café for a glass of rum and seltzer to calm his nerves.

Little by little the memory of the warning grew weaker, and he continued as before to give harmless consultations in his back room. But the mayor had it in for him; some colleagues were jealous. He had to watch his step. By putting Monsieur Bovary in his debt with his favors, he hoped to gain his gratitude and preclude his talking should he notice something later. And so, every morning, Homais would deliver the paper to the doctor and often would leave the pharmacy a minute in the afternoon to visit him and chat.

Charles was despondent. There were no patients. He would sit silently for long hours, fall asleep in his consulting room, or watch his wife sewing. To distract himself he became the handyman in his home and even tried to redo the attic with some paint that the painters had left behind. But money worries preoccupied him. He had spent so much for the repairs in Tostes, for Emma's wardrobe, and for the moving that the entire dowry, more than three thousand crowns, had dwindled away in two years. Then there were so many things damaged or lost in transit from Tostes to Yonville (including the plaster curé, which had fallen from the wagon because of a strong jar and smashed into a thousand pieces on the Quincampoix pavement).

Another, less trying, worry distracted him—his wife's pregnancy. As her term drew to a close, he cherished her more. It was another bond of the flesh between them and seemed to deepen their union and render it more complex. When he watched from afar her lumbering tread and the slow swaying of her uncorseted figure, when he looked at her at his ease as they sat facing each other and she relaxed wearily into her armchair, then his happiness could not contain itself. He would get up, kiss her, caress her face, call her "little mother," try to cajole her into dancing, and half laughing, half crying, utter all sorts of playful endearments that came to his mind. The idea of having begotten a child delighted him. Now he lacked nothing. He knew all there was to know about human existence, and he sat down before its table, as it were, with both elbows planted serenely.

Emma was at first bewildered, then she yearned for the child to be born in order to know how it felt to be a mother. But not being able to spend as freely as she wished—to have a cradle shaped like a boat with pink silk curtains and embroidered baby caps—she abandoned her dreams of a layette in an excess of bitterness and ordered the entire outfit from a village seamstress without choosing or discussing anything. And so she did not enjoy those preparations that stimulate maternal tenderness, and her affection from the beginning was perhaps weakened on that account.

However, since Charles spoke about the child at every meal, she soon thought about it in a more sustained way.

She hoped for a son; he would be strong and dark and she would call him Georges. The thought of having a male child was an anticipatory revenge for all her earlier helplessness. A man, at least, is free. He can explore passions and countries, surmount obstacles, taste the most exotic pleasures. But a woman is continually held back. Inert and flexible at the same time, she has both the susceptibilities of the flesh and legal restrictions against her. Her will, like the veil of her hat that is tied by a ribbon, reacts to every wind; there is always some desire to respond to, some convention that restricts action.

She gave birth one Sunday, at about six A.M., as the sun rose.

"It's a girl!" said Charles.

She turned her head away and fainted.

Madame Homais ran over almost immediately and kissed her, as did old Madame Lefrançois of the Golden Lion. The pharmacist, as became a man of discretion, merely addressed some provisional congratulations through the half-open door. He asked to see the child and found it well formed.

During her confinement she spent a lot of time seeking a name for her daughter. At first she reviewed all those with Italian endings, such as Clara, Louisa, Amanda, Atala; she was rather partial to

Galsuinde and even more to Yseult or Léocadie. Charles wanted the child to be named for his mother; Emma was against it. They went through the calendar of saints' names from one end to the other and consulted strangers.

"Monsieur Léon," said the pharmacist, "with whom I was talking about it the other day, is surprised that you don't choose Madeleine. It's very much in style now."

But Madame Bovary senior protested strongly against this sinner's name. As for Monsieur Homais, he had a predilection for all names that recalled a great man, a famous deed, or a generous conception, and it was in this vein that he had baptized his four children. Thus Napoleon represented glory, and Franklin liberty. Irma perhaps was a concession to romanticism, but Athalie paid homage to the greatest masterpiece of the French theater. Homais's philosophical convictions did not interfere with his artistic tastes; the thinker in him did not stifle the man of sensibility. He knew how to discriminate, where to draw the line between imagination and fanaticism. In Racine's tragedy, for example, he abhorred the idea but admired the style, he cursed the conception but applauded all the details, and although detesting the characters, waxed enthusiastic at their speeches. He was transported when he read the great passages, but when he remembered that the priests were taking advantage of them for their own purpose, he was desolate; and with these confusions of sentiment in which he was thrust, he wanted at the same time to set a laurel wreath on Racine's head with his two hands and to argue with him for a good quarter of an hour.

Finally, Emma remembered that at the Vaubyessard château she had heard the marquise call some young woman Berthe. From that point on the name was decided, and as father Rouault could not come, they asked Monsieur Homais to be godfather. His gifts were all products from his establishment, to wit: six boxes of jujubes, an entire jar of racahout, three tins of marshmallow, and half a dozen sticks of sugar candy that he had found in a cupboard. There was a festive dinner the evening of the ceremony. The curé attended, and excitement ran high. Over the liqueur Monsieur Homais quoted from Béranger's *Le Dieu des bonnes gens*, Monsieur Léon sang a barcarolle, and Madame Bovary senior, who was the godmother, sang a ballad from the days of the Empire. Then Monsieur Bovary senior asked that they bring down the baby and began to baptize her once more with a glass of champagne that he was pouring from above on her head. This mockery of the first sacraments infuriated Abbé Bournisien. Old Bovary countered by citing a passage from the *La Guerre des dieux;* the curé rose to leave. The ladies pleaded; Homais intervened, and they managed to reseat the clergyman, who quietly sipped his half-finished demitasse of coffee.

Monsieur Bovary senior remained one more month in Yonville, where he dazzled the inhabitants by a superb silver-trimmed police cap that he wore in the morning while smoking his pipe in the square. Since he also had a habit of drinking a lot of brandy, he would often send the maid to the Golden Lion to buy him a bottle, which they charged to his son's account; and he used up his daughter-in-law's entire supply of eau-de-cologne to scent his scarves.

Emma was not at all displeased by his company. He had traveled throughout the world; he spoke of Berlin, Vienna, Strasbourg, of his days as an officer, of his old mistresses, of the elegant dinners he had attended. Moreover, he was attentive and would clasp her by the waist occasionally on the staircase or in the garden and shout: "Look out for yourself, Charles!"

Then Madame Bovary senior began to worry about her son's happiness, and fearing that eventually her husband would have an immoral influence on the young woman's notions, she made haste to leave. Her apprehensions may have been more serious. Monsieur Bovary was not a man to respect anything.

One day Emma was suddenly smitten with the desire to see her small daughter, who had been put to nurse with the carpenter's wife. So without checking the almanac to see if the six weeks of the Virgin were over, she set out toward the Rollet dwelling, which was at the end of the village, at the bottom of the hill, between the main road and the meadows.

It was noon. The houses had their shutters closed and the slate roofs that gleamed under the harsh glare of the blue sky seemed to be sending off sparks from the gabletops. A sultry wind was blowing. Emma felt herself weakening as she walked; the pebbles of the sidewalk hurt her; she hesitated, wondering whether to return home or stop in somewhere and sit down.

At that moment, Monsieur Léon came out of a nearby door with a bundle of papers under his arm. He walked over to greet her and placed himself in the shadow in front of Lheureux's store under the gray awning that projected outward.

Madame Bovary said that she was on her way to see her child but that she was beginning to feel tired.

"If—" Léon began, not daring to say more.

"Are you going somewhere?" she asked.

On the clerk's negative reply, she asked him to accompany her. By evening, this was known in Yonville, and Madame Tuvache, the mayor's wife, announced in her maid's hearing that "Madame Bovary was compromising herself."

To arrive at the wet nurse's home, it was necessary to turn left at the end of the street in the direction of the cemetery and follow a narrow path lined with privet that ran between some tumbledown cottages and yard walls. The privets were in bloom, as were the veronica, the dog roses, the nettles, and the slim brambles thrusting forth from the bushes. Through the gaps in the hedges could be seen, outside the huts, pigs on a manure heap and some tethered cows rubbing their horns against the tree trunks. The two of them walked leisurely side by side, she leaning on his arm and he adjusting his pace to hers. A swarm of flies buzzed before them in the warm air.

They recognized the house by an old nut tree that shaded it. Low built and covered with brown tile, it had a string of onions hanging on the outside under the attic window. Some sticks of firewood propped against the thorn hedge surrounded a lettuce patch, a few lavender bushes, and some sweet peas trained on sticks. Dirty water was trickling over the grass, and all around were strewn nondescript garments—knitted stockings, a red calico nightdress, and a large coarse sheet spread out over the hedge. At the sound of the gate, the nurse appeared, holding in one arm an infant she was suckling. With the other hand she was pulling a puny little boy with scabs covering his face, the son of a Rouen hatmaker whose parents, too preoccupied with their business, had left him in the country.

"Come in," she said. "Your little girl is asleep."

The downstairs bedroom, the only one in the house, contained a large, uncurtained bed placed against the back wall, and the kneading trough was set against the side with the window, one pane of which was patched with a blue-paper star. In the corner, behind the door, a row of boots with shiny hobnails was lined up under the drainboard near a bottle of oil with a feather in its neck, and a Mathieu Laensberg almanac lay on the dusty mantelpiece among gunflints, candle ends, and bits of tinder. The final luxury in the room was a picture of Fame blowing her trumpets, no doubt cut out of some perfume advertisement and nailed to the wall with half a dozen shoe nails.

Emma's child was asleep on the floor in a wicker cradle. She picked her up in the cover she was wrapped in and began to sing softly and sway.

Léon was walking about in the room. It seemed strange to him to see this woman in a nankeen dress in the heart of all this misery. Madame Bovary blushed; he turned away, thinking that his eyes perhaps had revealed some impertinence. Then she replaced the child, who had just thrown up on her collar. The nurse came over immediately to wipe it off, insisting that it wouldn't show.

"She gives me plenty more," she said, "and I spend all day washing her! Perhaps you'd be kind enough to tell Camus the grocer to let me have some soap when I need it? It'll be even easier for you if I don't have to keep bothering you."

"Certainly," said Emma. "Good-bye, Madame Rollet!"

Emma's child was asleep on the floor in a wicker cradle. She picked her up in the cover she was wrapped in and began to sing softly and sway.

And she left, wiping her feet on the doorstep.

The good woman accompanied her through her yard, speaking of the trouble she had of getting up during the night.

"I'm so exhausted from it sometimes that I fall asleep on my chair. Maybe you could give me a pound of ground coffee that I can take in the morning with some milk. It will last me a month."

After acknowledging her thanks, Madame Bovary started off. She had barely moved down the path when the sound of clogs made her turn her head. It was the wet nurse.

"What's the matter?"

The woman, pulling her aside under an elm tree, began to speak of her husband, who, with his job and the six francs a year that the captain—

"Get to the point faster," Emma said.

"Very well!" the wet nurse continued, sighing between each word. "I'm afraid that he'll feel bad seeing me take coffee all by myself. You know how men are—"

"You'll have some," Emma repeated. "I'll give you enough! You're annoying me!"

"Oh dear, my lady, he has terrible pains in his chest from his wounds. He says that even cider weakens him."

"Do hurry up, Madame Rollet."

"So," the latter continued, dropping a curtsy, "if it weren't asking too much of you"—she curtsied one more time—"if you would"—and she implored with a look—"a small jug of brandy," she finally said, "and I'll rub some on your little girl's feet; they're as tender as your tongue."

Rid of the nurse, Emma took Monsieur Léon's arm again. She walked rapidly for a while; then she slowed down and her wandering gaze met the young man's shoulder. His frock coat had a black velvet collar over which fell his chestnut hair, smooth and well combed. She noticed his nails, which were longer than were worn in Yonville. One of the clerk's great occupations was to keep them manicured. He kept a penknife for this very purpose in his writing desk.

They came back to Yonville along the river. During warm weather the riverbank grew wide. They could see the bases of the garden walls, which had short staircases leading toward the water. The river flowed noiselessly, rapid and cold to the eye. Large thin grasses bent together, swaying to the current like abandoned green wigs spread out over the clear water. Here and there, on the tip of a reed or on the leaf of a water lily, a fine-footed insect would alight or crawl. Sun rays pierced through the small blue bubbles the waves made as they broke; the old, branchless willows reflected their gray bark in the water. All around the meadow seemed empty for miles. It was dinnertime on the farms, and the young woman and her companion heard nothing as they walked but the rhythm of their steps on the path, the words they were uttering, and the rustling of Emma's dress.

The garden walls, their copings stuck with pieces of broken bottles, were as warm as greenhouse windows. Wallflowers had pushed between the bricks, and with the tip of her open parasol Madame Bovary, as she walked, scraped some of their faded petals, which disintegrated into yellow dust; or some overhanging branch of honeysuckle or clematis would catch on the fringes for a moment.

They were talking about a Spanish dance company soon expected in the Rouen theater.

"Will you be going?" she asked.

"If I can," he answered.

Had they nothing else to say to each other? Yet their eyes were full of more serious statements; and while they sought for commonplace sentences, they each felt the same languor. It was like a murmur of the soul, profound and continuous, dominating that of the voices. Surprised at this unexpected sweetness, it did not occur to them to discuss the sensation or discover the cause. Future happiness, like tropical shores, projects over the vastness that precedes it, its innate indolence, and wafts a scented breeze that intoxicates and dispels any anxiety about the unseen horizon.

At one point the ground had been trampled by cattle; they had to step over large mossy rocks evenly spaced across the mud. She kept stopping to see where to place her shoe; and faltering on a shifting stone, elbows akimbo, body bent forward, looking unsure, she laughed out of fear of falling into the puddle.

When they reached her garden, Madame Bovary pushed open the small gate, ran up the steps, and disappeared.

Léon went back to his office. His employer was out; he glanced over the files, trimmed a pen, then picked up his hat and went off.

He went to the pasture, at the summit of the Argueil hill, near the forest entrance. He lay down on the ground under the pine trees and looked at the sky through his fingers.

"I'm so bored!" he said to himself; "so bored!"

He found it sad that he should have to live in this village, with Homais for a friend and Monsieur Guillaumin for an employer. The latter, completely occupied with business, with his gold-framed glasses and red sideburns over a white cravat, understood nothing about the subtleties of the spirit, although he affected a stiff British manner that had dazzled the clerk at the beginning. As for the pharmacist's wife, she was the best wife in Normandy; she was gentle as a lamb, cherished her children, her father, her mother, her cousins, cried over other people's troubles, made everything run smoothly in her household, and detested corsets; but she was so slow moving, so boring to listen to, so common in looks, and so limited in conversation that he would never have thought, even though she was thirty years old and he twenty, even though they slept next door to each other and he spoke to her each day, that she could be someone's wife, nor that she possessed anything of her sex other than her clothing.

And otherwise, what was there? Binet, a few tradesmen, two or three innkeepers, the curé, and finally, Monsieur Tuvache, the mayor, with his two sons; wealthy people, crude, thick headed, farming their land themselves, keeping their celebrations within the family, sanctimoniously pious, and completely insufferable socially.

But Emma's face detached itself from this background of human faces, isolated yet even further removed; for he sensed undefinable chasms between himself and her.

At the beginning, he had called on her several times in the pharmacist's company. Charles had not appeared very interested in receiving him; and Léon, between the fear of being indiscreet and the desire for an intimacy that he imagined almost impossible, did not know how to proceed.

I V

A s soon as the cold weather began, Emma abandoned her bedroom and moved into the parlor, a long, low-ceilinged room with a piece of branched coral spread out on the mantelpiece against the mirror. Sitting in her armchair near the window, she would watch the villagers walking along the sidewalk.

Léon went from his office to the Golden Lion twice a day. Emma heard him coming from afar; she would lean out while she listened, and the young man, always dressed the same way, would glide behind the curtain without turning his head. But at twilight she cupped her chin in her left hand, dropped her unfinished embroidery on her lap, and shuddered at the sudden appearance of this moving shadow. She would get up and order the table to be set.

Monsieur Homais would arrive during dinner. Skullcap in his hand, he entered on tiptoe in order not to disturb anyone and always repeated the same sentence: "Good evening, everyone!" Then, when he had settled in his place at the table, between husband and wife, he asked the doctor for news about his patients, and the latter would consult him about the chance of getting paid. Then they discussed the contents of the newspaper. By that hour Homais knew it almost by heart; and he would report it all, including the editorial comments and the stories of various catastrophes that had occurred in France or elsewhere. And when the subject began to peter out, he threw in some observations about the food he saw. Sometimes he would even half get up and delicately point out the tenderest bit to Madame, or turning to the maid, would offer her advice for the preparation of stews and the hygienic properties of seasonings; he spoke impressively about aroma, osmazome, natural juices, and gelatin. Moreover, his head being more filled with recipes than his pharmacy was with display jars, Homais excelled in making various jams, vinegars, and sweet liqueurs, and he also knew all the latest fuel-saving devices, the art of keeping cheese and of curing ailing wines.

At eight, Justin would come and call him to lock up the pharmacy. Then Monsieur Homais, having noticed that his pupil had a fondness for the doctor's house, looked at him knowingly, especially if Félicité happened to be there.

"My young friend," he would say, "is beginning to have ideas, and devil take me if he isn't in love with your maid!"

But a more serious fault, for which he reproached him, was that of constantly eavesdropping. On Sunday, for instance, one could not make him leave the drawing room into which Madame Homais had called him to take the children, who were falling asleep in the armchairs and disarranging the loose-fitting calico covers.

There were not many people who came to these gatherings at the pharmacist's home, his spiteful tongue and political opinions having alienated various respectable people in succession. The clerk never failed to be there. As soon as he heard the bell, he would run to meet Madame Bovary, take her shawl, and put away under the shop desk the thick list slippers she wore over her shoes when it snowed.

At first they played several games of trente-et-un, then Monsieur Homais would play a game of écarté with Emma; Léon, standing behind her, would offer advice. His hands on the back of her chair, he would look at the teeth of her comb biting into her chignon. Each time she moved to throw down the cards her dress would shift up on the right side. From her pinned-up hair a dark glow reflected down and gradually faded into the shadow. Her dress was draped over both sides of the chair in generous folds, spreading out to the floor. When Léon occasionally felt himself stepping on it, he would jump away as if he were stepping on someone.

When the card games were over, the pharmacist and the doctor would play dominoes, and Emma, changing her seat, would lean her elbows on the table and leaf through *L'Illustration*. She had brought her fashion magazine. Léon would station himself near her; they would look together at the illustrations and would await each other at the bottom of the page. She would often ask him to recite poetry to her; Léon would declaim in a drawling voice that he carefully allowed to expire at the love passages. But the noise of the dominoes irritated him; Monsieur Homais was good at them, he would beat Charles by a full double-six. When their three hundred was finished, they would both stretch before the hearth and lose no time in falling asleep. The fire died out among the embers; the teapot was empty; Léon would still be reading, Emma listening to him, absentmindedly turning the lampshade, on the gauze of which were painted clowns in carriages and tightrope walkers with their balancing poles. Léon would stop, pointing to his sleeping audience; then they spoke in low voices, and their conversation seemed sweeter to them because it was not overheard.

Thus a sort of relationship was established between them, a continual exchange of books and ballads; Monsieur Bovary, not a jealous type, did not wonder about it.

For his birthday he received a handsome phrenological head, marked with numbers as far as the thorax and painted blue. It was a thoughtful gesture from the clerk. He offered many others, even running errands for Charles in Rouen; and when some novelist's book launched a fad for cactus plants, he bought one for Emma, which he brought back on his lap in the Hirondelle, prickling his fingers on its spiky leaves.

She had a small railed window shelf built to hold her flowerpots. The clerk also had his hanging garden. They would see each other when they tended their flowers on the windows.

Among the village windows there was one even more often occupied; on Sunday, from morning until night, and every afternoon if the weather was clear, Monsieur Binet's thin profile could be seen as he leaned over his lathe. Its monotonous hum could be heard as far as the Golden Lion.

One evening when he came home, Léon found in his room a rug worked in velvet and wool, with a leaf design on a pale ground. He called Madame Homais, Monsieur Homais, Justin, the children, and the cook; he spoke about it to his employer. Everyone wanted to see the rug. Why was the doctor's wife making these "generous" gestures to the clerk? It seemed odd, and they thought it definite proof that she was "his good friend."

He spoke so often about her charms and her wit that he seemed to confirm it. In fact, Binet one time answered him rather brusquely: "What difference does it make to me? I'm not one of her friends!"

He tortured himself to discover how he could declare his feelings to her; and always hesitating between the fear of displeasing her and the fear of seeming weak willed, he wept tears of discouragement and desire. Then he made some energetic decisions; he wrote letters that he tore up, set himself deadlines that he would postpone. He would often start out with the intention of daring all; but his resolution would abandon him quickly in Emma's presence, and when Charles would appear and invite him to come along and visit some patient in the area with him, he would accept immediately, bid Madame farewell, and be off. After all, wasn't her husband part of her?

As for Emma, she didn't think she was in love with him. Love, she believed, should arrive all at once with thunder and lightning—a whirlwind from the skies that affects life, turns it every which way, wrests resolutions away like leaves, and plunges the entire heart into an abyss. She did not know that rain forms lakes on house terraces when the gutters are stopped up, and she remained secure in her ignorance until she suddenly discovered a crack in the wall.

V

It was a snowy Sunday afternoon in February.

They had all gone off—Monsieur and Madame Bovary, Homais, and Léon—to see a flax mill that was being built about a mile outside Yonville in the valley. The pharmacist took Napoleon and Athalie with him for the exercise. Justin came along with umbrellas on his shoulder.

Nothing, however, could have been less curious than this curiosity. A great expanse of empty ground in which several already rusted gear wheels could be found scattered among the piles of sand and pebbles surrounded a long, rectangular building, the walls of which were punctured by a number of small windows. The mill was not yet finished, and you could see the sky through the roof beams. Attached to the gable end was a bundle of straw mixed with wheat ears tied with tricolor ribbons flapping in the wind.

Homais was speaking. He was explaining to the group the future importance of this establishment, calculating the strength of the floors, the thickness of the walls, and very much regretting not having a measuring stick like Monsieur Binet's.

Emma, who had taken his arm, was leaning gently on his shoulder, looking at the solar disk gleaming whitely through the mist. Then she turned around. Charles was there, his cap pulled down over his eyebrows and his two thick lips quivering, which gave a rather stupid look to his face; even his back, his placid back, was irritating to see, and she found the flatness of his personality written all over his coat.

While she was looking at him, savoring in her impatience a sort of depraved voluptuousness, Léon moved a step forward. The chilly air that was making him pale seemed to soften his face; between his cravat and his neck the slightly loose collar of his shirt revealed the skin; a bit of ear escaped from under a lock of hair, and his big blue eyes lifted toward the clouds seemed to Emma more limpid and more beautiful than those mountain lakes in which the sky is reflected.

"Idiot!" the pharmacist shouted suddenly.

And he ran over to his son, who had just thrown himself into a heap of lime in order to whiten his shoes. Napoleon began to howl at the reproaches being poured on him while Justin was wiping his shoes with some straw. But a knife was needed; Charles offered his.

"Ah," she said to herself, "he carries a knife in his pocket, just like a peasant!"

The frost was beginning to fall and they headed back toward Yonville.

That evening Madame Bovary did not go to the neighbors', and when Charles had left, when she felt herself alone, the comparison began again with the clarity of an almost immediate sensation and with that lengthening of perspective that memory imparts to things. Looking from her bed at the fire burning brightly, she could still see, as if she were still there, Léon standing up, bending his walking stick in one hand and holding Athalie with the other as she sucked peacefully on a bit of ice. She found him charming; she couldn't get him out of her mind; she remembered his gestures of other days, things he had said, the sound of his voice, his entire person; and she repeated, thrusting her lips forward as for a kiss: "Yes, charming, charming! He must be in love," she told herself. "With whom? . . . But it's me!"

The proofs appeared before her all at once; her heart leaped. The flame from the fireplace was flickering merrily on the ceiling; she lay on her back and stretched out her arms.

Then the eternal lamentation began: "If only fate had willed it! Why can't it be? Who prevented it?"

When Charles returned at midnight, she pretended he had just awakened her, and as he made a noise while undressing, she pleaded a headache; then she asked nonchalantly what had happened during the evening.

"Monsieur Léon left early," he said.

She couldn't repress a smile. She fell asleep, her soul filled with a new enchantment.

The next day, at nightfall, she received a visit from Lheureux, the dry-goods merchant. The shopkeeper was a clever man.

Gascon by birth but Norman by adoption, he combined his southern loquaciousness with Cauchois shrewdness. His fat face, smooth and beardless, looked as if it had been colored by watered-down licorice juice, and his white hair heightened even more the hard brilliance of his small black eyes. No one knew what he had been before. Some said a peddler, others a banker. What was certain was that he could do complicated calculations in his head that frightened even Binet. Polite to the point of obsequiousness, he always stood slightly inclined in the posture of someone who is either greeting or inviting.

After leaving his crepebound hat at the door, he set down a green cardboard box on the table and began by lamenting to Madame, with a great show of politeness, that as of that day he had not obtained her confidence. A poor shop like his could never hope to attract "an elegant lady"—he dwelled on the word. She had but to order and he would make it his business to furnish her with whatever she wanted, both in cotton goods and lingerie, hats or novelties, since he went to the city four times a month regularly. He was in contact with the largest firms. One could ask about him at the Three Brothers, at the Golden Beard, or at the Great Savage; all those gentlemen knew him as well as the insides of their pockets! Today he had dropped in to show Madame an assortment of articles that he happened to have, thanks to an unusual opportunity. And he pulled a half dozen embroidered handkerchiefs out of the box.

Madame Bovary examined them.

"I don't need anything," she said.

Then Monsieur Lheureux delicately displayed three Algerian scarves, several packets of English needles, a pair of straw slippers, and finally four eggcups carved from coconut shells by convicts. Both hands on the table, leaning forward with his neck outstretched and his mouth open, he watched Emma as she hovered undecided over this merchandise. Occasionally, as if to brush off the dust, he would flick with his fingernail the silk of the scarves, which were unfolded to their entire length; and they would quiver with a light rustle while the golden threads in their fabric gleamed in the greenish twilight.

"How much are they?"

"A mere nothing," he answered, "a nothing. But there's no hurry. When you're ready. We aren't Jews."

She thought for a few minutes and ended by declining with thanks. Monsieur Lheureux replied without emotion: "Well! We'll come to an understanding later on. I've always worked things out with the ladies. Except with mine!"

Emma smiled.

"That is to say," he continued in jovial fashion after his joke, "it's not the money I worry about. I can give you some if you need it."

She started with surprise.

"Ah!" he said quickly, and in a low voice. "And I wouldn't need to go far to find you some. You can count on that!"

Then he began to ask about the health of old Tellier, the owner of the Café Français, whom Monsieur Bovary was caring for at the time.

"What's wrong with old Tellier? He coughs hard enough to shake the house and I'm afraid he may soon need a wooden overcoat instead of a flannel nightshirt. He carried on enough when he was young! Those people, Madame, did not have the slightest self-control, not the slightest discipline. He burned his insides out with brandy! But it's a sad thing all the same to see an acquaintance go off like that."

And while he was packing up his box, he chatted away in this fashion about the doctor's patients.

"It's the weather, no doubt," he said, looking with irritation out the window, "that causes all those illnesses. I don't feel quite right myself. I'll even have to come see Monsieur one of these days about a pain I have in my back. Well, au revoir, Madame Bovary. At your service. Your humble servant."

And he gently shut the door.

Emma had dinner served to her on a tray in her room, by the fireside. She took a long while to eat. Everything seemed good to her.

"How sensible I was!" she told herself, thinking about the scarves.

She heard steps on the staircase. It was Léon. She stood up and took from the top of the chest of drawers, among the dustcloths to be hemmed, the first one on the pile. She looked quite busy when he appeared.

The conversation languished, Madame Bovary abandoning it every minute while he himself seemed embarrassed. Seated on a low chair near the fireplace, he kept turning the ivory needle case with his fingers; she stitched away, occasionally puckering part of the fabric with her nail. She didn't say a word. He said nothing, as captivated by her silence as he would have been by her words.

"Poor boy," she thought.

"Why do I displease her?" he asked himself.

Léon finally ended by saying that he would have to go to Rouen on business within a few days.

"Your music subscription has run out. Shall I renew it?"

"No," she answered.

"Why?"

"Because—" And compressing her lips, she drew out slowly a long stitch of gray thread.

The embroidering bothered Léon. It seemed to be roughening the tips of her fingers.

He thought of something gallant to say, but didn't dare.

"You're giving it up?" he asked.

"What?" she asked quickly. "Oh, music? My God, yes! Don't I have my house to run, my husband to take care of, a thousand more important duties!"

She looked at the clock. Charles was late. Then she played the worrying wife. Two or three times she repeated: "He's so good."

The clerk liked Monsieur Bovary, but he found this tenderness annoying. Nevertheless he continued the praises he heard everyone sing, especially the pharmacist, he said.

"Ah, he's a good man," Emma said.

"True," said the clerk.

And he began to talk about Madame Homais, whose negligent manner of dressing usually gave them something to laugh about.

"What difference does it make?" Emma interrupted. "A good mother doesn't bother about her appearance."

Then she became silent once more.

She continued in this fashion during the following days; her conversation, her ways, everything changed. She was seen taking her household in hand, going to church regularly, and becoming stricter with her maid.

She took Berthe back from the wet nurse. Félicité would bring her down when visitors came, and Madame Bovary undressed her to show her legs. She asserted that she adored children; they were her consolation, her joy, her madness, and she accompanied her caresses with lyric expansiveness that to people other than the Yonvillites would have evoked memories of Sachette in *Notre-Dame de Paris.*

When Charles came home he would find his slippers warming near the embers. His waistcoats no longer lacked linings, nor his shirts buttons, and he even enjoyed the sight of all his cotton nightcaps arranged in equal piles in the cupboard. She did not look sour, as before, about taking walks in the garden; whatever he suggested was always agreed to, although she did not guess what it was that inspired her to submit without a murmur. And when Léon saw him near the fire after dinner, his two hands folded over his stomach, feet on the fender, flushed from digestion, eyes moist with happiness, while the child crawled on the rug and the slim-waisted woman leaned over the back of his chair to kiss him on the forehead, he told himself, "What madness! How could I ever have won her?"

She appeared so virtuous and inaccessible to him that any hope, even the most lingering, abandoned him.

But this renunciation set her in an extraordinary light. The carnal qualities that he could not obtain seemed extremely remote. She continually rose in his heart, detaching herself from it in the magnificent manner of a goddess soaring to heaven. It was one of those pure sentiments untroubled by the realities of life. One cultivates them because they are rare—and their loss would hurt more than the pleasure of possessing them.

Emma grew thin, her cheeks paled, her face lengthened. With her black hair, large eyes, straight nose, birdlike walk, and her continued silence, she appeared now to be moving through life hardly touching it and to be wearing on her forehead the vague mark of some sublime predestination. She was so sad and so calm, at the same time so sweet and so reserved, that one felt a glacial charm when near her, as one shivers in churches under the scent of flowers blended with the cold of the marble tiles. Even the others felt the power of her personality. The pharmacist said: "She's a woman of great talent who wouldn't be out of place in a subprefecture."

The women admired her thrift, the patients her politeness, the poor her charity.

But within she was full of envy, rage, and hatred. That dress with the straight folds hid a heart in turmoil, and those modest lips did not speak of her torment. She was in love with Léon and she longed for solitude in order to dream about him undisturbed. Even the sight of him troubled the voluptuousness of her meditation. Her heart pounded at the sound of his steps; but the emotion subsided in his presence, and only an immense wonder remained, which faded into sadness.

Léon did not know that when he left her home in despair she would watch him walk down the street. His movements made her anxious; she would steal glances at him, invent any story to visit his room. The pharmacist's wife seemed to her very lucky to sleep under the same roof, and her thoughts were constantly alighting on this house, like the pigeons of the Golden Lion that came to wet their pink feet and white wings in the gutters there. But the more Emma grew aware of her love, the more she repressed it, in order to hide and lessen it. She wanted Léon to suspect it, and she envisioned dangers, catastrophes, that would have revealed it. What held her back was no doubt laziness or fright, and also modesty. She thought that she had rejected him too strongly, that there was no more time, that all was lost. Then pride and the joy of telling herself "I am virtuous" and of looking at herself in the mirror while assuming poses of resignation consoled her a little for the sacrifice she believed herself to be making.

And then the fleshly appetites, desire for money, and the melancholy grip of passion combined into one agony. Instead of turning her thoughts from it, she dwelled on it more and more, wallowing in the pain and reaching out for it at all times. She would become irritated at a badly served dish or an unshut door, whimper about the velvet she didn't have, about the happiness she missed, about her unrealistic dreams, her cramped house.

What exasperated her was that Charles did not seem to suspect her suffering. His conviction that he was making her happy seemed an imbecilic insult to her, and his smugness about it sheer ingratitude. For whom then was she being virtuous? Was he not the obstacle to all happiness, the cause of all this misery, the sharp buckle, as it were, of the intricate strap that was binding her on all sides?

Therefore she brought to bear on him alone the intense hatred that resulted from her miseries, and each effort to lessen it served only to increase it; for this useless pain was added to her other motives for despair and contributed even more to the gulf between them. His very kindness to her made her rebel. Domestic mediocrity was pushing her to luxurious fantasies, matrimonial tenderness to adulterous desires. She wanted Charles to beat her so that she could hate him, take revenge. She amazed herself sometimes at the atrocious thoughts that came into her mind; and she had to continue to smile, hear herself repeat that she was happy, pretend to be happy, make others think she was.

But she was disgusted with this hypocrisy. She was filled with temptations to run off with Léon, somewhere, far away, to try a new destiny. But some unknown chasm would immediately open in her soul.

"Besides, he doesn't love me," she would think. "What will become of me? What rescue can I look forward to? What consolation, what lessening of my pain?"

She remained broken, breathless, inert, sobbing in a low voice, with tears flowing.

"Why not tell Monsieur?" the maid asked her when she would come in during these crises.

"It's nerves," Emma would answer. "Don't tell him about it. You'll make him unhappy."

"Ah, yes," Félicité would continue, "you're just like Mademoiselle Guérine, old Guérine's daughter, the Pollet fisherman I knew in Dieppe before coming to you. She was sad, so sad that to see her standing on her doorstep would remind you of a winding sheet hung in front of the door. It seems her trouble was a sort of fog in her head, and the doctors couldn't do anything about it, and the curé couldn't either. When it became too bad for her, she would go off all alone to the seashore, and the customs officer on duty would often find her flat on her belly on the shingles, crying away. It went away after her marriage they say."

"But with me," Emma said, "it began after my marriage."

V I

One evening as she was sitting at the open window and watching Lestiboudois, the sexton, trim the boxwood hedge, she suddenly heard the Angelus ringing.

It was the beginning of April, when the primroses are in bloom; a warm wind blows over the flower beds, and the gardens, like women, seem to be dressing for the summer holidays. Through the arbor lattice and all around beyond it, the river could be seen making its meandering way through the grassy meadow. The evening mist was passing through the leafless poplars, blurring their outlines with a violet haze, paler and more transparent than a fine gauze hung on their branches. Cattle were moving about in the distance; neither their steps nor their lowing was audible; and the bell, still ringing, continued its peaceful lamentation in the air.

At this repeated chiming, the young woman's thoughts strayed to her old memories of youth and school days. She remembered the candelabra, taller than the altar, the vases filled with flowers, and the tabernacle with its little columns. She wished she were still moving in that long line of white veils marked with black by the stiff coifs of the nuns kneeling on their *prie-Dieux*. When she lifted her head during Mass on Sunday, she would see the sweet face of the Virgin in the bluish clouds of incense that were rising. Then a tender emotion would suffuse her; she would feel all limp and abandoned like the down of a bird swirling in the tempest.

Without being aware of what she was doing at that moment, she headed toward the church, prepared for any act of devotion as long as she could give her soul up there and make her entire existence disappear.

In the square she met Lestiboudois, who was returning from church; for in order not to cut his day short, he preferred to interrupt his work and then resume it again. And so he sounded the Angelus at his convenience. Besides, the earlier ringing summoned the youngsters to the catechism class.

Several of them were already there and were playing marbles on the churchyard flagstones. Others, straddling the wall, were swinging their legs, crushing down with their wooden shoes the big nettles growing between the small wall and the most recent graves. It was the only patch of green; everything else was stone and continually covered with a fine powder despite the sexton's broom.

The children, wearing soft shoes, were running around as if on a floor made especially for them. Their voices could be heard across the booming of the bell, which diminished with the oscillations of the thick cord as it fell from the heights of the steeple and was dragged on the ground by its tip. Swallows were flying by and chirping, cutting through the air and rapidly returning to their yellow nests under the tiles of the eaves. A lamp was burning at the back of the church—that is, a wick of night light in a hanging glass. From afar its light looked like a whitish spot trembling over the oil. An elongated ray of sun was crossing the nave and casting the side aisles and the corners into even greater darkness.

"Where is the curé?" Madame Bovary asked a young boy who was jiggling the loosely latched gate.

"He's coming," he answered. And the door of the priest's residence squeaked open to reveal Abbé Bournisien. The children flew off into the church.

"Little scamps!" the priest grumbled. "Always the same." He picked up a tattered catechism that he had just stepped on. "They have no respect for anything!"

Then he noticed Madame Bovary: "Excuse me," he said, "I didn't notice you."

He tucked the catechism into his pocket and stood swinging the heavy vestry key with his hand.

The setting sun glowing down on his face bleached his woolen cassock. It was shiny at the elbows and frayed at the hem. Grease spots and tobacco followed the line of small buttons down his broad chest. There was a great accumulation of them near his clerical bands, on which the abundant folds of his red skin were resting. His complexion was dotted with yellow blemishes that disappeared under the stubble of his graying beard. He had just had his evening meal and was breathing heavily.

"How are you?" he added.

"Not well," Emma answered, "I am suffering."

"Ah, well, so am I," he answered. "These first hot spells weaken one terribly, don't they? Well, what do you expect? We are born to suffer, as Saint Paul says. What does Monsieur Bovary say?"

"He?" she said with a disdainful gesture.

"But hasn't he prescribed anything for you?" asked the priest, genuinely surprised.

"Ah," said Emma, "it isn't an earthly remedy that I need."

The curé kept glancing into the church, where the boys were squatting and bumping each other's shoulders; they were falling over like paper dolls.

"I would like to know——" she began.

"Just you wait, Riboudet," shouted the clergyman angrily. "I'm going to box your ears, you rascal!"

Then he turned to Emma: "He's the son of Boudet, the carpenter. His parents are well off and they let him do what he wants. He could learn rapidly if he only wanted, because he's very smart. And I sometimes joke by calling him Riboudet—like the hill you take to go to the Maromme—and I even say: 'Mon Riboudet.' Ha! ha! Mont Riboudet. The other day I told this to Monseigneur, who laughed; he condescended to laugh. . . . And how is Monsieur Bovary?"

She seemed not to hear him. He continued: "He's probably busy all the time. He and I are certainly the two busiest people in the parish. But he is the doctor of the body," he added with a heavy laugh, "and I of the soul."

She looked at the priest with mournful eyes. "Yes," she said, "you comfort all suffering."

"Ah, you don't have to tell me, Madame Bovary. This very morning I had to go to Bas-Diauville to see a cow that had swelled up; they thought it was bewitched. All their cows, I don't understand how— Oh, excuse me. Longuemarre and Boudet! Quiet! Enough of that!" And he leaped into the church.

The boys were crowding around the large lectern, climbing over the precentor's stool, looking into the missal. Others were tiptoeing

She looked at the priest with mournful eyes. "Yes," she said, "you comfort all suffering."

up to the confessional. But the curé suddenly distributed a volley of slaps right and left. Picking them up by the scruff of the neck, he lifted them off the ground and set them heavily down on their knees in the choir, as if he were going to plant them there.

"Well, now," he said when he returned to Emma, unfolding his large calico handkerchief and putting a corner of it between his teeth, "the farmers have their troubles."

"So have others," she answered.

"Of course! Workers in the city, for example."

"Not them—"

"Please! I've known poor mothers with families, virtuous women, I assure you, truly sainted, who didn't even have bread."

"But," Emma continued (and the corners of her mouth twitched as she spoke), "what about those, Monsieur, who have bread and who don't have—"

"Fire in the winter?" said the priest.

"Oh, what's the difference!"

"What do you mean, what's the difference? It seems to me that when one is properly warmed, well fed— Because, after all—"

"My God, my God," she sighed.

"Do you feel sick?" he asked, coming closer with an anxious air. "Probably something you ate. You ought to go home, Madame Bovary, and drink a little tea. It will strengthen you. Or perhaps a glass of cold water with some brown sugar."

"What for?" She looked like someone who awakes from a dream.

"You were passing your hand over your forehead. I thought you had a dizzy spell." Then, remembering: "But you asked me something. What was it now? I seem to have forgotten."

"Me? Nothing. Nothing," Emma repeated.

Her wandering gaze settled on the old man in the cassock. They stared at each other in silence.

"Madame Bovary," he said finally, "excuse me, but duty calls. You know I must look after my rascals. The first Communions will be here pretty soon. I'm afraid we won't be ready. From Ascension on I'm going to keep them an extra hour every Wednesday without fail. Those poor children! You can't start them too early in the Lord's path, as He Himself ordered through the mouth of His Divine Son. Good day, Madame. My respects to your husband."

And he walked into the church, genuflecting near the door.

Emma watched him disappear between the double line of benches, walking heavily, his head slightly bent toward one shoulder, his hands dangling down.

Then she turned around woodenly, like a statue on a pivot, and headed home. But the curé's gruff voice and the shrill sounds of the boys kept reaching her ear as she walked: "Are you a Christian?"

"Yes, I am Christian."

"What is a Christian?"

"A Christian is one who, being baptized—baptized—baptized—"

She walked up her staircase holding on to the banister and sank into an armchair when she reached her room.

The white light came in gentle undulations through the windowpane. The pieces of furniture seemed to be even more fixed in their place. They blended into the shadows as into a murky ocean. The fire was out, the clock ticked away, and Emma felt vaguely surprised that there could be such outward calm while there was so much turmoil within her. Little Berthe was standing between the window and the work table, tottering on her knitted booties and trying to get near her mother to pull the ends of her apron.

"Leave me alone!" she said, shoving her away with her hand.

The child soon came back, even closer. She leaned her arms on Emma's lap and lifted her big blue eyes toward her while a rivulet of saliva flowed out of her mouth onto the silk of the apron.

"Will you leave me alone!" she said with fury.

The expression on her face frightened the child, who began to cry.

"Go away!" she said, emphasizing the statement with her elbow.

Berthe fell against the chest of drawers, striking the brass curtain hook; she cut her cheek on it, and it started to bleed. Madame Bovary ran over to pick her up, ripped the bell pull, shouted for the maid at the top of her lungs, and was about to start cursing herself when Charles appeared. He was just coming home for dinner.

"Look, darling," Emma said in a calm voice, "the baby was playing and cut her cheek."

Charles assured her it wasn't serious and went off to find some adhesive plaster.

Madame Bovary did not go down to the parlor; she wanted to remain alone and take care of her child. Her anxiety gradually disappeared as she watched her sleeping, and she thought she had been both foolish and virtuous to worry about so little. Berthe had stopped bleeding. Her breath was now imperceptibly lifting the cotton coverlet. Great big tears were hovering in the corners of her half-closed eyelids. Two pale, deep-set pupils could be seen through the lashes; the sticking plaster on her cheek was pulling the taut skin to one side.

"Strange," Emma thought, "how ugly this child is."

When Charles came back from the pharmacy at eleven (he had gone there after dinner to return the remainder of the plaster), he found his wife standing near the cradle.

"I told you it was nothing," he said, kissing her on the forehead. "Don't worry about it, darling, you'll make yourself sick."

He had remained quite a while at the pharmacist's. Although he did not seem too frightened, Monsieur Homais nevertheless kept trying to bolster his morale, to "raise his spirits." Then they spoke about the various dangers that threatened childhood and about the stupidity of maids. Madame Homais knew something about it; she still bore on her chest the marks of some hot embers that a cook had once dropped down her smock. And so these devoted parents were extremely cautious. The knives were never sharpened, floors never waxed. There were iron bars on the windows and heavy guards at the fireplace. The Homais children, despite their independent ways, could not budge without someone to keep an eye on them; at the slightest cold their father loaded them down with cough medicine, and until they were four they were tightly bundled up in quilted garments. True, this was an eccentricity of Madame Homais about which her husband worried in silence, fearing the effect on the mind of such compression. He even ventured to ask her: "Do you intend to make Caribs or Botocudos out of them?"

Charles had tried several times to terminate the conversation.

"I'd like to talk to you," he whispered into the clerk's ear. The latter began to lead the way upstairs.

"Does he suspect something?" Léon asked himself. His heart began pounding as he wondered.

Charles shut the door and asked him, finally, to find out in Rouen what a good daguerreotype might cost. It was to be a romantic surprise for his wife, a token of affection—his portrait in his black suit. But he wanted to know what it would cost him beforehand. This errand should not take Monsieur Léon too much out of his way since he went to the city almost every week.

Why did he go? Homais suspected some "youthful carrying-on," some affair. But he was wrong. Léon was not involved in any romantic pursuit. He was unhappier than he had ever been. Madame Lefrançois realized this from the amount of food he left on his plate these days. She questioned the tax collector to get more information. Binet answered, in a knowing tone, that he was "not an informer paid by the police."

His dinner companion seemed quite strange to him, nevertheless, Léon would often lean back in his chair, stretch his arms, and complain vaguely about life.

"You don't have enough distractions," said the tax collector.

"Such as?"

"If I were in your shoes, I'd get a lathe!"

"But I don't know how to use one," the clerk answered.

"I guess that's right," the other said, stroking his chin with an air of smug superiority.

Léon was tired of being in love without results. He began feeling the despondency brought on by the unvarying repetition of the same life, when there is no motivating interest and no sustaining hope. He was so bored with Yonville and the Yonvillites that the sight of certain people and certain houses irritated him beyond endurance, and the pharmacist, as friendly as he was, seemed to have become absolutely unbearable. Yet the prospect of a new situation frightened him as much as it tempted him.

The apprehension soon turned into impatience and then he could hear the distant noises of Paris: the fanfare of its masked balls and the laughter of its grisettes. He was supposed to finish his law studies there. Why not go now? What was holding him back? And inwardly he started making preparations; he arranged his occupations in advance, he furnished his rooms in his imagination. He would lead the life of an artist; take guitar lessons; own a dressing gown, a beret, blue velvet slippers! He visualized already two crossed foils and a skull and the guitar on his Parisian mantelpiece.

The difficulty was in obtaining his mother's consent; yet nothing seemed to him more reasonable. His employer had even been suggesting that he change to another office where he could learn more.

Léon compromised by trying to find a position as second clerk in Rouen but found none. He finally wrote his mother a long, detailed letter in which he outlined his reasons for moving to Paris right away. She gave her consent.

He did not rush off. Every day, for one whole month, Hivert carried his boxes, valises, and packages from Yonville to Rouen, from Rouen to Yonville, and when Léon had replenished his wardrobe, had his three armchairs reupholstered, bought a new supply of scarves, in other words, made more arrangements than for a trip around the world, he kept putting off his move from week to week until his mother sent a second letter suggesting that he go now if he expected to pass his examination before vacation time.

When the moment for farewells came, Madame Homais cried, Justin sobbed, Homais, as befitted a man of dignity, hid his emotion. He wanted to carry his friend's overcoat up to the lawyer's gate. The lawyer was taking Léon to Rouen in his carriage. Léon had only enough time to say good-bye to Monsieur Bovary.

When he reached the top of the staircase, he stopped, out of breath. Madame Bovary started up when he walked in.

"I'm still here!" Léon said.

"I knew you'd come!"

She bit her lip and blushed red from the roots of her hair to the edge of her collar. She remained standing, leaning against the paneling.

"Your husband's not home?" he said.

"He's away." She repeated: "He's away."

Then there was a silence. They looked at each other, and their thoughts, coming together in the same anguish like two pounding hearts, were inextricably united.

"I'd like to kiss Berthe," Léon said.

Emma went down a few steps to call Félicité.

He looked around quickly at the walls, the shelves, the mantelpiece, as if to penetrate into everything, take everything with him.

Then she came back and the maid brought in Berthe, who was dangling a windmill upside down at the end of a string.

Léon kissed her several times on the neck.

"Good-bye, little one, good-bye, sweet child!" And he handed her back to her mother.

"Take her back," the latter said to the servant.

They were alone.

Madame Bovary had her face pressed against a windowpane, her back to him. Léon was holding his cap in his hand and tapping it gently against his thigh.

"It's going to rain," Emma said.

"I have a coat," he answered.

"Oh."

She turned back, chin down and forehead forward. The light was gleaming on it as if it were marble, as far as the arch of the brows. It was impossible to guess what she was looking at in the distance, nor what she was thinking in her heart of hearts.

"Well, good-bye," he said with a sigh.

She looked up quickly.

They drew closer. He held out his hand. She hesitated.

"English style, then," she said, extending hers and trying to smile.

Léon enclosed her hand in his and the very substance of his entire being seemed to pour into this moist palm.

Then he relaxed his grip. Their eyes met one more time and he disappeared.

When he reached the marketplace, he stopped and hid behind a pillar in order to look at that white house with its four green shutters one last time. He thought he could distinguish a shadow behind the bedroom window, but the curtain, slipping out of its holder by accident, slowly shook out its long slanting folds and fell straight down, as immobile as a plaster wall. Léon began to run.

He noticed his employer's carriage standing on the highway, some distance off. Beside him was a man in a shop-apron holding the horse. Homais and Monsieur Guillaumin were talking. They were waiting for him.

"Embrace me," said the pharmacist with tears in his eyes. "Here is your coat, dear boy. Do be careful of the cold! Take good care of yourself. Don't overwork!"

"Come on, Léon, let's go," said the lawyer.

Homais leaned over the mudguard and sobbed out two sad words: *"Bon voyage!"*

"Good-bye to you," answered Monsieur Guillaumin. "We're off!"

They drove away and Homais returned home.

Madame Bovary had opened the window that overlooked the garden and she was looking at the clouds.

They were massing in the west, toward Rouen. Their black wreathlike shapes moved along briskly, pierced by shafts of sunlight that resembled golden arrows stuck into a mounted trophy. The unclouded portion of the sky was as white as porcelain. Then a gust of wind bent the poplars and the rain came suddenly, pattering on the green leaves. The sun soon came out again, and the hens cackled, the sparrows rustled their wings against the wet shrubbery, and the water trickling over the gravel carried away pink acacia blossoms.

"He must be so far away by now," she thought.

As usual Monsieur Homais arrived at six-thirty, during dinner.

"Well," he said as he sat down, "we've sent our young man off!"

"So it seems," answered the doctor. Then he swiveled around in his chair: "What's new with you?"

"Nothing much. My wife was a little upset this afternoon. You know, women can be bothered by trifles. Especially mine. And there's no point complaining about it since their nervous system is much more sensitive than ours."

"Poor Léon!" said Charles. "I wonder how he will manage in Paris. Will he get used to it?"

Madame Bovary sighed.

"Come on, now!" the pharmacist said, clicking his tongue. "Little dinner parties in a restaurant, masked balls, champagne! He'll manage beautifully, I assure you."

"I don't think he'll run wild," Bovary objected.

"Nor do I," Monsieur Homais answered quickly, "even though he will have to go along with his friends or else be taken for a Jesuit. And you don't know the kind of life these young men lead in the Latin Quarter with the actresses! Besides, students are greatly esteemed in Paris. As long as they show a little ability to get along, they're received in the best circles. There are even women of the Faubourg Saint-Germain who fall in love with them, and that kind of an affair helps them make very good marriages later on."

"But, I'm afraid that he may—that he may—" said the doctor.

"You're right," the apothecary interrupted; "it's the other side of the coin! You have to keep your hand on your pocket all the time. Let's say you're in a public garden; a stranger appears, well dressed, even decorated, the type you could mistake for a diplomat. He comes over, you talk, he makes himself friendly, offers you some snuff or picks up your hat for you. Then you get even friendlier; he takes you to a café, invites you to visit his country home, introduces you to all sorts of acquaintances while you're drinking, and three quarters of the time it's only to grab your purse or lead you into evil ways."

"You're right," Charles said, "but I was really thinking about illnesses—typhoid fever, for instance, which attacks students from the provinces."

Emma shuddered.

"Because of the change of diet," the pharmacist continued, "and the disturbance it causes in the general bodily condition. And that Paris water, you know! And restaurant food—all those spicy dishes end up overheating your blood. No matter what they say, they're not worth a good stew. I myself have always preferred home cooking. It's much healthier. When I was studying pharmacy in Rouen, I lived in a boardinghouse and ate with the teachers."

He continued expatiating on his opinions in general and his personal preferences until Justin came to fetch him to prepare an eggnog that had been prescribed.

"Never a moment's rest," he grumbled, "always on call. I can't go out for a second. Always sweating blood like a workhorse. I labor under a real yoke of drudgery."

Then, when he was at the door, he said: "By the way, have you heard the news?"

"No, what?"

"It's very likely," said Homais, raising his eyebrows and taking on a most solemn look, "that the Seine-Inférieure Agricultural Show will be held in Yonville-l'Abbaye this year. At least the rumor is making the rounds. The newspaper mentioned it this morning. It would be a real honor for our community. But we'll talk about that later on. Thank you, I can see my way; Justin has the lantern."

VII

The next day was a day of mourning for Emma. A black cloud seemed to hover over everything and envelop everything, and unhappiness burrowed into her soul like a winter wind whistling hollowly through an abandoned château. It was the mood brought on by a permanent rupture, the lassitude that overcomes you after something is over—the sadness engendered by the interruption of a customary pattern of action, the abrupt cessation of a long-continuing vibration.

She was suffering the same lifeless melancholy, the same numb despair she had suffered after their return from La Vaubyessard, when the quadrilles were whirling in her head. Léon reappeared, taller, handsomer, more charming—and slightly out of focus. Although he was separated from her, he had not left her; he was still there and the walls seemed to retain his shadow. She could not take her eyes from the rug on which he had walked, from the now empty furniture on which he had sat. The river still flowed and rippled gently along the smooth bank. They had walked along it many times, to this same murmur of the waves, over the moss-covered pebbles. The sun had been so wonderful. And those lovely afternoons alone in the shade at the foot of the garden! With his head bare he would read aloud as he sat on a footstool of dried sticks. The fresh breeze from the meadow would blow on the pages and on the nasturtiums in the arbor. And now he was gone, the one pleasure of her life, the one possible hope for happiness. Why hadn't she seized this happiness when it first appeared? Why hadn't she held him back with her hands or by begging on her knees when he wanted to leave? She cursed herself for not having loved him. She thirsted for his lips. She yearned to run to him, to throw herself into his arms, to tell him: "Take me, I'm yours." But the anticipated difficulties forestalled any action, and her desires, heightened by regret, became even more ardent.

From that point on, the memory of Léon was the focal point of her boredom. It sparkled there more strongly than the fire of travelers abandoned in the snowy Russian steppes. She would rush toward it, revel in it, delicately revive the dying embers. She would seek out anything that could make it glow more brightly, and she utilized everything—the earliest memories and the most recent, her emotions and her thoughts, her craving for luxury and her plans for happiness that were snapping in the wind like dead branches, her sterile virtues and her shattered dreams, the domestic monotony—she seized on everything, to rekindle her misery.

Nevertheless the flames died down, either from an insufficience of emotion or an excess. Little by little absence caused love to die away and habit smothered regret. The firelight that crimsoned her pale sky became clouded over with shadow and was slowly eclipsed. Her sluggish conscience even mistook the aversion to her husband for yearning toward her lover and the passion of hatred for a renewal of tenderness, but since the storm kept brewing and the passion burning down to its embers with no help in sight, with no sunshine bursting through, there was a total night—and she was overcome by a fearful chill, which permeated her entire body.

Then the bad days of Tostes came back. She felt much more unhappy now because along with the experience of unhappiness, she now had the knowledge that it would never end.

A woman who had sacrificed so much could certainly indulge herself in some whims. She bought a Gothic *prie-Dieu*, purchased fourteen francs' worth of lemons in one month to clean her nails, sent to Rouen for a blue cashmere dress, purchased the most beautiful shawl in Lheureux's store, tied it around her waist over her dressing gown, and dressed thus, would lie on the sofa all day long with the shutters closed and a book in her hand.

She would keep changing her hair style, would arrange it Chinese fashion, in soft waves, in braids, would part it on one side and roll it under, like a man.

She decided to learn Italian. She bought dictionaries, a grammar, and a supply of white paper. She tried reading serious books on history and philosophy. Sometimes at night Charles would start up from his sleep, thinking someone had come to fetch him for a patient. "I'm coming," he would say sleepily.

It would be the noise of a match Emma was striking to relight her lamp. But her readings ended like her half-worked tapestries, which were filling up her cupboard; she would start them, drop them, and move on to new ones.

She had moods in which she almost went wild. She announced to her husband one day that she could easily drink a large glass of brandy, and when Charles was foolish enough to challenge her, she swallowed it down to the last drop.

Despite her "flighty" airs (as the Yonvillites called them), Emma did not appear to be happy. She habitually set the corners of her mouth in that pursed look that contracts the faces of old maids and frustrated people. She was extremely pale, as white as a sheet, and the skin on her nose was pulled taut toward the nostrils. Her eyes shifted about. When she discovered three gray hairs on her temples, she spoke about her old age.

She would frequently feel dizzy. One day she even spat blood and when Charles revealed his anxiety by his attention, she said, "Bah! What's the difference?"

Charles went to take refuge in his office. And he cried, sitting in his armchair under the phrenological head with his elbows on the table.

Then he wrote to his mother asking her to come. They spoke about Emma at length.

What would they do? What could be done with her refusal to submit to any treatment?

"You know what your wife needs?" his mother asserted. "To be forced to work. Manual labor. If she had to earn a living, like so many other women, she wouldn't have those spells that come from the ideas she stuffs into her head because she doesn't have enough to do."

"But she keeps busy," said Charles.

"Keeps busy! Doing what? Reading novels, evil books, books against religion where they make fun of priests by quoting Voltaire. But that goes far, my poor child, and a person without religion will always end up bad."

And so it was decided that Emma should be prevented from reading novels. The task did not seem easy. The good lady assumed responsibility: she was to go in person to the lending library when she passed through Rouen and tell them that Emma was canceling her subscription. Wouldn't they have the right to call the police if the bookstore persisted in poisoning her?

The farewells between mother- and daughter-in-law were curt. During the three weeks they had been together they had not exchanged four words outside of household matters or acknowledgments at meals or bedtime.

Old Madame Bovary left on a Wednesday, which was a market day in Yonville.

From morning on, the square was filled with a line of carts that extended along the houses from the church to the inn, with their ends uptilted and shafts in the air. On the opposite side there were canvas booths selling cotton goods, coverlets and wool stockings, halters for horses, and packs of blue ribbon whose tips were streaming into the wind. Heavy hardware goods were spread out over the ground between pyramids of eggs and hampers of cheese (from which wisps of sticky straw protruded); near the farm tools, some clucking hens poked their heads through the bars of their coops. The people were crowding into one spot and not budging—the pharmacist's window was in imminent danger of being smashed in. The store never emptied on Wednesdays. People pushed their way in, less for medicine than for consultations, so great was Homais's reputation in the neighboring villages. His hearty, reassuring air had fascinated the country people. They considered him a greater doctor than all the real ones.

Emma was sitting at the window as she often did, the window in the provinces substituting for theaters and walking paths, enjoying the rustic crowd when she noticed a gentleman dressed in a green velvet frock coat. Despite the heavy gaiters on his legs, he wore elegant yellow gloves. He was heading toward the doctor's house, followed by a peasant walking with his head down, a pensive look on his face.

"May I see the doctor?" he asked Justin, who was talking to Félicité on the doorstep.

Assuming that he was the house servant, he added: "Tell him that Monsieur Rodolphe Boulanger, of La Huchette, is here."

The visitor had mentioned his estate, not out of land-owning vanity but rather to introduce himself more fully. La Huchette was an estate near Yonville whose château he had just acquired. It contained two farms that he himself was cultivating in a rather casual way. He lived a bachelor life and was reputed to have "an income of at least fifteen hundred pounds."

Charles came into the parlor. Monsieur Boulanger introduced his man, who wanted to be bled because he "felt as if there were ants crawling up and down his body."

"It will take them away," the peasant maintained against all arguments.

Bovary therefore began preparing a bandage and a basin, asking Justin to assist him. Then he said to the villager, who was already quite pale: "Don't be afraid, my boy."

"Not me," the other answered. "Go ahead." And he held out his muscular arm with an air of bravado. The blood spurted out at the prick of the lancet and splattered all over the mirror.

"Hold the basin closer!" Charles exclaimed.

"Look at that!" said the peasant. "You'd swear it was a little fountain the way it runs. Look how red my blood is. Must be a good sign, isn't it?"

"Sometimes," said the doctor, "you don't feel anything at first and then you faint away. Especially people as healthy as you."

At these words the man dropped the little box that he had been turning with his fingers. His shoulders jerked so rapidly that they made the back of his chair crack. His hat fell off.

"I thought so," said Bovary, placing his finger over the vein.

The basin began trembling in Justin's hands. His knees shook and he became pale.

"Emma! Emma!" Charles called.

She came running down the stairs.

"Some vinegar," he cried. "Good God, two of them at once!"

He was so upset he could hardly apply the compress.

"It's all right," Monsieur Boulanger said calmly, supporting Justin in his arms. He propped him up on the table with his back against the wall.

Madame Bovary began removing his cravat. There was a knot in his shirt strings, and for a few minutes she moved her fingers lightly over the boy's neck. Then she poured vinegar on her batiste handkerchief and patted his temples gently, blowing on them softly.

The farmhand awoke, but Justin's fainting spell persisted and his pupils were disappearing into their pale eyeballs like blue flowers in milk.

"We'd better hide that from him," Charles said.

Madame Bovary picked the basin up to put it under the table. As she bent down, her dress (a yellow summer frock with four flounces, long-waisted and wide-skirted) billowed around her over the floor. She was slightly unsteady on her legs as she stooped and stretched her arms, and the folds of the fabric collapsed in a few places in response to her gestures. Then she went for a jug of water. She was dissolving some lumps of sugar when the pharmacist arrived. In the general confusion the maid had gone to call him, and when he saw that his apprentice's eyes were open, he took a deep breath. Then he turned him around, looking him over from head to toes.

"Fool!" he said. "Little fool! Fool in four letters! A bleeding is such a big affair? And a strapping lad like you who's afraid of nothing, who climbs up trees after nuts like a squirrel! Well, say something! What will you do later on when you're a pharmacist? What if you're called on to give evidence in court in a serious case— to help the magistrates make their minds up? You'll have to stay cool and calm then, remain logical and be a man or else they'll think you're an idiot!"

Justin said nothing. The apothecary continued: "Who asked you to come? You're always bothering Monsieur and Madame! Besides, I need you around on Wednesdays. There are twenty people in the house now. I left everything to see about you. All right, run along now. Hurry! I'll be back soon. Keep an eye on the jars."

Justin dressed himself and left, and they spoke for a few more minutes about fainting spells. Madame Bovary had never had one.

"That's very strange for a lady," said Monsieur Boulanger. "Some people are very delicate. I've seen a second pass out at a duel just from the noise of the pistols being loaded."

"Other people's blood doesn't bother me a bit," said the apothecary. "But just the thought of mine flowing would make me feel weak if I thought about it too long."

Monsieur Boulanger dismissed his servant, advising him to calm down now that his whim was satisfied.

"It did give me a chance to become acquainted with you," he added, looking at Emma as he spoke.

Then he placed three francs on the corner of the table, nodded casually, and went off.

He was soon on the other side of the river (it was the road back to La Huchette), and Emma could see him in the meadow, walking under the poplars and slowing down occasionally as if he were thinking.

"She's very pleasing," he told himself. "Very pleasing, that doctor's wife. Pretty teeth, black eyes, a well-turned foot, and manners like a Parisienne. Where the devil did she come from? Where did that coarse fellow find her?"

Monsieur Rodolphe Boulanger was thirty-four years old. He was hardhearted and extremely intelligent, had spent a lot of time in female company, and was very knowledgeable about women. He liked this new one and therefore thought about her and her husband.

"I find him dull. She must be tired of him. He's got dirty fingernails and a three-day growth of beard. He trots off to his patients, and she stays home darning his socks. And so bored! Longing to live in town and dance a polka every night. Poor little woman. Gasping for love, like a carp on a kitchen table gasping for water. Three flattering words and she'd adore me, I'm sure. How tender and charming it would be. But how would I get rid of her later?"

At that point the complications connected with pleasure, considered in their true perspective, made him think by contrast, about his mistress. She was an actress in Rouen. The very thought of her made him feel sated. "Madame Bovary is much prettier," he said to himself. "And fresher, especially. Virginie is definitely putting on weight and she's so tiresome with her constant high spirits. Plus that passion for shrimp!"

The countryside was deserted and Rodolphe heard nothing but the steady swish of his feet through the grass and the distant sound of grasshoppers among the oats. He pictured Emma in the room, first dressed as he had seen her and then nude.

"I'll have her!" he exclaimed, grinding his stick into a clump of earth. He began working out the strategy of the enterprise and asked himself: "Where should we meet? How? We'll have the brat on our necks all the time—and the maid and the neighbors and the husband. All kinds of irritations. Damn!" he said. "I'll lose too much time."

Then he started again: "But those eyes of hers go right through to your heart. And that pale skin. I adore pale women."

By the time he reached the summit of Argueil Hill, his mind was made up: "I'll have to look for opportunities. I'll stop by there occasionally, send them some game and poultry. I'll be bled, if I have to. I'll invite them to my place. Ah, of course," he added; "the Agricultural Show is coming! She'll be there and I'll see her. We'll start off boldly—it's the best way!"

VIII

The day of the famous Agricultural Show finally arrived. On that great occasion all the inhabitants stood on their doorsteps from early morning on, discussing the preparations. They had festooned the front of the Town Hall with ivy; a tent had been set up in one of the meadows for the banquet; and in the middle of the square, in front of the church, a sort of cannon was set up to herald the arrival of the prefect and salute the names of the winning farmers. The Buchy National Guard (there was none in Yonville) had come to join the fire brigade, of which Binet was the captain. He was wearing a collar even higher than usual and was buttoned so tightly into his tunic that his chest appeared stiff and motionless. The only parts of him that seemed to be alive were his two legs, rising and falling with one continuous movement as he marked time. Since a rivalry existed between the tax collector and the colonel, they were drilling their men separately in order to demonstrate their individual talents.

Red epaulets and black starched shirt fronts kept marching forward and facing about in a continuous beginning with no finish. There had never been such a display of pomp. Several villagers had washed their houses the night before. Tricolor flags hung from the open windows. All the inns were filled with people. In the fine weather the starched bonnets, gold crosses, and colored neckerchiefs glistened in the glaring sunshine and relieved with their splashes of color the somber monotony of the frock coats and the blue smocks.

The farmers' wives from the neighboring districts undid the large pins with which they had draped their dresses tightly around the body to avoid being splashed, while their husbands, on the contrary, in order to keep their hats on, had tied handkerchiefs around them and kept the corners in place between their teeth.

The crowd swarmed onto the main street from both ends of the village, pouring out from side streets, lanes, and houses. From time to time you could hear a door knocker banging behind a village woman in cotton gloves as she stepped out to watch the goings-on. The main attractions were two long triangular frames covered with Chinese lanterns, flanking the platform on which the authorities were to sit. Against each of the four pillars of the Town Hall stood a pole bearing a small green canvas standard adorned with inscriptions in gold letters. One said "Trade," another "Agriculture," the third "Industry," and the fourth "Fine Arts."

But the glow of delight on everyone's face seemed to make Madame Lefrançois, the innkeeper, quite gloomy. She was standing on her kitchen steps muttering under her breath: "Foolishness! Foolishness with that tent of theirs. Do they think the prefect will be comfortable eating there like a strolling player? They say such stupidities are for the good of the community! It certainly wasn't worth going to Neufchâtel to fetch that wretched cook. For whom? For cowherds and tramps!"

The pharmacist walked past. He was wearing a black dress coat, nankeen trousers, beaver shoes, and, most surprising for him, a hat—a hat with a low crown.

"Greetings!" he called out. "Excuse me, I'm in a hurry."

The fat widow asked him where he was going.

"Seems strange to see me out, doesn't it? I who always stick closer to my laboratory than a rat does to cheese."

"What cheese?" asked the landlady.

"Nothing, nothing," Homais continued. "I merely meant to explain to you, Madame Lefrançois, that I usually stay home like a hermit. Today, however, in view of the circumstances, I must—"

"Aha! So you're going off there?" she said disdainfully.

"Yes, I'm going," answered the pharmacist with surprise. "Am I not a member of the arrangements committee?"

The Widow Lefrançois stared at him a few minutes, then replied with a smile: "That's another story! But what's your connection with farming? Do you know anything about it?"

"Of course I do, since I'm a pharmacist, that is to say, a chemist. And chemistry, Madame Lefrançois, having as its goal the knowledge of the reciprocal and molecular action of nature's bodies, it follows that agriculture is included in its domain. After all, the composition of manure, fermentation of liquids, analyses of gas, and the influence of miasmas—what is all that, I ask you, if not chemistry pure and simple?"

The innkeeper said nothing. Homais continued: "Do you think that it is necessary to till the soil yourself or feed poultry in order to be an agronomist? One must rather be familiar with the composition of the substances they contain, with geological movements, atmospheric conditions, the quality of the soil, minerals and waters, the densities of different bodies and their capillary attraction. And so on. And one must have a thorough knowledge of all the principles of hygiene in order to direct and criticize the construction of buildings, the feeding of animals and servants. And also, Madame Lefrançois, one must possess a knowledge of botany, be able to distinguish among plants you see. Know which are the beneficial ones, which are harmful, which are unproductive, and which nutritional; if it's a good idea to pull some from one spot and plant them elsewhere; or to cultivate some and destroy others. In short, you must keep up with science by reading scientific papers and government pamphlets, be constantly on the watch to point out improvements—"

The landlady kept staring at the door of the Café Français. The pharmacist continued: "Would to heaven that our farmers were chemists, or at least that they heeded the advice of science more closely. For example, I recently wrote a substantial little paper, a memorandum of more than seventy-two pages entitled 'On Cider: Its Manufacture and Effects with Several New Comments on This Topic,' which I sent to the Agricultural Society of Rouen. It even earned me the honor of being received as a member in the agricultural section, pomology subsection. Ah! If only my work had had a wider publicity—" But the apothecary stopped short since Madame Lefrançois appeared quite preoccupied.

"Just look at them," she said. "I don't understand. To call *that* an eating place."

She shrugged her shoulders so that the stitches in her sweater stretched over her bosom and pointed with both hands to her rival's establishment, from which singing could be heard.

"Anyway, he won't have it much longer," she added. "It'll all be finished in a week."

Homais seemed shocked. She walked down the three steps and whispered into his ear: "Didn't you know? He's going to be taken over this week. Lheureux is foreclosing him. He drove him into bankruptcy."

"What a dreadful catastrophe!" exclaimed the apothecary, who always had the proper expression for any conceivable circumstance.

The landlady began to tell him the story, which she had gotten from Theodore, Monsieur Guillaumin's servant; and even though she loathed Tellier, she blamed Lheureux. He was a wheedling, groveling, loathsome man.

"There he is," she said, "in the market. He's bowing to Madame Bovary, who's wearing that green hat. See, she's holding on to Monsieur Boulanger's arm."

"Madame Bovary!" exclaimed Homais. "I must pay my respects. She might like to have a seat in the enclosure under the colonnade."

And ignoring Madame Lefrançois, who was calling him back in order to continue her story, the pharmacist walked off hurriedly, his mouth fixed in a smile, his bearing erect, distributing a quantity of greetings to the right and to the left, taking up a great deal of space with the large tails of his black frock coat, which floated behind him in the wind.

Rodolphe noticed him from afar and consequently started walking faster. But Madame Bovary was soon out of breath and so he slowed down, smiling at her as he said in a gruff manner, "Let's get away from that terrible man; you know, the pharmacist."

She nudged him with her elbow.

"What's that supposed to mean?" he asked himself, looking at her out of the corner of his eye as they walked.

Her profile was so calm that nothing could be guessed from it. It stood out in the bright sunlight against the oval shape of her bonnet, which was tied with light-colored reedlike ribbons. Her eyes, with their long curving lashes, were directed straight ahead, and even though they were wide open, they seemed slightly narrowed by the cheekbones because of the blood pulsing gently beneath her delicate skin. There was a pinkish tinge across the bridge of her nose. She was leaning her head a bit to one side, and the pearly edges of her white teeth were visible between her lips.

"Is she laughing at me?" Rodolphe wondered.

But Emma's gesture had only been a warning because Monsieur Lheureux was at their side. He kept addressing them every once in a while, trying to engage them in conversation.

"What a magnificent day! Everyone's out. The wind's coming from the east."

Neither Madame Bovary nor Rodolphe made any comment, while he, at their slightest movement, would come closer and say, "I beg your pardon?" and tip his hat with his hand.

When they had reached the blacksmith's, instead of continuing along the road as far as the gate, Rodolphe turned abruptly into a pathway, pulling Madame Bovary along with him. He shouted: "Good-bye, Monsieur Lheureux. See you soon."

"What a way to get rid of him," she said with a laugh.

"Why let people bother you?" he said. "Especially when I have the pleasure of being with you today——"

Emma blushed. He did not complete his sentence. Then he began to speak about the lovely weather and the delight of walking on the grass. A few daisies were up.

"Nice little daisies," he said, "enough to provide prophecies for all the girls around here who are in love."

"What would you say if I picked one?" he added.

"Are you in love?" she asked with a slight cough.

"Who knows?" Rodolphe answered.

The meadow was beginning to fill up, and the people were being jostled by housewives with their huge parasols and baskets and their babies. It was often necessary to move out of the way of a long row of farm girls, blue-stockinged servant girls with flat shoes and silver rings who reeked of milk when you drew near them. They would walk along, holding hands, and were spread out in this fashion all across the meadow, from the line of aspens as far as the banquet tent. Then the time arrived for the judging, and the farmers, one after another, filed into a sort of arena formed by a long rope supported by stakes.

The animals were already there, muzzles facing the rope, rumps of varying sizes more or less aligned. The drowsy pigs were sinking their snouts into the ground; the calves were lowing; the sheep bleating; the cows with their legs folded under were resting their bellies on the ground, and while they slowly chewed their cuds, blinked their heavy eyelids at the flies buzzing around them. Carters with their sleeves rolled up were holding the halters of rearing stallions, which were loudly whinnying in the direction of the mares, who were standing quietly by, stretching their necks, their manes dangling. Their foals rested in their shadows, occasionally approaching to suck. Along the tightly packed line of these undulating bodies could be seen a few white manes flowing in the breeze like waves or a pair of pointed horns jutting forth over the heads of men who were running. Away to one side, about a hundred feet outside the arena, stood a huge black bull, muzzled, with an iron ring through his nostrils, as motionless as a bronze statue of an animal. A child in tatters held him by a rope.

Meanwhile, between the two rows, several gentlemen were walking along with heavy gait, examining each animal and then talking together in low voices. One of them, who seemed more important than the others, was taking notes in a notebook as he walked. He was the president of the jury: Monsieur Derozerays de la Panville. As soon as he noticed Rodolphe, he walked over quickly and said to him with a friendly smile: "Are you deserting us, Monsieur Boulanger?"

Rodolphe assured him that he was going to join them. But when the president had disappeared, he said, "Good grief! I'm not going to go. I prefer your company to his."

Although he poked fun at the show, Rodolphe showed the guard his blue ticket so that they could move about more freely. He even stopped occasionally to admire some interesting exhibit, which Madame Bovary did not find at all to her liking. Realizing this, he began to make jokes about the way the Yonville ladies dressed; then apologized for his own negligence about clothes. His clothes were that hodgepodge blend of ordinary and elegant in which the common man thinks he discerns eccentricity of behavior, lack of disciplined emotions, subservience to the tyranny of art, and a general scorn for social convention. This he finds either very alluring or thoroughly exasperating. Thus, Rodolphe's cambric shirt with its frilled cuffs would puff out through the opening of his gray drill waistcoat when the wind blew, and his broad-striped trousers reached only to his ankles, revealing nankeen boots with patent leather uppers polished so brightly that they reflected the grass. He trampled over the horse dung with them, one hand in his jacket pocket and his straw hat tilted to one side.

"Besides," he said, "when you live in the country—"

"It's all a waste," Emma continued.

"It is," Rodolphe replied. "Just think, not one of these good souls could appreciate the cut of a coat."

And so they spoke about provincial mediocrity, of the lives it stifled, the illusions it killed.

"And I bury myself, in my sadness," Rodolphe said.

"You!" she said with surprise. "I thought you were gay!"

"I am, on the surface, because I wear my jester's mask in public, and yet how many times have I asked myself, seeing a cemetery in the moonlight, if I wouldn't be better off joining those who sleep there."

"What about your friends?" she said. "Don't you think of them?"

"My friends? Which ones? Do I have any? Who cares about me?"

He accompanied these last words with a hissing sound.

Then they had to be separated because of a large scaffolding of chairs being carried by a man behind them. He was so loaded down that only the tips of his wooden shoes and of his outstretched arms were visible. It was Lestiboudois, the gravedigger, transporting the church chairs through the crowd. Always ready with ideas for anything regarding his interests, he had discovered this method of profiting from the show. His notion was succeeding so well he no longer knew which way to turn. The villagers, affected by the heat, were arguing over these straw-filled chairs smelling of incense and leaning against their sturdy backs, soiled by candle wax, with a certain feeling of veneration.

Madame Bovary took Rodolphe's arm again. He kept on speaking, as though to himself: "I've missed so many things! Always alone! If I had only had a goal in my life, if I'd fallen in love, found someone—I would have applied all my energy, overcome everything, surmounted every obstacle!"

"I still think," said Emma, "that you're hardly to be pitied."

"Oh?" said Rodolphe.

"Because—after all," she said, "you're free." She hesitated, "and rich."

"Don't make fun of me," he answered.

She assured him that she wasn't making fun. Just then there was a blast from the cannon. There was an immediate surge of people toward the village.

It was a false alarm. The prefect was not yet there, and the members of the jury found themselves in a very awkward situation, unsure whether they should begin the proceedings or keep on waiting.

Finally, at the far end of the square, a large hired landau appeared, pulled by two scrawny horses that a coachman in a white hat was whipping with all his might. Binet had only enough time to shout "Fall in!" and the colonel to follow suit. The men made a dash for the piled guns, some even forgetting to fasten their collars in their hurry. But the prefect's equipage seemed to be aware of the confusion and the two sorry nags, dawdling at their coupling chain, ambled up to the entrance of the Town Hall just as the National Guard and the Fire Brigade were deploying to the roll of drums.

"Mark time!" Binet shouted.

"Halt!" shouted the colonel. "Left face!"

And after a "Present Arms!" the clatter of which sounded like a copper kettle bumping down the stairs, all the rifles were lowered again.

Then a gentleman in a short, silver-trimmed jacket was seen alighting from the carriage. He had a bald forehead with a shock of hair behind, a pale complexion, and an appearance of extreme benevolence. His large, heavy-lidded eyes were narrowed as he looked at the assemblage, his pointed nose was high in the air, and there was a smile on his sunken mouth. He recognized the mayor by his sash and informed him that the prefect had not been able to come. He himself was one of the counselors of the prefecture. He added a few words of apology. Tuvache answered with some polite clichés, the other declared himself overwhelmed. And thus they stood, face to face, foreheads almost touching, surrounded by the members of the jury, the municipal council, the notables, the National Guard, and the crowd. The counselor, holding his small black three-cornered hat against his heart, reiterated his greetings while Tuvache, bending like a bow, smiled, stammered, groped for things to say, and declared his devotion to the monarchy and his appreciation of the honor that was being rendered to Yonville.

Hippolyte, the groom from the inn, came limping up on his clubfoot to take the coachman's horses by the bridle and led them through the gates of the Golden Lion, where many of the peasants were gathered to look at the carriage. The drum rolled, the howitzer thundered, and the gentlemen filed onto the platform, seating themselves in the armchairs of red Utrecht velvet that Madame Tuvache had lent them.

They all looked alike. Their pale, flabby faces, slightly bronzed by the sun, had the color of sweet cider, and their bushy whiskers stuck out above their stiff high collars, which were held in place by white cravats tied in generous bows. All the waistcoats had velvet lapels; every watch had an oval cornelian seal at the end of a long ribbon. And they all sat with both hands resting on their thighs, legs carefully spread, the unsponged cloth of their trousers shining more than the leather of their heavy boots.

Their ladies were behind them, between the columns of the vestibule, while the common horde faced them, standing or seated on the chairs that Lestiboudois had actually brought over from the meadow. He kept running every minute into the church to look for more. He was causing such a bottleneck with his business that it was very difficult to gain access to the platform steps.

"It seems to me," said Monsieur Lheureux (addressing the pharmacist, who was walking past to get to his place), "that they should have put up a couple of Venetian mats with something rich and a little severe in the way of drapery. It would have been rather eye-catching."

"You're right," said Homais. "But what do you expect? The

mayor took charge of everything. He has no taste to speak of, poor Tuvache. Completely lacking in what you might call artistic sense."

During this time Rodolphe had gone up with Madame Bovary to the council chamber on the first floor of the Town Hall. Since it was empty, he said that it would be quite a comfortable spot from which to watch the proceedings at their ease. He took three stools that were set around the oval table under the bust of the king and set them near one of the windows. They sat down side by side.

There was some commotion on the platform, a great deal of whispering and discussing. The counselor finally arose. His name, it had been learned, was Lieuvain and people were repeating it through the crowd. When he had arranged several sheets of paper and brought them closer to his eyes to see better, he began: "Gentlemen: May I begin—before addressing you on the subject of this meeting today, and this sentiment will, I am quite sure, be shared by all of you—may I begin, I say, by paying my just respects to the national administration, to the government, to the king, gentlemen, to our sovereign, to that beloved king to whom no branch of prosperity, either private or public, is indifferent, and who steers the ship of state with a hand both firm and wise amid the ceaseless perils of a stormy sea—who knows, moreover, how to inculcate respect for peace as well as war, for industry, commerce, agriculture, and the fine arts. . . ."

"I ought to move back a bit," said Rodolphe.

"Why?" Emma asked.

Just then the counselor's voice boomed out in an extraordinary manner. He was declaiming: "The days have passed, gentlemen, when civil strife spilled blood on our public places, when the land-owner, the tradesman, and even the worker, falling peacefully asleep in the evening, trembled lest they be awakened by the noise of incendiary tocsins, when the most subversive theories were boldly undermining the foundations. . . ."

"I can be seen from here," said Rodolphe, "and it would take me two weeks to clear myself. With my bad reputation—"

"You're too hard on yourself," said Emma.

"No, it's really dreadful, I assure you."

"But gentlemen," the counselor continued, "if I cast those gloomy images from my memory and focus my eyes on the present situation in our fair land, what do I see? Commerce and the arts flourish everywhere, everywhere new systems of communication, like so many new arteries in the body of the State, are establishing new relationships; our great manufacturing centers have regained their activity; religion, more firmly established than heretofore, smiles at every heart; our ports are full, confidence is reborn, and France is finally breathing with ease!"

"Besides," Rodolphe added, "people may be right."

"How so?" she said.

"Well," he said, "don't you know that there are certain souls in perpetual torment? They are constantly in need of either a dream or some occupation, the purest of passions, the most passionate of pleasures, and they throw themselves into all kinds of daydreams and madness."

At that she looked at him as one stares at a traveler who has passed through exotic lands, and said: "We poor women don't even have that distraction."

"A sad distraction in which you don't find any happiness."

"But does one ever find happiness?" she asked.

"Yes, someday," he answered.

"And this is what you have understood," said the councilman. "You farmers and farmhands, you peaceful pioneers in a true task of civilization, you, men of progress and morality. You have understood, I repeat, that political storms remain more to be feared than atmospheric disorders. . . ."

"It appears one fine day," Rodolphe repeated, "suddenly, when you are most despairing. Then the heavens open up and it's as if a voice cried out: 'Here it is!' You feel you must confide your life to that person, confide everything. You don't discuss feelings, you sense them. You've already met in your dreams." And here he looked at her. "Finally there it is, the treasure so long searched for, before you; shining and sparkling. And yet you still doubt, you're afraid to believe. You remain dazzled by it as if you had stepped out of the shadows into the light."

As he finished these words, Rodolphe added pantomime to his speech. He passed his hand over his face in the gesture of a man stunned; then he dropped it onto Emma's. She pulled hers away.

The councilman was still reading: "And who will be surprised at it, gentlemen? Only he who is so blinded, so steeped—I do not fear to say it—so steeped in the prejudices of another age that he cannot comprehend even today the spirit of our farm populations. Where is a more faithful patriotism to be found than in the countryside, more devotion to the public welfare, more intelligence, in a word? And I do not refer, gentlemen, to that superficial intelligence that is the vain adornment of idle minds, but rather that deep and reasoning intelligence that applies itself above all else to the pursuit of necessary goals, contributing in this fashion to the welfare of all, to the public betterment and to the maintenance of the state—the fruit of respect for law and the fulfillment of duty."

"Still at it," Rodolphe said. "Always duty. I'm fed up with those words. They're a bunch of old fogies in flannel waistcoats, bigoted old ladies with foot warmers and beads, who keep singing into our ears, 'Duty! Duty!' Our duty is to discern the great and cherish the beautiful and not to accept all those conventions of society with the ignominies it imposes on us."

"But—but—" Madame Bovary was objecting.

"No! Why argue against the passions? Aren't they the only beautiful things on the earth, the inspiration for heroism, enthusiasm, poetry, music, art, for everything?"

"But you have to go along with society to some extent, and respect its morality," Emma said.

"Ah, but there are two moralities," he answered. "The petty, conventional morality, the morality of men, which is constantly changing and which makes such a loud noise, floundering about on the earth like this collection of imbeciles you see before you. But the other, the eternal morality, is all around and above us like the countryside that surrounds us and the blue sky that sends down its light."

Monsieur Lieuvain had just wiped his mouth with his pocket handkerchief. He went on: "And who am I, gentlemen, to show you here the usefulness of agriculture? After all, who is it who supplies our needs? Who furnishes our food? Is it not the farmer? The farmer, my friends, who, sowing with a weary, hard-working hand the fruitful furrows of the land, brings forth the wheat, which, crushed and ground into powder by means of ingenious machinery, from which it emerges under the name of flour, is transported from there into the cities and soon delivered to the baker, who makes from it a food for poor as well as rich. Is it not the farmer who also fattens his abundant sheep in the pastures for our clothing needs? For how would we dress ourselves and how would we eat without agriculture? And gentlemen, must we go so far to seek examples? Who has not often thought about the importance we derive from that modest animal, the adornment of our farmyards, who furnishes us with soft pillows for our sleep, a succulent meat for our tables, and eggs? But I would never finish if I had to enumerate every single one of the different products that the well-cultivated earth, like a generous mother, lavishes on its children. Here it is the vine, elsewhere, cider apples; in other places, rapeseed; farther on, cheese; and flax—gentlemen, let us not forget flax! Flax, which has made considerable strides these last few years and to which I would particularly like to draw your attention."

He did not have to draw it; every mouth in the crowd was open as if to drink in his words. Tuvache, beside him, was listening with his eyes wide open; Monsieur Derozerays would occasionally close his eyes gently. Farther down, the pharmacist with his son Napoleon between his knees had his hand cupped behind his ear in order not to miss a single syllable. The other members of the jury were nodding their chins slowly into their waistcoats to signify assent. The firemen stood leaning on their bayonets at the foot of the platform, and Binet, motionless and with his elbow sticking out, had his saber pointing into the air. He may have been listening, but he could not have seen anything because the visor of his helmet came down over his nose. His lieutenant, Tuvache's younger son, had his visor at an even more exaggerated angle; he wore an enormous one that wobbled unsteadily on his head, revealing an edge of his calico kerchief. Beneath it he was smiling with a childlike meekness, and his small, pale face, beaded with sweat, revealed an expression of pleasure blended with exhaustion and sleepiness.

The square was crowded as far back as the housefronts. You could see people leaning out of every window, others standing on every doorstep, and Justin, in front of the pharmacy window, appeared to be fixedly contemplating some object. Despite the silence, Monsieur Lieuvain's voice did not carry through the air. It reached you only in fragments of sentences, interrupted here and there by the creaking of chairs in the crowd, or a sudden long lowing of a bull behind you, or of the lambs bleating to each other from the corners of the streets. The cowherds and shepherds had driven their animals out there where they kept up their lowing while snatching with their tongues at some bit of foliage hanging above their muzzles.

Rodolphe had drawn closer to Emma and was speaking rapidly in a low voice: "Doesn't this conspiracy of society revolt you? Is there one ounce of feeling that it does not condemn? The most noble instincts, the purest emotions, are persecuted and slandered, and if two poor souls finally meet, everything is organized so that they cannot unite. But they will keep trying, beating their wings, calling out to each other. And, sooner or later, in six months or ten years, they will reunite and love each other because destiny demands it and they were born for each other."

He sat with his arms closed on his lap, looking up at Emma and gazing at her closely, steadily. In his eyes she could distinguish small flecks of gold irradiating all around his black pupils and could even smell the perfume of the pomade that made his hair shine. Then a sudden weakness overcame her; she remembered the viscount who had waltzed with her at Vaubyessard and from whose beard emanated the same odor of vanilla and lemon; mechanically, she shut her eyes in order to smell it better. But as she straightened up in her chair, she glimpsed in the distance the old diligence, the Hirondelle, slowly descending Leux Hill and trailing a long plume of dust behind it. It was in this yellow carriage that Léon had so often come back to her and by that road that he had left forever! She had a vision of him across the way, at his window, then everything seemed to be topsy-turvy, clouds passed over her; she seemed to be still turning to that waltz in the viscount's arms—Léon was not far off, he was going to come—and yet she did not stop being aware of Rodolphe's head beside her. The sweetness of this sensation mingled with her old desires, and like grains of sand when the wind blows, they were tossed about in the subtle gusts of perfume settling on her soul. She opened her nostrils wide, wider, to take in the freshness of the ivy winding around the tops of the columns. She drew off her gloves, dried her hands, then fanned her face with her handkerchief while through the throbbing of her temples she could hear the murmurs of the crowd and the voice of the counselor.

He was saying: "Keep going! Persevere! Heed not the promptings of routine nor the overhasty advice of rash empiricism. Apply your-selves especially to improving the soil, enriching your fertilizers, to the development of the equine, bovine, and porcine breeds! May this Show be unto you as a peaceful arena in which the victor, as he leaves, stretches out his hand in friendship to the vanquished, wishing him luck for next time. And you, venerable servitors, humble domestic help, whose painful labors no government until now has taken into consideration, come take the reward for your silent virtues and be assured that the state henceforth shall keep its eyes on you, that it encourages you, protects you, that it will do justice unto your rightful claims and will lighten, as much as it is in its power, the burden of your painful sacrifices."

Monsieur Lieuvain sat down again. Monsieur Derozerays arose, beginning a new speech. His was not quite as flowery as the counselor's, but this was compensated for by a more positive style, that is, by a more specialized knowledge and more exhalted reflections. Thus, praise of the government was stressed less and religion and agriculture more. The relation between the latter two was brought out, and also how they had always worked together in the interests of civilization. Rodolphe was talking to Madame Bovary about dreams, omens, and magnetic attraction. Going back to the cradle of civilization, the orator was depicting those fierce times when men lived on acorns deep in the forest. Later they exchanged the skins of animals for cloth garments, learned to plow the fields and cultivate the vine. Was this for man's good or was there not more inconvenience than advantage in this discovery? Monsieur Derozerays asked himself this question. From magnetic attraction, little by little, Rodolphe had arrived at the affinities, and while the president was citing Cincinnatus at his plow, Diocletian planting his cabbages, and the emperors of China ushering in the new year by sowing the seed, the young man was explaining to the young woman that the cause of these irresistible attractions derived from some previous existence.

"Take us, for example," he was saying. "Why did we meet? What chance determined it? It is surely because our particular selves inclined us toward each other across the distance, like two rivers that gradually converge toward one another."

He took her hand. She did not take it back.

"Grand prize! To the best all-around farmer!" shouted the president.

"The other day, for example, when I came to your house—"

"To Monsieur Bizet of Quincampoix."

"Did I know that I would be spending today with you?"

"Seventy francs!"

"I've wanted to go off a hundred times, but I've kept by your side, stayed with you."

"Manures."

"As I will remain this evening, tomorrow, all the other days all my life!"

"To Monsieur Caron of Argueil, a gold medal."

"For I have never found anyone's company as charming as yours."

"To Monsieur Bain of Givry-Saint-Martin!"

"And so I will cherish the thought of you."

"For a merino ram—"

"But you'll forget me. I shall pass away like a shadow."

"To Monsieur Belot of Notre-Dame—"

"Oh no. Tell me I will remain in your thoughts, in your life."

"Pig class: a prize of sixty francs divided between Messieurs Lehérissé and Cullembourg."

Rodolphe held her hand tightly; he felt it warm and trembling like a captive dove trying to resume its flight. She moved her fingers either because she was trying to free them or replying to the pressure and he exclaimed: "Thank you. You aren't rejecting me. You're so good. You understand that I am yours. Just let me look at you, gaze at you."

A gust of wind coming in through the window disturbed the tablecloth. Below, in the square, the large headdresses of all the countrywomen soared upward like the wings of white butterflies.

"Oil-cake," the president continued. He began to go faster: "Flemish fertilizer—flax—drainage—long leases—domestic service—"

Rodolphe was no longer speaking. They were looking at one another. A supreme desire was causing their dry lips to quiver. Gently, without effort, their fingers intertwined.

"Catherine-Nicaise-Elisabeth Leroux, of Sassetot-la-Guerrière, for fifty-four years of service in the same farm: a silver medal—value, twenty-five francs!"

"Catherine Leroux. Where is she?" the counselor repeated.

She did not come forward. People were whispering: "Go on!"

"No."

"To the left." "Don't be afraid." "How silly she is!"

"Well, where is she?" shouted Tuvache.

"Here she is!"

"Come now, come forward."

Then, to the platform came a frightened-looking little old lady who seemed shrunken in her shabby garments. On her feet were heavy wooden clogs and around her hips a large blue apron. Her scrawny face, framed by a borderless cap, was more wrinkled than a shriveled apple, and bony knuckles dangled from the sleeves of her red bodice. They were so encrusted, roughened, and gnarled from barn dust, soapsuds and grease from sheep's wool that they seemed dirty even though they had been washed in clean water. They remained half bent from having worked so long, humble witnesses of so much suffering. The expression on her face was of an almost nunlike inflexibility. Having lived in the company of animals, she had acquired their muteness and placidity. This was the first time that she found herself in the midst of such a numerous group, and inwardly frightened by the flags and drums, by the gentlemen in frock coats, and by the counselor's Cross of Honor, she remained stock-still, not knowing whether to move forward or run off, nor why the people were pushing her and the examiners smiling. There, before these expansive townspeople, stood this half century of servitude.

"Come forth, venerable Catherine-Nicaise-Elisabeth Leroux!" said the counselor, who had taken the list of winners from the president's hands. "Come up, come up," he repeated in a paternal tone, alternately looking at the sheet of paper and the old woman.

"Are you deaf?" said Tuvache, hopping up from his chair.

He began to shout in her ear: "Fifty-four years of service! A silver medal. Twenty-five francs. For you."

When she was finally holding her medal, she looked at it carefully and a blissful smile spread over her face. She could be heard muttering as she walked off: "I'll give it to our curé to say Mass for me."

"What fanaticism!" exclaimed the pharmacist, leaning toward the notary.

The proceedings were over. The crowd dispersed. Now that the speeches had been read, everyone reassumed his station and things reverted to normal. Masters spoke sharply to their servants, and the servants struck the animals, indolent winners returning to the stable with a green wreath set between their horns.

Meanwhile the National Guard had ascended to the first floor of the Town Hall, with rolls impaled on their bayonets, and the battalion drummer was carrying a basketful of bottles. Madame Bovary took Rodolphe's arm. He accompanied her home, and they separated at her door. Then he walked alone through the meadow, awaiting the hour of the banquet.

The meal was long, noisy, and badly served. They were so crowded that there was virtually no elbow room, and the narrow planks that served as benches almost broke under the weight of the guests. They ate huge quantities of food, everyone gorging himself. Perspiration was pouring down every face, and a white vapor, like river mist on an autumn day, was hovering above the table between the hanging lamps. Rodolphe, leaning back against the side of the tent, was concentrating so much on Emma that he heard nothing. Behind him, on the lawn, the servants were stacking the dirty dishes; his neighbors addressed him, but he did not answer. His glass was filled and, despite the increasing volume of the sound, in his mind there was silence. He was dreaming about what she had said and the shape of her lips; her face, as in a magic mirror, was shining on the badges of the military caps. The folds of her dress were draping the walls, and days of love unfurled unto infinity in the perspective of the future.

He saw her again that evening during the fireworks; but she was with her husband, Madame Homais, and the pharmacist, the latter tormenting himself about the danger of stray rockets. He kept leaving his party every minute to give Binet his suggestions.

The fireworks had been sent in care of Monsieur Tuvache, who had locked them in his cellar in an excess of caution, and so the humid powder barely ignited. The principal display, which was to be a dragon biting its tail, failed completely. An occasional lone Roman candle would go off to a clamor from the gaping mass, which included the squeals of women whose waists were being squeezed in the dark. Emma, in silence, was leaning gently against Charles's shoulder, looking up at the luminous track of the rocket in the black sky. Rodolphe looked at her by the light of the Chinese lanterns.

These died down slowly, and the stars appeared. A few drops of rain began to fall. Emma tied her scarf over her unprotected head.

Just then the counselor's carriage came out from the direction of the inn. The coachman, who was drunk, suddenly fell asleep, and from afar, above the hood, between the two lanterns, the hulk of his body could be seen swaying from right to left to the pitching of the vehicle.

"Really," said the pharmacist, "we must deal harshly with intoxication. I would like to see a weekly *ad hoc* list put up on the Town Hall of all those who became drunk on alcohol during the week. Besides, from a statistical point of view we would have a public record, which might do— Oh, excuse me."

And he ran off once more toward the captain, who was going home, to look again at his lathe.

"It might not be a bad idea," Homais said to him, "to send one of your men or go yourself—"

"Leave me alone," the tax collector answered. "There's no danger."

"It's all right," said Homais when he returned to his friends. "Monsieur Binet assured me that all possible measures were taken. No stray spark will fall. The pumps are filled. Let's go home to sleep."

"Lord knows I need it," said Madame Homais, yawning widely. "Never mind, we had a beautiful day for our celebration."

Rodolphe repeated softly, with a tender expression: "Ah, yes, very beautiful."

They bade each other good night and went their separate ways.

Two days later, in the *Rouen Beacon*, there was a lengthy article about the Show. Homais had written it with enthusiasm on the next day:

"Why all these festoons and flowers and garlands? Whither ran this crowd like the waves of an enraged sea, under a tropical sun beating down over our fields?"

He went on to speak about the plight of the peasants. The government was indeed doing a great deal, but not enough! "Be brave!" he advised. "There are a thousand indispensable reforms. Let us accomplish them."

Then, discussing the counselor's arrival, he forgot neither "the martial air of our militia" nor "our sprightly village lasses" nor the bald-headed old men, "those patriarchs who attended, the remnants of our immortal legions, their hearts still beating to the manly roll of the drums." He listed himself among the leading members of the jury, and even mentioned in a note that Monsieur Homais, pharmacist, had sent a memorandum on cider to the Society of Agriculture.

When he reached the distribution of the prizes, he painted the winners' joy in dithyrambic strokes. "Father embraced son, husband wife, brother brother. More than one displayed his humble medal with pride, and doubtless, on his return home, was to hang it in tears upon the modest walls of his humble cottage.

"At six o'clock, a banquet, set out in Monsieur Liégeard's meadow, assembled the principal personalities of the Show. The greatest cordiality reigned throughout. Several toasts were offered; Monsieur Lieuvain proposed the King's health, Monsieur Tuvache that of the prefect; Monsieur Derozerays the farmers' and Monsieur Homais those two sisters industry and the fine arts. Monsieur Leplichey offered his toast to progress. In the evening a brilliant fireworks display suddenly illuminated the heavens. It was a veritable kaleidoscope, a setting for an opera. For a moment our little town believed itself transported to the heart of an Arabian Nights dream.

"Let us note that no untoward event occurred to mar this family reunion."

He added: "However, the absence of the clergy was noted. Doubtless the gentlemen of the cloth understand progress in a different way. As you will, revered followers of Loyola!"

I X

Six weeks went by. Rodolphe did not return. He finally appeared one evening.

"It would be a mistake to return too soon," he had said to himself. And he went off on a hunting trip the week after the Show.

After the hunt he thought it was too late, and then he reasoned: "If she loved me that first day, her impatience to see me again must be increasing her love. We'll keep this up awhile."

He realized that his reasoning had been sound when he saw Emma turn pale as he entered the room.

She was alone in the fading light. The short muslin curtains along the windowpanes intensified the twilight; the gilt on the barometer, touched by a ray of sunshine, was reflecting sparks onto the mirror hanging between the fretted coral.

Rodolphe remained standing. His opening remarks were conventionally polite; Emma barely answered them.

"I've been busy," he went on, "and ill."

"Nothing serious?" she asked quickly.

"No," he said, sitting down near her on a stool. "I just didn't want to come back."

"Why?"

"You can't guess?"

He looked at her with such intensity that she lowered her head and blushed. He began again: "Emma—"

"Sir!" she said, pulling back a little.

"Ah, you can see," he said in a melancholy tone, "I was right not to come back, since you refuse me that name, that name that courses through my soul and that just escaped from me! 'Madame Bovary!' Everyone calls you that. And it's not even your name, it's someone else's. Someone else's," he repeated, and he hid his face in his hands. "Yes, I think of you all the time. The memory of you drives me to despair. Forgive me. I'll leave you. Good-bye. I shall go far away, so far that you will never hear about me again. And yet—today—I don't know what power still impelled me toward you. You can't fight fate, or resist the smile of an angel! You let yourself be lured by what is beautiful, charming, and adorable!"

This was the first time Emma had heard such things, and her pride, like someone who lets himself relax in a steam bath, stretched luxuriously and without reservations in the warmth of his words.

"But even if I didn't come," he continued, "if I couldn't see you, at least I studied your surroundings closely. I arose and came here every night, looked at your house, at the roof gleaming in the moonlight, at the trees in the garden swaying near your window, and at that tiny light shining through the window into the shadows. Ah! Little did you guess what was there, so near and yet so far, a poor miserable—"

She turned toward him with a sob.

"You are so good!" she said.

"No, I love you, that is all. You don't doubt it? Tell me, say one word, one single word!"

And Rodolphe let himself slip imperceptibly from the stool onto the floor. But the sound of clogs was heard from the kitchen, and he noticed that the door was open.

"It would be so kind of you," he continued, getting up, "to satisfy a whim of mine."

This was to visit her house. He wanted to know it well.

Madame Bovary saw nothing out of the way in this, and they were both standing up when Charles came in.

"Good day, doctor," said Rodolphe.

Charles, flattered by the unexpected title, became extravagantly obsequious. The other took advantage of this to regain his composure. He said, "Your wife was telling me about her health—"

Charles interrupted him. He had many worries on that score; his wife's attacks of breathlessness were beginning again. Rodolphe asked if horseback riding would not be a good idea.

"Certainly! Excellent! Perfect! A fine idea! You ought to look into it, dear."

She objected that she did not own a horse. Monsieur Rodolphe offered one of his. She refused, and he did not insist. Then, to justify his visit, he mentioned that his carter, the man who had been bled, was still suffering from dizzy spells.

"I'll stop by," said Bovary.

"No, I'll send him here. We can come together. It will be more convenient for you."

"Fine. Thank you very much." When they were alone: "Why don't you accept Monsieur Boulanger's suggestion? It was very considerate."

She began to pout, searched about for a quantity of excuses, and finally declared that "it might look strange."

"I don't care if it does!" said Charles, turning on his heel. "Health above all. You're wrong."

"How do you expect me to go horseback riding when I have no riding habit?"

"We'll have to order one for you." The riding habit decided her.

When the outfit was ready, Charles wrote to Monsieur Boulanger that his wife awaited his convenience and that they were counting on his kindness.

At noon the next day Rodolphe arrived at Charles's door with two riding horses. One had pink pompons on its ears and a buckskin sidesaddle.

Rodolphe was wearing high soft-leather boots. He told himself that she had probably never seen their like. Emma was indeed charmed by his appearance when he appeared on the landing in his long velvet coat and his white tricot riding breeches. She was ready and waiting for him.

Justin slipped out of the shop to see her, and the apothecary himself also stopped work. He offered some advice to Monsieur Boulanger: "An accident happens so fast. Take care. Your horses may be spirited."

Emma heard a noise up above. It was Félicité tapping on the panes to amuse little Berthe. The child threw a kiss from afar. Her mother answered with a wave of her riding crop.

"Have a good ride," shouted Monsieur Homais. "Be careful! Be very careful."

He waved his newspaper as he watched them ride off.

Emma's horse broke into a gallop as soon as it felt soft ground. Rodolphe kept alongside. They would exchange an occasional word. With her head slightly lowered, her hand held high, and her right arm outstretched, she abandoned herself to the rhythmic rocking movement on the saddle.

Rodolphe let go the reins at the foot of the hill and they went off together as one. The horses stopped short at the summit, and her large blue veil fell back down.

It was the beginning of October. A mist lay over the countryside, and there were long wisps of vapor along the hills silhouetted against the horizon. Clouds would break apart, float upward, and disappear. Occasionally, when the haze parted, the rooftops of Yonville could be seen in the distance, gleaming in the sun with the gardens along the river's edge, the barnyards, the walls and the church steeple. Emma squinted as she tried to make out her house. This wretched village in which she lived had never appeared so small to her. From the heights on which they were standing, the entire valley seemed to be a pale, immense lake, evaporating in the air. Occasional clumps of trees jutted out like black rocks, and the tall lines of the poplars, extending out of the mist, looked like the windswept shores of the lake.

A brown light hovered in the warm air between the pines. The earth, red-brown like tobacco, muffled the sound of the horses' hooves as they pushed fallen pinecones before them with their iron shoes.

Rodolphe and Emma skirted around the wooded area. She kept turning her head away in order to avoid his gaze, and then she would see nothing but the evenly spaced trunks of the pine trees, the unbroken succession of which made her slightly dizzy.

The sun came out just as they entered the forest. "God is protecting us," Rodolphe said.

"You think so?" she asked.

"Come," he said. He clicked his tongue, and the two horses moved rapidly.

Tall ferns at the side of the road kept catching in Emma's stirrup. Rodolphe would lean over and pull them off as they moved along. At other times, in order to push aside the branches, he came closer, and Emma felt his knee rubbing against her leg. The sky had turned blue and the leaves were still. There were large stretches of heather in bloom. Patches of violets alternated with the tangled undergrowth of the trees, which was gray, fawn colored, or gold, varying according to the tree.

They would often hear a soft flutter of wings beneath the bushes or the hoarse, soft cry of the rooks as they flew off among the oaks.

They dismounted. Rodolphe tethered the horses. She walked ahead of him over the moss between the car tracks.

But her long riding habit hampered her, even though she was holding it up. Rodolphe, walking behind her, feasted his eyes on the bit of white stocking that showed like naked flesh between the black of the cloth and the boot.

She stopped. "I'm tired," she said.

"Just a little more; keep trying!" he said. "Be brave!"

She stopped again, a few yards farther. The veil slanting down to her hips over her man-styled hat lent a bluish cast to her face, as if she were floating in azure waters. "Where are we going?"

He didn't answer. She was panting slightly. Rodolphe looked about, biting his mustache.

They reached a more spacious clearing in which young trees had been felled and sat down on a log. Rodolphe began telling her of his love.

He avoided frightening her at the beginning by too many compliments. He was calm, serious, and melancholy.

Emma listened to him with her head lowered, pushing at wood shavings on the ground with her toe.

But when he said: "Aren't our destinies united now?" she answered "No! You know they aren't. It's impossible."

She arose to leave. He grasped her by the wrist. She stopped. Then, after she had looked at him for a while, her eyes moist with love, she said quickly: "Let's not talk about it anymore. Where are the horses? Let's go back."

He reacted with an angry gesture of annoyance. She repeated: "Where are the horses?"

Then he moved toward her with his arms outstretched, smiling strangely. There was a fixed look in his eyes, and his teeth were clenched. She trembled as she retreated from him, stammering: "You're frightening me. You're hurting me. Let's go back."

"If we must," he said, changing his expression. And once more he became respectful, fond, and shy. She took his arm and they turned back. He said: "What's the matter? What is it? I don't understand. You must have mistaken my intentions. In my soul you are a Madonna on a pedestal, exalted, secure, and immaculate. But I need you to survive. I need your eyes, your voice, your thoughts. Be my friend, my sister, my angel!"

He stretched his arm around her waist. She tried feebly to free herself. He supported her thus as they walked.

They heard the two horses munching leaves.

"Stay awhile," Rodolphe said. "Let's not go back. Stay!"

He led her farther along, around a small pond where the green duckweed covered the water. Wilted water lilies lay motionless

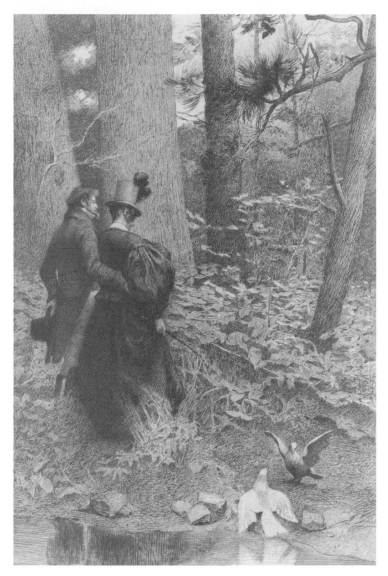

He led her farther along, around a small pond where the green duckweed covered the water.

among the reeds. At the sound of their steps through the grass, frogs jumped up to find cover.

"I shouldn't, I shouldn't," she said. "I'm mad to listen to you."

"Why? Emma—Emma—"

"Oh, Rodolphe!" the young woman said slowly, leaning on his shoulder.

The cloth of her habit clung to the velvet of his coat. She threw back her head, her white throat swelled in a sigh, and without resisting, tears streaming, with a long shudder and her face hidden, she gave herself to him.

Evening shadows were falling; the horizontal sun, passing through the branches, was blinding her eyes. All around her, in the leaves and on the ground, were luminous shimmering patches, as if hummingbirds had shed their feathers in flight. All was silent; gentleness seemed to emanate from the trees; she could feel her heart beating again, and the blood circulating like a milky river through her body. Then she heard, off in the distance beyond the woods, over the other hills, a vague, prolonged cry, a drawn-out voice to which she listened in silence as it mingled like music with the waning vibrations of her throbbing nerves. Rodolphe, a cigar in his mouth, was fixing one of the two broken bridles with his knife.

They returned to Yonville along the same road. They saw the traces of their horses side by side in the mud; the same bushes, the same stones in the grass. Nothing had changed around them; and yet, for her, something had happened of greater importance than if the mountains had shifted place. Rodolphe would occasionally pick her hand up and kiss it.

She was charming on horseback! Erect, her waist narrow, her knee bent on her horse's mane, and slightly flushed from the fresh air in the glow of evening.

As they entered Yonville, she made her horse prance over the pavement. People looked at her from the windows.

During dinner her husband remarked that she looked very well; but she seemed not to hear him when he asked about her outing; and she remained with her elbow at the edge of her plate, between the two lighted candles.

"Emma!" he said.

"What?"

"You know, I spent this afternoon with Monsieur Alexander; he has an old mare that is still very handsome, only a little broken at the knees. We could have it for a hundred crowns, I'm sure." He added: "I thought you'd be pleased and I said we'd take it. I bought it. Was I right? Tell me."

She moved her head in a sign of assent; then, a quarter of an hour later: "Are you going out tonight?" she asked.

"Yes. Why?"

"No reason, dear."

As soon as she was rid of Charles, she went up to her room and shut herself in.

At first she was in a state of confusion; she saw the trees, the paths, the ditches, Rodolphe, and she could still feel the tightness of his embrace while the leaves rustled and the reeds whistled.

But when she saw her reflection in the mirror, she was astounded at her appearance. Her eyes had never been so large, so black, nor of such a depth. She was transfigured by some subtle change permeating her entire being.

She kept telling herself, "I have a lover! A lover!" relishing the thought like that of some unexpected second puberty. So she was finally going to possess those joys of love, that fever of happiness, of which she had so long despaired. She was entering into something marvelous where all would be passion, ecstasy, delirium; she was enveloped in a vast expanse of blue, the peaks of emotion sparkling in her thoughts. Ordinary existence seemed to be in the distance, down below, in the shadows, between the peaks.

Then she remembered the heroines in the books she had read, and the lyrical legion of these adulterous women began to sing in her memory with sisterly voices enchanting her. She herself became a part of these fantasies. She was realizing the long dream of her adolescence, seeing herself as one of those amorous women she had so long envied. Moreover, Emma was feeling a sensation of revenge. Had she not suffered enough? But now she was triumphing, and love, so long contained, burst forth in its entirety with joyous effervescence. She was savoring it without remorse or anxiety, without feeling troubled.

The next day brought new delight. They made promises to each other. She told him her troubles. Rodolphe interrupted her with his kisses; and she asked him, looking at him through half-closed eyelids, to repeat her name again and to tell her once more that he loved her. Like the preceding day, this took place in the forest, in a clogmaker's hut. The walls were of straw and the roof came down so low that they had to stoop. They sat side by side on a bed of dried leaves.

From that day on they wrote each other regularly every evening. Emma would carry her letter to the back of the garden, near the river, to a crevice in the wall. Rodolphe would come for it and leave another, which she always complained was too short.

One day, when Charles had gone out before dawn, she was seized with the yearning to see Rodolphe right away. She could go quickly to La Huchette, remain an hour, and be back in Yonville while everyone was still asleep. The notion made her pant with desire; she soon found herself walking rapidly through the meadow without a backward glance.

Day was beginning to break. Emma recognized her lover's home in the distance. Its two swallow-tailed weathervanes were silhouetted black in the pale light of dawn.

Beyond the barnyard there was a building that was probably the château. She walked in as if the walls had parted at her approach. A long straight staircase led up to a corridor. Emma lifted a door latch and suddenly, at the back of the room, she saw a man sleeping. It was Rodolphe. She uttered a cry.

"You!" he said. "You! How did you get here? Your dress is all wet!"

"I love you," she answered, twining her arms around his neck.

This first risk having succeeded, each time from then on that Charles left early, Emma would dress rapidly and walk stealthily down the flight of steps leading to the water's edge.

But when the plank for the cows was taken away, she had to walk along the walls beside the water; the bank was slippery; to keep from falling, she would grasp the tufts of faded wallflowers. Farther on, she would turn into the plowed fields, where she would stumble as her thin boots sank deep and filled with mud. Her kerchief, tied around her head, would flutter in the wind of the meadows; she was afraid of the oxen and would begin to run; she would arrive out of breath, her cheeks flushed, and her body exuding a fresh fragrance of sap, verdure, and open air. Rodolphe would be still sleeping at that hour, and it was as if a spring morning had come into his bedroom.

Through the yellow curtains along the windows a heavy light softly penetrated. Emma blinked, groping her way, while the drops of dew on her hair resembled a topaz halo around her face. Rodolphe would laughingly pull her to him and hold her close to his chest.

Later she would look around the room, open the furniture drawers, comb her hair with his comb, and stare at herself in the shaving mirror. Often she placed between her teeth the stem of a large pipe that was on the night table, along with the lemons and the sugar lumps, near a water pitcher.

They needed a good fifteen minutes for their good-byes. Emma would cry; she didn't want to leave him ever again. Something stronger than herself was pushing her toward him, so that one day, seeing her appear unexpectedly, he frowned as if he were annoyed.

"What's the matter?" she asked. "Are you ill? Tell me!"

He declared, very gravely, that her visits were becoming imprudent and that she was compromising herself.

X

Gradually Rodolphe's fears began to affect her. At first she had been so drunk with love that she thought of nothing beyond it. But now that it was so indispensable to her life, she was terrified that it might be disturbed or even destroyed. She would look around anxiously when returning from his house, stare at every shadow on the horizon and each attic window in the village from which she might be seen. She strained her ears for the sound of footsteps, shouts, the noise of plows; and she would stop short, more pale and quivering than the poplar leaves swaying above her.

As she was returning home in this state of mind one morning, she suddenly thought she saw the long barrel of a gun pointing directly at her. It was sticking out at an angle from a small barrel half hidden in the grass at the edge of a ditch. Although she was frightened almost to the point of fainting, Emma kept on walking. A man came out of the barrel like a jack-in-the-box. He had leggings buckled at his knees and a cap pulled down over his eyes. His teeth were chattering and his nose red. It was Captain Binet, hunting for wild duck.

"You should have called out before you came so close," he shouted. "When you see a gun, you should always give warning."

The tax collector was trying to cover up the fright he had just received. A decree from the prefect had outlawed duck hunting except from boats, and Monsieur Binet, despite his respect for the law, was acting illegally. He expected to hear the game warden arrive at any moment. But the danger added spice to his enjoyment, and all alone in his barrel he congratulated himself on his luck and his cunning.

When Emma appeared he looked greatly relieved and began to chat: "It's certainly not warm; there's a definite chill in the air."

Emma said nothing. He continued: "You're up so early?"

"Yes," she said with a stammer, "I've been to see my daughter at her nurse's."

"Ah, I see, I see. I've been here since daybreak; but the weather's so foul that unless you have your bird right at the end of your gun—"

"Good day, Monsieur Binet," she interrupted, turning away from him.

"Your servant, Madame," he answered curtly, and climbed back into his barrel.

Emma regretted having left the tax collector so abruptly. He would surely become suspicious. The story about the nurse was the worst possible excuse, since everyone in Yonville knew that the Bovary child had been home with her parents for a year. Besides, no one lived in this direction; the road led only to La Huchette. Binet had therefore guessed where she was coming from, and he would not keep quiet. He would certainly talk! She spent the entire day torturing herself, thinking up all kinds of plausible lies, continually haunted by the face of this fool with his game bag.

Charles noticed her worried air and wanted to distract her after dinner by taking her to the pharmacist's. The first person she met in the pharmacy was the tax collector himself! He was standing at the counter in the light of the red jar and saying: "Give me half an ounce of vitriol, please."

"Justin!" shouted the apothecary. "Bring some sulfuric acid." Then to Emma, who was about to go upstairs to Madame Homais: "No, don't bother. Stay here, she's coming down. Warm up at the stove while you're waiting. Excuse me. Good evening, doctor (the pharmacist loved pronouncing the word *doctor,* as if in addressing another person, some of the glory in it reflected back on himself). Don't upset those mortars, boy! Go get some chairs from the sun parlor! You know you're not supposed to move the living-room furniture!"

And Homais was halfway out from behind the counter to put his armchair back where it belonged when Binet asked him for half an ounce of sugar acid.

"Sugar acid?" the pharmacist repeated with contempt. "I don't know what that is. Perhaps you mean oxalic acid? It is oxalic, isn't it?"

Binet explained that he needed an abrasive to make a solution of copper with which he could remove the rust from his hunting gear. Emma shuddered. The pharmacist said: "I guess the weather's been bad, what with all this humidity."

"Well," said the tax collector with a sly look, "some people don't seem to mind it."

She was stifling.

"And I also want—"

"He'll never go!" she thought.

"Half an ounce of resin and some turpentine, four ounces of beeswax, and an ounce and a half of animal black, please, to polish the patent leather on my gear."

The apothecary was beginning to cut the wax when Madame Homais appeared with Irma in her arms, Napoleon at her side, and Athalie following behind. She sat down on the plush-covered bench beneath the window. The boy squatted on a footstool while his older sister hovered around the jujube box near her darling papa, who was filling containers, corking them, pasting labels, and tying parcels. No one spoke to him, and the only sound was the occasional clink of the weights on the scale and a few whispered words from the pharmacist instructing his pupil.

"How's your little girl?" Madame Homais suddenly asked.

"Quiet!" said her husband, who was entering figures in the notebook.

"Why didn't you bring her?" she continued in softer tones.

"Ssh!" Emma said, pointing to the pharmacist.

But Binet, completely involved in checking the bill, had probably heard nothing. He finally left, and Emma heaved a deep sigh of relief.

"You're breathing so heavily," Madame Homais said.

"It's so warm," she answered.

The next day they decided, because of the incident, to arrange their meetings better. Emma wanted to bribe his maid by a gift, but he felt it would be still better to find some discreet house in Yonville. Rodolphe promised to look for one.

All through the winter, three or four times a week, he came to the garden in the dead of night. Emma had purposely removed the key from the garden gate. Charles thought it was lost.

Rodolphe would announce his presence by throwing a handful of gravel against the shutters. She would jump up. Sometimes she had to wait because Charles had a habit of sitting by the fireside and chattering interminably.

She would rage with impatience. If looks could have done it, she would have pushed him out the window. Finally she would begin undressing, then pick up a book and start quietly reading with obvious pleasure. Charles, already in bed, would call to her.

"Emma, come to bed, it's late," he would say.

"I'm coming," she would answer.

But as the candles were too bright for his eyes, he would turn toward the wall and fall asleep. Then, holding her breath, she would sneak out of the room, a smile on her face and her heart pounding, half undressed.

Rodolphe had a voluminous cloak that he would wrap around her. He would wind his arms around her waist and lead her silently to the back of the garden.

They would stay in the arbor on the same bench of rotting wood where in the old days Léon had looked at her so lovingly in the summer nights. She rarely thought of him now.

The stars shone through the leafless jasmine branches. They could hear the river flowing behind them and an occasional crackling of dry reeds on the bank. Great masses of shadow loomed up against the obscurity and sometimes, rising as if with a shudder, they would advance like huge black waves ready to engulf them. The cold of the night made them hold each other even more tightly; the sighs emerging from their lips seemed louder; their eyes, which they could discern only with difficulty, seemed even larger; and in the midst of the silence, their whispered words fell crystal clear on their souls and echoed and reechoed with continuing vibrations.

When it rained, they took shelter in the consulting room, between the shed and the stable. She would light one of the kitchen candles, which she had hidden behind the books. Rodolphe would make himself as comfortable as if he were at home. The sight of the bookcase and the desk, of the entire room, intensified his gaiety; he could not refrain from making various jokes at Charles's expense, which Emma found embarrassing. She wanted him to be more serious and even more dramatic on occasion. Once, for example, she thought she heard approaching footsteps in the lane.

"Someone's coming!" she said.

He blew out the light.

"Do you have your pistols?"

"What for?"

"To—to defend yourself," Emma said.

"Against your husband? That poor fellow!" And Rodolphe finished his sentence with a gesture signifying: "I could crush him with a flick of the finger."

She was amazed at his courage, although she sensed in it an indelicacy and blatant vulgarity that she thought shocking.

Rodolphe thought a long while about this talk of pistols. If she had meant it seriously, it would be the height of idiocy, even odious, for he personally had no reason to hate good old Charles. Rodolphe was not a man "devoured with jealousy." Besides, in this connection Emma had made a solemn promise to him that, moreover, he did not find in the best of taste.

She was also becoming quite sentimental. They had had to exchange miniatures and locks of hair and now she wanted a ring, an actual marriage band as a sign of eternal union. She would often speak to him of the bells of evening or of the "voices of nature." She would talk to him about her mother and his. Rodolphe had lost his mother twenty years before. Emma, nevertheless, consoled him with the gushing language one uses to a bereaved child. She even said to him, sometimes, looking up at the moon: "I'm sure that they're together up there, smiling down on our love!"

But she was so pretty! He had had few mistresses as unspoiled as she was. This love without guile was something new to him. It had taken him out of his free-and-easy ways, flattered his pride, and quickened his sensuality. Emma's emotional raptures, which his middle-class common sense disdained, seemed charming to him, deep down, since he was the recipient. Then, when he was sure of being loved, he stopped trying to please her, and his ways changed imperceptibly.

He no longer used words so sweet that they made her cry, as he had in the old days; nor were his caresses so ardent that they drove her mad. So the great love affair in which she had plunged seemed to diminish under her like the water of a river being absorbed into its own bed, and she began to see slime at the bottom. She didn't want to believe it and redoubled her tenderness. Rodolphe hid his indifference less and less.

She did not know if she regretted having given in to him or if she wished, on the contrary, to love him even more. The humiliation of feeling how weak she was where he was concerned turned into a resentment tempered only by sensual pleasure. It was not an attachment, but a permanent seduction. He was subjugating her. She was almost afraid of him.

The surface, however, was calmer than ever, Rodolphe having succeeded in conducting the affair to suit his whims, and when half a year had gone by and springtime came, they were like a married couple peacefully tending the domestic fires.

It was the time of year when old Rouault sent his turkey in memory of Charles's setting his leg. The gift always arrived with a letter. Emma cut the cord tying it to the basket and read the following lines:

My dear children,

I hope that this letter will find you in good health and that the bird is as good as the others. It looks a bit more tender, if I may say so, and larger. Next time I'll send you a cock for a change, unless you would rather stick to the gobblers, and send back the basket please with the two from before. I had trouble with the cart shed. The roof flew off into the trees one night when it was very windy. And the harvest hasn't been very good. Anyhow, I don't know when I'll be coming to see you. It's so hard for me to leave the house now that I'm all alone, Emma dear!

There was a space after these lines, as if the old man had dropped his pen to dream for a while.

As for me, I'm fine except for a cold I caught the other day at the Yvetot Fair, where I went to hire a shepherd. I sent mine off because he was too fussy about food. What trouble these rascals cause us! And he wasn't honest either.

I heard from a peddler who traveled through your district this winter and had a tooth pulled that Bovary is still working hard. I'm not surprised. He showed me his tooth, and we had a cup of coffee together. I asked him if he saw you and he said no, but that he'd seen two horses in the stable, so I imagine that business is good. Welcome news, dear children. May God send you all possible happiness.

I'm very unhappy that I don't know my beloved granddaughter, Berthe Bovary, as yet. I've planted a plum tree for her in the garden under your window, and I won't let anyone near it except to make jam for her, which I can put aside in my cupboard for her visit.

Good-bye, my dear children. I kiss you, daughter, and you, dear son-in-law, and the little one, on both cheeks.

With much love,

Your devoted father,
Theodore Rouault

She sat for a few minutes holding the coarse paper in her hands. There were many spelling errors, and Emma followed the loving thoughts that cackled through them like a hen half hidden in a thorn hedge. He had blotted the writing with ashes from the fireplace, because some gray dust fell off the letter onto her dress. She could almost see her father bending over the hearth to pick up the tongs. How long it was since she had sat with him on the bench near the fireplace, burning a stick in the blazing furze fire as it crackled! She remembered summer evenings filled with sunshine. The foals would whinny as you passed, and run and run. Under her window there was a beehive, and sometimes the bees flying around in the sunlight would strike against her windowpanes like golden balls. She had been so happy in those days! Days of freedom and hope, filled with illusions! There were no illusions left now. She had gradually spent them in all the adventures of her soul, in all her successive conditions, in her virginity, in her marriage, and in love; losing them continually as she grew older, like a traveler who leaves part of his money in every inn along the highway.

But what was making her so unhappy? Where was the extraordinary calamity that had overwhelmed her? She lifted her head and looked around as if to seek the cause of her suffering.

An April sunbeam was glowing over the china figures on the cabinet; the fire was blazing. She felt the softness of the rug through her slippers. The day was clear and warm and she could hear her child laughing.

The little girl was rolling on the lawn while the grass was being cut. She was face down on top of a haystack while her nursemaid held onto her skirt. Lestiboudois was raking on one side, and each time he came near she leaned forward, flailing her arms through the air.

"Bring her here," said her mother, rushing out to kiss her. "I love you so much, my darling child, so much!"

Then she noticed that the tips of her ears were slightly dirty. She rang for warm water at once and washed her, changing her underwear, stockings, and shoes and asking a thousand questions about her health, as if she had returned from a trip. Finally, still kissing her and crying a little, she handed her back to the maid, who was quite amazed at this excess of affection.

Rodolphe found her more serious than usual that evening.

"It will pass," he told himself. "It's a mood."

And he missed three meetings in a row. When he returned, she was cold and almost disdainful.

"You're wasting your time, my pet!" And he pretended to notice neither her melancholy sighs nor the handkerchief she pulled out.

And then Emma repented.

She even asked herself why she loathed Charles so, and if it would not be better to be able to love him. But there was very little he could offer for the return of her affection, and she remained quite bewildered about her impulse to sacrifice until the pharmacist showed up at the right moment to provide her with an opportunity.

XI

Homais had recently read an article praising a new method for curing clubfoot; and since he was an enthusiast for progress, he thought up the patriotic notion that Yonville, "to put itself on the map," should have some operations for talipes, as he called it.

"After all, what's the risk?" he asked Emma. "Let's see"—he ticked off on his fingers the advantages of such an attempt—"an almost certain success, relief and improved appearance of the patient, and a rapid rise to fame for the surgeon. Why, for example, wouldn't your husband want to help poor Hippolyte from the Golden Lion? He wouldn't fail to tell all the travelers about his cure, you know, and besides," here Homais lowered his voice and looked around, "what's to stop me from sending a short article about it to the paper? And, by God, an article gets around; people talk about it; it begins to snowball! And then, who knows? Who knows?"

It was true: Bovary might well succeed. Emma had no reason to think he wasn't a capable doctor, and what a satisfaction for her were she to get him to take a step that would increase his reputation and his fortune. She wanted desperately something more substantial than love to lean on.

Urged on by her and by the apothecary, Charles let himself be convinced. He ordered Doctor Duval's book on clubfoot from Rouen and would bury himself in it every evening, holding his head in his hands.

While he was studying the various forms of talipes—equinus, varus, and valgus—scientifically called *strephocatopodia, strephendopodia,* and *strephexopodia* (or, in more simple terms, the different ways the foot deviates—downwards, inwards, or outwards), as well as *strephypopody* and *strephanopody* (in other words, torsion downward or upward), Monsieur Homais was urging the stableboy, with all kinds of reasons, to let himself be operated.

"You'll probably feel almost nothing, just a little pain. It's just an injection, like being bled, less than removing certain kinds of corns."

Hippolyte rolled his eyes stupidly and tried to think.

"Besides," the pharmacist continued, "it's not for me. It's for you, purely out of goodwill. I'd like to see you rid of your ugly deformity, my friend, and that lumbar region of yours straightened out. No matter how much you say, I'm sure it hurts you terribly in your work."

Then Homais pointed out to him how much more cheerful and agile he would feel later on, and even hinted that he would find himself more likely to please women. The stableboy began to grin sheepishly. Then he played on his vanity: "Aren't you a man, damn it! Suppose you had to join the army and fight to defend our flag? Ah, Hippolyte!"

And Homais walked away, asserting that he could not understand this stubbornness, this blindness in refusing to benefit from science.

The poor soul finally gave in, yielding to what became a veritable conspiracy against him. Binet, who never meddled in other people's affairs, Madame Lefrançois, Artémise, the neighbors, and even Monsieur Tuvache, the mayor—everyone approached him, lectured him, shamed him; but what finally convinced him was that "it wouldn't cost a cent." Bovary took it upon himself to provide the apparatus for the operation.

Emma had thought of this generous gesture, and Charles consented, thinking to himself that his wife was an angel.

With the pharmacist's advice, and after two false starts, he had the carpenter, aided by the locksmith, construct a boxlike contraption, weighing about eight pounds, in which neither iron, wood, sheet metal, leather, screws, nor nuts were spared.

Then, in order to decide which of Hippolyte's tendons to cut, it was necessary to figure out first which sort of clubfoot he had.

His foot was in an almost completely straight line with his leg; nevertheless, this did not stop it from being turned inward. So it was an equinus with slight varus characteristics, or, alternatively, a slight varus with pronounced equinus characteristics. But with this equinus, as large as a horse's hoof, with rough skin, brittle tendons, thick toes, and blackened toenails resembling the nails of a horseshoe—on that foot the taliped raced about from day to night like a deer. He was constantly to be seen in the square, hopping around the carts, putting his bad foot forward. He actually seemed stronger on that foot than on the other. By dint of having been used, it had in a sense acquired the moral qualities of patience and energy, and when he was given some heavy work, he actually preferred to shift his weight onto it.

Now, since it was an equinus, the Achilles tendon had to be cut first, and later the anterior tibial muscle, to take care of the varus; for the doctor did not dare to risk two operations at once, and he was even trembling already, afraid of interfering with some important area of the foot that he did not know.

Neither Ambrose Paré, applying an immediate ligature to an artery for the first time since Celsus, after an interval of fifteen hundred years; nor Dupuytren, opening an abscess through a thick layer of brain; nor Gensoul, performing the first removal of an upper maxillary, could have suffered such palpitations of the heart, such trembling hands, such mental strain as did Monsieur Bovary when he approached Hippolyte, with his tenotomy knife in his hands. And, as in a hospital, on a table at his side were a pile of lint, waxed thread, a quantity of bandages—a pyramid of bandages, all the bandages there were in the pharmacist's shop. It was Monsieur Homais who had been organizing all these preparations since early morning, as much to bedazzle the crowd as to inflate his own ego. Charles pierced the skin; a brittle snap was heard. The tendon was cut, the operation finished. Hippolyte could not get over his surprise; he leaned over Bovary's hands to cover them with kisses.

"Calm down," said the pharmacist. "You'll show your gratitude to your benefactor later!"

And he went down to announce the results to five or six curious souls lingering in the yard who imagined that Hippolyte would appear walking properly. Charles, having strapped his patient into the mechanical motor, went home, where Emma was anxiously awaiting him on the doorstep. She threw herself at him; they went in to eat. Charles ate with gusto and even asked for a cup of coffee with dessert, an extravagance he permitted himself only on Sundays when they had company.

The evening passed beautifully, filled with talk, with daydreams in common. They spoke about their future fortune, about improvements they would make in the house; he foresaw his reputation increasing, his prosperity growing, his wife loving him always; and she felt happy to revive herself with a healthier emotion, a better and different one, to feel, finally, some affection for this poor boy who adored her. The thought of Rodolphe passed through her head at one moment, but she looked at Charles and even noticed with surprise that his teeth were not at all bad.

They were in bed when Monsieur Homais, despite the cook's protests, walked right into the bedroom holding a newly written sheet of paper in his hand. It was the publicity article he was going to send to the *Rouen Beacon*. He had brought it to read to them.

"Read it to us," said Bovary.

He read: " 'Despite the network of prejudices that still covers part of the map of Europe, light is nevertheless beginning to penetrate our countrysides. And so, last Tuesday, our small city of Yonville was the scene of a surgical experiment that is, at the same time, an act of great philanthropy. Monsieur Bovary, one of our most distinguished doctors——' "

"That's too much, too much," said Charles, choking with emotion.

"Not at all! Please! '. . . operated on a clubfoot. . . .' I didn't use the scientific term because in a newspaper, you know, not everyone would understand; the masses need——"

"Exactly," said Bovary. "Continue."

"I'll start over," said the pharmacist. " 'Monsieur Bovary, one of our most distinguished doctors, operated on the clubfoot of one Hippolyte Tautain, stableboy for the past twenty-five years at the Golden Lion Hotel, overlooking the Place d'Armes, run by the Widow Lefrançois. The novelty of the attempt and the interest inherent in the subject had attracted so many people that there was a veritable crush at the door of the building. The operation, moreover, was carried out beautifully and there were only a few drops of blood on the skin, as if to bear witness that the rebellious tendon had finally yielded to the surgeon's art. The patient, strange to say (we can report this as eyewitnesses), seemed to feel no pain. Everything leads us to think that the convalescence will be of short duration. Who knows, perhaps at the next village festival we shall see our brave Hippolyte taking part in the Bacchic dances in a ring of jolly companions, and thus proving to all eyes his complete recovery by his liveliness and his capers.

" 'All honor to our generous men of science! All honor to those untiring souls who deprive themselves of sleep for the improvement or the healing of their fellow men! All honor to them! Should we not cry aloud that the blind will see, the deaf hear, and the crippled walk? But what fanaticism once promised to its elect, science shall now accomplish for all mankind! We shall keep our readers informed of the further stages of this remarkable cure.' "

None of this prevented Madame Lefrançois, five days later, from arriving in fright and screaming: "Help! He's dying! I'm going out of my mind."

Charles rushed over to the Golden Lion. The pharmacist, seeing him hasten through the square without his hat, left his store and appeared, out of breath, red in the face, and anxious, asking everyone going up the stairs: "What's wrong with our interesting taliped?"

The taliped was twisting about in dreadful convulsions; the apparatus in which his foot was encased was hitting the wall hard enough to smash it.

Taking many precautions so as not to disturb the position of the limb, they pulled off the box. A hideous sight was revealed. The foot was swollen to an unrecognizable shape, the skin seemed about to burst open. It was covered with black and blue marks caused by the famous machine. Hippolyte had already complained that it hurt him, but no one had heeded him. They had to admit that he wasn't entirely wrong and left him alone for a few hours. But hardly had the swelling subsided when the two scientists decided it was time to put the foot back in the apparatus. They even tightened it to obtain quicker results. Finally, three days later, when Hippolyte could not endure it any longer, they removed the mechanism once more. They were greatly surprised at the result which greeted them. A livid tumescence was spread all over the leg, dotted with blisters oozing a dark liquid. Things were taking a serious turn. Hippolyte was beginning to fret and Madame Lefrançois settled him into the small parlor, near the kitchen, so that he would at least have some distraction.

But the tax collector, who dined there daily, complained bitterly about such a neighbor. And so they moved Hippolyte into the billiard room.

There he lay, moaning under his heavy blankets, pale, unshaven, eyes sunken, from time to time turning his perspiring face over the filthy pillow, on which the flies were settling. Madame Bovary came to visit him. She brought him linen for his poultices; she comforted him, tried to encourage him. He did not lack for other company either, especially on market days, when the farmers pushed their billiard cues all around him or fenced with them while smoking, drinking, singing, and shouting.

"How are you?" they would ask, clapping him on the shoulder. "You don't look very good. But it's your fault. You should have—"

And they would tell him stories of people who had all been cured by remedies other than his; then, as a consolation, they would add: "You're coddling yourself. Come on, get up! You're treating yourself like a king. Ah, never mind, old boy. You don't smell very good."

The gangrene was actually moving higher and higher. Bovary himself was sick of it. He came every hour, every minute. Hippolyte would look at him with fear-filled eyes and sob and stammer: "When will I be cured? Save me, please! I feel awful! I feel awful!"

And the doctor would go off, always telling him to eat lightly.

"Don't listen to him, my poor boy," said Madame Lefrançois. "They've made enough of a martyr out of you. You'll get even weaker. Here, swallow this."

And so she would offer him some tasty bouillon, a slice of lamb, a rasher of bacon, and occasionally tiny glasses of brandy which he lacked the strength to bring to his lips.

Abbé Bournisien, hearing that he was growing worse, asked to see him. He began by offering his regrets for the illness, all the while declaring that he ought to rejoice over it since it was the Lord's will and take quick advantage of the opportunity to reconcile himself with heaven.

"Because," said the clergyman in a fatherly tone, "you were neglecting your religious duties a bit; you were rarely seen at Mass; how many years has it been since you came to Communion? I realize that your occupations, amid the distractions of the world, lured you away from thinking about your salvation. Now is the time to think about it. Don't despair. I've known really great sinners who, when they were about to appear before God—you aren't anywhere near that point, I know—begged for mercy and who certainly died in a state of grace. Let us hope that like them you will set us a good example! And so, as a precaution, what's to prevent you from reciting 'Hail Mary, full of grace' morning and evening and an 'Our Father, who art in heaven'? Yes, do it. For me. To make me happy. What will it cost you? Will you promise me?"

The poor devil promised. The curé came back the following days. He chatted with the landlady and even told humorous anecdotes and puns that Hippolyte did not understand. Then, when the opportunity presented itself, he reverted to religion, his face taking on an appropriate expression.

His zeal seemed to be succeeding because the taliped soon expressed his desire to go on a pilgrimage to Bon-Secours if he recovered—to which Abbé Bournisien answered that he saw no objection; two precautions were worth more than one. "You wouldn't lose anything by it."

The apothecary grew angry at what he called the "priest's maneuvers." They were harming Hippolyte's convalescence, he claimed. "Leave him alone," Homais told Madame Lefrançois. "You damage his morale with that mysticism of yours."

But the good lady refused to heed the apothecary any longer. He was "to blame for the whole thing." Out of contrariness she even hung a basin filled with holy water and a sprig of boxwood at the invalid's bedside.

But religion seemed to be helping him no more than surgery, and the gangrene kept spreading relentlessly from the extremities toward the trunk. In vain did they vary the medicines and change poultices; the muscles grew more lax each day, and finally, with a nod of his head, Charles assented when Madame Lefrançois, out of desperation, asked if she could send for Monsieur Canivet, who was quite a famous surgeon in Neufchâtel.

An M.D., fifty years old, of fine standing and great self-assurance, Charles's colleague did not bother to conceal a contemptuous laugh when he uncovered the gangrenous leg, infected all the way to the knee. Then, having flatly stated that he would have to amputate, he crossed over to the pharmacist's shop to rail against the idiots who could have reduced an unfortunate man to such a state. Taking hold of Monsieur Homais by the button of his coat, he boomed out all over the pharmacy: "Those are your Paris inventions for you! Now you see the ideas of the gentlemen from the capital! It's like strabismus, chloroform, and lithotripsy—a bunch of nonsense the government ought to forbid! But they care only about being clever, and they load you down with remedies without worrying about the consequences. We aren't as clever as all that here in the country; we aren't specialists, and we don't dress up like dandies! We practice medicine, we cure, and we never think of operating on someone who's perfectly healthy! Straighten a clubfoot indeed! Is it possible to straighten a clubfoot? It's like wanting to make a hunchback straight!"

Homais suffered as he listened to this speech, hiding his discomfort under an obsequious smile. It was necessary to curry favor with Monsieur Canivet, whose prescriptions were sometimes brought into Yonville to be filled; and so he did not defend Bovary, nor even comment, and abandoning his principles, sacrificed his dignity to the weightier interests of his business.

This amputation at the thigh by Doctor Canivet was an event of considerable importance in the village. All the villagers arose early that day, and the main street, despite being filled with people, had a certain gloomy air about it, as if an execution were to take place. At the grocer's, people talked about Hippolyte's condition; the stores made no sales, and Madame Tuvache, the mayor's wife, did not budge from the window in her impatience to see the surgeon.

He arrived in his gig, which he drove himself. The spring on the right side had given way to his corpulence over the years and the carriage tilted slightly to one side as it moved, revealing, on the cushion at his side, a large red leather case, its three brass clasps gleaming with authority.

After he had entered the yard of the Golden Lion like a whirlwind, the doctor, shouting loudly, ordered his horse unhitched, then went into the stable to see if the animal was being well fed. He took care of his mare and his gig first when he arrived at his patients' homes. People commented about this: "Ah, that Canivet is a character!" And they respected him all the more for this imperturbable coolness. The population of the entire world could expire to the last man before he would change a single one of his habits.

Homais came in.

"I'm counting on you," said the doctor. "Are we ready? Let's go."

But the apothecary turned red and announced that he was too sensitive to be present at such an operation.

"When you're just a spectator," he said, "your imagination takes hold of you, you know. And I have such a sensitive nervous system that———"

"Nonsense!" interrupted Canivet. "You look to me more inclined to apoplexy. Although it doesn't surprise me. You pharmacists are always cooped up in your kitchens, which probably affects your constitution in the long run. Now take me. I get up at four every morning, shave with cold water, never feel chilly. Never wear flannel, never have a sniffle. Body sound as can be! I manage any old way, like a philosopher; eat whatever comes along. That's why I'm not so delicate like you, and it's all the same to me if I carve up a

Christian or any old chicken that's available. And you'll probably say it's habit, just habit."

Then, with no consideration whatever for Hippolyte, who was perspiring with terror under the bedclothes, the gentlemen began a conversation in the course of which the apothecary compared a surgeon's coolheadedness to that of a general. The comparison pleased Canivet, who launched into a discussion of the demands of his profession. He looked upon it as a sacred calling, even though the health officers were dishonoring it. Finally, getting back to the present patient, he examined the bandages Homais had brought (the same ones that had appeared at the operation) and asked for someone to hold the leg for him.

They sent for Lestiboudois, and Monsieur Canivet, having rolled up his sleeves, went into the billiard room, while the pharmacist remained with Artémise and the landlady, both whiter than their aprons, and all three with their ears glued to the door.

During this time Bovary did not dare budge from his house. He remained downstairs, in the parlor, seated near the empty fireplace, his chin sunk on his chest, hands clasped, his eyes staring. "What a misfortune!" he thought. "What a disappointment!" And yet he had taken every conceivable precaution. Fate intervened. But what difference did it make? If Hippolyte were to die later on, he would be the assassin. And what answer would he give in his visits later on when people asked him questions? Perhaps he *had* nevertheless made a mistake somewhere? He sought to find one, but could not. But the greatest surgeons made mistakes. No one would believe that now. They would laugh at him, gossip about him. The story would spread all the way to Forges, to Neufchâtel, Rouen, everywhere! Some of his colleagues might attack him. There would be a controversy; he'd have to reply in the newspapers. Hippolyte might even sue him. He saw himself dishonored, ruined, lost. And his imagination, assailed by so many fears, was tossed about among them like an empty barrel washed out to sea, rolling over the waves.

Emma sat opposite, looking at him. She was not sharing his

humiliation, but enduring a private one, that of having imagined that such a man could be worth something. As if she had not already clearly perceived his mediocrity twenty times over.

Charles was pacing back and forth in the room; his boots creaked on the floor.

"Sit down," she said. "You're making me nervous."

He sat down again.

How could she—she who was so intelligent!—have fooled herself one more time? Moreover, what deplorable mania had made her ruin her life by these constant sacrifices? She recalled all her yearnings for luxury, all the privations to which she had subjected her soul, the sordidness of her marriage, of the household, her dreams falling into the mud like wounded swallows, everything she had wanted and denied herself, everything she could have had! Why? Why?

In the midst of the silence that filled the village, a piercing cry shattered the air. Bovary turned pale and seemed about to faint. She frowned, with a nervous twitch, then went on: yet it was for him, for this creature, for this man who understood nothing, who felt nothing! There he was, quite calm, not even suspecting that the ridicule henceforth attaching itself to his name would now smear her as well. She had tried to love him and had even repented in tears her affair with another man.

"Maybe it was a valgus!" Bovary, who had been lost in thought, suddenly exclaimed.

Emma started at the unexpected shock of this statement crashing into her thoughts like a lead bullet into a silver dish. She looked up to see what he meant; and they stared at each other in silence, almost astonished to see each other, so far apart were they in their respective meditations.

Charles looked at her with the troubled gaze of a drunken man. At the same time, he was numbly listening to the last cries of the amputee, which followed each other in drawn-out waves interspersed by sharp screams, like the far-off howling of some animal being slaughtered. Emma bit her pale lip, rolled between her fingers some bits of the coral she had broken off, and fixed the blazing centers of her eyes, like two fiery arrows about to be released, on Charles. Everything about him irritated her now, his face, his clothes, the things he didn't say, his entire person, his very existence. She lamented her virtuous past as if it had been a crime, and whatever virtue still remained collapsed beneath the fury of her pride. She reveled in all the evil ironies of adultery triumphant. The memory of her lover returned to her with dizzying attraction; she threw her soul into her longing, surging toward it with a new enthusiasm. Charles seemed detached from her life, forever gone, as impossible and annihilated as if he were dying and passing away before her eyes.

There was a noise of steps on the sidewalk. Charles looked out; across the lowered blinds he could see, at the edge of the square, in the sunlight, Doctor Canivet wiping his forehead with his scarf, and Homais behind him, carrying a large red box. They were both heading toward the pharmacy.

Then, out of a sudden impulse of tenderness and discouragement, Charles turned toward his wife and said: "Kiss me, darling."

"Leave me alone!" she exclaimed, scarlet with anger.

"What's wrong? What's wrong?" he repeated, dumbfounded. "Calm down, pull yourself together. You know how I love you. Come here."

"Enough!" she cried with a terrible look. And she ran from the room, closing the door so violently that the barometer fell from the wall and crashed into pieces on the floor.

Charles sank into his armchair, overwhelmed, trying to puzzle out what was wrong with her, imagining some nervous ailment, crying, and vaguely sensing something dire and incomprehensible hovering around him.

When Rodolphe reached the garden that night, he found his mistress awaiting him at the foot of the stairs. They embraced, and all their bitterness melted away like snow in the warmth of their kiss.

XII

They fell in love all over again. Often Emma would write to him suddenly even in the middle of the day. Then she would signal through the window to Justin, who would untie his apron quickly and fly off toward La Huchette. Rodolphe would come; she wanted to tell him that she was bored, that her husband was hateful and life unbearable.

"What can I do about it?" he asked impatiently one day.

"If you only wanted to—"

She was seated on the ground leaning against his knees, her hair ribbons undone, staring into a void.

"Wanted to what?" Rodolphe asked.

She sighed: "We could go and live elsewhere—somewhere—"

"You're really mad!" he said, laughing. "How could we?"

She repeated her thought. He seemed not to understand and changed the subject. What he didn't understand was all this fuss over something as simple as love. She had a motive, a reason, a kind of impetus to her affection.

This love increased each day in proportion to the revulsion she felt for her husband. The more she gave herself to the one man, the more she loathed the other. Never did Charles appear so repulsive to her, to have such coarse fingers, such a dull mind, such common manners, as when they happened to be together after her meetings with Rodolphe. At such moments, while she was outwardly playing the part of a virtuous wife, she would be burning within at thoughts of that head of black hair curling over a suntanned forehead, of that body that was both robust and elegant at the same time, of this man who was so mature in judgment and so passionate in love. Because of him she filed her fingernails with the precision of an engraver, because of him there was never enough cold cream on her skin, nor

When he was expected, she filled her two big blue glass vases with roses . . .

enough scent of patchouli in her handkerchiefs. She loaded herself down with bracelets, rings, and necklaces. When he was expected, she filled her two big blue glass vases with roses and arranged her room and her person like a courtesan awaiting a prince. The maid had to keep washing her underthings. Félicité did not budge from the kitchen all day long. Little Justin, who often kept her company, would watch her work.

His elbow on the long board on which she was ironing, he would look avidly at all the female garments strewn around him: dimity petticoats, fichus, muslin collars, and pantaloons with drawstrings, voluminous around the hips and tapering near the bottom.

"What's this for?" the boy would ask, stroking a crinoline or fingering some hooks.

"Haven't you ever seen anything?" Félicité replied with a laugh. "As if your mistress, Madame Homais, didn't wear these same things."

"Oh, Madame Homais—" And he added, thinking out loud: "As if she were a lady like Madame!"

But Félicité was getting impatient at the sight of him hovering around her. She was six years older than he, and Theodore, Monsieur Guillaumin's manservant, was beginning to court her.

"Leave me alone!" she said, picking up her starch pot. "Why don't you go grind some almonds? You're always snooping around women's affairs. Wait till you have a beard on your chin before you mix into such matters, you nasty little boy."

"Don't get angry; I'm going to do *her* boots for you."

And he immediately reached up to the doorsill for Emma's shoes, encrusted with dried mud—mud from their meetings—that crumbled away at his touch and the particles of which he watched float upward into a sunbeam.

"How frightened you are of spoiling them!" said Félicité, who didn't go to so much trouble when she herself cleaned them, because Emma would hand them on to her as soon as the fabric lost its freshness.

Emma had a supply of them in her wardrobe that she was recklessly using up, pair by pair, without Charles's allowing himself the slightest comment.

He also had to spend three hundred francs for a wooden leg that she felt should be given as a gift to Hippolyte. Its top was trimmed with cork; it had joints and levers set on springs, a complicated mechanism covered with a black trouser leg ending in a patent-leather boot. But Hippolyte, not daring to use such a beautiful leg every day, begged Madame Bovary to get him another, more simple one. The doctor of course bore the expense of this new one as well.

The stableboy gradually resumed his work. He could be seen as before wandering around the village. When Charles heard from afar the sharp tap of his cane on the pavement, he would quickly change his route.

Monsieur Lheureux, the merchant, had taken care of the order; this gave him the opportunity to associate with Emma. He chatted with her about the new goods from Paris, about a thousand feminine trifles, made himself extremely obliging, and never asked for money. Emma abandoned herself to this easy way of satisfying all her whims. She wanted, for example, a very handsome hunting crop that was in an umbrella store in Rouen—as a gift for Rodolphe. Lheureux placed it on her table the following week.

But the very next day he turned up at her home with a bill for 270 francs, not counting the centimes. Emma was very embarrassed: all the drawers of the writing desk were empty, they owed more than two weeks' wages to Lestiboudois, six months' wages to the maid, and many other items as well. Bovary was impatiently awaiting a remittance from Monsieur Derozerays, who was in the habit of paying him once a year around the end of June.

She managed to put Lheureux off for a while. Finally he lost patience: he was being pressed, he had no ready funds, and if he didn't collect some of his debts, he'd be forced to take back all the things he had brought her.

"Then take them back!" Emma said.

"Oh, I was only joking," he answered. "I'm only sorry about the hunting crop. I think I'll ask Monsieur if I may have it back."

"No!" she cried.

"Aha! I've got you!" thought Lheureux.

And sure that he had discovered her secret, he left, saying to himself under his breath, with his usual slight wheeze: "All right. We'll see. We'll see."

She was dreaming up ways to extricate herself from the situation when the cook came in and placed on the mantelpiece a small roll of blue paper. "From Monsieur Derozerays," she said. Emma pounced on it and opened it. It contained fifteen napoleons, payment in full. She heard Charles on the stairs; she threw the gold pieces into her drawer and took the key.

Lheureux reappeared three days later.

"I have a suggestion for you," he said. "If, instead of the amount agreed on, you would be willing to take—"

"Here it is!" she said, handing him fourteen napoleons.

The merchant was dumbfounded. To mask his disappointment, he multiplied apologies and offers of service, all of which Emma declined. Afterward she stood for a few moments fingering in the pocket of her apron the two five-franc pieces he had given her in change. She resolved to economize so that she would be able to restore the money later.

"Never mind!" she thought. "He won't think about it again."

Besides the hunting crop with a silver-gilt handle, Rodolphe had received a seal with the motto *Amor nel cor,* a scarf to be used as a muffler, and finally a cigar case identical to the viscount's, the one Charles had picked up on the road and which Emma had been saving. However, the gifts humiliated him. He refused several others. She insisted and he finally gave in, finding her high-handed and too demanding.

She was also filled with strange notions: "At the stroke of midnight," she would say, "you must think of me."

If he confessed that he hadn't thought of her, there were countless reproaches, which always ended in the eternal question: "Do you love me?"

"Of course I love you," he would answer.

"Very much?"

"Certainly!"

"You've never loved any other women?"

"Do you think I came to you a virgin?" he would exclaim with a laugh.

Emma would cry and he would try to console her, enlivening his protestations with little jokes.

"Oh, how I love you!" she would continue. "I love you so much I couldn't live without you, do you realize? I sometimes want to see you so badly that I feel torn apart. I ask myself: 'Where is he? Perhaps he's talking to other women? They're smiling at him. He's going up to them—' Oh no! Tell me it isn't so. No one else pleases you. There are women who are prettier than I am, but I know how to love better. I'm your servant and your mistress. You're my king, my idol. You're so good, so handsome, so intelligent, so strong!"

He had heard these things so many times that they no longer held any interest for him. Emma resembled all his old mistresses, and the charm of novelty, falling away little by little like articles of clothing, revealed in all its nakedness the eternal monotony of passion, which always assumes the same forms and speaks the same language. This man, who was so experienced in love, could not distinguish the dissimilarity in the emotions behind the similarity of expressions. He couldn't really accept Emma's lack of guile, having heard similar sentences from the mouths of venal and immoral women. One should be able to tone down, he thought, those exaggerated speeches that mask lack of feeling—as if the fullness of the soul did not sometimes overflow into the emptiest of metaphors. No one can ever express the exact measure of his needs, or conceptions, or sorrows. The human language is like a cracked kettle on which we beat out a tune for a dancing bear, when we hope with our music to move the stars.

But with that superior critical ability of those who hold themselves back from any and all involvements, Rodolphe found other pleasures to exploit in this love. He discarded the last shreds of modesty and treated her without consideration, making her into something compliant and corrupt. It was an idiotic, one-sided attachment, filled with admiration for him, and sensual satisfaction for herself. She was in a blissful state of numbness. Her soul sank deeper into this inebriation and was drowned in it, shriveled up like the Duke of Clarence in his butt of malmsey.

Madame Bovary's manner changed as a result of her constant indulgence in love. Her gaze became bolder, her talk freer. She even had the audacity to parade with Monsieur Rodolphe, a cigarette in her mouth, "as if to defy everyone." Finally, those who were still in doubt doubted no more when she was seen one day, stepping down from the Hirondelle, wearing a masculine-styled, tight-fitting waistcoat. Madame Bovary senior, who had come to seek refuge with her son after a frightful scene with her husband, was as scandalized as the other women in town. Many other things displeased her. First of all, Charles had not taken her advice about banning novels from the house. Also, the "way the house was run" did not suit her. She offered unasked-for advice and they quarreled, once in particular about Félicité.

While crossing the hallway the night before, Madame Bovary senior had surprised the maid in the company of a man—a man with dark chin whiskers, about forty years of age, who escaped through the kitchen at the sound of her steps. Emma began to laugh about it, but the good woman lost her temper and declared that unless one scoffed at morals, one should keep an eye on those of one's servants.

"What sort of world do you live in?" asked her daughter-in-law, so impertinently that Madame Bovary inquired if she were not really defending her own behavior.

"Get out!" said the young woman, jumping up.

"Emma! Mama!" Charles exclaimed, trying to reconcile them.

But each fled in exasperation. Emma trembled with rage and kept repeating: "What a lack of manners! What a peasant!"

He ran to his mother; she was seething. She stammered: "She's an insolent, irresponsible woman! And maybe worse!"

She threatened to leave immediately if Emma did not apologize. Charles returned to his wife and begged her to give in. He went down on his knees. She finally said: "All right. I'll go."

She offered her hand to her mother-in-law with the dignity of a marquise, saying: "Excuse me, Madame."

Then, back in her own room, she threw herself onto the bed and cried like a child, her head buried in her pillow.

She and Rodolphe had agreed that in case anything unusual happened, she would attach a small piece of white paper to the shutter so that if he should by chance happen to be in Yonville he would hurry to the lane behind the house. Emma hung out the signal; she had been waiting for three quarters of an hour when she suddenly noticed Rodolphe at the corner of the market. She was tempted to open the window and call to him, but he had already disappeared. She sank back in despair.

Soon, however, she sensed that someone was walking along the sidewalk. It was surely he. She went downstairs, crossed the yard. He was there, outside. She threw herself into his arms.

"Be careful," he said.

"If you only knew!" she answered.

She began to tell him everything, in haste, without sequence, exaggerating some facts, inventing others, and introducing so many parenthetical remarks that he did not understand her story.

"There, there, my poor angel, be brave! Cheer up, be patient."

"I've been patient for four years now and look how I'm suffering! We should be able to declare a love like ours to the world! They're torturing me. I can't stand it anymore. Save me!"

She clung to him tightly. Her eyes, filled with tears, sparkled like flames under water, her throat rose and fell rapidly as she gasped for air; he had never loved her so much, so much that he lost his head and said: "What should we do? What do you want?"

"Take me away," she sobbed. "Take me away. Please!"

She kissed him passionately, as if to draw the unexpected consent from his mouth.

"But—" he said.

"But what?"

"Your daughter?"

She thought for a while, then answered: "We'll take her. It can't be helped."

"What a woman!" he thought, watching her go off. For she had just run off into the garden. Someone was calling her.

Mother Bovary was amazed at the change in her daughter-in-law in the days that followed. Emma really appeared to be more amenable and even extended her deference to the point of consulting her about a recipe for pickling gherkins.

Was it in order to dupe the two of them more easily? Or rather did she want, by a kind of voluptuous stoicism, to taste more profoundly the bitterness of the things she was about to leave? It could not be the latter, for she was paying no attention to them; she lived as if lost in the anticipated enjoyment of her approaching happiness. It was a constant subject for discussion with Rodolphe. She would lean on his shoulder and murmur: "Just think! When we're in the mail coach! Do you think about it? Is it possible? It seems to me that the moment I feel the carriage start off, it will feel as if we're going up in a balloon, soaring toward the clouds. Do you know that I'm counting the days? Are you?"

Never had Madame Bovary been so beautiful as now. She had that indefinable beauty that comes from joy, enthusiasm, and success, a beauty that is but the blending of temperament with circumstances. Her desires, her regrets, her experience of sensual pleasure, and her continually youthful illusions had nurtured her gradually, as fertilizer, rain, wind, and sunshine nurture a flower, and she finally blossomed forth in all the fullness of her being. Her eyelids seemed purposely shaped for her long amorous gazes, in which the pupils disappeared, while her heavy breathing caused her delicately chiseled nostrils to flare and raised the fleshy corners of her upper lip (which was lightly shaded by a slight black down). One would have said that some artist skilled in depravity had arranged the coil of hair on the nape of her neck. It was wound carelessly, in a heavy mass, and loosened every day by the chance meetings with her lover. The inflections of her voice became more languid, and also her body. A certain penetrating subtlety detached itself even from the folds of her dress and the instep of her foot. As he had during the first days of their marriage, Charles now found her delicious and completely irresistible.

When he would come home in the middle of the night, he was afraid to wake her. The porcelain night lamp threw a flickering circle of light on the ceiling, and the drawn curtains of the small cradle were like a white tent billowing out in the dark at the edge of the bed. Charles would look at them. He thought he could hear his daughter's gentle breathing. She was going to grow up now; each season would bring quick progress. He already saw her coming back from school in the late afternoon, laughing gaily, her blouse ink-stained, her basket dangling from her arm. Then he would have to send her to boarding school, which would be expensive. How would he do it? He pondered. He thought about renting a small farm in the area that he himself could supervise every morning as he went out to see his patients. He would save the profits and deposit them in the bank. Later he would purchase stock somewhere, it didn't matter where. Besides, his clientele would increase. He was counting on it because he wanted Berthe to be well brought up, to be talented, to learn to play the piano. Ah! How pretty she would be later on, at fifteen, when, resembling her mother, she would wear great big straw hats like hers in the summertime. From afar they would be taken for two sisters. He pictured her to himself working near them in the evening under the lamplight. She would embroider slippers for him, busy herself with household chores, fill the whole house with her engaging ways and her gaiety. Eventually they would think about getting her settled. They would find her some fine young man with a solid business who would make her happy. It would last forever.

Emma was merely pretending to be asleep. While he dozed off at her side, she awoke to other dreams.

For the last week she had galloped off with the speed of four horses toward a new land from which she and Rodolphe would never return. Farther, farther, they went, arms entwined, without saying a word. Often, from atop a mountain, they would suddenly see some splendid city with domes, bridges, ships, forests of lemon trees, and white marble cathedrals whose pointed steeples sheltered stork nests. They would stroll leisurely because of the large flagstones, and there would be bouquets of flowers on the ground offered by women in red bodices. They could hear the bells ringing and mules braying, the murmur of guitars and fountains. The mist from the fountains would spray the pyramids of fruit arranged at the feet of the pale statues that seemed to smile under the streams of water. Then they would arrive in a fishing village one evening where brown fishnets were drying in the wind along the cliff and in front of the huts. There they would settle. They would live in a low, flat-roofed house in the shade of a palm tree, bordering on a bay near the sea. They would float off in a gondola, swing in a hammock; and their existence would be as relaxed and easy as their silk clothes, as warm and starry as the gentle nights they would contemplate. Nevertheless, in the vastness of this future she was creating for herself, nothing in particular stood out. The days, all magnificent, resembled each other like waves. They seemed to sway against the horizon, infinite, harmonious, tinted with blue, awash with sunshine. But the baby in her cradle began to cough or Bovary would snore harder and Emma would not fall asleep until morning, when the dawn was bringing light in through the windows and little Justin was already in the square opening the shutters of the pharmacy.

She sent for Monsieur Lheureux and told him: "I'm going to need a cloak, a large lined one with a deep collar."

"You're taking a trip?" he asked.

"Not at all! Only— Never mind. I can rely on you for it, can't I? And quickly?"

He bowed.

"I'll also need a trunk," she continued, "not too heavy—roomy."

"Yes, I understand. About three feet by a foot and a half, they're made now."

"And an overnight bag."

"There's definitely something fishy going on," thought Lheureux.

"And here," said Madame Bovary, unfastening her watch from her belt, "take this, you can pay for the things you get me out of it."

But the merchant protested that she was mistaken. They knew each other. Didn't he trust her? What childishness! She insisted however that he at least take the chain, and Lheureux had already put it into his pocket and was walking off when she called him back.

"You will leave everything at your place. As for the cloak," she seemed to reflect for a moment, "don't bring that either. Just give me the address of the tailor and tell him to hold it for me."

They were to go off the following month. She would leave Yonville as if she were going shopping in Rouen. Rodolphe would have booked passage, obtained passports, and even written to Paris so as to have the entire coach to themselves as far as Marseille. There they would buy a carriage and continue without a stop along the road to Genoa. She would send her baggage to Lheureux, to be taken directly to the Hirondelle, in such a way that no one would be suspicious. In all of this, there was never any mention of her daughter. Rodolphe avoided discussing her; perhaps Emma wasn't thinking about her any longer.

He needed two more weeks to wind up some business. Then,

after one week had passed, he asked for two more. Then he said he felt ill. Then he took a trip. The month of August passed. After all these delays, they decided that it would be, without fail, Monday, September 4.

The Saturday preceding the fatal day arrived.

Rodolphe came in the evening, earlier than usual.

"Is everything ready?" he asked.

"Yes."

They walked around a flower bed and sat down on the edge of the wall near the terrace.

"You're sad," Emma said.

"No. Why?" Yet he was looking at her in an unusually tender way.

"Is it because you're going away?" she continued, "leaving things you're attached to, your life here? Oh, I understand. But I have nothing in the world. You're everything for me. And I'll be everything for you. I'll be your whole family, your country. I'll take care of you. I'll love you."

"What a darling you are," he said, taking her into his arms.

"Really?" she asked with a sensuous laugh. "Do you love me? Swear it."

"Do I love you? Do I love you! I adore you, my dearest!"

The full orange moon rose out of the earth on the other side of the meadow. It quickly climbed between the branches of the poplar trees that obscured it here and there, as if it were shining through a torn black curtain. Then it burst forth into the empty sky, lit it with a blaze of white, and then, becoming more subdued, dropped a great patch of light onto the river. The patch splintered into an infinity of stars and their silvery light seemed to slither all the way down like a headless snake covered with luminous scales. It resembled, too, a monstrous candelabrum dripping with molten diamonds running together. The lovely night was all around them, patches of shadow hovering over the foliage. Emma, her eyes half closed, was breathing the cool breeze with great gulps. They were so lost in their dreams that they didn't say a word. The tenderness of the old days came back to them, abundant and silent as the flowing river, as soft as the perfume of the syringa. It projected shadows into their memories, shadows more distorted and melancholy than those of the motionless willows on the grass. Occasionally some night animal, a hedgehog or weasel, would begin to run and make the leaves rustle. From time to time they would hear a ripe peach falling from a tree.

"What a lovely night," said Rodolphe.

"We'll have many more," she answered, and as if she were speaking to herself: "Yes, it will be good to travel. Then why am I so sad? Is it the fear of the unknown? Because I'm leaving behind this life I'm used to? Or what? No! It's from too much happiness! How weak I am. Forgive me."

"There's still time," he said. "Think carefully; you may regret it."

"Never," she said impetuously. And she drew closer to him: "What harm can come to me? There is no desert, no precipice, no ocean that I wouldn't cross with you. Each day that we live together will be like a tighter, more complete embrace. We'll have nothing to bother us, no worries, nothing in our way. We'll be alone, all to ourselves, forever. Say something, answer me."

He kept saying "Yes, yes," at regular intervals. She ran her fingers through his hair and repeated in a childlike voice through large tears that were flowing from her eyes: "Rodolphe! Rodolphe! Oh Rodolphe, my dearest Rodolphe!"

Midnight struck.

"It's midnight!" she said. "It's already tomorrow. One more day!"

He arose to go. Emma suddenly came alive, as if this movement were the signal for their flight. "You have the passports?"

"Yes."

"You won't forget anything?"

"No."

"You're sure?"

"Positive."

"You'll be waiting for me at the Hotel de Provence? At noon?"

He nodded.

"Until tomorrow then!" said Emma with one last caress.

And she watched him walk away.

He didn't turn back. She ran after him, leaned over the water between the bushes and cried: "Until tomorrow!"

He was already on the other side of the river, striding quickly through the meadow.

Rodolphe stopped after a few minutes. When he saw her in her white dress gradually fading into the dark like a ghost, his heart began to beat so wildly that he had to lean against a tree to keep from falling.

"What a fool I am," he said, cursing furiously. "Ah well! She was a pretty mistress."

Emma's beauty suddenly reappeared in front of his eyes and he thought of all the pleasures of their love. At first he softened, then he became angry at her.

"After all," he exclaimed with a gesture, "I can't become an expatriate, and be saddled with a child."

He talked aloud, looking for more reasons to reassure himself.

"And besides, the bother, the expense— No, no, absolutely not! It would be too stupid!"

XIII

As soon as Rodolphe arrived home, he sat down abruptly at his desk, under the stag's head hanging on the wall. But when he had the pen in his hand he could find nothing to write, and so he leaned on his two elbows and began to think. Emma seemed remote to him, in the distant past, as if the decision he had taken had suddenly placed an immense time gulf between them.

In order to recapture something of her, he went to get an old Rheims biscuit box in the wardrobe at the head of his bed. In it he always saved the letters he received from women. It exuded an odor of damp dust and withered roses. The first thing he saw was a handkerchief covered with faint stains. It was one of hers. She once had had a nosebleed while they were out walking—he no longer remembered when. Nearby, knocking against the corners of the box, was the miniature Emma had given him: her clothes seemed pretentious to him and the ogling look in her eyes in the most lamentable taste. Emma's features slowly blurred in his memory as he stared at the picture and at the same time evoked the memory of Emma herself. It was as if the living face and the painted one, rubbing against each other, had erased each other. Finally he read some of her letters. They were short, factual, and as urgent as business letters, full of details about their trip. He wanted to see the longer ones again, those written in the old days. In order to find them at the bottom of the box, Rodolphe shuffled together all the others and began to search mechanically through the pile of papers and objects, finding a varied assortment of bouquets, a garter, a black mask, pins, locks of hair—so many locks! Brunette ones, blonde ones: some were even stuck to the hinges of the box and broke off when it was opened.

Browsing in this fashion among his souvenirs, he studied the handwriting and styles of the letters, as varied as the spelling. Some letters were tender, some gay, others humorous or sad. Some asked for love and some for money. One word would bring back a face, a gesture, the sound of a voice; sometimes, however, he could remember nothing.

Actually, these women rushing into his thoughts at the same time tended to get in one another's way. They faded into the background, as if equalized on the same level of love.

Rodolphe took up a random handful of letters and amused himself for a few minutes by letting them cascade from his right hand to his left. Finally, bored and tired, he put the box back into the cupboard, saying to himself: "What a collection of non-sense!"

This summed up his opinion, because pleasures, like children in a schoolyard, had so trampled on his heart that nothing green could grow there. What did pass through was more thoughtless than schoolchildren: it did not even leave, like them, a name scribbled on the wall.

"All right," he said to himself, "let's begin."

He wrote: "Courage, Emma, courage! I don't want to ruin your life."

"It's really true," he thought. "I'm acting in her interest. I'm being honest."

"Have you seriously considered your decision? Do you know what an abyss I was dragging you into, my poor angel? No, you don't, do you? You were going off, rashly confident, believing in happiness, in the future. Ah! What wretched, insane creatures we are!"

Rodolphe paused here in order to think up some good excuse.

"Suppose I tell her my entire fortune is lost? No, that wouldn't stop anything. It would start all over again later on. Is there any way to make such women listen to reason?"

He pondered, then added: "You must believe me when I say I shall never forget you. I shall continue to feel a deep affection for you. But one day sooner or later, our passion would doubtless have lessened—that is the way things are in life. We would have grown weary. I might even have had the terrible pain of witnessing your remorse and even of sharing it since I caused it. The mere thought of the unhappiness you are undergoing tortures me, Emma. Forget me. Why did I have to know you? Why were you so beautiful? Is it my fault? Oh my God! No, no, fate alone is to blame!"

"A word that is always effective," he said to himself.

"Ah! Had you been one of those frivolous women, I would certainly have been able, by sheer egotism, to try an experiment. And it would have been without danger for you. But your wonderful exaltation, which is both your charm and your undoing, has prevented you, adorable creature that you are, from understanding the falsity of our future position. Nor did I think about it clearly at first. I was relaxing in the shade of our ideal happiness as if it were some poisonous tree of the tropics, without giving a thought to the consequences."

"She may think I'm giving her up out of stinginess. Well, what can I do? It's too bad but I've got to end it."

"The world is cruel, Emma. It would have pursued us everywhere we went. You would have had to endure indiscreet questions, slander, disdain, actual insults perhaps. Insults to you! And I who wanted to seat you on a throne, who will carry away the memory of you like a talisman. For I am punishing myself for all the evil I have done to you by going into exile. I am leaving. Where? I have no idea. I feel I am losing my mind. Farewell! Always remain as good as you are. Do not forget the unhappy man who has lost you. Teach my name to your child so that she will repeat it in her prayers."

The candles flickered. Rodolphe arose to shut the window. When he sat down again, he said to himself: "I think that's all. No, let's add this so she won't come back for me":

"I shall be far away when you read these sad lines. I wanted to flee as quickly as possible in order to avoid seeing you again. I won't weaken! I shall return later on and perhaps after that we will chat together, without passion, about our former love. Farewell!"

And there was one last farewell separated into two words: "Fare well!" which he deemed to be in excellent taste.

"How shall I sign?" he wondered. "Your devoted— No. Your friend? Yes, that will do."

"Your friend."

He reread the letter and found it good.

"Poor little woman," he thought, feeling tender. "She's going to think me harder than a rock. It needs a few tears on it, but unfortunately I just can't cry." He poured some water into a glass, dipped his finger into it, and let a big drop fall on the letter. It made a pale splotch on the ink. Then, looking for a seal for the letter, he came upon the one: *Amor nel cor.*

"It hardly suits the occasion. Oh, well, what's the difference?"

After which he smoked three pipes and went to bed.

The next day, after he was up (toward two in the afternoon—he had slept late), Rodolphe had some apricots picked and placed in a basket. He placed the letter at the bottom, under the vine leaves, and immediately ordered his plowboy, Girard, to bring it to Madame Bovary. This was his usual way of corresponding with her, sending her fruit or game according to the season.

"If she asks about me," he said, "tell her that I've left on a trip. You must put the basket into her hands. Go along now. Be careful!"

Girard put on his new shirt, tied his kerchief around the apricots, and set off tranquilly along the road to Yonville, taking long heavy strides in his hobnailed clogs.

When he reached the house, he found Madame Bovary and Félicité sorting a bundle of laundry on the kitchen table.

A feeling of dread seized her. While she groped in her pocket for some small change, she kept looking at the peasant with a frightened stare. He in turn gazed at her with astonishment, unable to comprehend why such a gift should move someone so much. At last he left. Félicité remained. Emma couldn't bear it any longer. She ran into the living room as if to bring the apricots there, turned the basket upside down, ripped away the leaves, and found the letter, opened it, and fled toward her bedroom, terror-stricken, as if there were some terrible fire behind her.

Charles was there; she saw him. He spoke to her; she heard nothing and continued to climb the stairs rapidly; she was breathless, lost, and drunk, still clutching in her fingers that horrible sheet of paper that rattled in her fingers like a sheet of tin. On the second floor, she stopped in front of the attic door, which was closed.

She tried to calm down, then thought about the letter. It had to be finished. But she didn't dare. Besides, where? How? She would be seen.

"No," she thought, "I'll be safe here."

Emma pushed open the door and walked in.

The oppressive heat, rising from the roof slates, closed in around her temples and stifled her. She dragged herself to the closed shutters of the dormer and pulled the bolt; the dazzling sunlight rushed in.

Beyond the rooftops the countryside spread out as far as the eye could see. Down below, the village square was empty, the cobblestones of the pavement sparkled, the weathervanes of the houses were lifeless. At the corner of the street, some sort of strident whirring noise came from a lower floor. It was Binet, turning his lathe.

She leaned against the window frame, rereading the letter with sneers of anger. But the more she tried to concentrate on it, the more confused she became. She could see him in front of her, hear him; she was wrapping her arms around him. Her heart was pounding like a sledgehammer, furiously, irregularly, constantly accelerating. She looked all around her, hoping that the earth would crumble. Why not end it all? Who was keeping her back? She was free. She moved forward, concentrating on the pavement, and said: "Now! Now!"

The beam of sunlight reflecting directly up at her from below was pulling the weight of her body into an abyss. She felt as if the square were swinging to and fro, its ground climbing the walls. The floor was tilting at one end like a vessel in a storm. She was right at the edge, almost hanging out, surrounded by a great vastness. The blue of the sky flooded over her; the air rushed through her hollow brain. All she had to do was give in, let herself go. The whirr of the lathe kept on unceasingly, like a furious voice summoning her.

"Emma! Emma!" Charles shouted.

She stopped.

"Where are you? Come down!"

The thought that she had just escaped death almost made her faint from terror. She closed her eyes. Then she shivered as a hand touched her sleeve. It was Félicité.

"Monsieur is waiting for you, Madame. The soup is ready."

And she had to go down—had to seat herself at the table.

She tried to eat, but the food choked her. Then she unfolded her napkin as if to examine the darns. She began to concentrate on this, to count the threads in the fabric. Suddenly she thought about the letter again. Had she lost it? Where was it? But she felt such a weariness of the spirit that she could not bring herself to invent an excuse to leave the table. Then she became frightened, afraid of Charles. He knew everything. She was sure of it. And he did utter these strange words: "It seems we aren't likely to see Monsieur Rodolphe again soon."

"Who told you?" she asked with a start.

"Who told me?" he repeated, slightly surprised at her sharp tone. "Girard. I met him a few minutes ago at the door of the Café Français. He's gone off on a trip, or he's about to leave."

She caught her breath with a sob.

"What's so surprising about it? He occasionally goes off like this for some distraction. I must say, I approve. When you're rich and a bachelor! Besides, he has himself a good time, our friend. He's a bit of a rake. Monsieur Langlois told me—"

He stopped talking because the maid had just come in. She put the apricots, which had been scattered on the sideboard, back into the basket. Charles did not notice his wife's redness. He had the fruit brought to him, took one, and bit into it.

"Perfect," he said. "Here, taste one." And he held out the basket, which she pushed away gently.

"Smell that fragrance," he said, moving it back and forth under her nose.

"I'm choking," she cried, jumping up. But she managed to gain control of the spasm. "It's nothing," she said, "nothing. Just nerves. Sit down and eat."

She was afraid he might question her, pay attention to her, not leave her alone.

Charles sat down again in order to please her. He was spitting the apricot pits into his hand and then placing them on his plate.

Suddenly a blue tilbury passed rapidly through the square. Emma moaned once, then fell back on the floor and lay there rigidly.

Rodolphe, after much thought, had decided to leave for Rouen. But since there was no other road from La Huchette to Buchy except the one through Yonville, it was necessary for him to cross the village. Emma had recognized him by the light of the lanterns that cut through the twilight like a streak of lightning.

The pharmacist, hearing the commotion, rushed to the house. The table and all the plates were overturned. Sauce, meat, knives, salt shaker, and oil cruet littered the room. Charles was shouting for help. Berthe was frightened and crying. Félicité, with trembling hands, was unlacing her mistress, whose entire body shuddered convulsively.

"I'll run back to my laboratory and get some aromatic vinegar," said the apothecary.

When she opened her eyes after inhaling from the bottle, he said: "I was sure of it. This stuff would awaken the dead."

"Speak to me," said Charles; "talk to me. Pull yourself together. It's I, Charles—I love you. Don't you know me? Look, here's our little girl. Kiss her."

The child tried to place her arms around her mother's neck, but Emma turned her head away and said in a quivering voice: "No, no—no one!" Then she fainted again and they carried her to bed.

There she remained, stretched out, mouth agape, eyes shut, hands open and motionless. She was as white as a waxen image. Two rivulets of tears flowed slowly out of her eyes over the pillow.

Charles was standing at the back of the alcove. The pharmacist stood near him, maintaining that thoughtful silence that is appropriate to life's serious moments.

"Don't worry," he said, nudging Charles with his elbow. "I think the crisis is over."

"Yes, she's resting a little now," answered Charles, who was watching her as she slept. "Poor thing! Poor thing! Look how weak she is."

Homais asked how the incident had happened. Charles answered that it had seized her suddenly while she was eating apricots.

"Extraordinary!" said the pharmacist. "But it is possible that the apricots caused the fainting spell. Some natures are so sensitive to certain smells. It would even be a rather interesting phenomenon to study, from the pathological as well as the physiological aspects. The priests know how important it is. They've always introduced aromatic spices into their ceremonies. They do so in order to stupefy the senses and induce a state of ecstasy—a condition, moreover, that is easier to obtain in women, who are more delicate than men. I've heard cases of people fainting at the smell of burnt hartshorn, or fresh bread."

"Be careful, don't wake her!" said Bovary in a low voice.

"And not only are humans susceptible to these anomalies," continued the pharmacist, "but animals are also. You are of course aware of the powerful aphrodisiac effect produced by *Nepeta cataria*, commonly known as catnip, on the feline race? Furthermore, to cite an example that I will vouch for as authentic, Bridoux—an old friend of mine who's currently in business on the Rue Malpalu—owns a dog that falls into convulsions as soon as he's offered a snuffbox. Bridoux even performs the experiment quite often for his friends at his summer home in Bois-Guillaume. Would you believe that a simple sneezing powder could cause such havoc in a quadruped's body? Extremely curious, isn't it?"

"Yes," said Charles, who wasn't listening.

"Which proves to us," continued the other, smiling with an air of benign self-satisfaction, "the innumerable irregularities of the nervous system. Insofar as Madame is concerned, she has always seemed to me, I must admit, genuinely sensitive. Nor will I suggest to you at all, my friend, any of those so-called remedies that, under the guise of attacking symptoms, attack one's constitution. No, no useless medication! Diet alone. Sedatives, emollients, dulcifiers. And don't you think perhaps that we should stir up her imagination?"

"In what way? How?" asked Bovary.

"Ah, that's it! That's just it. 'That is the question,' " he quoted in English, "as I was reading in the newspaper the other day."

But Emma, awakening, cried out: "The letter! The letter!"

They thought she was delirious, and she was, from midnight on. Brain fever had broken out.

Charles did not leave her side for forty-three days. He neglected all his patients. He no longer slept, was constantly feeling her pulse, applying mustard plasters, cold compresses. He would send Justin as far as Neufchâtel to fetch ice. The ice would melt on the way. He would send the boy back. He called Monsieur Canivet into consultation, had Dr. Larivière, his old teacher, come from Rouen. He was in despair. What frightened him most was Emma's state of prostration; she didn't speak, appeared not to hear, and even seemed not to suffer—as if body and soul were now resting together after all their exertions.

Toward the middle of October she could sit up in bed propped up by pillows. Charles cried the first time he saw her eating bread and jam. Her strength returned. She would get up for a few hours in the afternoon. One day when she was feeling better, he tried to take her for a walk in the garden, supporting her on his arm. The sand of the paths was disappearing from sight under the dead leaves. She took one step at a time, dragging her slippers, and continued to smile as she leaned on Charles's shoulder.

They walked in this manner to the back of the garden, near the terrace. She straightened up slowly and shielded her eyes with her hand in order to look about. She stared as far as possible into the distance, but against the horizon there were only huge grass fires smoking on the hillsides.

"You'll get tired, darling," said Bovary. He pushed her gently into the arbor. "Sit down on this bench. You'll be comfortable."

"No, not there, not there," she said in a faltering voice.

She had a dizzy spell. That very evening her illness began again, in a much less clearly defined way, it is true, and with more complex symptoms. Sometimes it was her heart that pained her, then her chest, head, or limbs; she had vomiting spells in which Charles thought he saw the first signs of cancer.

And besides all this, the poor young man was worried about money!

XIV

In the first place, he didn't know how he could reimburse Homais for all the medicines he had supplied; and although as a doctor he didn't have to pay, he still felt embarrassed. Then too, now that the cook was mistress, the household expenses were becoming frightening; bills poured into the house, the tradespeople grumbled. Lheureux in particular was dunning him. He had even, when Emma was at the critical point in her illness, taken advantage of the circumstance to increase his bill; he had quickly delivered the cloak, traveling bag, two trunks instead of one, and a number of other things as well. Charles protested vainly that he didn't need them. The shopkeeper answered with arrogance that all the items had been ordered from him and he wouldn't take them back. Besides, if he did, it might be detrimental to Madame in her convalescence. Monsieur ought to think about it. In brief, he was determined to bring him into court rather than give up his rights and take the merchandise back. Charles then ordered the goods to be returned to the store; Félicité forgot, Charles had other worries, and they thought no further about it. Monsieur Lheureux resumed the attack and managed, by alternating whines and threats, to maneuver Bovary into signing a promissory note to be paid within six months. The ink was barely dry on the note when Charles had a daring thought. This was to borrow a thousand francs from Lheureux. And so he asked with embarrassment if he could borrow them, adding that the loan would be for one year and at the stipulated rate of interest. Lheureux ran to his store, brought back the money, and dictated another note, on which Bovary declared that he had to pay to his order, on September 1 following, the sum of thousand seventy francs, which, with the 180 already stipulated, made an even 1,250. Thus, lending at six percent, plus twenty-five percent commission, and with the goods bringing in another third at least, he would have 130 francs' profit in a year. He was hoping that the matter wouldn't stop there, that Charles wouldn't be able to pay the notes and that they would be renewed, and that his meager funds, having nourished themselves at the doctor's expense like a patient in a rest home, would return to him one day considerably plumper, and fat enough to burst his moneybag.

Besides, everything was going his way. He had the contract for supplying cider to the Neufchâtel poorhouse; Monsieur Guillaumin had promised him shares in the Grumesnil peat bogs; and he was thinking about establishing a new coach line between Argueil and Rouen, which would certainly put a quick end to the rickety old Golden Lion carriage and which with its greater speed, lowered prices, and greater baggage capacity would concentrate all the business of Yonville in his hands.

Charles kept wondering how he would be able to pay back so much money the following year; he tried to think up various schemes—such as turning to his father or selling something. But his father would turn a deaf ear, and he personally had nothing to sell. Then the difficulties began to loom so large that he thrust the unpleasant thoughts from his mind. He reproached himself for forgetting Emma as if he owed her all of his thoughts and were robbing her by thinking of other matters.

It was a severe winter. Emma's convalescence made slow progress. When the weather was good, they would push her chair over to the window, the one overlooking the square, because she hated the garden now and the shutter on that side was always closed. She wanted the horse sold; everything she had once loved now displeased

When the weather was good, they would push her chair over to the window, the one overlooking the square . . .

her. She seemed able to think only of her own state of health. She
remained in bed eating little meals, then would ring for the maid to
inquire about her medicinal tea or to chat. Meanwhile the snow
would cast a still, white light into the room. Then the rains came.
And Emma would await, almost anxiously, the inevitable recurrence
of some trifling daily event, even when it did not concern her. The
most important was the arrival of the Hirondelle each evening. Then
the landlady would cry out and other voices would answer, while
Hippolyte's lantern would glow like a star as he hunted among the
boxes in the baggage compartment. Charles would come in at noon.
Afterwards he would leave and she would have her broth, and then at
sunset, around five o'clock, the children returning from class would
drag their wooden shoes over the sidewalks and take turns running
their rulers along the shutters.

Abbé Bournisien came to see her at that hour. He would ask
about her health, bring her the news, and try to nudge her toward
religion with some unctuous gossip that was not without charm. The
very sight of his cassock comforted her.

One day, at the height of her illness, she believed herself dying
and asked for Communion; and as the preparations for the sacrament
went on in her room, as they arranged the dresser with its clutter of
medicine bottles into an altar and Félicité scattered dahlia petals over
the floor, Emma sensed something powerful passing over her, freeing
her from all her pains, from all perception and feeling. Her body,
freed of its burden, no longer thought; another life was beginning; it
seemed to her that her being, ascending toward God, was going to be
destroyed in that love like a burning incense that is dissolved in
smoke. They sprinkled holy water over the sheets; the priest took the
white wafer from the holy pyx; and she nearly fainted with a celestial
joy as she offered her lips to receive the body of the Saviour. The
curtains of her alcove swelled out gently, like clouds, and the rays of
the two candles burning on the chest of drawers seemed to her to be
two dazzling haloes. Then she dropped her head, thinking she could
hear the far-off song of heavenly harps and see God the Father on a

golden throne in an azure sky, in the midst of saints bearing green palms, a God radiant with majesty, signaling to angels with flaming wings to descend to earth and take her off in their arms.

This splendid vision remained in her memory as the most beautiful dream imaginable, so much so that she kept trying to recapture the sensation, which continued with the same sweetness, albeit less intensely. Her soul, aching with pride, was at last reposing in Christian humility; she relished the pleasure of having succumbed and studied the destruction of her will within herself, which was to allow free entry of heavenly grace. And so there existed greater joys than mere happiness, another love above all other loves, with neither interruption nor end, which would grow eternally! In her illusions born of hope she envisaged a state of purity floating above the earth, blending with the heavens, into which she longed to be absorbed. She wanted to become a saint. She bought rosaries and wore amulets; she wanted an emerald-studded reliquary at her bedside so that she could kiss it every night.

The curé was delighted at this condition, although he felt that Emma's religious leanings, because of their very fervor, might end in heresy, even extravagance. But since he was not very well versed in these matters once they passed a certain limit, he wrote to Monsieur Boulard, bookseller to the bishop, to send him "something really worthwhile for a lady with a fine mind." The bookseller, as casually as if he were sending hardware off to some ignorant savages, sent a random collection of his current accumulation of religious tracts. There were little manuals of questions and answers, arrogant-sounding pamphlets in the style of Monsieur de Maistre, and a certain type of cloying novel with pink binding, turned out by sentimental seminarists or penitent blue-stockings, like *Think It Over; The Man of the World at Mary's Feet, by Monsieur de——, Holder of Several Decorations; Some Errors of Voltaire, For the Benefit of the Young;* etc.

Madame Bovary was not yet mentally well enough to apply herself seriously to anything at all; besides, she plunged into the books with too much haste. She grew annoyed at the rules of ritual;

the arrogance of the written polemics displeased her by their pitiless attacks on people she didn't know; and the secular tales, with their religious touches, seemed to have been written out of such ignorance of the world that imperceptibly they drove her away from the truths she was seeking. She persisted, however, and when the book would fall from her hands, she believed herself permeated with the most refined Catholic melancholy that could enter an ethereal soul.

As for the memory of Rodolphe, she had buried it in the very bottom of her heart and it remained there, more solemn and motionless than a royal mummy in a subterranean tomb. A fragrance was emanating from this great embalmed love that suffused with tenderness the atmosphere of immaculate purity in which she wanted to live. When she knelt at her Gothic *prie-Dieu,* she addressed to the Lord the same fond words she had formerly murmured to her lover in the ecstasies of adultery. She was trying to entice faith. But no joy descended from the heavens, and she would stand up with her legs aching and the vague feeling that it was all a huge fraud. She told herself that this search would earn her even more credit, and in the pride of her devotion, she compared herself to those great women of yesteryear whose glory she had dreamed of over a portrait of La Vallière, and who had retired into solitude (trailing their lace-edged trains with so much majesty) to pour out at the feet of Christ all the tears of a heart wounded by life.

Then she became excessively charitable. She would sew clothes for the poor, she sent wood to women in labor, and one day on his return home Charles found three tramps sitting at the kitchen table and drinking soup. She had her little daughter, whom Charles had sent back to the nurse during her illness, brought home. She wanted to teach her to read. Berthe could cry and cry, she did not let it upset her. She had made up her mind to be resigned, and was indulgent toward everyone. Her language was continually filled with lofty phrases. She would ask the child: "Is your stomachache better, my angel?"

Madame Bovary senior found nothing to criticize in Emma except perhaps her zealousness in knitting undershirts for orphans instead of mending her own dishcloths. The good woman, beset by constant quarrels at home, felt comfortable in this peaceful house. She even remained until after Easter in order to avoid the sarcastic comments of old Bovary, who invariably ordered pork sausages on Good Friday.

Apart from the company of her mother-in-law, whose correctness of judgment and dignified ways lent her moral support, Emma received different guests almost every day. Mesdames Langlois, Caron, Dubreuil, and Tuvache came, and the goodhearted Madame Homais would come every afternoon from two to five. She had never wanted to believe any of the gossip about her neighbor. The Homais children also visited, Justin accompanying them. He would go up to the room with them and remain standing near the door, motionless and silent. Often Madame Bovary would start dressing without paying any attention to him. She would begin by taking out her comb and shaking her head rapidly. The first time the poor boy saw the mass of black ringlets fall to her knees, it meant to him a sudden entry into some extraordinary new country, the splendors of which terrified him.

His silent ardor and his shyness were lost on Emma. She never dreamed that the love that had disappeared from her life was throbbing so close to her, under that homespun shirt, in that adolescent heart so receptive to the emanations of her beauty. Besides, everything seemed indifferent to her now. She would speak with affection but look with disdain. Her conduct was so contradictory that it was impossible to distinguish selfishness from charity, corruption from virtue. One evening, for example, when the maid was asking permission to go out and stammering out an excuse, she grew angry. Then she suddenly asked, "So you love him?" And without awaiting an answer from the blushing Félicité, she added sadly, "Well, run along. Have a good time."

She had the garden completely rearranged at the beginning of spring, despite Bovary's objections; but he was happy to see her finally showing some signs of will. She showed more as she grew stronger. First she managed to get rid of Madame Rollet, the nurse, who had fallen into the habit, during Emma's convalescence, of going into the kitchen too often with her two foster-children and her little boarder, who had a more voracious appetite than a cannibal. Then she saw less and less of the Homais family, dismissed the other visitors one by one, and even attended church less regularly, which earned her the warm approval of the apothecary. He commented, in a rather friendly fashion, "You were taken in a bit by all that rigmarole!"

Abbé Bournisien, as before, showed up every day after the catechism class. He preferred to stay outside in the fresh air "in the grove," as he called the arbor.

Charles came home at that hour, and the men (who felt warm) would be served sweet cider. They drank to Emma's complete recovery.

Binet was present, a bit further down, that is, leaning against the terrace wall fishing for crayfish. Bovary would invite him over for some refreshment. He was an expert at uncorking wine bottles.

He would look around smugly at the countryside and say: "The bottle should be placed this way, straight up on the table, and when the wires are cut, the cork should be removed a little at a time, gently, gently, the way they handle seltzer in restaurants."

But the cider often spurted forth right in their faces during his demonstration. The priest never missed his chance to make the same joke with a heavy laugh: "Its goodness just jumps right out at you."

The abbé was really a good sort and was not even scandalized one day when the pharmacist advised Charles to distract Emma a bit by taking her to the theater in Rouen to hear Lagardy, the famous tenor. Homais, surprised at his silence, asked what he thought, and the priest asserted that he considered music less dangerous to morals than literature. Then the pharmacist began to defend the latter. The theater, he claimed, served to expose prejudice and taught virtue under the guise of pleasure.

"*Castigat ridendo mores,* Monsieur Bournisien! Consider the majority of Voltaire's tragedies, for example. They are cleverly larded with philosophical reflections that provide the people with a veritable education in morality and diplomacy."

Binet said: "I once saw a play. It was called *The Urchin from Paris,* and it portrayed an old general to a T. He slaps down a young man of society who seduces a working girl, who ends by——"

"Of course," Homais continued, "there is bad literature as there is bad pharmaceutical practice, but to condemn *in toto* the most important of the fine arts seems to me a stupid error, a Gothic notion worthy of those awful days when they imprisoned Galileo."

"I'm sure," the curé protested, "that there are good works and good authors, but the mere fact of people of both sexes being brought together in seductive surroundings decorated with worldly pomp, with pagan disguises and cosmetics, flaming lights and effeminate voices—all of that must in the long run give rise to a certain mental abandon and inspire dishonest thoughts and impure temptations. At least this is the opinion of all the Fathers. Finally," he added, suddenly assuming an unctuous tone while he rolled a pinch of snuff between his fingers, "if the Church has condemned theatrical performances, she has her reasons; we must submit to her decrees."

"Why does she excommunicate actors?" asked the pharmacist. "At one time they openly took part in religious ceremonies. In fact they acted out right in the middle of the choir certain types of farcical plays called mysteries in which the laws of decency were often offended."

The clergyman contented himself with a low moan, and the pharmacist continued: "It's like it is in the Bible. There is—you know—more than one spicy detail of really—lively—things."

And in reply to a gesture of irritation from Abbé Bournisien: "Ah! You'll agree that it's not a book to put into the hands of the young and I would be angry if my daughter, Athalie——"

"But it's the Protestants, not us, who recommend the Bible," the other exclaimed with impatience.

"It doesn't matter," Homais said. "I'm surprised that in our time, in an enlightened century, we still persist in forbidding an intellectual relaxation that is inoffensive, edifying, and even sometimes therapeutic, isn't it, doctor?"

"I suppose so," the doctor answered casually, either because, sharing the same ideas, he didn't want to offend anyone or else because he didn't have any ideas.

The conversation seemed over when the pharmacist saw fit to make one last jab.

"I've known priests who dressed in street clothes to go see dancing girls wriggling around."

"That's ridiculous!" said the curé.

"Yes, I've known some." And, drawing out his sentence, Homais repeated: "I—have—known—some."

"Well, then, they were wrong," said Bournisien, resigned to hearing anything.

"Believe me, they do more than that!" exclaimed the apothecary.

"Monsieur!" the clergyman retorted, looking so fierce that the pharmacist was finally intimidated.

"I only mean," the other answered in a less antagonistic tone, "that toleration is the surest way to attract people to religion."

"True, true," the curé conceded, sitting down again in his chair. But he only stayed two more minutes.

Then, as soon as he was gone, Homais said to the doctor: "That's what I call a real argument! Did you see how I won! Anyway, take my advice and take Madame to the theater, if only to irritate one of those old crows for once in your life! If someone could take my place I'd go with you myself. But hurry! Lagardy is giving only one performance; he's been engaged for England at a very impressive fee. From what I hear, he's quite a fellow—he's rolling in money and travels with three mistresses and a cook. All those great artists burn the candle at both ends. They need a wild life to stimulate their imagination. But they die in the poorhouse because they didn't have the foresight to save their money in their youth. Well, hearty appetite! See you tomorrow."

The idea of the theater grew quickly in Bovary's mind; he mentioned it to his wife right away. She at first refused, pleading the fatigue, discomfort, and expense. But for once Charles did not give in, so much did he think the relaxation would do her good. He foresaw no difficulties; his mother had sent them three hundred francs that he had not counted on, the current debts were not very large, and the due date of Lheureux's notes was so far off that he didn't have to worry about them. Besides, thinking that she was refusing out of consideration for him, he insisted all the more and she finally gave in to his arguments. So the next day, at eight o'clock, they set off in the Hirondelle.

The apothecary, who had nothing to keep him in Yonville, but felt himself unable to budge from there, sighed as he saw them off.

"Bon voyage!" he called out to them. "You're lucky people!"

Then he said to Emma, who wore a blue silk dress with four flounces: "You're as lovely as a goddess. You'll make quite an impression in Rouen."

The stagecoach stopped at the Red Cross Hotel, on the Place Beauvoisine. It was one of those inns that are found in all provincial towns, with huge stables and tiny bedrooms, where the yard is filled with chickens pecking oats under the mud-spattered gigs of the traveling salesmen—a solid old house with a worm-eaten wooden balcony that creaked in the wind on winter nights; always filled with people, noise, and eating; with black tables sticky from spilled brandy-laced coffee; thick windows yellowed by the flies; and damp towels stained by wine. Always smelling of the village, like farmhands dressed in city clothes, such hotels have a café on the street side and a vegetable garden on the country side. Charles went out immediately. He mixed up the stalls with the gallery, the pit with the boxes, asked for explanations that he didn't understand, was sent from the box office to the manager, came back to the inn, returned to

The stagecoach stopped at the Red Cross Hotel, on the Place Beauvoisine.

the box office, and thus several times covered the entire length of the town from the theater to the boulevard.

Madame Bovary bought a hat, gloves, and a bouquet. Charles was very frightened of missing the opening, and without stopping for even a bit of soup, they walked to the theater and found the doors still closed.

XV

The crowd outside was gathered against the wall, which was symmetrically enclosed between the railings. At the corner of the neighboring streets huge posters announced in ornate letters: *"Lucia de Lammermoor—Lagardy—Opéra—*etc." It was lovely outside but warm, and perspiration dampened hairdos. Handkerchiefs were removed from pockets, mopping red foreheads. An occasional warm breeze coming from the river would gently flutter the border of the canvas awnings hanging over the doors of the bars. A bit farther along, people were cooled by an icy draft of air smelling of tallow, leather, and oil. This was the smell from the Rue des Charrettes, filled with large black buildings in which barrels were stored.

Afraid of looking ridiculous, Emma suggested taking a walk along the promenade before they went in. Bovary kept the tickets cautiously in his hand, and the hand in his trousers pocket, pressing it against his stomach.

Emma's heart began to beat as soon as they neared the foyer. She involuntarily smiled with self-satisfaction at seeing the crowd rushing toward the right, through the other corridor, while she ascended the staircase to the reserved seats. She was as thrilled as a child when she pushed the large tapestried doors with her finger; she took in the dusty odor of the corridors with a deep breath, and when she was seated in her box, she leaned forward with the ease of a duchess.

The hall was beginning to fill up, opera glasses were being removed from their cases, and the subscribers, glimpsing each other, bowed across the distance. They came to relax in the theater from the anxieties of business; but not forgetting work entirely, they were still talking of cottons, brandy alcohol, or indigo. There were faces of old people, impassive and peaceful, which resembled, with their white hair and coloring, silver medals tarnished by leaden fumes. The handsome young men were strutting about in the pit, showing off pink or apple-green cravats above their waistcoats. Madame Bovary admired them from above as they rested the open palms of their yellow gloves on their golden-knobbed canes.

Then the orchestra lights were lit, the chandelier, let down from the ceiling, cast a sudden gaiety over the room with the sparkles from its crystals; the musicians filed in one at a time. At first there was a lengthy din of rumbling basses, squeaking violins, blaring cornets, piping flutes and flageolets. Then came three knocks on the stage; there was a roll of drums, the brass section played some chords, and the curtain rose to reveal a country setting.

It was a crossroads in a wood with a fountain on the left, shaded by an oak tree. Peasants and lords with plaids on their shoulders were singing a hunting song together. Then a captain appeared, lifting his two arms to heaven and calling down the angel of evil. Then another character appeared, they went off together, and the hunters took over.

She felt transported to the readings of her childhood—to the books of Walter Scott. She felt as if she could hear, across the fog, the sound of Scottish bagpipes echoing through the heather. Moreover, her recollection of the novel made it easier for her to understand the libretto, and she kept pace with the action phrase by phrase, while elusive thoughts crossing her mind were quickly dispelled by the gusts of music. She gave herself up to the lulling melodies, felt herself vibrating with all her being, as if violin bows were being drawn over her nerves. Her eyes were not large enough to take in the costumes, the sets, the actors, the painted trees trembling at the slightest footsteps, the velvet hats, cloaks, swords—all these fantasies floating together in harmony as if in another world. But a young woman stepped forth, throwing a purse to a squire in green. She was left alone and then a flute was heard, like the murmur of a fountain or the warbling of birds. Lucia, looking solemn, launched into her cavatina in G major. She bemoaned love, and yearned to have wings. Emma, too, would have wanted to escape from life and fly off in an embrace. Suddenly, Edgar Lagardy appeared.

He had that splendid pallor that lends something of the majesty of marble to the passionate races of the south. His vigorous body was encased in a brown doublet; a small carved dagger hung against his left thigh. He was posing languorously and displaying his white teeth. It was said that a Polish princess, hearing him sing one night on the beach at Biarritz, where he mended boats, had fallen in love with him. She had ruined herself for him. Then he left her for other women, and this romantic fame had but served to enhance his reputation as an artist. The publicity men always took care to slip into his advertisements some poetic phrase about his fascinating personality and the sensitivity of his soul. A beautiful voice, complete self-possession, more temperament than intelligence and more bombast than true lyricism—thus was constituted this admirable charlatan, in whose nature there was a blend of hairdresser and toreador.

He had the audience with him from the very first scene. He pressed Lucia to his chest, left her, came back, appeared to be desperate; he burst out in anger, then sang throaty elegies of infinite sweetness. Notes filled with sobs and kisses escaped from his bare throat. Emma leaned over to see him, digging her nails into the plush of the box. Her heart filled with the melodious lamentations that were drawn out to the accompaniment of the double basses, like the cries of the drowning amid the tumult of a storm. She recognized all the intoxication and anguish of which she had nearly died. The voice of the soprano seemed but the echo of her own conscience, and this illusion enchanting her as something of her own life. But no one on earth had loved her with such a love. *He* did not cry like Edgar that last night in the moonlight when they told each other: "Until tomorrow! Until tomorrow!" The theater rang with bravos; they repeated the entire passage; the lovers spoke about the flowers on their grave, of oaths, exile, fate, hope, and when they uttered the final adieu, Emma let out a sharp cry that blended into the sound of the last chords.

"Why is that lord persecuting her?" Bovary asked.

"No, no," she answered. "He's her lover."

"But he's swearing to revenge himself on her family while the other one, the one who came only a few minutes ago, said 'I love Lucia and I think she loves me.' And besides, he went off with her father arm in arm. He is her father, isn't he, the ugly little man with a cock feather in his hat?"

Despite Emma's explanations, as soon as the recitative duet began in which Gilbert reveals to his master, Ashton, his detestable machinations, Charles, seeing the false engagement ring that is to trick Lucia, thought that it was a token of love sent by Edgar. Indeed, he confessed he couldn't understand the story—because the music drowned out much of the words.

"What's the difference?" Emma said. "Be quiet!"

"But I like to understand what's going on; you know that," he said, leaning on her shoulder.

"Do be quiet!" she said with impatience.

Lucia came forward, half supported by her ladies, an orange wreath in her hair and paler than the white satin of her dress. Emma dreamed of her wedding day; she could see herself down there, in the middle of the cornfields, on the tiny path, as they walked toward the church. Why had she not resisted, implored, like Lucia? On the contrary, she had been happy, without perceiving the abyss into which she was rushing. Ah! If, in the freshness of her beauty, before the defilements of marriage and the disillusionments of adultery, she had been able to offer her life to some generous, solid heart. Then virtue, tenderness, sensual delights, and duty would have mingled. Never would she have fallen from such high happiness. But such happiness, no doubt, was a lie invented to cause the despair of all desire. Now she knew the petty quality of the passions that art exaggerated. Making an effort to turn away from such thoughts, Emma saw this reconstruction of her sorrows as nothing but a colorful fantasy, an entertaining spectacle for the eyes. And she even smiled to herself with disdainful pity when a man in a black cloak appeared under the velvet curtains at the back of the stage.

His large Spanish hat fell at a single gesture. Immediately the instruments and singers began the sextet. Edgar, flashing rage, dominated all the others with his clear voice; Ashton flung the homicidal provocations at him in deep tones; Lucia emitted her shrill lament; Arthur sung his asides in middle-register notes; and the chaplain's baritone boomed out like an organ, while the voices of the women, repeating his words, sang in a delightful chorus. Now they were all lined up and gesticulating; anger, vengeance, jealousy, terror, mercy, and amazement issued forth at the same time from their open mouths. The outraged lover brandished his unsheathed sword; his lace ruffle rose and fell with the heaving of his chest; and he walked from right to left across the stage, taking large steps, clicking on the floor the silver-gilt spurs of his soft boots that widened out at the ankles. He must, she thought, have an inexhaustible love to pour so much out over the crowd, and so effusively. All her critical objections faded away under the poetry of the role that was absorbing her, and attracted to the man by the fictional character he was portraying, she tried to imagine his life, that glamorous life, out of the ordinary and splendid and yet one that she could have led if fate had so willed it. They might have met and loved! With him she would have traveled from capital to capital through all the kingdoms of Europe, sharing his weariness and his pride, picking up the flowers thrown at him, she herself embroidering his costumes. Then, each evening, at the back of a box, sitting open-mouthed behind the golden trellis work, she would have breathed in the outpourings of this soul who would sing only for her; he would look for her from the stage, even while acting. Then a mad notion struck her; he was looking at her, she was sure of it! She wanted to run into his arms, to take refuge in his strength as in the incarnation of love itself, and to say to him, to cry out: "Take me away, take me with you, let us go! I am yours, yours; all my passion and all my dreams are yours!"

The curtain fell.

The smell of gas mingled with that of human breathing; the stir of the fans made the atmosphere seem even more stifling. Emma wanted to go out; people were crowding the corridors and she fell back into her chair with stifling palpitations. Charles, afraid that she was going to faint, ran to the bar to get her a glass of barley water. He had a difficult time getting back to the box; his elbows were jostled at every step because of the glass he was carrying in both hands. He even spilled three fourths of it on the shoulders of a Rouen lady in short sleeves, who, feeling the cold liquid trickling down her back, screamed like a peacock, as if she were being assassinated. Her husband, a mill owner, began to shout at the clumsy oaf. While she was dabbing at the spots on her lovely cherry-colored taffeta dress with her handkerchief, he muttered with anger about damages, coats, and reimbursement. Charles finally reached his wife and gasped: "I thought I'd never get back! Such a crowd!" He added: "Guess who I saw over there? Monsieur Léon."

"Léon?"

"Yes, Léon. He's coming over to say hello." Just as he finished these words, the one-time Yonville clerk entered the box.

He extended his hand with aristocratic nonchalance; and Madame Bovary mechanically offered hers, no doubt obeying the attraction of a stronger will. She had not felt that hand since the spring evening when the rain was dropping on the green leaves and they had bade each other farewell standing near the window. But she quickly reminded herself of the propriety of the situation and with an effort shook off the old memories. She began chattering rapidly.

"Why, hello! What a surprise! What are you doing here?"

"Quiet!" cried a voice from the pit, for the third act was beginning.

"You're in Rouen?"

"Yes."

"Since when?"

"Put them out!" People were staring at them. They stopped talking.

But from that moment on, she listened no longer to the music; and the chorus of the guests, the scene between Ashton and his attendant, the great duet in D major—for her everything took place in the distance, as if the instruments had been muffled and the characters moved farther off. She remembered the card games at the pharmacist's house, the walk to the wet nurse's, the readings in the arbor, the tête-à-têtes by the fireside, all of that pathetically calm and long-enduring love, so discreet and tender, which she had nevertheless forgotten. Why had he come back? What combination of events was bringing him back into her life? He stood behind her, leaning his shoulder against the wall of the box, and she quivered occasionally at the warm breath from his nostrils blowing into her hair.

"Are you enjoying this?" he said, leaning so close to her that the tip of his mustache brushed against her cheek.

She answered casually: "Lord no, not very much!"

Then he suggested that they leave the theater and stop somewhere for an ice.

"Oh, not yet," said Bovary. "Let's stay. Her hair's come undone; it looks as if it's going to be tragic."

But the mad scene did not interest Emma at all, and the soprano's acting seemed overdone.

"She's shouting too loud," she said, turning toward Charles, who was listening.

"Yes, maybe—a bit," he answered, undecided between his own genuine pleasure and his respect for his wife's opinions.

Then Léon said with a sigh: "It's so warm—"

"Unbearable, isn't it?"

"Are you uncomfortable?" asked Bovary.

"Yes, stifling. Let's go."

Carefully, Monsieur Léon placed her long lace shawl around her shoulders, and the three of them went off to sit near the waterfront, in the open air, on a café terrace. At first they talked about her illness, even though Emma kept interrupting Charles for fear, she said, that they were boring Monsieur Léon; and then the latter told them that he had come to Rouen to spend two years in a large office in order to gain experience in Normandy, where business methods were different from those in Paris. Then he asked about Berthe, about the Homais family, about the Widow Lefrançois; and since they had nothing more to say to each other in the husband's presence, the conversation soon died.

People coming out of the theater passed by on the sidewalk, humming or yelling as loud as possible: *"O bel ange, ma Lucie!"* Then Léon, playing the dilettante, began to talk of music. He had seen Tamburini, Rubini, Persiani, and Grisi. Compared to them, Lagardy, despite his powerful outbursts, was nothing.

"But," said Charles, who was taking small licks of his rum sherbet, "they say he was just wonderful in the last act. I'm sorry we left before it was over. It was just beginning to amuse me."

"Anyway," said the clerk, "there will be another performance."

But Charles answered that they were leaving the next day.

"Unless you want to stay alone, my kitten," he added, turning to his wife.

Changing his tactics in the face of this unexpected opportunity, the young man began praising Lagardy in the final number. It was something superb, sublime. Then Charles insisted: "You can come back Sunday. Go on, make up your mind. You'll make a mistake by leaving if you feel this will do you the least good."

The tables around them were beginning to empty; a waiter approached discreetly, taking up a position near them. Charles, who understood, pulled out his purse; the clerk held back his arm and did not even forget to leave a couple of silver coins for the waiter, which he noisily tossed on the table.

"I'm really sorry," Bovary murmured, "about the money that you're—"

The other made a nonchalant, extremely cordial gesture and picked up his hat, saying, "It's agreed, then, isn't it, tomorrow at six?"

Charles explained once more that he couldn't stay away any longer but that nothing prevented Emma . . .

"But—" she stammered, with a peculiar smile, "I really don't know—"

"Well, think about it. We'll see. The night will bring counsel." Then to Léon, who was walking along with them: "Now that you're back in our part of the world, you'll drop in for dinner once in a while, I hope?"

The clerk said that he certainly would, especially since he had to go to Yonville on some office business. And they said good night at the Passage Saint-Herbland, just as the cathedral clock struck half past eleven.

PART THREE

I

While studying law, Monsieur Léon had also been a fairly frequent visitor to the Chaumière cabaret, where he even did rather well with the grisettes, who thought him "distinguished." He was the most personable of the students: he wore his hair neither too short nor too long, did not spend his whole quarter's allowance on the first day of the month, and managed to stay on good terms with his professors. And he always avoided going to excesses in his behavior, as much from timidity as from fastidiousness.

Often when reading in his room or when sitting in the evening under the linden trees of the Luxembourg Gardens, he would let his law book fall to the ground, and he would think of Emma. But the feeling gradually lessened in intensity, and other sensual desires replaced it. Nevertheless the old sentiment still persisted, for Léon had not lost all hope. The idea remained for him like some vague promise dangling in the future, a golden fruit hanging on some imaginary tree.

Then, seeing her after three years' separation, his passion revived. This time, he thought, he must finally make up his mind to possess her. Moreover, his shyness had worn off in the gay company he had kept, and he returned to the provinces despising everyone who had not trod the Paris boulevards with a polished boot. In the presence of an elegant Parisienne in the drawing room of some decorated doctor who owned a carriage, the poor clerk would doubtless have trembled like a child; but here in Rouen, on the river front with this wife of a country doctor, he felt at ease, sure in advance that he would dazzle her. Self-possession depends on one's environment; one doesn't speak in a drawing room as one does in an attic, and a rich woman's virtue seems to be protected by the thought of all her bank notes that she wears, like so much armor, in the lining of her corset.

When he had taken leave of Monsieur and Madame Bovary that evening, Léon followed them at a distance in the street until he saw them stop at the Red Cross Hotel. Then he turned around and spent the whole night working out a plan.

The next day, at about five o'clock, his throat constricted, his cheeks pale, and with that cowardly determination that stops at nothing, he entered the inn's kitchen.

"Monsieur is not in," answered a maid.

That seemed to him a good omen. He went upstairs.

Emma was not disturbed by his coming; on the contrary, she apologized for having forgotten to tell him where they were staying.

"I guessed," said Léon.

"How?"

He pretended that he had been guided to her by chance, by instinct. She began to smile, and Léon in order to make up for his foolishness quickly told her that he had devoted the morning to looking for her in all the hotels of the city, one by one.

"So you decided to stay?" he added.

"Yes," she said, "and I made a mistake. I shouldn't get used to impractical pleasures, I who have a thousand responsibilities."

"Oh! I can imagine."

"No, you can't! You're not a woman." But men also have their troubles, and the conversation began with a few philosophical reflections. Emma commented at length about the futility of earthly affections and the eternal isolation in which every heart remains.

Either to sound impressive or in a naïve imitation of her melancholy mood, the young man declared that he had been dreadfully bored with his studies. Legal procedure irritated him, other professions attracted him, and his mother kept tormenting him anew in each letter. They became more specific about the causes of their unhappiness as they spoke, and freer with their confidences. Sometimes they stopped short before the completion of their thought and then groped for some phrase that could translate it. She omitted any mention of her passion for another; nor did he say that he had forgotten her.

Perhaps he no longer recalled his suppers after fancy-dress balls with costumed girls; and she no doubt no longer remembered the meetings of earlier days, when in the morning she ran through the grass to her lover's château. The sounds of the town barely reached them. The room seemed tiny, as if to emphasize their solitude. Emma, dressed in a dimity dressing gown, was leaning her head against the back of the old armchair. The yellow wallpaper lent her a golden background; and her bare head was reflected in the mirror, with the white center part in the middle and the tips of her ears showing from under her hair.

"You must forgive me for talking like this," she said. "I'm boring you with my continual complaints."

"Not in the least!"

"If you only knew," she continued, lifting to the ceiling her beautiful eyes, in which tears were forming, "all the things I've dreamed of."

"And I too! Oh, I've suffered so! I would often go out, walk off, and dawdle along the waterfront trying to lose myself in the noise of the crowd, unable to drive out the obsession pursuing me. There's a print seller on the boulevard who has an Italian engraving that shows a Muse. She is draped in a tunic and looking at the moon, with forget-me-nots in her flowing hair. Something drove me there time and again; I spent hours on end there." Then, in a trembling voice: "She resembled you a little."

Madame Bovary turned her head away so that he would not notice the irrepressible smile she felt on her lips.

"Often," he went on, "I wrote you letters and then tore them up."

She was silent. He went on: "I sometimes imagined that we would meet by some chance. I thought I saw you on street corners. I would run after all the carriages from which a shawl or veil like yours fluttered from the window. . . ."

She seemed determined to let him talk without interruption. Crossing her arms and lowering her head, she studied the rosettes on her slippers and wiggled her toes occasionally under the satin.

Then she sighed: "The saddest thing of all, it seems to me, is to drag out, as I do, a useless existence. If our misfortunes were of use to someone, we could console ourselves with the thought of sacrifice."

He began to praise virtue, duty, and silent sacrifices. He himself had an incredible need for self-sacrifice that he couldn't satisfy.

"I would dearly love," she said, "to be a nursing sister in a poorhouse."

"Unfortunately," he replied, "men don't have such sacred missions, and I see no occupation anywhere—unless perhaps that of a doctor."

With a slight shrug of her shoulders, Emma interrupted to regret that she had not died of her illness. A pity she hadn't died; she wouldn't be suffering now. Léon immediately envied "the peace of the grave." He had even written his will one evening, asking that he be buried in that handsome velvet-striped coverlet she had given him. This was how they wanted to be, each of them imagining an ideal toward which they would now readjust their past lives. Besides, the spoken word is like a rolling machine that draws feelings out.

At his made-up story of the coverlet, she asked, "But why?"

"Why?" He hesitated. "Because I loved you so."

And congratulating himself on having overcome that hurdle, Léon studied her face out of the corner of his eye.

It resembled the sky when a gust of wind chases away the clouds. The mass of sad thoughts that had darkened her blue eyes seemed to go away: her entire face was radiant.

He waited. Finally she answered: "I always thought so. . . ."

Then they talked over the trivial events of that far-off time, the pleasures and the sorrows which they had just evoked in a single word. He remembered the clematis arbor, the dresses she had worn, the furniture in her room, her house.

"And our poor cactuses? What's happened to them?"

"They died of frost last winter."

"Ah! You don't know how often I've thought of them. I've imagined them as they used to be on summer mornings when the sun was beating down on the shutters—and I saw your two bare arms among the flowers."

"Poor boy," she said, holding out her hand.

Léon quickly pressed his lips to it. Then, when he had taken a deep breath: "In those days you were, to me, some mysterious force captivating my life. Once, for example, I came to your home; but you don't remember, do you?"

"Of course I do," she said. "Go on."

"You were downstairs in the hall, about to go out, standing on the bottom step. You even had on a hat with little blue flowers; and without being invited, in spite of myself, I accompanied you. And each minute I grew more and more aware of my foolishness, yet I kept walking near you, not daring to follow you completely and yet not wanting to leave you. When you went into a shop, I stayed in the street and watched you through the windowpane as you took off your gloves and counted your change on the counter. Then you rang Madame Tuvache's bell and went in, and I remained like an idiot in front of the big heavy door that had just slammed behind you."

Madame Bovary, listening to him, was surprised at feeling so old.

All these things reappearing seemed to enlarge her life. They offered her, in a sense, vast sentimental areas to wallow in; and she kept repeating in a low voice, with her eyelids half shut: "Yes, you're right, that's how it was—you're right."

They heard eight o'clock strike from the various clocks around the Place Beauvoisine, which is filled with boarding schools, churches, and large deserted mansions. They no longer spoke, but as they looked at each other they felt a throbbing in their heads as if some vibrating impulse were in their mutual glances. They had just joined hands; and past and future, memory and dreams—everything mingled in the sweetness of this ecstasy. Night was darkening the walls on which there still gleamed, half lost in the shadow, the loud colors of four prints representing four scenes from the *Tour de Nesle*, with captions on the bottom in Spanish and French. A patch of black sky between gabled roof-tops showed through the window.

She rose to light two candles on the chest of drawers, then sat down again.

"Well?" asked Léon.

"Well?" she answered.

He was groping for a way to renew the interrupted conversation when she said: "Why has no one ever spoken to me like this before?"

The clerk warmly explained that ideal natures were difficult to understand. He had loved her at first sight and he was in despair when he realized the happiness he would have had if, by the grace of fate, they had met earlier and been indissolubly bound to each other.

"I thought about it sometimes," she said.

"What a dream!" Léon murmured. And delicately fingering the blue binding of her long white belt, he added:

"What's stopping us from starting all over again?"

"No, my friend," she answered. "I am too old—you are too young—forget me! Others will love you—you will love them."

"Not as I love you," he cried.

"What a child you are! Come now, let's be sensible. I want us to be."

She pointed out the impossibility of their love and said that they could still remain, as before, on terms of fraternal friendship.

Was she serious when she said this? No doubt herself did not know, involved as she was with the charm of the seduction and the need to defend herself; and giving the young man a tender look, she gently repulsed the timid caresses his trembling hands were attempting.

"Ah! Forgive me," he said, pulling back.

Emma was seized by a vague fear at this timidity, more dangerous for her than Rodolphe's boldness when he advanced with his arms outstretched. Never had any man appeared so handsome to her. She sensed an exquisite candor emanating from him. He lowered his long, fine, curling lashes. His smooth-skinned cheek was blushing with desire for her body, she thought—and Emma felt an unquenchable longing to place her lips on it. Then, leaning toward the clock as if to see the time, she said, "My goodness, how late it is. We've been such chatterboxes."

He understood the hint and looked around for his hat.

"I've even forgotten about the opera. And poor Bovary left me here especially for it. Monsieur Lormeaux, who lives on Ruc Grand Pont, was to take me with his wife."

And the opportunity was lost, since she was leaving the next day.

"Definitely?" asked Léon.

"Yes."

"But I must see you again," he said. "I have something to tell you."

"What?"

"Something important, serious. Well, no, anyway you can't leave, it's impossible. If you only knew—Listen—haven't you understood me? Haven't you guessed?"

"But speak plainly enough," she said.

"Oh! Please don't joke! Please, pity me, let me see you once more—only once."

"Very well," she said, and then stopped as if changing her mind, "but not here!"

"Anywhere you want."

"Would you—" She seemed to reflect, then said briefly, "Tomorrow, at eleven, in the cathedral."

"I'll be there!" he exclaimed, grasping her hands. She pulled them away.

As they were both standing, he behind her and she with her head lowered, he leaned toward her neck and kissed her lingeringly on the nape.

"You're mad, absolutely mad!" she said with little bursts of laughter, while the kisses multiplied.

Then he leaned over her shoulder and seemed to be seeking her consent in her eyes. But she gazed back at him with icy majesty.

Léon stepped backward to go out. He stopped on the threshold and then whispered in a trembling voice: "Until tomorrow!"

She replied with a nod and disappeared like a bird into the next room.

That evening Emma wrote the clerk an endless letter in which she canceled their meeting; everything was now at an end and they were not to meet anymore, for the sake of their happiness. But when the letter was sealed, she found herself in quite a predicament. She didn't know Léon's address.

"I'll give it to him myself," she thought. "He'll be there."

The next day, humming on his balcony with his window open, Léon applied several layers of polish to his pumps. He donned white trousers, fine socks, a green coat, poured all the scent he had over his handkerchief, and then, having curled his hair, uncurled it in order to give it a more natural elegance.

"It's still too early," he thought, looking at the cuckoo clock, which was striking nine.

He read an old fashion magazine, went out, smoked a cigar,

walked up three streets, thought that it was time, and headed slowly toward Notre Dame.

It was a lovely summer day. Silverware gleamed in jewelers' windows, and the light slanting down on the cathedral made the gray stones glitter. A flock of birds was whirling around in the blue sky around the trefoiled bell turrets. The square, echoing with cries, was fragrant with the flowers that lined its pavement—roses, jasmine, carnations, narcissus, and tuberoses, irregularly laid out between watered greenery, catmint, and chickweed for the birds. The fountain gurgled; and in the center, beneath large umbrellas, among the cantaloupes piled up in pyramids, bareheaded flower women were wrapping bunches of violets in paper.

The young man took one. It was the first time he had bought flowers for a woman, and as he sniffed them his chest swelled with pride, as if the homage intended for her were reflecting back on him.

However, he was afraid of being seen; so he resolutely entered the church.

The verger was just then standing on the doorstep, in the middle of the left doorway beneath the figure of the Dancing Marianne, with plumed hat on his head, rapier at his side, and cane in his hand, more majestic than a cardinal and shining like a pyx.

He walked over toward Léon and asked, with that benevolent wheedling smile that priests use when they question children, "You are a stranger to these parts, I believe? Would you care to see the curiosities of the church, sir?"

"No," said Léon.

At first he went around a side aisle. Then he went back to look at the square. Emma was not in sight. He went up into the choir.

The filled holy-water fonts reflected the nave, the beginning of the arches, and some sections of the stained-glass windows. The reflection of the painted windows broke off at the edge of the marble and continued over the flagstones like a many-colored carpet. The daylight streamed into the church in three enormous rays through the three open portals. A sacristan would pass through the far end occasionally, genuflecting before the altar in the half-turned fashion of worshipers in a hurry. The crystal chandelier hung motionless. A silver lamp was burning in the choir, and from the side chapels and dark places in the church there would sometimes be heard sounds like the heaving of a sigh and a clanging noise as a grating was shut, its echo reverberating beneath the vaulted roof.

Léon was walking near the walls with measured steps. Life had never appeared so good to him. She would soon be there—charming, high spirited, glancing behind her to see if she were being followed—and with her flowered dress, her golden lorgnette, and narrow boots, with all sorts of elegant touches that he had never enjoyed, and with the ineffable allure of virtue succumbing. The church, like an immense boudoir, spread out around her; the arches bent over to receive in the shadows the confession of her love; the windows shone resplendent to illuminate her face and the censers were going to burn so that she would appear like an angel amid clouds of perfume.

But she did not appear. He sat down on a chair and his eyes fell upon a blue window depicting boatmen carrying baskets. He looked at it for a long time, attentively, counted the scales of the fish and the buttonholes in the doublets, while his thoughts wandered off in search of Emma.

The verger, standing off to one side, was secretly angry at this man who allowed himself to admire the cathedral alone. It seemed to him a monstrous sort of conduct, as if he were robbing him in some way and almost committing sacrilege.

But there was a rustle of silk over the flagstones, the brim of a hat, a black cape. . . . It was she! Léon arose and ran toward her.

Emma was pale. She walked rapidly. "Read it," she said holding a paper out to him. "Oh, no!" And she abruptly pulled her hand back, entered the chapel of the Virgin, where, kneeling down against a chair, she began to pray.

The young man was irritated by this whim of piety, but then he found a certain charm in seeing her in the midst of their rendezvous as lost in prayer as an Andalusian *marquesa*. But he soon grew bored, for she seemed to be going on endlessly.

Emma was praying, or rather forcing herself to pray, hoping that some sudden strength of will would descend from heaven; and in order to win divine help, she filled her eyes with the splendors of the tabernacle, inhaled the perfume of the white blossoms in the huge vases, and intently heeded the silence in the church, which only intensified the tumult in her heart.

She stood up, and they were about to leave when the verger approached them rapidly, saying: "Madame is probably not from around here? Madame would like to see the curiosities of the church?"

"Absolutely not!" exclaimed the clerk

"Why not?" she said. For in her wavering virtue she was clutching at the Virgin, the sculptures, the tombs, at anything.

Then, in order to proceed "in proper order," the verger led them as far as the entrance near the square, where, indicating with his cane a large circle of black paving blocks, with neither inscription nor engravings: "There," he declared majestically, "is the circumference of the beautiful bell of Amboise. It weighed forty thousand pounds. Its like does not exist in all of Europe! The worker who cast it died of joy. . . ."

"Let's leave," said Léon.

The old man moved on; when he came back to the chapel of the Virgin, he extended his arms in an all-embracing gesture and said, prouder than a country squire showing off his fruit trees: "This simple stone marks the grave of Pierre de Brézé, lord of Varenne and Brissac, grand marshal of Poitou, and governor of Normandy, killed in the battle of Monthéry, July 16, 1465."

Léon bit his lips and fumed.

"And to the right, that gentleman all encased in iron, on the prancing horse, is his grandson, Louis de Brézé, lord of Breval and Montchauvet, count of Maulevrier, baron of Mauny, king's chamberlain, knight of the order, and also governor of Normandy, died July

23, 1531, on a Sunday, as the inscription notes; and below, that man about to descend into the tomb, is the same one. It is not possible, is it, to see a more perfect representation of man's mortality."

Madame Bovary took up her lorgnette. Léon, motionless, stared at her, no longer trying to speak or make any gesture, so discouraged did he feel at this deliberate combination of chatter and indifference.

The never-ending guide continued: "Near him, that kneeling woman in tears is his wife, Diane de Poitiers, countess of Brézé, duchess of Valentinois, born 1499, died 1566; and to the left, the woman carrying the child is the Holy Virgin. Now, turn this way; here are the graves of the Amboises. They were both cardinals and archbishops of Rouen. That one was a minister of King Louis XII. He was a great benefactor of the cathedral. In his will he left thirty thousand gold crowns for the poor."

And without stopping, talking all the while, he ushered them into a chapel filled with railings, pushed a few of them aside, and uncovered a sort of block that might have been a badly carved statue.

"It once decorated," he said with a profound sigh, "the tomb of Richard the Lion-Hearted, king of England and duke of Normandy. The Calvinists, sir, reduced it to this condition. They buried it for spite in the ground under the episcopal seat of Monseigneur. See, this is the door through which Monseigneur goes home. Let us move on to the gargoyle windows."

But Léon quickly pulled some silver from his pocket and grasped Emma's arm. The verger was struck dumb, not understanding this premature generosity, when the stranger still had so much to see. Then calling him back: "But Monsieur, the steeple! The steeple!"

"No, thank you," said Léon.

"You are mistaken, sir! It is four hundred forty feet high, nine less than the Great Pyramid of Egypt. It is all cast, it—"

Léon fled. It seemed to him that his love, which for the past two hours had been kept as stationary in the church as the stones themselves, was now going to evaporate like smoke through that truncated funnel, that oblong cage, that open chimney, that rises so grotesquely from the cathedral like the fantastic invention of some imaginative metal worker.

"But where are we going?" she asked.

He continued to walk rapidly without replying. Madame Bovary was already dipping her finger into the holy water when they heard behind them a panting breath punctuated at regular intervals by the tapping of a cane. Léon turned around.

"Monsieur!"

"Yes?" He recognized the verger, carrying under his arms and balancing against his stomach about twenty heavy paperbound books. These were works "about the cathedral."

"Imbecile!" Léon growled, dashing out of the church.

A street urchin was playing on the pavement. "Get me a cab!" The child flew off like a shot, through the Rue des Quatre-Vents. They remained alone for several minutes, facing each other and slightly embarrassed.

"Ah! Léon, really—I don't know—if I ought—" she simpered. Then, with a more serious expression: "It's very improper, you know."

"How so?" answered the clerk. "It's done in Paris!" And that statement convinced her. It was an irresistible argument.

The cab was slow to appear. Léon feared she might go back into the church. Finally the cab came.

"At least go out through the north portal!" shouted the verger, who had remained on the threshold, "to see the *Resurrection*, the *Last Judgment*, Paradise, King David, and the *Damned in the Flames of Hell.*"

"Where to, sir?" asked the coachman.

"Anywhere!" Léon said, pushing Emma into the carriage. And the lumbering vehicle started off.

It went down the Rue Grand-Pont, crossed the Place des Arts, the Quai Napoléon, the Pont Neuf, and stopped short before the statue of Pierre Corneille.

"Keep going," cried a voice from within.

*The cab was slow to appear. Léon feared she might go back into the church.
Finally the cab came.*

The carriage started off again, and as soon as it reached the Carrefour La Fayette, headed downhill, galloping toward the railroad station.

"No, straight ahead!" cried the same voice.

The cab emerged through the gate, and when it reached the boulevard, trotted gently beneath the large elms. The driver mopped his forehead, put his leather cap between his legs, and drove the vehicle beyond the sidelines near the meadow to the water's edge.

It traveled along the length of the river, moving over the cobbled towing path and went for a long time in the direction of Oyssel, beyond the islands.

But suddenly it made a leap across Quatre-Mares, Sotteville, the Grande-Chaussée, the Rue d'Elbeuf, and made its third stop before the botanical gardens.

"Will you keep going?" shouted the voice with greater anger.

And immediately resuming its course, it passed by Saint-Sever, along the Quai des Curandiers, the Quai aux Meules, once more over the bridge, through the Place Champ-de-Mars, and behind the poorhouse gardens, where the old men in black coats were walking in the sun along a terrace green with ivy. It went up the Boulevard Bouvreuil, along the Boulevard Cauchoise, then crossed the whole of Mont-Riboudet as far as the Deville hills.

Then it came back, and with neither fixed plan nor direction, wandered about at random. It was seen at Saint-Paul, at Lescure, Mont Gargan, at Rouge-Mare, and at the Place du Gaillardbois; in the Rue Maladrerie, the Rue Dinanderie, in front of various churches—Saint-Romain, Saint-Vivien, Saint-Maclou, Saint-Nicaise—in front of the customs house—at the Basse-Vieille-Tour, at the Trois-Pipes, and the Cimetière Monumental. Occasionally the coachman on his box would cast looks of despair at the cafés. He did not understand what kind of a rage for locomotion inspired these people, who did not want to stop. He attempted to a few times and immediately heard angry outbursts at him from behind. Then he lashed his two sweating nags even more furiously, without paying attention to the jolts, bumping into things here and there, not caring, demoralized, and almost weeping from thirst, fatigue, and unhappiness.

And at the harbor, amid the wagons and the barrels in the streets, the inhabitants at the corners were wide-eyed with astonishment at this most extraordinary spectacle in a provincial town—a constantly reappearing cab with closed blinds, shut up more tightly than a tomb and tossing about like a boat.

Once, in the middle of the day, in the open country, at a moment when the sun beat strongest against the old silver-plated lanterns, a bare hand reached out under the little yellow homespun curtains and threw out some scraps of paper that scattered in the wind, to alight farther along like white butterflies on a field of red clover in bloom.

Then, about six o'clock, the carriage stopped in a side street of the Beauvoisine section and a woman stepped down, walking away with her veil pulled down and without looking back.

I I

Madame Bovary was surprised at not seeing the stagecoach when she reached the inn. Hivert had waited for her for fifty-three minutes and finally gone off.

Yet nothing forced her to leave except that she had promised she would come back that evening. Besides, Charles was expecting her; and she already felt in her heart that cowardly submissiveness that is, for many women, both the punishment and the atonement of their adultery.

She packed quickly, paid the bill, took a cab in the yard, and hurrying the driver, urging him on, asked the time and elapsed distance every minute. They managed to catch up with the Hirondelle as it neared the outskirts of Quincampoix.

She was barely seated in it when she closed her eyes and did not open them until they arrived at the foot of the hill, where she recognized Félicité from afar. The girl was stationed outside the blacksmith's, on the watch for her. Hivert pulled up the horses, and the maid, standing on tiptoe to talk to her through the window, said mysteriously, "Madame, you must go to Monsieur Homais's right away. It's very important."

The village was silent as usual. There were small pink mounds smoking in the gutters, for it was jelly-making time and everyone in Yonville made his year's supply the same day. But in front of the pharmacist's shop there was a much larger mound, which surpassed all the others: a laboratory must always be superior to ordinary home ovens; a general demand must take precedence over private tastes.

She walked in. The large armchair was overturned and even the *Rouen Beacon* lay scattered over the floor between the two pestles. She pushed open the hall door, and in the middle of the kitchen, amid the brown jars filled with stemmed currants, powdered sugar, and lump sugar, amid the scales on the table and pots on the fire, she saw the entire Homais family, big and little, with aprons reaching to their chins and forks in their hands. Justin stood with his head lowered, and the pharmacist was shouting: "Who told you to look for it in the capharnaum?"

"What's the matter? What happened?"

"What happened?" answered the apothecary. "We're making jelly; it's simmering but the supply was just about to overflow because it was boiling too much. I asked for another pan. So this blockhead, out of sheer laziness, went to my laboratory and took from the hook the key to the capharnaum!"

This was what the druggist called a room under the roof filled with tools and supplies. Often he spent long hours there all by himself, labeling, decanting, repacking; and he considered it not a simple storeroom but a true sanctuary from which would emerge later on, made by his own hands, all sorts of pills, boluses, infusions, lotions, and potions, destined to spread his fame far and wide. No one else in the world set foot in there, and he respected it so much that he even swept it himself. If the pharmacy, open to all visitors, was the place where he displayed his pride, the capharnaum was the refuge where, selfishly secluding himself, Homais delighted in the exercise of his professional talents. So Justin's stupidity appeared to him a monstrous bit of irreverence; and redder than the currants, he repeated: "Yes, the capharnaum! The key that locks up the acids and caustic alkalies! To go in there and take a spare pan! A pan with a lid! One I may not ever use! Everything has its importance in the delicate operations of our art! But devil take it, one must make distinctions and not employ for near-domestic uses what is meant for prescriptions! It's as if one were to behead a fowl with a scalpel; as if a judge were to——"

"Don't get excited," said Madame Homais.

And Athalie, tugging at his coat, cried: "Papa! Papa!"

"No! Leave me alone," he shouted, "leave me alone. Damn it! Might as well set myself up as a grocer, I swear! Go on! Don't respect a thing! Break everything! Let the leeches go! Burn the marshmallow! Pickle cucumbers in my medicine jars! Tear the bandages!"

"You did want to——" said Emma.

"Just a minute! Do you know the risk you were running? Didn't you see something in the corner to the left on the third shelf? Answer me, say something!"

"I—don't—know," the boy stammered.

"Ah! You don't know. But *I* do. You saw a blue bottle sealed with yellow wax that contains a white powder. And on it, I myself wrote 'Dangerous!' And do you know what was inside it? Arsenic! And you touch it! You take a pan standing beside it!"

"Beside it," cried Madame Homais, clasping her hands. "Arsenic? You could have poisoned us all!"

And the children began to cry as if they already felt atrocious pains in their insides.

"Or poisoned one of the patients!" continued the apothecary.

"Did you want me to be brought to court and put in the prisoner's dock? Did you want to see me dragged to the scaffold? Have you never noticed the care I take in handling things, even though I've done it time and again? Sometimes I get frightened at myself when I think of my responsibility! The government hounds us, and the absurd laws restricting us are a veritable sword of Damocles hanging over our heads!"

Emma had given up asking what they wanted of her, as the pharmacist went on breathlessly: "See how you pay back all the kindness we have shown you. See how you reward me for the fatherly care I've lavished on you. Where would you be without me? What would you do? Who would give you food and education and clothing and every opportunity to become one day a respectable member of society? But you have to pull hard on the oar for that—and get, as they say, callouses on your hands. *Fabricando fit faber, age quod agis.*"

He was so furious that he was quoting Latin. He would have quoted Chinese or Icelandic had he known those two languages, for he found himself in one of those crises in which the entire soul reveals everything that is in it, like the ocean, which, in storms, opens wide to reveal the seaweed on its shores as well as the sands of its greatest depths.

And he continued: "I'm beginning to be terribly sorry that I ever promised to take care of you! I would have been much better off if I had left you to rot in your misery and in the filth you were born in! You'll never be good for anything except taking care of the cows! You have no talent for science! You hardly know how to paste on a label! And you live here in my home, snug as a parson, like a pig in clover!"

But Emma, turning toward Madame Homais: "They told me to come here—"

"Oh, dear Lord!" the good lady interrupted sadly. "How can I possibly tell you? It's a tragedy!"

She did not finish. The apothecary thundered: "Empty it! Scour it! Take it back! And hurry up!" And as he shook Justin by the collar of his blouse, a book dropped out of his pocket.

The boy stooped down, but Homais was faster, and when he picked up the book he stared at it, his eyes wide open and mouth agape.

"Conjugal—Love!" he said, pronouncing the two words slowly. "Ah, very good, very good, a pretty state of affairs! And illustrations! Oh, this is just too much!"

Madame Homais drew nearer.

"No! Don't touch it!"

The children wanted to see the pictures.

"Out of here!" he said imperiously. And they filed out.

First he paced back and forth, taking big steps, holding the open book between his fingers, rolling his eyes, choking, puffing, apoplectic. Then he walked up to his apprentice and planted himself before him with folded arms: "So you have all the vices, eh, you little monster? Take care, you're going downhill fast. Did it ever occur to you that this wicked book might fall into the hands of my children, inflame their thoughts, sully Athalie's purity, corrupt Napoleon? Physically, he's already built like a man. Are you at least sure that they have never read it? Can you swear to me?"

"Monsieur Homais, once and for all," Emma said, "do you have something to tell me?"

"Ah, yes, Madame! Your father-in-law is dead."

Actually, Charles's father had suddenly died two nights before, of an attack of apoplexy as he was finishing his dinner: and Charles had asked Monsieur Homais to reveal the terrible news to Emma gently, being worried about how she might take it.

He had pondered the announcement he would make, rounded it out, polished it, made it rhythmic; it was to be a masterpiece of discretion and transition, of subtle and delicate phrasing. But anger had swept rhetoric away.

Emma, giving up any hope of hearing details, left the pharmacy because Homais had resumed his vituperations. He was calming down, however, and now grumbled in a fatherly way, all the while fanning himself with his skullcap.

"It's not that I disapprove entirely of the book! The author was a doctor. There are certain scientific aspects in it that are not bad for a man to know—which, I dare say, a man should know. But later, later! At least wait until you're a man and your character's formed."

At Emma's knock, Charles, who had been awaiting her, advanced with his arms outstretched, and said to her with tears in his voice: "Oh, my dearest darling—" And he leaned forward gently to kiss her. But at the touch of his lips, the memory of Léon took hold of her and she passed her hand over her face, shuddering. But she did manage to say: "Yes, I know, I know."

He showed her the letter in which his mother told what had happened, without any sentimental hypocrisy. She only regretted that her husband had not received the consolations of religion, since he had died at Doudeville in the street at the door of a café after a patriotic banquet with old army-officer friends.

Emma handed the letter back to him; then, at dinner, out of politeness she pretended she had lost her appetite. But as he insisted, she began to eat heartily while Charles, sitting opposite her, remained motionless, looking stunned with grief.

He would occasionally lift his head and look at her mournfully, lingeringly. Once he sighed: "If only I had seen him once again!"

"How old was your father?"

"Fifty-eight."

"Ah!"

And that was all.

Fifteen minutes later he added: "My poor mother. What's to become of her now?"

She shrugged her shoulders in a gesture of ignorance.

Seeing her so taciturn, Charles assumed she was upset and restrained himself from talking in order not to revive her sorrow, which he found moving. Then, shaking off his own grief, he asked: "Did you have a good time yesterday?"

"Yes."

Bovary did not budge after the table had been cleared. Nor did Emma; and as she looked at him, the monotony of the sight banished little by little all the pity in her heart.

He seemed so weak and puny to her, a nonentity—in short, a contemptible man in every respect. How could she rid herself of him? What an interminable evening! Something stultifying, like opium fumes, engulfed her.

From the hall they heard the dry tap of a stick on the floor. Hippolyte was bringing in Emma's luggage. In order to set it down, he painfully described a ninety-degree angle with his stump.

"Charles doesn't even think of him anymore," she told herself, looking at the poor devil whose mop of red hair was dripping with perspiration.

Bovary was looking for a coin at the bottom of his purse. He seemed unaware of all the humiliation there was for him in the mere presence of this man who stood there like a living reproach to his incurable ineptness.

"That's a pretty bouquet you have," he said, noticing Léon's violets on the mantelpiece.

"Yes," she said casually, "I bought it as I was leaving—from a beggar woman."

Charles picked up the violets and refreshed his tear-reddened eyes against them, sniffing them delicately.

She pulled them quickly from his hand and went to put them into a glass of water.

The next day Madame Bovary senior arrived. She and her son wept copiously. Emma left them to themselves, claiming she had household chores.

The following day they all had to consult about the mourning.

They sat down—the women with their workbaskets—at the water's edge under the arbor.

Charles was thinking about his father and was amazed to feel so much affection for the man. Until now, he had thought he cared only slightly about him. His mother thought of her husband. The worst days of the past seemed enviable to her now. Everything was softened by a kind of instinctive regret after such a long-time relationship; and occasionally as she plied her needle, a big tear would slide down her nose and hang there from its tip for a moment.

Emma was thinking that barely forty-eight hours ago they had been together, far from the world, intoxicated and unable to gaze enough at each other. She tried to recapture the slightest details of that vanished day. But the presence of her mother-in-law and her husband interfered. She wanted to hear nothing and see nothing: she wanted to be alone to enjoy the memory of her love, which was dwindling away under the impact of external impressions no matter what she did to recapture it.

She was ripping out the lining of a dress, and the pieces of material were scattered around her. Mother Bovary was using the scissors without once looking up, and Charles, in his cloth slippers and the old brown frock coat that he used as a dressing gown, kept his hands in his pockets and also said nothing. Near them, Berthe, in a tiny white apron, was shoveling the gravel in the walk with her spade.

Suddenly they heard Monsieur Lheureux, the dry-goods merchant, enter through the gate.

He had come to offer his services "in view of the sad circumstances." Emma replied that she thought they could do without them. The merchant refused to take no for an answer.

"I beg your pardon," he said. "I was hoping to have a private talk with you." Then, in a lowered voice: "It's about that matter—you know which one?"

Charles blushed to the tips of his ears. "Oh, yes—of course."

And in his agitation he turned to Emma and said: "Darling, could you——?"

She seemed to understand him, for she arose. "It's nothing," Charles said to his mother. "Some household detail, I suspect."

He did not want her to know the story of the note, since he feared her comments.

The moment they were alone, Monsieur Lheureux began congratulating Emma quite openly on the inheritance. Then he chatted about unimportant matters, about fruit trees, the harvest, his own health, which was "merely so-so, with continual ups and downs." As a matter of fact he was working like a slave and still didn't earn even enough to butter his bread, despite what people said about him.

Emma let him talk on. She had been so bored these last two days!

"And you're all better again?" he continued. "I tell you, your poor husband was in a very unhappy state! He's a fine fellow, even though we've had our difficulties."

"What difficulties?" she asked, for Charles had concealed from her the dispute over the goods she had ordered.

"But you must know!" said Lheureux. "Over those notions of yours—the luggage for the trip."

He had pulled his hat down over his eyes, and his hands were behind his back as he smiled and softly whistled. He was staring into her face in an intolerable manner. Did he suspect something? She was lost in all sorts of apprehensions. Finally, however, he said: "We managed to get together, and I came to suggest another arrangement to him."

This was to renew the note signed by Bovary. Of course the doctor would do as he thought best; he mustn't be upset, especially now that he was going to have all kinds of bothersome things on his mind.

"He might do best by turning them all over to someone like you, for example; with a power of attorney it would be easily arranged, and then you and I would manage our little affairs together. . . ."

She didn't understand. He stopped talking. Then, returning to his dry-goods business, Lheureux announced that Madame must certainly need something from him. He would send her a dozen meters of black barège for a dress.

"The one you're wearing is good enough for the house. But you need another one for going out. I noticed that as soon as I came in. I have as sharp an eye as an American."

Instead of sending the fabric, he brought it. Then he came for the measurements; then again on different pretexts, each time trying to show how amiable and helpful he was, "ingratiating himself," as Homais would have said, and always slipping some hint to Emma about the power of attorney. He didn't mention the note and she forgot about it. Charles, at the beginning of her convalescence, had told her something about it, but so much had passed through her head since then that she no longer remembered. Besides, she was careful not to mention money; her mother-in-law was surprised at this and attributed her changed attitude to the religious feelings she had acquired during her illness.

But as soon as her mother-in-law left, Emma lost no time in amazing Bovary by her solid good sense. They were going to have to obtain information, verify mortgages, see if they should consider an auction or a liquidation.

Technical terms rolled off her tongue. She pronounced impressive words—"order," "future," and "foresight"—and continually exaggerated the troubles attendant on settling wills; and she did so thorough a job that one day she even showed him the form of a general authorization to "manage and administer his business matters, effect all loans, sign and endorse all notes, pay all sums, etc." She had profited by Lheureux's lessons.

Charles naïvely asked her where the document came from.

"From Monsieur Guillaumin." And with the utmost coolness, she added: "I don't trust him too much. Notaries have such bad reputations. We might perhaps consult— We know no one who—no one, really."

"Léon might—" Charles replied, thinking out loud.

But it was hard to make things clear by letter. So she offered to take the trip. Charles was grateful but reluctant to let her go. She insisted. It was a duel of mutual politeness. Finally, she exclaimed in a tone of mock rebellion: "No, I insist, I'll go!"

"How good you are!" he said, kissing her on the forehead.

The next day she set out in the Hirondelle to go to Rouen and consult Monsieur Léon; and there she remained three days.

III

They were three exquisitely full days, glorious days, a real honeymoon.

They stayed at the Hotel de Boulogne on the riverfront. And they lived there, with shutters closed and doors locked, with flowers on the floor and iced fruit drinks brought up from morning on.

In the evening they took a covered boat and went to dine on one of the islands.

It was the time of day when caulking hammers could be heard ringing against hulls in every shipyard. The tar fumes rose up between the trees and on the river there were large oily patches undulating unevenly in the scarlet light of the setting sun, like floating plaques of Florentine bronze.

They rowed among the moored boats, whose long, slanting cables grazed the top of their boat.

Imperceptibly the city noises faded away: the rattle of the wagons, the tumult of voices, the yapping of dogs on the boat decks. She untied the ribbon of her hat and they landed on their island.

They sat in the low-ceilinged room of a tavern, on whose door hung black fishnets. There they ate fried smelts and cream and cherries. Later they lay down on the grass and embraced in the shade of the poplar trees. They wanted to live forever in this tiny spot, like a couple of Robinson Crusoes. In their joy it seemed to them the most magnificent place on earth. It was not the first time that they had seen trees and blue sky and grass, that they had heard water flowing and the wind rustling through the leaves, but they had certainly never before admired all these things so much. It was as if nature had not existed before or had only begun to be beautiful since the gratification of their desires.

They returned at nightfall. The boat skirted the edge of the islands. They sat in the stern, hidden in the shadow without talking. The square-tipped oars grated in the iron oarlocks and punctuated the silence like a metronome, while the rope trailing behind them rippled gently in the water.

One night the moon appeared and so they proceeded to invent beautiful phrases about the melancholy, poetical orb. She even began to sing:

> *Do you remember the evening we drifted . . .*

Her weak but musical voice died away on the water; and the wind carried off the trills that Léon heard flutter all around him like wings.

She sat facing him, leaning against the bulkhead, the moon coming down on her through one of the open shutters. Her black dress, fanning out around her, made her appear thinner and taller. Her head was raised and her hands clasped. She was staring at the sky. Occasionally the shadows of the willows hid her completely, then she reappeared suddenly like a vision in the moonlight.

Léon, sitting beside her on the bottom of the boat, came upon a bright red silk ribbon.

The boatman looked at it awhile and then said: "Ah, it must belong to a group I took out the other day. A lively bunch of jokers, gentlemen and ladies, came on board with cakes and champagne and musical instruments and Lord knows what else! There was one handsome man, specially, a tall man with a tiny mustache. He was very funny. They kept saying to him, 'Come on, tell us a story, Adolphe'—Dodolphe, I think."

She shuddered.

"Are you uncomfortable?" Léon said, coming closer.

"It's nothing. Probably the chill of the night."

"And that gentleman doesn't have to worry about not having ladies either," the old boatman added softly, thinking he was complimenting the stranger.

Then he spat into his hands and picked up his oars.

But finally they had to part! The farewells were sad. He was to send his letters in care of Madame Rollet, the wet nurse. She was so precise in her details about using a double envelope that he greatly admired her shrewdness in love matters.

"So, you're sure that everything is all right?" she said during the last kiss.

"Yes, of course!"

"But why is she so insistent about that power of attorney?" he asked himself later as he walked back alone through the streets.

I V

Léon soon assumed an air of superiority in front of his friends, kept aloof from their company, and completely neglected his work.

He awaited her letters, read them over and over again. He wrote her, evoking all the power of his passion and his memories. Instead of diminishing with absence, the desire to see her grew so strong that finally one Saturday morning he had to get away from his office.

When from the top of the hill he saw down in the valley the Yonville church steeple with its tin flag turning in the wind, he felt that combination of delight, vanity triumphant, and condescending sentimentality that must be the emotion of a millionaire returning to visit his native village.

He wandered around her house. A light was shining in the kitchen. He sought her shadow behind the curtains. No one appeared.

The Widow Lefrançois exclaimed loudly when she saw him that he was "taller and thinner," whereas Artémise, on the contrary, thought him "stouter and darker."

He dined in the small dining room, as in the old days, but alone, without the tax collector, because Binet, tired of waiting for the Hirondelle, had permanently advanced his meal by an hour and now ate at five o'clock sharp. He still complained that the "broken-down old clock was slow."

Léon finally made up his mind; he knocked on the doctor's door. Emma was in her room and only emerged a quarter of an hour later. The doctor appeared delighted to see him but did not leave the house that whole evening or all the next day.

He saw her alone late at night in the lane behind the garden—the same lane where she had been with Rodolphe! A storm was raging and they spoke under an umbrella, catching glimpses of each other by the flashes of lightning.

The thought of separation was becoming unbearable.

"I'd rather die," Emma said. She was writhing in his arms, in tears.

"Good-bye, good-bye! When will I see you again?"

They turned back to kiss once more; and it was then that she promised him to find some permanent way, and quickly, by whatever means necessary, to see him freely at least once a week. Emma was sure she could. Moreover, she was full of high spirits. She was going to have some money.

And so she bought a pair of yellow curtains with wide stripes for her room that Monsieur Lheureux had proclaimed a bargain; she yearned for a rug, and Lheureux, commenting that, "it won't be *that* hard a job," politely took it on himself to find her one. She could no longer do without his services. Twenty times a day she sent for him and he would immediately drop what he was doing without a murmur of protest. Nor did anyone understand why Madame Rollet lunched at her house every day and even paid her private visits.

Toward this period—at the approach of winter—she seemed smitten by a passion for music.

One evening as Charles was listening to her, she started the same piece four times in a row and always with great irritation, while he, without noticing the difference, exclaimed: "Bravo! Very good. You're wrong to stop. Keep going."

"I can't. It's terrible. I'm all thumbs."

The next day he asked her to "play something for him again."

"All right, if it makes you happy."

And Charles had to admit that she had lost some of her ability. She played the wrong notes, stumbled, and then stopped short: "That's enough! I really should take lessons, but—" She bit her lips and added: "Twenty francs a session is much too expensive."

"Yes, it is—a bit—" said Charles, snickering a bit. "But you might be able to get someone for less. There are artists who aren't famous who are sometimes better than celebrities."

"Find them!" said Emma.

When he came home the next day he looked at her slyly and finally couldn't resist saying: "You can be so stubborn sometimes! I went to Barfeuchères today and Madame Liégeard assured me that her three girls, at the Miséricorde school, take lessons for fifty sous an hour, and from a well-known teacher too!"

She shrugged her shoulders and did not open the piano again. But when she passed near it (if Bovary were in the room) she would sigh: "Ah, my poor piano!"

And when visitors came, she made sure to inform them that she had given up music and could no longer take it up again, for very good reasons. Everyone pitied her. What a shame! She had such a fine talent! They even spoke about it to Bovary, and embarrassed him, especially the pharmacist: "You're making a mistake. One should never neglect nature's gifts. Besides, think of it, my friend, by letting your wife study, you'll save later on when it comes to your daughter's musical education. I think that the mothers should teach their children themselves. It's one of Rousseau's theories, perhaps still a bit new, but it will win out in the end, I'm sure, like mothers' breast-feeding and vaccination."

And so Charles brought up the question of the piano once more. Emma answered caustically that it was better to sell it. But Charles felt that if that poor old piano, which had pleased her vanity so much, were taken away, it would be like a partial suicide of his wife.

"If you really wanted—" he said. "A lesson now and then wouldn't be that ruinous."

"Lessons are worthwhile only when they're taken regularly," she answered.

And that was how Emma managed to obtain her husband's permission to go to the city once a week to see her lover. People even commented, at the end of a month, that she had made considerable progress.

V

Her day was Thursday. She got up and dressed silently to avoid waking Charles, who would have commented that she was getting ready too early. Then she paced back and forth, stationed herself at the windows, and looked at the square. Dawn would be breaking through the pillars of the marketplace, and in the early morning light you could read the block letters of the pharmacist's sign standing out against the closed shutters.

When the clock pointed to seven-fifteen, she walked over to the Golden Lion, where a yawning Artémise opened the door for her, and then raked out the embers for her. Emma remained alone in the kitchen, occasionally stepping outside. Hivert harnessed the horse leisurely, while listening at the same time to Madame Lefrançois. The widow, with her nightcap still on, stuck her head out through a window and was giving him instructions on what to buy and elaborate explanations that would have tried the patience of any other man. Emma tapped her feet against the cobblestones in the yard.

Finally, when he had swallowed his soup, pulled on his driving coat, lit his pipe, and picked up his whip, he would calmly get up on the seat.

The Hirondelle started off at a slow trot and stopped frequently for the first mile to pick up the passengers watching for it along the road outside their gates. Those who had reserved seats the night before kept it waiting; some were even still at home in bed. Hivert would call out, shout, and swear. Then he would step down from his seat and knock furiously on the doors while the wind blew through the cracked blinds.

Finally the four benches filled up and the carriage rolled along, row after row of apple trees appearing to file past; and the road, running between two long ditches filled with yellow water, seemed endless, dwindling off toward the horizon.

Emma knew it from one end to the other; she knew that after a certain meadow there was a signpost, then an elm, a barn, or a road repairer's hut; she would sometimes shut her eyes to try to surprise herself, but she never lost her true sense of the remaining distance.

Finally the brick houses grew more frequent, the ground rang out beneath the wheels, the Hirondelle glided between the gardens where an opening would reveal statues, arbors, clipped yew trees, and a swing. Then, suddenly, the city appeared.

Sloping down like an amphitheater, drowned in the fog, it sprawled amorphously beyond the bridges. Then the open country climbed monotonously upward until it seemed in the distance to touch the faint edge of the pale sky. From this height, the entire landscape looked as still as a painting; the boats at anchor were crowded into a corner; the river curved around the foot of the green hills and the oblong-shaped islands looked like large, motionless black fish on the water. The factory chimneys belched forth huge brown plumes of smoke that drifted away in the breeze. The roar of foundries mingled with the clear ringing of chimes from churches that loomed in the mist; leafless trees on the boulevard formed violet patches in the midst of the houses, and the rooftops, glistening with rain, gave off reflections that varied according to the height of the different parts of town. An occasional gust of wind would carry the clouds off toward Sainte-Catherine's Hill, like airborne waves breaking in silence against a cliff.

The thought of the people huddled below gave her a feeling of dizziness. Her heart swelled as if the 120,000 souls who pulsated there had sent forth, all at once, the breath of the passions she attributed to them. Her love expanded before this vastness and filled with the tumult of the vague hum rising from the valley. She poured it back again, over the squares, the walking paths, and the streets, and the old Norman city spread out before her eyes like an immense metropolis, a Babylon into which she was entering. She leaned out the window, holding on with both hands, and breathed in the air. The three horses galloped, the stones were heard grinding in the mud, the coach swayed, and Hivert hailed the wagons along the way from afar, while townfolk who had spent the night in Bois-Guillaume descended the hill slowly in their small family traps.

They stopped at the city gate. Emma unbuckled her overshoes, pulled on a fresh pair of gloves, adjusted her shawl, and stepped down from the Hirondelle twenty steps farther on.

The city was waking up. Clerks in caps were dusting showcase windows, and women with baskets on their hips were periodically shouting loud cries from the street corners. She walked along, looking down, keeping close to the house walls, and smiling with pleasure beneath her lowered black veil.

For fear of being seen, she usually did not take the shortest road. She plunged into dark alleys and would arrive covered with perspiration at the lower end of the Rue Nationale near the fountain. This is the theater section, with its cafés and prostitutes. Often a wagon would pass near her, carrying shaky pieces of stage scenery. Waiters in aprons were scattering sand over the flagstones between the tubs of green bushes. There was a mingled smell of absinthe, cigars, and oysters.

She turned a corner and recognized his curly hair escaping from under his hat.

Léon would keep walking along the sidewalk. She would follow him to his hotel. He would go up, open the door, and go in; and then, what a passionate embrace!

After the kisses came an outpouring of words. They told each other all the woes of the past week, their misgivings, their anxieties about letters; but now all that was forgotten and they looked at each other laughing with sensual delight and uttering terms of endearment.

The bed was a large mahogany one shaped like a boat. The red silk curtains that hung from the ceiling were bunched very low near the bell-shaped headboard—and nothing in the world was as beautiful as her dark hair and white skin standing out against the deep red when she covered her face with her two hands in a gesture of modesty and revealed her nude arms.

The warm room with its noise-muffling rug, its gay ornaments, and soft light, seemed exactly right for the intimacies of passion. The arrow-shaped curtain rods, brass hooks, and large oak bowls gleamed when the sun suddenly entered. Between the candlesticks on the mantelpiece there were two of those large pink shells that echo the sound of the sea when held next to the ear.

How they loved that dear room filled with gaiety, despite its slightly faded splendor. They always found the furniture as they had left it, and sometimes even found hairpins beneath the base of the clock that she had forgotten the previous Thursday. They would sit and eat by the fire on a small table inlaid with rosewood. Emma would carve the food and put the pieces into his plate, chattering all the while, and she would laugh loudly and dissolutely when the champagne froth spilled over the fragile glass onto the rings on her fingers. They were so completely lost in each other that they actually believed they were living in their own house and would remain there until death like a couple eternally young. They said *our room, our rug, our armchairs;* she even said *our slippers.* They were a gift from Léon, in response to a whim of hers—pink satin slippers trimmed with swansdown. Her leg dangled in midair when she sat on his lap, since she was too short for it to reach the floor; and the charming backless little slipper was held on solely by the toes of her bare foot.

For the first time in his life he was tasting the inexpressible subtlety of feminine grace. He had never before encountered this refinement of speech, this quiet elegance of dress, these poses of a soothed dove. He admired the raptures of her spirit and the laces of her petticoat. Moreover, wasn't she "a woman of the world"—and a married woman? In other words, a real mistress.

She awoke a thousand desires in him, evoked instincts or reminiscences by her changing moods. She was in turn mystic or gay, chattering or taciturn, wildly passionate or casual. She was the *amoureuse* in every novel, the heroine of every drama, the vague "she" of every book of poetry. He found her shoulders glowing with amber, like "Odalisque at Her Bath"; she was long waisted like the feudal châtelaines, and she resembled "The Pale Lady of Barcelona"—but above all she was an angel!

Often, as he looked at her, it seemed to him that his soul, reaching out toward her, was spreading like a wave over the outline of her head and was being drawn down into the whiteness of her bosom.

He would sit on the floor at her feet with his elbows on his knees and look up at her with a smile.

She would lean over toward him murmuring, as if suffocating with passion: "Don't move! Don't say a word! Just look at me! There's a sweetness in your eyes that I adore!"

She called him "child": "Child, do you love me?" And she barely heard his answer in the rush of his lips to meet her mouth.

On the clock there was a small bronze Cupid with a simpering smile, who curved his arms beneath a gilded garland. They laughed at it many times. But when they had to part, everything became serious.

Motionless they faced each other, saying: "Until Thursday! Until Thursday!" Suddenly she would take his head in her hands, kiss him quickly on the forehead while sobbing "Adieu!" and rush off into the hall.

She headed toward a hairdresser's on the Rue de la Comédie, to have her hair done. Night would be falling, and they would light the gas in the shop.

She could hear the theater bell calling the performers to their rehearsal; and she could see, across the street, men with whitened faces and ladies in faded finery entering the stage door.

It was always stuffy in this little low-ceilinged room, where the stove hummed amid the wigs and the hair cream. The odor of the curling irons and the oily hands working over her head never failed to soothe her into somnolence, and she would doze off awhile in her wrapper. The hairdresser, while combing her hair, would often ask her to buy tickets for a masked ball.

Afterwards she would start for home. She would go up the streets toward the Croix-Rouge, pick up the overshoes she had hidden in the morning beneath one of the benches, and settle into her seat among the impatient passengers. A few of them got off at the other side of the hill. She would be left alone in the carriage.

Each turn in the road revealed more of the lights of the city. They glowed like a broad luminous mist above the blurred-looking houses. Emma would kneel on the cushions and gaze at the dazzling sight. She would sob, call out to Léon, and send him tender words and kisses that would be lost in the wind.

On the hill a poor wandering beggar with a cane appeared right in the middle of all the carriages. He wore a mass of rags, and a battered old beaver hat, shaped like a basin, hid his face; but when he pulled it off, he revealed two gaping bloody orbits where the eyelids should have been. His skin was peeling away in red strips; liquid matter flowed from it, hardening into green scabs as far as his nose, the black nostrils of which sniffed convulsively. When he wanted to speak he would throw back his head with an idiot's laugh, and then his blue pupils would roll continuously toward the temples, close to the live wound.

He would sing a little song while trailing after the coaches:

> *Often the warmth of a lovely day*
> *Makes a girl dream of love.*

The rest of it was about birds, sunshine, and leaves.

Sometimes he would suddenly appear bareheaded behind Emma. She would start back with a cry, but Hivert would joke with him, tell him to take a boat to the Saint-Romain Fair, or sometimes ask him with a laugh how his girl friend was.

Often while they were moving, his hat would suddenly enter the coach through the window while he clung with one arm to the footboard between the mud-spattering wheels. His voice, at first low and moaning, would become shrill. It would echo into the night like an indistinct wail of distress; and through the ringing of the bells, the murmur of the trees, and the rumble of the empty coach, it had a kind of far-off quality that terrified Emma. It plunged deep into her soul like a whirlwind in a chasm and swept her away into an expanse of limitless melancholy. But Hivert, who noticed the weight behind, would lash out at the blind man with his whip. The thong would cut into his wounds and he would fall into the mud shrieking.

Afterwards the remaining occupants of the Hirondelle would fall asleep, some of them with their mouths open, others with their chins sunk down, leaning on a neighbor's shoulder or with an arm passed through the strap, all the while swaying rhythmically with each jolt; and the reflection of the lantern swinging outside above the rumps of the horses penetrated into the interior through the chocolate-colored calico curtains, sending a blood-red light over all these motionless people. Emma, numb with sadness, would shiver under her clothes and grow continually colder down to her feet, with death in her soul.

Charles would be waiting for her at home; the Hirondelle was always late on Thursday. Emma would finally arrive, then give her child a cursory kiss. Dinner was not ready. It did not matter! She forgave the maid. Now the girl was allowed to do anything.

Her husband would often notice her pallor and ask her if she felt ill.

"No," Emma would say.

"You seem so strange this evening," he would comment.

"Oh, it's nothing! Nothing!"

There were even days when she went straight to her room as soon as she came in; Justin would be there and would walk on tiptoes. He was better at serving her than the best of maids. He would set down the matches, candlestick and book, then prepare her nightdress and turn down the bed.

"All right," she would say, "that will do. You may go now." For he would remain standing there, arms dangling and eyes wide open as if enmeshed in countless threads of a sudden dream.

The next day was always terrible and the following ones even more unbearable because of Emma's impatience to be happy again— hers was a burning desire, inflamed by all her memories, and it exploded on the seventh day at Léon's caresses. His own raptures were shown by his expressions of wonder and gratitude.

Emma savored this love in a discreet and intense way, cultivating it with all the artifices of her sentiment and trembling all the while that later on it might end.

She would often say to him, with a sweet, melancholy voice: "Ah! You'll leave me, you will. You'll marry. You'll be like the others."

"Which others?" he asked.

"Men, all of them," she said. Then she added, pushing him away with a languid gesture: "You're all heartless!"

One day as they were talking philosophically about earthly disillusionments, she happened to say (to test his jealousy, or perhaps giving in to some inordinate need for confession) that once before him she had loved someone. "Not like you!" she immediately went on, swearing on her daughter's head that "nothing ever happened."

The young man believed her but nevertheless asked her who the man was.

"He was a ship's captain, darling."

Wasn't this done to prevent any inquiries, and at the same time gain impressive status by a pretended involvement with a man who by nature must have been strong willed and accustomed to being worshiped?

The clerk then felt the lowliness of his own position; he envied epaulets, crosses, titles, things that were probably pleasing to her, he suspected, knowing her expensive tastes.

And yet Emma suppressed many of her extravagant notions, such as the yearning for a blue tilbury drawn by an English horse and driven by a groom in top boots to take her to Rouen. Justin had inspired this fancy in her by begging her to take him on as a footman; and while the privation did not lessen the pleasure of arriving at each rendezvous, it definitely increased the bitterness of the return trip.

Often when they were talking about Paris, she would murmur: "Ah! We'd be so happy living there!"

"Aren't we happy?" the young man would say softly, caressing her hair.

"Yes, of course," she would say; "I'm being silly. Kiss me."

She was more charming than ever to her husband, prepared pistachio creams for him, and played waltzes after dinner. He considered himself the most fortunate of mortals, and Emma lived in tranquillity until suddenly one evening: "It's Mademoiselle Lempereur you're taking lessons from, isn't it?"

"Yes."

"Well I saw her today at Madame Liégeard's," Charles said, "and mentioned you to her. She doesn't know you."

It was like a thunderbolt. Yet she answered in a natural tone: "She's probably forgotten my name."

"There may be several ladies named Lempereur in Rouen who teach piano," the doctor said.

"It's possible." Then quickly: "But I have her receipts. Wait a minute! Here." And she went to the secretary, looked through all the drawers, and finally became so agitated that Charles begged her not to trouble herself so much about those silly receipts.

"Oh, I'll find them," she said.

And actually on the following Friday as he was pulling on one of his boots in the dark little room where his clothes were kept, he felt a piece of paper between the leather and his sock, pulled it out, and read: "Received, for three months of lessons and various supplies, the sum of sixty-five francs. Félicie Lempereur, music teacher."

"How the devil did this get into my boot?"

"It probably fell from the old bill box on the edge of the shelf." From that moment on, her existence was a continuous string of lies, in which she wrapped her love as if in layers of veiling in order to hide it.

Lying became a need, a mania, a pleasure, so much so that if she said she had walked along the right side of the street yesterday, one had to assume it had been the left.

One morning, just after she left, dressed lightly as usual, a sudden snow started falling; and as Charles stood at the window watching it fall he noticed Monsieur Bournisien sitting in Monsieur Tuvache's cart, which was to take him to Rouen. And so he went down to give the priest a heavy shawl to be transmitted to Emma at the Croix-Rouge. As soon as Bournisien arrived at the inn, he asked for the wife of the Yonville doctor. The landlady replied that she spent very little time there. In the evening, when the curé met Madame Bovary in the Hirondelle, he mentioned his difficulty, without appearing to attach any great importance to it; for he began praising a preacher who was causing a sensation in the cathedral and whom all the women were running to hear.

But even if he had not asked for explanations, others, later on, might be less discreet. And so she deemed it advisable to stop at the

Croix-Rouge each time so that the good people from her village, seeing her on the staircase, would suspect nothing.

One day, however, Monsieur Lheureux met her leaving the Hotel de Boulogne on Léon's arm. She was afraid, thinking he would talk. He was not so stupid.

Three days later, he came into her room, shut the door and said: "I want some money."

She declared she had none to give him. Lheureux burst into complaints and reminded her of all his past favors.

In fact, of the two notes signed by Charles, Emma had paid only one as of this moment. As for the second, the merchant had consented, on her plea, to replace it by two others, which had also been renewed for a very long term. Now he pulled from his pocket a list of unpaid goods, to wit: curtains, the rug, fabric for the armchairs, several dresses, and various toilet articles, the total value of which came to about two thousand francs.

She lowered her eyes. He went on: "But if you don't have cash, you do have property."

And he mentioned a miserable little shack in Barneville, near Aumale, which brought in almost nothing. It had once been part of a little farm sold by old Bovary: Lheureux knew all about it, even the number of acres and the names of the neighbors. "If I were you," he said, "I'd get rid of it and even have some money left over."

She protested that it would be difficult to find a buyer. He offered to find one for her. Then she asked how she would be able to sell it.

"Don't you have the power of attorney?" he asked. The phrase seemed to her a breath of fresh air.

"Leave me the bill," Emma said.

"Oh, don't bother about it," said Lheureux.

He came back the following week and boasted that he had found, after several false starts, a man named Langlois who had been eying the property for some time without offering a price.

"The price doesn't matter," she exclaimed.

On the contrary, he said: they should wait to smoke out the

gentleman in question. It was worth the trouble of a trip, and since she couldn't make it, he offered to go and discuss the matter with Langlois. When he returned, he announced that the buyer was offering four thousand francs.

Emma was overjoyed at this news.

"Frankly," he added, "it's a good price."

Half the money was paid immediately, and when she offered to settle her bills the merchant said: "It hurts me, honestly, to see you part with such a large sum as that all at once."

Then she stared at the bank notes and dreamed of the countless number of meetings these two thousand francs represented. "But what—" she stammered. "What do you mean?"

"Oh," he said, laughing amiably, "you can put any sum you want on the sales receipts. Don't you think I know about household finances!" And he stared hard at her as he ran his fingers up and down over two long documents. Finally, opening his pocketbook, he spread out on the table four promissory notes, each one for one thousand francs.

"Sign these for me," he said, "and keep everything."

She uttered a shocked cry.

"But if I give you the balance," Lheureux answered with brazen effrontery, "am I not doing you a favor?"

And taking a pen, he wrote at the bottom of the account: "Received of Madame Bovary, four thousand francs."

"What are you worrying about? In six months you'll receive the balance due on the shack, and I've placed the due date of the last note after that payment."

Emma was a bit confused by his calculations, and her ears rang as if pieces of gold, bursting forth from their sacks, had clanked all around her on the floor. Finally Lheureux explained that he had a friend named Vinçart, a Rouen banker, who was going to discount these four notes and then he himself would remit to her the payment of the real debt.

But instead of two thousand francs, he brought back only eighteen hundred, for friend Vinçart (as was "only fair") had taken two hundred as his commission and expenses.

Then he casually asked for a receipt. "In business, you understand—sometimes—And please date it."

A horizon opened up before Emma—a horizon of dreams she could now realize. She was careful enough to put aside three thousand francs with which the first three notes were paid, when they fell due, but the fourth one by chance came to the house on a Thursday, and a stunned Charles patiently awaited his wife's return for some explanation.

She hadn't told him about the note because she wanted to spare him domestic worries; she sat down on his knees, caressed him, cooed, enumerated at length all the indispensable items she had bought on credit: "And you must admit that the amount isn't so high when you consider the number of items."

Charles, at his wits' end, soon had recourse to the indispensable Lheureux, who promised to straighten matters out if Monsieur would sign two notes for him, one for seven hundred francs, payable in three months. In order to be able to meet it, he wrote a pathetic letter to his mother. Instead of sending an answer, she herself came, and when Emma asked if he had managed to get something from her, he said, "Yes, but she wants to see the bill."

At daybreak the next morning Emma ran to Monsieur Lheureux to ask him to make up another note not to exceed a thousand francs, for if she showed the one for four thousand, she would have to explain that she had paid two thirds, and consequently reveal the sale of the property, which had been so well handled by the merchant that it was not discovered until later.

Despite the low price for each article, Madame Bovary senior quickly found that she had spent too much. "Couldn't you do without a rug? Why did you have the armchairs reupholstered? In my day, you had one armchair in a house, for older people—at least that's how it was in my mother's home, and she was a proper woman, I assure you. Everyone can't be rich! There's no fortune will last if you fritter it away. I would blush to pamper myself the way you do, and yet I'm old and need care. Look at this! Repairs, frills! What nonsense! Silk for lining at two francs a yard! When you can find perfectly suitable cotton for ten sous, and even eight!"

Emma lay on the lounge and answered in the calmest manner possible: "All right, Madame, that's enough!"

The other woman continued to lecture, predicting that they would end up in the poorhouse. But it was Bovary's fault. Fortunately he had promised to cancel the power of attorney.

"What?"

"He swore he'd do it," the woman answered.

Emma opened the window and called out to Charles. The poor fellow was forced to admit the promise his mother had wrested from him.

Emma disappeared and then returned quickly, holding out a large sheet of paper with an imperious manner.

"Thank you," said the old woman, and she threw the document into the fire.

Emma began to laugh—a strident, shrieking, hysterical laugh; she was suffering an attack of nerves.

"Dear Lord," cried Charles, "you're wrong too. You shouldn't have come to make scenes."

His mother, shrugging her shoulders, claimed that "it was all play-acting."

But Charles, rebelling for the first time in his life, took his wife's part—and so well that his mother decided to leave. She left the next day, and as he was trying to get her to stay, she said on the doorstep, "No, you love her more than you love me and you're right. That's how it should be. Besides, so much the worse for you. You'll see. Stay well. It'll be a long time before I come back here to 'make scenes,' as you call it."

Yet Charles felt no less guilty toward Emma. She made no effort to hide the bitterness she felt for his lack of confidence in her. He had to plead at great length before she would consent to take back the power of attorney, and he even accompanied her to Monsieur Guillaumin's to have him prepare a second one, just like the first.

"I understand," said the notary, "a man of science cannot be bothered with the practical details of life."

Charles felt comforted by this smug comment, which flattered his weakness, and made it look like a lofty virtue.

What a scene there was the following Thursday in the hotel, in the room with Léon! She laughed, cried, sang, danced, ordered sherbets sent up, wanted to smoke cigarettes—she seemed wild to him, but adorable and superb.

He did not know what there was within her that drove her recklessly toward the pleasures of life. She was becoming irritable, greedy, and voluptuous. She would walk with him in the streets, her head held high, without fear of being compromised, she said. Occasionally, however, Emma would shudder at the sudden thought of meeting Rodolphe; for it seemed to her that even though they were separated forever, she was not completely liberated from his power over her.

One evening she did not go back to Yonville. Charles was out of his mind with worry, and little Berthe, who did not want to go to bed without seeing her mama, sobbed as if her heart were breaking. Justin had gone off along the road to look for her. Even Homais left his pharmacy.

Finally, at eleven, not being able to stand it any longer, Charles harnessed his cart, jumped into it, whipped the horse, and arrived at the Croix-Rouge at about two in the morning. No sign of her. He thought that Léon might have seen her; but where did he live? Happily, Charles remembered his employer's address. He hurried there.

Day was beginning to break and he could make out the signs above a door. He knocked. Someone shouted out the information he wanted, without opening the door, meanwhile loudly cursing those who disturbed people during the night.

The house in which the clerk lived had neither bell, knocker, nor porter. Charles banged against the shutters with all his strength. A policeman passed by; he became frightened and went off.

"I'm mad," he told himself, "she probably stayed with the Lormeaux family after dinner." But the Lormeaux family no longer lived in Rouen.

"She must have stayed to take care of Madame Dubreuil. But Madame Dubreuil died ten months ago! So where can she be?"

A thought came to him. He asked for the directory in a café and quickly looked up the name of Mademoiselle Lempereur, who lived at 74 Rue de la Renelle-des-Maroquiniers.

Just as he turned into that street, Emma herself appeared at the other end. He threw himself at her, more in a lunge than an embrace, exclaiming: "What kept you yesterday?"

"I didn't feel well."

"What was it? Where? How?"

She passed her hand over her forehead and answered: "At Mademoiselle Lempereur's."

"That's what I thought! I was going there."

"Well, don't bother," said Emma. "She just went out. But in the future, don't worry. I won't feel free, you know, if I have to remember that the slightest delay worries you so much."

This was a sort of permission she was giving herself in order not to be hampered in her future escapades. And she took free and full advantage of this. When she had a sudden desire to see Léon, she would leave at the slightest excuse, and since he would not be expecting her that day, she would call for him at his office.

At first it made him very happy. But soon he told her that his employer was very displeased by these intrusions.

"So what!" she would say. "Come along." And he would slip out.

She wanted him to dress all in black and grow a pointed beard on his chin to resemble the portraits of Louis XIII. She wanted to see his rooms, found them mediocre. He blushed at the remark. She didn't notice and advised him to buy curtains like hers. And when he objected to the expense: "You do pinch your pennies!" she laughed.

Each time Léon had to tell her everything that had happened during the week. She asked for poetry, poetry written just for her, "a love poem" in her honor. He could never find a rhyme for the second line and would end up copying a sonnet from a keepsake.

This was less out of vanity than from a desire to please her. He did not argue about any of her notions; he accepted all her tastes, becoming her mistress rather than she being his. She offered tender words and kisses that drove him mad. Where, where had she learned this corruption, so deep and yet so disguised that it appeared almost disembodied?

V I

When he traveled to Yonville to see her, Léon often dined at the pharmacist's home, and he felt obliged out of politeness to reciprocate an invitation.

"Gladly!" Homais had replied. "I really should take a bit of a plunge. I'm getting fossilized here. We'll go to a show and eat in a restaurant. We'll carry on a bit!"

"Oh dear!" Madame Homais murmured affectionately, frightened by the vague perils to which he was exposing himself.

"Why, what's the matter? You think I don't ruin my health enough living with those constant fumes from the pharmacy? That's the female character for you—they're jealous of science, yet they're opposed to one's enjoying the most legitimate distractions. Never mind, you can definitely expect me. One of these days I'll turn up in Rouen and we'll throw our money around!"

In the old days the apothecary would not have used such an expression; but nowadays he was using a colloquial and Parisian way of speech that he considered to be in the best of taste; and like his neighbor Madame Bovary, he questioned the clerk curiously about the life in the capital, even using slang to dazzle the "bourgeois," saying such things as *turne, bazar, chicard, chicandard, Breda-Street* and "I'll cut along now" for "I'm leaving."

And so Emma was surprised one Thursday to see Monsieur Homais in the Golden Lion kitchen. He was dressed in his traveling clothes, that is, enveloped in an old cloak that no one had seen before, carrying a valise in one hand and the foot warmer from his shop in the other. He had told no one of his plan, fearing that the public would become uneasy in his absence.

The thought of revisiting the places in which he had spent his youth probably excited him because he did not stop talking during the entire trip. The moment they arrived, he jumped from the carriage to go off in search of Léon. The clerk protested in vain. Homais dragged him toward the Café de Normandie, where he entered with great self-importance, not removing his hat since he felt it was very provincial to be bareheaded in a public place.

Emma waited for Léon for three quarters of an hour. Finally she ran to his office. Then, lost in all sorts of conjectures, accusing him of indifference and reproaching herself for her weakness, she spent the afternoon with her forehead glued to the windowpanes.

At two o'clock they were still at the table. The large dining room was emptying. The stovepipe shaped like a palm tree spread its gilt leaves on the white ceiling; near them, inside the café window, in the bright sunlight, a small fountain was gurgling in a marble basin where, among the watercress and the asparagus, three torpid lobsters stretched their claws toward a heap of quail.

Homais was in seventh heaven. Even though he was drunk more on the luxury than the good fare, the Pommard did go to his head a little. And when the rum-flavored omelet appeared he put forth some immoral theories about women.

What attracted him above all was chic. He adored an elegant manner of dress in a well-furnished apartment, and in the matter of physical attributes he didn't dislike a "pleasingly plump little morsel."

Léon looked at the clock—in despair. The apothecary went on drinking, eating, talking.

"You must be rather hard up here in Rouen," he suddenly said. "But then, your love's not far from here."

And as the other blushed: "Come now, admit it. Will you deny that in Yonville—"

The young man stammered something.

"At Madame Bovary's, weren't you courting—"

"Whom?"

"The maid!" He wasn't joking. But vanity conquering caution, Léon denied it vehemently, despite himself. Besides, he liked only dark women.

"You're right," said the pharmacist. "They have more temperament." And leaning over toward his companion's ear, he listed the signs by which a woman with temperament can be recognized. He even launched into an ethnic digression. German women were moody, French women wanton, and Italians passionate.

"And Negro women?" asked the clerk.

"They're preferred by artists," said Homais. "Waiter! Two demitasses!"

"Shall we go?" Léon finally asked with impatience.

"Yes," said Homais in English.

But before they left he wanted to see the owner of the place and offer his congratulations.

Then the young man pleaded, in order to get rid of him, that he had a business appointment.

"I'll go with you!" Homais announced. And as they walked down the streets together, he spoke about his wife, his children and their future, and the pharmacy, talking about the state of disrepair he had found it in—and the height of perfection to which he had brought it.

When they reached the Hotel de Boulogne, Léon abruptly left

him and ran up the stairs, where he found his mistress in a highly excited state.

She grew furious at the mention of the pharmacist's name. But he sought to justify himself. Had it been his fault? Didn't she know Homais? Could she believe that he would prefer his company to hers? She turned away. He took hold of her, and falling to his knees, put his arms around her waist in a languorous pose full of desire and pleading.

She stood with her large flashing eyes looking at him seriously, almost fiercely. Then they were clouded by tears, her reddened eyelids lowered, she let her hands fall, and Léon brought them to his lips. Just then a servant appeared to tell Léon that someone was asking for him.

"You'll come back?" she said.

"Yes."

"When?"

"Right away."

"It's a trick," the pharmacist said, seeing Léon. "I wanted to get you away from that appointment. I thought you weren't very happy about it. Let's go to Bridoux's and have a glass of cordial."

Léon insisted he had to go back to his office. The apothecary became facetious about legal paperwork and legal procedure.

"Forget about your Cujas and Barthole for a while! Devil take it! Who's stopping you? Buck up, man! Come along to Bridoux's. You'll see his dog—it's very odd." And when the clerk proved stubborn: "Then I'll go with you. I'll read a newspaper while waiting, or I'll leaf through a law journal."

Léon, bewildered by Emma's anger and Homais's incessant talk, and perhaps affected by the heavy lunch, stood undecided and as if under the spell of the pharmacist, who kept repeating: "Let's go to Bridoux's! It's only two steps from here—on Rue Malpalu."

Then, out of cowardice or foolishness or that elusive feeling that commits us to the actions we dislike most, he let himself be taken to Bridoux's. They found him in his small yard, keeping an eye on three workers who were panting as they tugged at the big wheel of a seltzer-making machine. Homais gave them a few suggestions and embraced Bridoux, and they had their drinks. Twenty times Léon was on the point of leaving, but Homais would tug at his arm and say, "I'm leaving too; wait a minute! We'll go to the *Rouen Beacon* and see the people there. I'll introduce you to Thomassin."

He did manage to get rid of him, however, and rushed to the hotel. Emma was no longer there.

She had just left in exasperation. Now she detested him. His failure to keep his promise about their rendezvous seemed an outrage to her. She kept looking for other reasons to break with him: he was incapable of heroism, weak, commonplace, banal, softer than a woman, stingy, and what is more, cowardly.

Then, calming down, she finally realized that she had probably unjustly condemned him. But the disparagement of those we love always erodes a bit of the affection. One must not touch idols; the gilt rubs off on one's hands.

From now on, matters apart from their love entered into their correspondence. Emma's letters to him talked of flowers, poetry, the moon and the stars, naïve expedients of a weakening passion trying to revive itself by external devices. She kept promising herself a profound joy for their next meeting; then she would admit to herself that she had felt nothing extraordinary. This disappointment soon gave way to a renewed hope, and Emma would return to him more impassioned and avid. She would undress savagely, tearing at the thin lacing of her corset, which fell down around her hips like a gliding snake. She would tiptoe on her bare feet to see once more if the door were locked, then she would drop all her clothes in one movement—and pale, without speaking, solemn, she would fall against his chest with one long shudder.

Yet there was something wild, something strange and tragic in this forehead covered with cold sweat, in those stammering lips and wildly staring eyes, in the embrace of those arms—something that

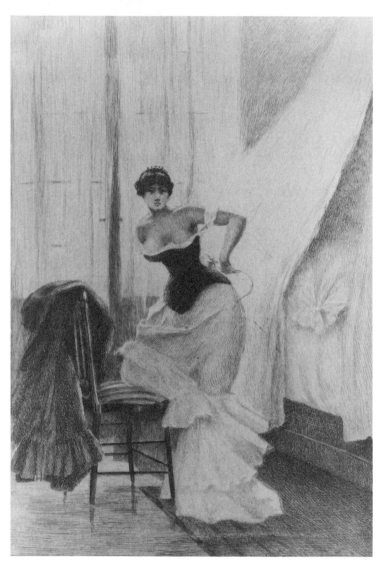

She would undress savagely, tearing at the thin lacing of her corset, which fell down around her hips like a gliding snake.

seemed to Léon to be coming between them subtly as if to tear them apart.

He did not dare question her, but seeing how experienced she was, he told himself that she must have known all the extremes of suffering and pleasure. What had once charmed him now frightened him a little. He was also rebelling against the increasing encroachment upon his personality. He resented Emma for this permanent victory over him, even tried not to want her; and then at the sound of her footsteps he felt himself grow weak like an alcoholic at the sight of strong liquor.

She did not fail, it is true, to lavish all sorts of attentions on him, from choice foods to tricks of dress and languishing looks. She brought roses from Yonville in her bosom, and tossed them at him. She became anxious about his health, advised him on his conduct, and in order to bring him closer to her, hoping perhaps that heaven would help, she slipped a medal of the Blessed Virgin around his neck. Like a virtuous mother, she would ask about his friends. She told him: "Don't see them, don't go out, think only of us. Love me!"

She wanted to be able to keep track of his life, and it occurred to her to have him followed in the streets. There was always some sort of vagabond near the hotel who accosted travelers and who would not refuse. But her pride asserted itself. "Too bad, then! Let him deceive me, what of it? Do I really care?"

One day when they had parted early, she was walking alone along the boulevard. She noticed the walls of her convent and sat down on a bench in the shade of the elm trees. How calm those days had been! How wistful she was about the indescribable ideas of love she had tried to imagine for herself from books.

The first months of her marriage, her horseback rides in the forest, the viscount waltzing, and Lagardy singing—all of this passed before her eyes. And Léon suddenly appeared to be as far from her as the others. "But I love him!" she told herself. Nonetheless she was not happy, had never been happy. Why then was life so inadequate? Why did she feel this instantaneous decay of the things she relied on?

If there existed somewhere a strong and handsome being, a valiant nature imbued with both exaltation and refinement, the heart of a poet in the shape of an angel, a lyre with strings of bronze, sounding elegiac nuptial songs toward the heavens—why, why could she not find him? How impossible it seemed! And anyway, nothing was worth looking for; everything was a lie. Each smile hid a yawn of boredom, each joy a curse, each pleasure its aftermath of disgust, and the best of kisses left on your lips only the unattainable desire for a higher delight.

A metallic clang rang through the air and there were four strokes from the convent clock. Four o'clock! And it seemed to her that she had been there on that bench for eternity. But an infinity of passions can be contained in a minute, like a crowd in a tiny space.

Emma lived only for her passions, no more concerned about money than an archduchess.

One day, though, a puny little man, red-faced and bald, came to her house and declared that he had been sent by Monsieur Vinçart of Rouen. He removed the pins that closed the side pocket of his long green frock coat, stuck them into his sleeve, and politely held out a paper.

It was a note for seven hundred francs, signed by her, that Lheureux, despite all her protests, had endorsed over to Vinçart.

She sent her maid to fetch him. He couldn't come.

Then the stranger, who had remained standing and glancing about left and right (his curiosity concealed by his heavy blond lashes), asked with a naïve air: "Is there any message for Monsieur Vinçart?"

"Well, tell him—" said Emma, "tell him—that I don't have the money! It will be paid next week. Ask him to wait. Yes, next week." And the man went off without a word.

But at noon on the next day she received a summons; and the sight of the stamped paper, over which was written in several places in large letters "Maître Hareng, Bailiff at Buchy," frightened her so that she quickly ran to the dry-goods merchant.

She found him in his shop, tying up a package. "At your service, Madame," he said, but did not stop his work. He was assisted by a girl of about thirteen, slightly hunchbacked, who worked as both salesgirl and cook.

Then, his clogs clattering over the shop's floor, he preceded Emma one flight up the stairs and escorted her into a narrow room. Here there was a large fir desk on which were several ledgers secured by locked metal bars. Against the wall beneath some calico samples was a safe so large that it probably contained something besides notes and money. Monsieur Lheureux, as a matter of fact, also acted as a pawnbroker, and it was there that he had put Madame Bovary's golden chain, along with Tellier's golden earrings. The poor old man had been finally forced to sell out, and had bought a little grocery store in Quincampoix, where he was dying of catarrh among tallow candles less yellow than his face.

Lheureux sat down in his large rattan armchair, saying: "What's new?"

"Look!" And she showed him the paper.

"Hmm, well. What can I do?" Then she became angry, remembering the promise he had given her not to endorse her notes. He acknowledged it. "But I myself was forced to. The knife was at my throat."

"And what's going to happen now?" she asked.

"Oh, it's simple enough; a court judgment and then a seizure — and that's it!"

She had to restrain herself from hitting him. Then she asked quietly if there were no way to placate Monsieur Vinçart.

"What! Placate Vinçart! You don't know him. He's fiercer than an Arab."

But Monsieur Lheureux simply had to do something!

"Listen to me," he said, "I think I've been nice enough to you until now." And he opened one of his ledgers: "Look," working up the page with his finger: "Let's see—August 3, 200 francs—June 17, 150, March 23, 46—April—" He stopped as if afraid of committing a blunder. "And I'm not even mentioning the notes signed by your husband, one for seven hundred francs and another for three hundred! As for your little payments on account and the interest, we'll never get through with them, they're so tangled up. I'm not going to involve myself anymore!"

She cried, she even called him "my good Monsieur Lheureux." But he kept referring to that "scoundrel Vinçart." Besides, he didn't have a centime, no one was paying him right now, they were taking the shirt off his back; a poor shopkeeper like him couldn't lend money.

Emma stopped talking, and Lheureux, who was nibbling on the feathers of a quill, seemed worried by her silence because he said: "At least, if one of these days some money came in—I could—"

"Anyhow," she said, "as soon as the balance on Barneville—"

"What?" He seemed very surprised to learn that Langlois had not yet paid. Then, in honeyed tones: "And we can agree, you say—"

"On anything you want!"

Then he closed his eyes to think, jotted down some figures, and asserting that it would be a lot of trouble to him, that it was a tricky business, and that he was "bleeding himself," he wrote out four notes for 250 francs each, one payable every month.

"If Vinçart will only listen to me. Anyway, we're all agreed. I don't play around. I'm as straight as a die!"

Then he casually showed her some new merchandise, though none of it was good enough for her in his opinion.

"When I think that this is dress goods at seven sous a meter, and guaranteed color fast! And they believe it! Of course, you realize I don't tell them what it really is," he said, hoping by this confession of skullduggery toward others to convince her of his honesty toward her.

Then he called her back to show her three lengths of lace he had recently come upon "in a sale."

"So handsome!" said Lheureux. "They use a lot of it now for

antimacassars; it's the style." And more rapidly than a juggler he wrapped the lace in blue paper and placed it in Emma's hands.

"At least tell me how much—"

"Oh, later!" he said, turning quickly away from her.

She began pressing Bovary that very evening to write his mother to send them the entire balance of his inheritance immediately. The mother-in-law answered that she had nothing more; the estate was settled, and except for Barneville, there remained for them an annual income of six hundred francs, which she would forward regularly.

Then Emma sent off bills to two or three patients and before long had frequent recourse to this method, which worked well for her. She was always careful to write as a postscript: "Don't mention this to my husband; you know how proud he is. . . . Please forgive me. . . . Your humble servant." There were a few complaints. She intercepted them.

To make some money she began selling her old gloves, hats, household utensils; and she drove hard bargains, her blood inciting her to gain. Then, during her trips to the city she would pick up trifles that Lheureux would certainly buy from her if no one else did. She bought ostrich feathers, Chinese porcelain, and old chests; she borrowed from Félicité, from Madame Lefrançois, from the landlady of the Croix-Rouge, from everyone, no matter who. With the money she finally received from Barneville, she paid off two notes; the other fifteen hundred francs were frittered away. She signed new notes, and so it went on.

Sometimes she did try to add some figures, but she uncovered such exorbitant sums that she couldn't believe it. So she began again, became quickly confused, stopped working at it, and thought no more about it.

The house was very sad now. The tradesmen left with furious faces. Handkerchiefs were left lying on the stoves; and little Berthe, to Madame Homais's great horror, had holes in her stockings. If Charles timidly made some comment, Emma answered harshly that it wasn't her fault.

Why these fits of rage? He attributed it all to her old nervous ailment and reproached himself for having considered her infirmities as faults. He accused himself of selfishness, felt like running over to her and kissing her.

"I mustn't," he told himself; "I'll irritate her." And so he held back.

After dinner, he would walk alone through the garden, take Berthe on his knees, and unfolding his medical journal, would try to teach her to read. The child, who had never had any schooling, soon opened two large sad eyes and cried. Then he would console her by going off to find water in the sprinkling can to make rivers in the sand; or he would break off branches from the privet hedge to plant trees in the flower beds. They didn't really harm the garden, as it was all clogged up with weeds. They owed Lestiboudois for so many days' work! Later the child would feel cold and ask for her mother.

"Call the maid," Charles would say. "You know, child, that Mama doesn't want to be bothered."

Autumn was already beginning and the leaves were falling, just like two years ago when she was sick! When would all of this end? And he would keep on walking, his hands behind his back.

Emma would stay in her room. No one went up. She would remain there all day long, in a torpor, only half dressed, burning incense that she had bought in Rouen in an Algerian shop. She managed by enough fussing to relegate Charles to the second floor, so that she wouldn't have to sleep next to him. All night long she would read sensational books in which there were orgies and gory situations. Often she would be terrified by a sudden thought and scream. Charles would come running.

"Oh, go away," she would say.

At other times, burning violently from her adulterous passion, panting and shaking, throbbing with desire, she would open her window, breathe in the cold air, let down her heavy mass of hair, and stare at the stars, yearning for the love of a prince. She would think of *him*, of Léon. At that moment she would have given anything for one of those meetings that sated her desires.

Those were her festive days—when they met. She wanted them to be splendid, and when he alone could not pay for them, she freely paid the difference. This happened nearly every time. He tried to make her understand that they would be just as comfortable elsewhere, in a more modest hotel, but she always objected.

One day she pulled from her bag six little silver-gilt spoons (the wedding gift from her father, old Rouault), asking him to go immediately to the pawnbroker's for her. Léon obeyed, even though this business displeased him. He was afraid of compromising himself.

Thinking about it later, he found that his mistress was taking on strange ways. Perhaps the people who wanted him to leave her weren't so wrong.

As a matter of fact, someone had sent his mother a long anonymous letter, warning her that he "was ruining himself with a married woman," and immediately the good lady—visualizing that eternal threat to families, the insidious pernicious creature, the siren, lurking like a fantastic monster in the depths of love—wrote to Monsieur Dubocage, his employer, who behaved splendidly in the circumstances. He talked to Léon for three quarters of an hour, trying to open his eyes for him, to warn him away from the chasm. Such an intrigue would later be harmful to his career. He begged Léon to break it up, and if he wouldn't make this sacrifice for his own sake, at least to do it for him, for Dubocage!

Léon finally swore not to see Emma again, and he reproached himself for not having kept his word when he considered all the trouble and blame this woman could still bring upon him, not to mention the jokes of his fellow clerks as they sat around the stove. Besides, he was going to be head clerk and this was the moment of decision. And so he gave up his flute, his elevated sentiments, and his dreams. Every bourgeois in the heat of his youth has believed himself capable—if only for a single day, a single moment—of tremendous passions and noble exploits. The most mediocre rake has dreamed of sultanas; every notary carries within himself the remains of a poet.

Now he was bored when Emma would suddenly sob on his chest; and his heart, like people who can stand only a certain amount of music, languished with indifference amid the stridency of a love whose subtleties left him cold.

They knew each other too well to feel those mutual revelations of possession that multiply its joys a hundredfold. She was as sated with him as he was tired of her. Emma was finding in adultery all the banalities of marriage.

But how could she break free? Though she felt humiliated by the base quality of such happiness, she clung to it out of habit or depravity. Each day she clung more desperately to it, thus destroying all happiness by demanding too much of it. She blamed Léon for her disappointed hopes as if he had betrayed her, and she even wished for some catastrophe that would cause their separation since she lacked the courage to bring it about herself.

Nevertheless, this did not stop her from continuing to write him loving letters, in line with the idea that a woman should always be writing to her lover.

But even as she wrote she perceived another man, a phantom fabricated from her most ardent memories, her most beautiful literary memories, her strongest desires; and he finally became so real and accessible that she trembled with amazement, yet without being able to visualize him clearly, since he was so hidden, like a god, under his many attributes. He inhabited that enchanted country where silken ladders swing from balconies among flowers, by the light of the moon. She felt him near her; he would come and sweep her away in one kiss. Then she fell back to earth, broken, for her surges of imaginary love tired her more than wild debauches.

She was now living in a state of chronic and complete wretchedness. She would often receive summonses, official documents she barely glanced at. She wished she were dead, or continually asleep.

The day of Mid-Lent she did not return to Yonville, but went to a masked ball in the evening. She wore velvet trousers and red stockings, a wig and a cocked hat over one ear. She danced all night to the wild sound of the trombones. People formed a circle around her, and she found herself in the morning in front of the theater entrance with five or six masked figures dressed like longshoremen and sailors—friends of Léon who were talking about getting something to eat.

The neighboring cafés were full. They found a second-rate restaurant down by the river where the proprietor showed them to a little room on the fifth floor.

The men whispered in one corner, probably discussing the expenses. There were a clerk, two medical students, and a shop assistant. What company for her! As for the women, Emma quickly realized from their voices that almost all of them were from the dregs of society. Then she grew frightened, pushed back her chair, and lowered her eyes.

The others began to eat. She couldn't. Her forehead was on fire, her eyes smarted and she felt an icy coldness on her skin. She could still feel the floor of the ballroom in her head, resounding under the rhythmic beat of a thousand dancing feet. Then the odor of punch mingled with cigar smoke made her dizzy. She fainted, and they carried her to the window.

It was growing light and a large reddish patch showed against the pale sky toward Sainte-Catherine hill. The blue river quivered in the wind. There was no one on the bridges. The streetlights were going out.

Eventually she came to and began thinking of Berthe, who was sleeping somewhere out there, in the maid's room. Then a wagon loaded with long strips of iron passed by, causing a deafening metallic clang against the walls of the houses.

She slipped away abruptly, removed her costume, told Léon that she had to go back, and finally remained alone at the Hotel de Boulogne. She found everything, herself included, unbearable. She yearned to escape like a bird, to go somewhere and recapture her youth, somewhere far off, in the immaculate expanse of space.

She went out, crossed the boulevard, the Place Cauchoise, and the outskirts of the city, and came to an open street overlooking some gardens. She was walking rapidly, the fresh air soothing her; and gradually the faces of the crowd, the masks, the quadrilles, the chandeliers, the supper, and those women she had been with—all disappeared like mist floating off. Then, having returned to the Croix-Rouge, she threw herself on her bed in the little third-floor room where the Tour de Nesle prints hung. Hivert woke her at four in the afternoon.

When she returned home Félicité showed her a gray sheet of paper behind the clock. She read: "By virtue of the seizure, in due and legal execution of the judgment—"

What judgment? As a matter of fact, the day before, they had brought another document, which she had not seen, and so she was stunned by these words: "Ordered on behalf of the King, the law, and the courts to Madame Bovary—"

Then, skipping several lines, she read: "Within twenty-four hours, without fail—"

What?

"To pay the total sum of eight thousand francs."

And lower down, it even said: "She will be constrained thereto by the full power of the law and notably by the seizure of her furniture and effects."

What could she do? In twenty-four hours. That meant tomorrow! Lheureux, she thought, probably wanted to frighten her still more. Now suddenly she understood all his maneuvers, the end goal of all his favors. What reassured her, however, was the very enormity of the sum.

However, by dint of all her buying, and not paying, borrowing, signing promissory notes, then renewing the notes, which swelled each time they fell due, she had finally built up a capital for Monsieur Lheureux, who was impatiently awaiting it to use in his speculations.

She walked into his house as casually as she could. "Do you know what has happened to me? It must be a joke."

"No."

"What do you mean?"

He turned away slowly and said to her, crossing his arms: "Did you think, dear lady, that I was going to be your source of supply and your banker until the end of time, just out of sheer affection? I really have to get my money back; let's be fair!"

She protested the amount.

"That's too bad! The court acknowledged it. There's been a judgment. They've summoned you. Anyway, it's not me, it's Vinçart."

"Can't you do—"

"Nothing at all."

"But—still—let's talk —" And she began stammering: she hadn't known anything—it was a complete surprise—

"Whose fault is it?" Lheureux said, bowing low with irony. "While I work like a slave, you have yourself a good time."

"Don't you preach morality to me!"

"It never hurts," he retorted.

She lost all shame, she implored him; she even placed her lovely long white hand on the merchant's knee.

"Leave me alone! One would think you were trying to seduce me."

"You're a monster!" she cried.

"Oh! How you do go on," he said with a laugh.

"I'll let people know what you are. I'll tell my husband—"

"Is that so? Then I'll show your husband something!" And Lheureux took from the safe a receipt for eighteen hundred francs that she had given him after Vinçart discounted the note.

"Do you think he won't see through your little theft," he said, "that poor, dear man?"

She sank back, more stunned than if she had been hit by a club. He was pacing up and down between the window and the desk, saying: "Ah! I'll show him good and proper—good and proper."

Then he walked over to her and said in a less harsh tone: "It's not pleasant, I know. But after all, no one ever died from it, and since it's the only way left for you to repay me my money—"

"But where will I find the money?" Emma said, wringing her hands.

"Bah! With the friends you have?" And he looked at her in such a knowing and terrible way that her whole being shuddered.

"I promise you," she said. "I'll sign—"

"I've had enough of your signatures!"

"I'll sell—"

"Come now!" he said, shrugging his shoulders. "You have nothing left." And he shouted through the peephole that opened onto the store: "Annette! Don't forget the three remnants of Number 14."

The servant appeared. Emma understood and asked, "How much money would it take to stop the legal action?"

"It's too late!"

"But if I brought you several thousand francs, a fourth of the sum, a third, nearly all?"

"No! It's a waste of time." He pushed her gently toward the staircase.

"I beg of you, Monsieur Lheureux, a few days more." She was sobbing.

"So! Now we have tears!"

"You're making me desperate!"

"As if I care!" he said, slamming the door.

VII

She appeared stoical the next day when Maître Hareng, the bailiff, appeared with two witnesses to draw up the inventory for the seizure.

They began with Bovary's consulting room but omitted the phrenological head, which was considered "a professional instrument";

however, in the kitchen, they counted the plates, pots, chairs, and lamps, and in her room all the articles on the whatnot. They examined her dresses, linen, and dressing room; and her entire existence, even in its most intimate details, was laid out at full length like a corpse being autopsied before the eyes of these three men.

Maître Hareng, buttoned up in a narrow black coat, with a white tie, and wearing tightly fastened bootstraps, kept repeating: "With your permission, Madame? With your permission?"

Often he would exclaim: "Charming! So pretty!" Then he would begin writing again, dipping his pen into the inkwell he held with his left hand.

When they finished with the various rooms they went up to the attic.

She kept a desk there in which Rodolphe's letters were locked. She had to open it.

"Ah! Personal correspondence!" said Maître Hareng with a discreet smile. "May I, please? I must make sure that the box doesn't contain anything else." He tilted the papers slightly, as if to shake out gold pieces. Then she grew indignant, seeing this coarse hand, with fingers reddened and as soft as slugs, touching the pages that had caused her heart to pound.

Finally they left! Félicité came back in. She had sent her to be on the lookout for Bovary, to keep him away; and they quickly installed the bailiff's watchman in the attic, where he promised to stay.

Charles, she thought, looked worried during the evening. Emma kept stealing anguished glances at him, thinking she could see accusations written in the lines on his face. Then, when her eyes fell on the mantelpiece adorned with Chinese screens, on the full curtains, on the armchairs, over all these things that had sweetened the bitterness of her life, she was overcome by remorse, or rather by an immense regret that stimulated passion, instead of suppressing it. Charles kept quietly poking the fire, his two feet on the fender.

At one moment the watchman, probably bored in his hiding place, made a bit of noise.

"Is somebody walking around upstairs?" Charles asked.

"No," she said. "It's an open window rattling in the wind."

The next day, Sunday, she left for Rouen in order to go to all the bankers whose names she knew. Most of them were in the country or away on trips. She was not discouraged, and asked those whom she did meet for money, insisting that she needed it and would repay it. A few laughed in her face; all refused.

At two o'clock she ran to Léon's and knocked on his door. No one came to open. Finally he appeared.

"What brings you here?"

"Am I disturbing you?"

"No—but—" And he said that the landlord did not like him to receive "women."

"I must speak to you," she said. Then he reached for his key but she stopped him. "No, let's go to our place."

And they went to their room at the Hotel de Boulogne.

When they got there she gulped down a large glass of water. She was very pale. "Léon, you'll have to do me a favor," she told him. Then shaking him by his hands, which she squeezed tightly, she added: "Listen, I need eight thousand francs."

"You must be mad!"

"Not yet." Quickly she told him the story of the seizure, revealing her distress to him. Charles was ignorant of the entire matter; her mother-in-law detested her; old Rouault could do nothing; but he, Léon, would have to go out and begin looking for that indispensable sum.

"How do you expect me to—?"

"What a coward you are!" she cried.

Then he said stupidly: "You're exaggerating the trouble. Maybe three thousand francs would calm him down."

All the more reason for trying to do something. It wasn't possible that they couldn't find three thousand francs. Besides, Léon could sign the notes for her. "Go ahead and try! You must! Run! Oh, try, please try! I'll love you so much."

He went out, came back after an hour, and said solemnly: "I went to three people—no use." Then they sat facing each other at the two sides of the fireplace, not moving, not speaking. Emma shrugged her shoulders, tapping her foot. He heard her murmur: "If I were in your place, I'd find the money."

"Where?"

"In your office." She looked intently at him. A criminal boldness was in her flaming eyes and her eyelids narrowed with voluptuous suggestiveness—so much so that the young man felt himself weakening before the mute will of this woman who was suggesting a crime to him. Then he grew afraid, and in order to avoid any explanations, struck his forehead and said: "Morel is due back tonight! He won't refuse me, I hope! (This was one of his friends, the son of a very wealthy businessman.) I'll bring it to you tomorrow," he added.

Emma did not appear to accept this hope of a solution with as much joy as he had thought. Did she suspect his lie? He continued, blushing: "But if you don't see me at three o'clock, don't wait for me anymore, darling. I must go. Forgive me. Good-bye!"

He pressed her hand but it felt completely lifeless. Emma no longer had the strength for any emotion.

Four o'clock struck and she arose to return to Yonville, obeying her habit pattern like an automaton.

It was a lovely day, one of those clear, sharp March days when the sun gleams in an all-white sky. Dressed in their Sunday best, the people of Rouen were walking along happily. She reached the Place du Parvis. Vespers had just ended; the crowd poured through the three portals like a river through the three arches of a bridge, and in the middle, motionless as a rock, stood the verger.

Then she remembered that day when, tremulous and filled with hope, she had entered under that tall nave that stretched out before her—yet not as lofty as her love; and she continued to walk, sobbing under her veil, dazed, stumbling, almost fainting.

"Look out!" shouted a voice as a carriage gate opened.

She stopped to let pass a black horse, prancing in the shafts of a tilbury being driven by a gentleman in a sable coat. Who was it? She knew him. The carriage rushed forward and disappeared.

It was he—the viscount! She turned around but the street was deserted. And she felt so overwhelmed and sad that she leaned against a wall in order not to fall.

Then she thought that she might have been mistaken. Besides, she wasn't sure of anything anymore. Everything, within her and without, was abandoning her. She felt herself lost, rolling beyond control in bottomless abysses; and it was almost with joy that she caught sight of good old Homais when she reached the Croix-Rouge. He was watching a large box filled with pharmaceuticals being loaded on the Hirondelle; in a handkerchief in his hand he carried six *cheminots* for his wife.

Madame Homais loved these heavy little rolls, shaped like turbans, which are eaten during Lent with salted butter—last remnants of medieval food, dating back to the century of the Crusades, on which the robust Normans of old gorged themselves, imagining they saw Saracen heads waiting to be devoured, by the light of the yellow torches between tankards of mead and huge joints of meat.

The apothecary's wife crunched them as they had done, heroically, despite the terrible condition of her teeth; and so every time that Homais went into the city he did not fail to bring some back for her. He always bought them from the large bakery on the Rue Massacre.

"Delighted to see you," he said, offering Emma his arm to help her into the Hirondelle. Then he hung the *cheminots* on the netting of the baggage rack and sat with his head uncovered and arms crossed in a pensive, Napoleonic pose.

But when the blind man, as usual, appeared at the foot of the hill, he exclaimed: "I don't understand why the authorities tolerate such goings-on! They ought to shut these unfortunates up and force them to work. My word, progress moves at a snail's pace. We are wallowing in sheer barbarism."

The blind man held out his hat, which flopped about at the window like a loose piece of upholstery.

"There, you see," said the pharmacist, "a scrofulous infection." And despite the fact that he knew the poor devil, he pretended to be seeing him for the first time, murmuring the terms, "cornea," "opaque cornea," "sclerotic," "facies," and then asking him in a paternal tone: "Have you had this dreadful infirmity a long time, my friend? Instead of getting drunk in the tavern, you'd be better off on a special diet." He advised him to take good wine, good beer, good roasts. The blind man continued to sing. In fact, he seemed to be almost an idiot. Finally Homais opened his purse.

"Here's a sou for you; take half and give me back my change. And don't forget my advice, you'll be better for it."

Hivert allowed himself to express some doubt about Homais's advice. But the apothecary was absolutely certain that he could cure the blind fellow with an antiphlogistic salve of his own making, and he gave his address: "Monsieur Homais, near the marketplace, known by all."

"Now then," said Hivert, "for all this trouble, you show us your act."

The blind man squatted down on his haunches, threw back his head, rolling his glaucoma-affected eyes, stuck out his tongue, and rubbed his stomach with both hands as he emitted a kind of low howl, like a starving dog.

Emma, filled with disgust, threw him a five-franc piece over her shoulder. It represented her entire fortune. She thought it a beautiful gesture to squander it like this.

The carriage had started off again when Homais suddenly leaned out the window and shouted: "No farinaceous foods or dairy products! Wear wool against the skin and expose the diseased portions to the fumes of juniper berries."

The familiar objects unfurling before her eyes distracted Emma gradually from her present misery. She was overcome by a heavy fatigue and arrived home numbed, discouraged, almost asleep.

"What will come will come!" she told herself. After all, who could tell? Why shouldn't some extraordinary event occur at any moment? Lheureux might even die.

At nine in the morning she was awakened by a noise of voices in the square. There was a crowd gathered in the marketplace to read a large notice attached to one of the posts, and she saw Justin climbing onto a stone and ripping it down. Just then the village policeman grabbed him by the collar. Monsieur Homais left the pharmacy and Madame Lefrançois seemed to be making a speech in the midst of the crowd.

"Madame! Madame!" Félicité cried as she rushed in. "It's terrible!" And in her distress the poor girl held out to her a yellow piece of paper that she had just torn from the door. Emma read at a glance that all her household furnishings were to be sold.

Then they looked at each other in silence. Servant and mistress had no secrets from each other. Finally Félicité sighed: "If I were you, Madame, I'd go see Monsieur Guillaumin."

"You think so?"

And this question meant: "You who know the Guillaumins via their manservant; do you know if the master has occasionally mentioned me?"

"Yes, do go. You'll be doing the right thing."

She dressed, put on her black dress and the bonnet with jet beads; and in order not to be seen (there was still a crowd of people in the square), she took the back road near the river, beyond the village.

She reached the notary's gate quite out of breath. The sky was dark and there was a light snow falling.

At the sound of the bell, Theodore, in a red vest, appeared on the porch; he let her in almost familiarly, as if he knew her well, and showed her into the dining room.

A large porcelain stove was humming beneath a cactus plant that filled the alcove. Framed in black wood, against the oak-grained wallpaper, were Steuben's "Esmeralda" and Schopin's "Potiphar."

Everything glistened with spotless English cleanliness, the table already set, the silver dishwarmers, the crystal doorknobs, the floor, and the furniture. The windows were decorated in each corner with colored glass.

"This is the kind of dining room I would like," Emma thought.

The notary entered, pressing his left arm tightly to his chest against his dressing gown embroidered with palm designs, while with the other hand he lifted and quickly replaced his chestnut-colored velvet skullcap. He kept it jauntily tilted to the right side. The ends of three blond tufts of hair, combed up from the back around his bald pate, dangled down.

He offered her a seat and sat down to his breakfast, apologizing profusely for his impoliteness.

"Monsieur," she said, "I would ask of you—"

"What, Madame? I'm listening."

She began to relate her predicament.

Maître Guillaumin knew all about it. He was secretly in league with the dry-goods merchant, from whom he always got capital for the loans on mortgages that he was asked to arrange. Therefore he knew (and better than she) the long history of these notes, small at first, which had had various endorsers, had been spaced out over long periods, and had been continually renewed until the day when, gathering together all the protests for nonpayment, the merchant had asked his friend Vinçart to institute the necessary proceedings in his own name since he did not want to appear a bloodsucker before his fellow townspeople.

She kept interrupting her tale with recriminations against Lheureux, recriminations to which the notary replied from time to time with some perfunctory remark. Eating his chop and drinking his tea, he buried his chin in his sky-blue cravat, secured by two diamond pins linked by a gold chain, and smiled strangely—a smile in which there were elements of unction and ambiguity. But noticing that her feet were damp, he said: "Come closer to the stove. Put your feet up higher, against the porcelain."

But she was afraid she would dirty it. The notary replied gallantly: "Beautiful things never do harm."

Then she tried to arouse his emotions, and became aroused herself. She told him of the lack of funds in her home, her difficulties, her needs. He could understand that: such an elegant lady! He had managed to turn toward her completely without ceasing to eat, and his knee rubbed against her shoe, the sole of which was curling up a little from the smoke of the stove.

But when she asked him for three thousand francs, he pursed his lips. Then he declared that he regretted very much not having been able to take charge of her fortune earlier, for there were a hundred easy ways, even for a lady, to earn a profit on her money. They could have made some excellent speculations, with almost no risk, either in the Grumesnil peatbogs or Le Havre building sites. And he let her eat her heart out with rage at the thought of the fantastic sums she would certainly have made.

"Why didn't you come to me?" he said.

"I just don't know."

"But why? Did I frighten you? It's I, on the contrary, who ought to pity myself. We hardly know each other! And yet I'm very devoted to you. You no longer doubt it, I hope?"

He stretched out his hand, took hold of hers, and covered it with a greedy kiss, then kept it on his knee. He played gently with her fingers, while paying her all sorts of compliments.

His monotonous voice droned on like a flowing brook. His eyes gleamed through his glasses and his hands were moving up into Emma's sleeves, caressing her arm. She felt a panting breath against her cheek. This man was repulsive to her.

She leaped up and said: "Monsieur, I am waiting!"

"For what?" asked the notary, who suddenly became very pale.

"The money."

"But—"

Then he gave in to the explosion of an irresistible desire: "Very well, yes!"

He was crawling on his knees to her, with no concern for his dressing gown: "Stay, please. I love you!" He grasped her around the waist.

Madame Bovary's face immediately flushed red. She recoiled with a terrible look on her face, exclaiming: "You're brazenly taking advantage of my distress, Monsieur! I am to be pitied, but I'm not for sale!"

And she went out.

The notary remained there, stunned, his eyes fixed on his handsome embroidered slippers. They were a gift from a mistress, and the sight of them finally consoled him. Besides, he felt that such an adventure might have involved him too deeply.

"What a monster! What an unspeakable cad!" she said to herself, running nervously beneath the aspens that lined the road. Disappointment at her lack of success intensified her indignation about her outraged honor. She felt that Providence was determined to hound her, and the thought strengthened her pride. Never had she had so much respect for herself or so much scorn for others. A kind of warlike emotion was transporting her. She wanted to fight all men, spit in their faces, crush them all; and she continued to walk rapidly, pale, trembling, and furious, scanning the empty horizon with tear-filled eyes and almost relishing the hatred that was stifling her.

At the sight of her house she suddenly felt paralyzed. She could not go forward, but she had to. Besides, where could she flee?

Félicité was waiting for her at the door.

"Well?"

"No!" Emma said. And for a quarter of an hour they went over the different people in Yonville who might be able to help her. But each time Félicité mentioned someone, Emma would reply: "Impossible! They wouldn't want to."

"But the doctor will be home soon."

"I know. Leave me alone now."

She had tried everything. Now there was nothing more to do. So when Charles appeared she was going to tell him: "Don't come in. That rug you're walking on is no longer ours. You don't have one piece of furniture left in your house, not a pin or a piece of straw— and I'm the one who's ruined you, poor man."

Then she would give one great sob, he would cry profusely, and finally, when he recovered from the shock, he would forgive her.

"Yes," she muttered, grinding her teeth. "He'll forgive me. Even if he offered me a million, I wouldn't forgive him for having known me. Never! Never!"

The thought of Bovary's having something over her enraged her. For whether she confessed or not, in a little while, today or tomorrow, he would get to know all about the catastrophe, and she had to look forward to that horrible scene and endure the weight of his magnanimity. A sudden impulse urged her to return to Lheureux. What for? Write to her father? It was too late. Perhaps she was sorry now for not having yielded to the notary—when she heard the sound of a horse trotting up the lane. It was he. He opened the gate. His face was whiter than the plaster on the wall. Running down the staircase, she quickly escaped across the square; and the mayor's wife, talking with Lestiboudois in front of the church, saw her enter the tax collector's house.

She ran to tell Madame Caron. The two ladies climbed up to the attic, and hidden by the laundry stretched out over the line, they posted themselves in a convenient spot from which they could see everything going on in Binet's house.

He was alone in his garret, making a wooden replica of one of those indescribable ivories that consist of crescents and spheres carved one inside the other, the whole straight as an obelisk and quite useless. He was just beginning to work on the last piece. The end was in sight!

In the dim light of the studio the white dust flew off from his tool like a shower of sparks beneath the hooves of a galloping horse. The two wheels turned and whirred. Binet was smiling, chin down, nostrils dilated; he seemed absorbed in one of those states of total happiness that come only with humble occupations—amusing the intelligence by easy difficulties and satisfying it with a complete sense of ultimate achievement.

"Ah! There she is!" said Madame Tuvache. But it was barely possible to hear what she was saying because of the lathe.

Finally the ladies thought they could make out the word "francs," and Madame Tuvache whispered quite low: "She's begging for more time to pay her taxes."

"Apparently!" said the other.

They saw her walking back and forth, examining the napkin rings on the wall, the candlesticks, the bannister knobs, while Binet stroked his chin with satisfaction.

"Do you suppose she's gone there to order something from him?" asked Madame Tuvache.

"But his things aren't for sale!" her neighbor objected.

The tax collector seemed to be listening. He was opening his eyes wide as if he didn't understand. She kept on in a gentle, pleading manner. She drew closer. Her breast was heaving. They stopped talking.

"Is she making advances to him?" said Madame Tuvache.

Binet was blushing to the tips of his ears. She took his hands.

"Oh, this is just too much!" She was probably making some outrageous proposal to him, for the tax collector—he was a brave man, had fought at Bautzen and Lutzen and the campaigns of France and had even been recommended for the Legion of Honor—suddenly drew back quite far as if he had caught sight of a snake and shouted: "Madame, what's got into you?"

"They ought to whip women like that!" said Madame Tuvache.

"Where is she?" said Madame Caron. For she had disappeared during his words. Then they saw her flying along the Grand Rue and turning to the right as if heading for the cemetery, and they lost themselves in all sorts of conjectures.

• • •

"Madame Rollet," she said, arriving at the wet nurse's home, "I'm choking! Unlace me!"

She fell on the bed and sobbed. Madame Rollet covered her with a petticoat and stood near her. Then, since Emma didn't speak the other woman moved away, sat down at her wheel, and began to spin flax.

"Stop it, please!" she murmured, thinking she was hearing Binet's lathe.

"What's the matter with her?" wondered the nurse. "Why did she come here?"

She had run there impelled by a sort of terror that drove her from home.

Lying motionless on her back, her eyes in a fixed stare, she could only vaguely discern the objects, even though she was trying to concentrate with a kind of idiot persistence. She focused her eyes on the peeling plaster on the wall, on two sticks smoking in the fire end to end, and on a large spider climbing above her head in a crack of the rafter. She finally collected her thoughts. She remembered— One day, with Léon— Oh, how far off it was! The sun was shining over the water and the clematis scenting the air. Then, carried off by her memories as if by a raging torrent, she soon remembered the previous day.

"What time is it?" she asked.

Madame Rollet walked outside, lifted the fingers of her right hand toward the brightest part of the sky, and walked back in slowly, saying: "Almost three o'clock."

"Oh, thank you! Thank you!"

He was going to come. She was sure of it! He would find the money. But he might go down there, to her house, not knowing that she was here; so she asked the nurse to run to her home and bring him back.

"Hurry!"

"I'm going, dear lady, I'm going!"

She was amazed now that she had not thought of him immediately. He had given his word yesterday, and he would not fail. She saw herself at Lheureux's already, spreading out on his desk the three bank notes. Then she would have to invent a story to explain things to Bovary. But what?

It seemed to be taking the nurse a very long while to return. But since there was no clock in the cottage Emma feared she might be exaggerating the time elapsed. She began to walk in the garden with measured steps, went down the path along the hedge, and came back quickly, hoping that the nurse would have come back by another road. Finally, tired of waiting, tortured by suspicions that she kept trying to repress, not knowing any longer whether she had been there for a century or a moment, she sat down in a corner, closed her eyes, and covered her ears with her hands. The gate squeaked. She leaped up. Before she spoke, Madame Rollet said to her: "There's no one in your house!"

"What?"

"No one! And your husband's crying. He's calling you. They're looking for you."

Emma did not answer. She was panting heavily and rolling her eyes around, while the peasant woman, frightened at the expression on her face, drew back instinctively, thinking her mad. Suddenly she struck her forehead and uttered a cry, for the thought of Rodolphe, like a great lightning flash in a dark night, had just passed through her soul. He was so good, so sensitive, so generous! And besides, if he hesitated to render her this service, she knew very well how to force him to do it, by reminding him with one flick of an eyelash of their lost love. And so she went off toward La Huchette, without realizing that she was running to offer herself—the very thing that had so outraged her a little while ago—and quite unaware that she was prostituting herself.

VIII

As she walked along, she asked herself: "What am I going to say? Where shall I begin?" And as she came closer, she recognized the bushes, the trees, the furze on the hill, and the château below. She was reliving the sensations of her first tenderness, and her poor constricted heart was expanding with the memory of love. A warm breeze played over her face. The melting snow was falling drop by drop from the young buds onto the grass.

As in the old days she walked in through the little park gate, then reached the courtyard that was lined by a double row of thickset linden trees. Their long branches rustled as they swayed. The dogs in the kennel barked, and though the sounds of their yapping echoed, no one appeared in sight.

She climbed the straight, wide staircase with its wooden banisters. It led to the corridor paved with dusty flagstones onto which several rooms in a row opened, as in a monastery or an inn. His was at the far end, on the left. When she finally placed her fingers on the latch, her strength suddenly left her. She was afraid he wouldn't be there, almost hoped he wouldn't be—and yet he was her only hope, her last chance for salvation. She held back a minute; then, mustering up her courage at the thought of the present necessity, she went in.

He was seated before the fire, his feet on the fender, smoking a pipe.

"You!" he said, jumping up.

"Yes, it's me. I came—to ask your advice, Rodolphe."

Despite her efforts to talk, it was impossible for her to go on.

"You haven't changed. You're as charming as ever."

"Oh," she replied with bitterness, "they must be dreary charms, my friend, since you were able to spurn them."

Then he launched into an explanation of his conduct, apologizing in vague terms, for lack of any better excuses.

She allowed herself to be taken in by his words, even more by his voice and his physical presence, so much so that she pretended to believe, or perhaps even did believe, in the excuse he gave for their rupture. He claimed it was a secret on which depended the honor and perhaps even the life of a third person.

"It doesn't really matter," she said, looking at him sadly. "I suffered enough."

He answered philosophically: "That's the way life is."

"Has it at least been good to you since our separation?" Emma asked.

"Neither good nor bad."

"It might have been better had we never separated."

"Yes—maybe."

"Do you really think so?" she said, drawing closer. And she sighed: "Oh, Rodolphe, if you only knew! I loved you so!"

Then she took his hand and they remained for a while with their fingers intertwined, like that first day at the Agricultural Show. Out of pride, he fought against any display of tenderness. But nestling against his chest, she said: "How did you expect me to live without you? One can't learn to do without happiness. I was desperate. I thought I would die. I'll tell you all about it. And you—you kept avoiding me."

It was true. For three years he had carefully avoided her, out of that natural cowardice that characterizes the stronger sex. Emma went on speaking, with coquettish movements of her head, as coaxing as an amorous kitten: "You love other women, admit it. Oh, I can understand them. I can. I forgive them. You seduced them as you seduced me. You're a man. You have all you need to make yourself loved. But we'll begin all over again, won't we? We'll love each other. See, I'm laughing. I'm happy! Say something!"

She was adorable to watch, with that expression in which a tear trembled, like a raindrop in a blue flower cup.

He pulled her onto his lap. With the back of his hand he caressed her smooth hair on which, in the twilight glow, there shimmered one last ray of sunlight like a golden arrow. She bent her head. He finally kissed her gently on her eyelids, with the tips of his lips: "But you've been crying?" he said. "Why?"

She burst into sobs. Rodolphe thought that it was the explosive violence of her love. As she said nothing, he took her silence to be a last show of modesty. Then he exclaimed: "Forgive me! You're the only one I care for. I was a fool and a monster! I love you, I'll always love you. What's wrong? Tell me."

He knelt down.

"All right, then— I'm ruined, Rodolphe. You've got to lend me three thousand francs."

"But—but—" he said, rising slowly, while his face took on a somber expression.

"You know," she went on quickly, "that my husband placed his entire fortune with a notary. Well, he's run off. We had to borrow money. The patients haven't paid. And the estate isn't settled yet. We'll have money later. But today, just for three thousand francs, we're going to be dispossessed. Right now, at this very moment. And I came here counting on your friendship."

"Ah," thought Rodolphe, who suddenly became very pale, "so that's why she came!"

Finally he said, very calmly: "Dear lady, I don't have it."

He was not lying. Had he had the money, he probably would have given it to her, even though as a rule he disliked doing such bighearted things. A demand for money, of all the winds blowing down on love, was the coldest and the most uprooting.

She stared at him for a few minutes.

"You don't have it!" She repeated several times: "You don't have it! I should have spared myself this last humiliation. You never loved me! You're no better than the others!" She was betraying herself, losing control over her words.

Rodolphe interrupted her, insisting that he himself was "hard up for cash."

"How I pity you!" Emma said. "Yes, I pity you very much!" She happened to glance at a damascened rifle gleaming in the gun rack, and said: "But when you're so poor, you don't put silver on the stocks of your guns. You don't buy clocks inlaid with tortoiseshell"—she continued, pointing to the Boulle clock—"or silver-gilt whistles for your whips"—she touched them—"or charms for your watch chains. Oh, you have everything, even a liquor stand in your room. How you love yourself. You live well. You have a château, farms, a forest. You ride to hounds, travel to Paris—Why, these alone," she cried, taking his cuff links from the mantelpiece, "the smallest of these knickknacks you could turn into money. But you can keep them, I don't want them!"

She threw the cuff links away so violently that their golden chain broke when it hit the wall.

"But I, I would have given you everything, sold everything; I would have worked with my hands, begged along the highways, for one smile, one look, just to hear you say 'Thank you.' And you sit there relaxed in your armchair, as if you haven't made me suffer enough already! Without you, do you know, I would have been able to live happily. What made you do it? Was it a bet? But you did love me. You said so—and again just now— You'd have done better to drive me away. My hands are still warm from your kisses. And here on the rug is the spot where you swore on your knees you would love me forever. You made me believe it. For two years you led me through the most magnificent, the sweetest dream. And our plans for a trip—do you remember them? And your letter, that letter! It broke my heart. And when I come back to him, to this man who is rich, happy, free—when I beg him for help that any stranger would give, pleading and reminding him of all my love, he refuses me, because it would cost him three thousand francs!"

"I don't have it," Rodolphe replied with that perfect calm that masks anger as if with a shield.

She left. The walls were trembling, the ceiling seemed to be crushing her. She walked down the long path, stumbling against the piles of dead leaves scattering in the wind. Finally she reached the ditch near the gate. She broke her nails against the latch, so eager was she to open it. A hundred yards beyond, she stopped, out of breath and nearly falling. And then, turning around, she took one last look at the impassive château, with its park and gardens, its three courtyards, and all the windows of its facade.

She stood there in a daze, conscious of herself only because of the beating of her pulse. She thought she could hear it escaping and merging with a deafening music filling the countryside. The ground beneath her feet was more yielding than water, and the furrows looked to her like immense dark waves breaking. All the memories and thoughts in her head rushed out in a single motion like the thousand bits of a fireworks display. She saw her father, Lheureux's office, their room in the Rouen hotel, a different landscape. Madness seized her. She took fright and managed to take hold of herself, but still in a state of confusion. She no longer remembered the cause of her dreadful state—the matter of money. She was suffering only from love, and felt that her soul was draining away at the thought of it—like the mortally wounded, who in their agony feel their lives ebbing away through the bleeding wound.

Night was falling. The crows were overhead.

Suddenly she felt as if the air were filled with balls of fire, bursting like bullets through the air, spinning around and around and flattening out as they melted in the snow among the tree branches. In the center of each one of them, Rodolphe's face appeared. They multiplied, crowded together, seemed to penetrate her. Then everything disappeared. She recognized the lights of houses, shining from afar through the mist.

She happened to glance at a damascened rifle gleaming in the gun rack . . .

Her troubles loomed before her like an abyss. She was panting as if her lungs would burst. Then, in a transport of heroism that made her almost joyful, she ran down the hill, crossed the cow plank, went past the path and the lane, reached the marketplace, and finally, came to the pharmacist's shop.

No one was there. She was about to enter but feared they might come at the sound of the bell. So she slipped through the gate, holding her breath and groping at the walls. She got as far as the entrance to the kitchen, where there was a candle burning on the stove. Justin, in shirt sleeves, was carrying out a platter.

"Ah, they're eating. I'll have to wait."

He came back. She rapped on the window. He came out.

"The key! The key for upstairs, where the—"

"What?" He looked at her, aghast at the pallor of her face, which stood out white against the blackness of the night. She seemed extraordinarily beautiful to him, with a ghostly majesty. Without understanding what she wanted, he had a premonition of something terrible.

But she quickly continued in a low voice, gentle and melting, "I want it. Give it to me!" Through the thin wall they could hear the rattle of forks on the plates in the dining room.

She pretended she had to kill some rats that were keeping her from falling asleep.

"I'll have to ask Monsieur."

"No! Stay here." Then, very casually, "Oh, don't bother. I'll tell him later. Come along. You can light the way for me."

She walked into the hall that led to the door of the laboratory. Hanging on the wall was a key marked "Capharnaum."

"Justin!" shouted the apothecary, who was becoming impatient.

"Let's go up!"

He followed her.

The key turned in the lock and she went straight to the third shelf—so well did her memory guide her—seized the blue jar, pulled out the stopper, plunged her hand in, and pulled it out filled with a white powder that she began to stuff into her mouth.

"Stop!" he shouted, hurling himself at her.

"Quiet! They'll hear us."

He was in despair and wanted to call for help.

"Don't say a word; your master will be blamed!"

Then she went back home, suddenly relieved and almost as serene as if she had done her duty.

When Charles, shocked by the news of the dispossession, came home, Emma had just left. He shouted, wept, fainted, but she did not come back. Where could she be? He sent Félicité to Homais, to Tuvache, Lheureux, to the Golden Lion, everywhere. In the calmer moments of his anguish he saw his reputation ruined, their fortune lost, Berthe's future shattered. Why? Not a word! He waited until six in the evening. Finally, unable to stand it any longer and imagining that she had left for Rouen, he went off on the highway for about a mile, found no one, waited a bit longer, then came back.

She had returned.

"What happened? Why? Tell me."

She sat down at her desk and wrote a letter that she slowly sealed, adding the date and the hour. Then she said solemnly: "You will read this tomorrow; from now until then, I beg you not to ask me a single question. No, not even one."

"But—"

"Oh, leave me alone!" And she stretched out on her bed.

A bitter taste in her mouth awoke her. She caught sight of Charles and closed her eyes again.

She was studying herself attentively to see if she was suffering. No, nothing yet. She heard the clock ticking, the flames crackling, and Charles breathing as he stood near her bed.

"It's really quite simple to die," she thought. "I'll fall asleep and it will all be over."

She drank some water and turned toward the wall. The loathesome taste of ink continued.

"I'm thirsty, so thirsty!" she sighed.

"What's the matter with you?" asked Charles, holding out a glass.

"Nothing! Open the window, I'm stifling." And she was seized by such a sudden attack of nausea that she barely had time to pull her handkerchief from under the pillow.

"Take it away!" she said quickly. "Throw it out!"

He questioned her. She didn't answer. She kept herself from moving, fearing that the slightest emotion would make her vomit. Then she felt a glacial chill creep up from her feet to her heart.

"Ah, it's beginning now," she murmured.

"What did you say?"

She twisted her head slowly, with anguish, continually opening her mouth as if she had something very heavy on her tongue. The vomiting started again at eight o'clock.

Charles noticed some sort of gritty white sediment clinging to the bottom of the basin.

"How strange," he said, "how very odd."

But she said in a loud voice: "No, you're wrong."

Then gently, almost caressingly, he passed his hand over her stomach. She let out a piercing cry. He drew back in terror.

Then she began to moan, at first feebly. Her shoulders heaved in a mighty shudder and she became paler than the sheet into which her taut fingers were digging. Her irregular pulse was almost imperceptible now.

Drops of sweat stood out on her face. It was bluish now and rigid, as if from the exhalation of some metallic vapor. Her teeth were chattering, her enlarged eyes roamed around vaguely, and she replied to all questions only by nodding her head. She even smiled two or three times. Then the groans grew louder. A muffled scream broke from her. She insisted she was feeling better and would soon get up. But convulsions seized her. She shouted out: "Oh, my God, it's horrible!"

He threw himself on his knees beside the bed.

"Tell me! What did you eat? Answer me for the love of God!" And he looked at her with a tenderness in his eyes such as she had never known.

"All right—there—over there," she said in a faltering voice.

He ran to the desk, broke the seal, and read out loud: "No one is guilty—" He stopped, passed his hands across his eyes, and read it again.

"What! Help! Help!" He was only able to repeat the word "Poisoned! Poisoned!" Félicité ran to Homais, who shouted it out as he crossed the square; Madame Lefrançois heard it at the Golden Lion; a few people rose from bed to tell it to their neighbors. No one in the village slept that night.

Dazed and mumbling, barely able to stand, Charles wandered around the room. He stumbled against the furniture and tore at his hair. The pharmacist had never thought he would see such a pathetic sight.

He went back home to write to Monsieur Canivet and Doctor Larivière. He couldn't concentrate and made more than fifteen drafts. Hippolyte left for Neufchâtel, and Justin spurred Bovary's horse so hard he was forced to leave it, foundered and all but dead, on the Bois-Guillaume hill.

Charles tried to leaf through his medical dictionary, but the lines danced so that he couldn't read them.

"Stay calm," said the apothecary. "We have only to administer a powerful antidote. What was the poison?"

Charles showed him the letter. It was arsenic.

"Well then," said Homais, "we'll have to make an analysis."

He knew that analyses were always necessary in cases of poisoning; and Charles, who did not understand, answered: "Do it, do it. Save her!"

He returned to her side, sank down on the rug, and remained sobbing with his head against the edge of the bed.

"Don't cry," she said. "Soon I won't torment you any longer."

"Why? What made you do it?"

"I had to, my dear," she answered.

"Weren't you happy? Is it my fault? But I did everything I could."

"Yes, I know. You're very good." And she caressed his hair slowly. The sweetness of this sensation was the last straw: he felt his whole being crumble in despair at the thought that he was going to lose her just now when she was showing more love for him than ever before. He could think of nothing to do. He did not know, did not dare—the urgent need for an immediate solution left him in utter confusion.

Now she was through, she thought, with treachery, baseness, and the endless desires that had ravaged her. She hated no one now; a twilight confusion was descending over her thoughts, and of all the sounds on earth, Emma could hear only the intermittent lament of this poor soul at her side, gentle and indistinct, like the last echo of a symphony dying away in the distance.

"Bring me the child," she said, raising herself on her elbow.

"You aren't feeling worse, are you?" asked Charles.

"No, no!"

The child was carried in by the maid. She wore a long nightdress from which her bare feet peeped out. She was solemn and still partially asleep. She stared with surprise at the sight of the disordered room and blinked her eyes, dazzled by the candles burning on the furniture. They probably reminded her of the mornings of New Year's Day or of Mid-Lent, when she was thus awakened early by the light of candles to come to her mother's bed to receive her presents, for she began to ask: "Where is it, Mama?" And when no one spoke: "But I don't see my little stocking."

Félicité held her over the bed while she continued to look toward the fireplace. "Did Nanny Rollet take it?" she asked.

At the mention of this name, which brought back to her the memory of her adulteries and miseries, Madame Bovary turned her head away as if in disgust at a poison even stronger than the one mounting into her mouth. Berthe remained on the bed. "Oh, Mama, your eyes are so big! And you're so pale. You're sweating."

Her mother looked at her.

"I'm afraid!" said the child, pulling back.

Emma took her hand to kiss it, but she struggled.

"Enough! Take her away!" said Charles, who was sobbing in the alcove.

The symptoms stopped for a moment. She seemed less agitated and at each insignificant word, at each more relaxed breath she took, he regained hope. When Canivet finally came in, he threw himself into his arms, crying: "Ah, it's you! Thank you. You're so kind. But she's getting better. See, look at her."

His colleague did not share his opinion at all, and without as he put it, beating around the bush, he prescribed an emetic in order to empty her stomach completely.

She soon began vomiting blood. Her lips pressed tighter together. Her limbs were tensed, her body was covered with brown patches, and her pulse quivered under the fingers like a taut thread, like a harpstring about to break.

Then she began to scream horribly. She cursed the poison, damned it, begged it to work faster, and pushed away with her stiffened arms everything that Charles, in greater agony than she, kept trying to get her to drink. He stood with his handkerchief to his lips and a hoarse rattle in his throat, crying, choked by sobs that shook his entire body. Félicité was running all over the room; Homais stood still, heaving great sighs, and Monsieur Canivet, although still maintaining his composure, was beginning to be worried.

"Damn it all! Yet she's been purged, and from the moment that the cause ceases—"

"The effect should cease," said Homais. "It's obvious."

"Save her!" cried Bovary.

Paying no attention to the pharmacist, who was venturing the hypothesis that "It might be a salutary paroxysm," Canivet was about to administer an antidote of theriaca when they heard the crack of a whip. All the windows rattled and a stagecoach drawn at full speed by three horses, mud spattered to the ears, came hurtling around the corner of the marketplace. It was Doctor Larivière.

The sudden appearance of a god would not have caused more excitement. Bovary lifted up both his hands, Canivet stopped short, and Homais pulled off his cap well in advance of the doctor's entrance.

He belonged to the great surgical school founded by Bichat, to that generation, now gone, of philosopher-practitioners who cherished their art with a fanatic love and exercised it with zeal and wisdom. When his anger was roused everyone in his hospital trembled, and his students revered him so deeply that they tried to imitate him as much as possible as soon as they began their own practice. So in every town for miles around there were replicas of his long merino overcoat and his full black frock coat, whose unbuttoned cuffs slightly covered his fleshy hands, handsome hands that were never gloved, as if to be the readier to plunge into misery. Disdaining honors, titles, and academies, hospitable and generous, like a father to the poor, practicing virtue without believing in it, he would almost have been taken for a saint had not the keen quality of his mind made him feared as a devil. His glance, more piercing than a scalpel, penetrated straight into your soul, cutting through every excuse and prudery to the underlying lie. And so he went his way, filled with that quiet majesty that comes of the consciousness of a great talent, of a fortune, and of forty years of hard work and irreproachable private life.

He frowned the moment he entered the room and saw Emma's cadaverous face as she lay stretched out on her back with her mouth open. While appearing to listen to Canivet, he passed his forefinger under his nose and kept saying: "Yes, yes."

But he shrugged his shoulders slowly. Bovary noticed it. They stared at each other, and this man, accustomed as he was to the sight of unhappiness, could not restrain a tear that dropped onto his shirtfront.

He tried to lead Canivet into the next room. Charles followed.

"She's very bad, isn't she? What about a mustard plaster? Anything! Just find something. You've saved so many others!"

Charles placed his two arms around him. There was a look of terrified supplication in his eyes, as he almost collapsed on his chest.

"Be brave, my poor boy! There's nothing more to be done." And Doctor Larivière turned away.

"Are you leaving?"

"I'll be back." He went out as if to give an order to the coachman. Doctor Canivet followed. He too did not care to see Emma die under his care.

The pharmacist joined them in the square. He was temperamentally unable to keep away from famous people. So he invited Doctor Larivière to do him the signal honor of having lunch with him.

They immediately sent to the Golden Lion for pigeons, to the butcher for all the chops he had, to Tuvache for cream, and to Lestiboudois for eggs. The apothecary himself helped in the preparations, while Madame Homais, pulling at the strings of her bodice, said: "You'll excuse us, sir, in our poor village, without a day's warning—"

"The wineglasses!" whispered Homais.

"At least in the city we could have served stuffed pigs' feet."

"Be quiet! Shall we sit down, doctor?"

After the first few mouthfuls, he deemed it appropriate to furnish some details about the catastrophe: "We had a dryness of the pharynx at first, then unbearable pains in the epigastrium, excessive vomiting, and coma."

"How did she poison herself?"

"I have no idea, doctor. I don't even know where she could have obtained the arsenious acid."

At that moment Justin, who was carrying in a pile of dishes, began trembling.

"What's the matter with you?" asked the pharmacist.

At this question the boy dropped everything to the floor, making a loud crash.

"Imbecile!" shouted Homais. "Clumsy fool! Blockhead! Jackass!"

But he quickly regained control of himself and said: "I wanted to do an analysis, doctor, and *primo*, I carefully introduced into a tube—"

"It would have been better," said the surgeon, "had you introduced your fingers into her throat."

Doctor Canivet said nothing. He had just received a severe scolding in private about his emetic; consequently poor Canivet, who had been so arrogant and talkative about Hippolyte's clubfoot, sat very quietly today, a fixed smile of approval on his lips.

Homais was blossoming out with pride at being a host. The painful thought of Bovary somehow added to his pleasure by a selfish contrast with his own lot. Moreover, the presence of the doctor enraptured him. He displayed his erudition, making all sorts of random remarks about cantharides, the upas, the manchineel, and the adder.

"I've even read that various people have been poisoned, doctor, really struck down suddenly by black puddings that had been smoked too much. At least so I read in a very impressive report drawn up by one of our leading pharmacists, one of our masters, the famous Cadet de Gassicourt!"

Madame Homais reappeared carrying one of those unsteady contraptions that have to be heated with a spirit lamp; for Homais believed in making his coffee at the table, having first roasted and ground the beans himself and then blended them.

"*Saccharum*, doctor?" he asked, passing the sugar.

Then he sent for all his children, curious to have the surgeon's opinion on their constitutions.

When Doctor Larivière was about to leave, Madame Homais

consulted him about her husband. He was "thickening his blood" by falling asleep every night after dinner.

"Oh, it's not his *blood* that's thick." And smiling a bit at his undetected joke at Homais, the doctor opened the door. But the pharmacy was crowded with people, and he had a great deal of trouble getting rid of Tuvache, who feared his wife had an inflammation of the lungs since she was always spitting into the fire; then of Binet, who sometimes had hunger pangs; of Madame Caron, who suffered from a prickling sensation; of Lheureux, who had dizzy spells; of Lestiboudois, who had rheumatism; and of Madame Lefrançois, who had heartburn. After the three horses finally went off, the consensus was that he had not been very gracious.

Public attention was distracted by the appearance of Monsieur Bournisien walking through the marketplace with the holy oils.

Homais, out of obligation to his principles, compared priests to crows attracted by the smell of death. The sight of a priest was personally distasteful to him: the cassock reminded him of a shroud and he cursed the one partly out of fear of the other.

Nevertheless, not flinching before what he called "his mission," he returned to the Bovary house with Canivet, whom Monsieur Larivière, before leaving, had strongly urged to remain; and had his wife not objected, he would have taken his two sons with him in order to accustom them to painful situations and to give them an object lesson, a solemn spectacle that they would remember later on.

When they entered the bedroom, they found it filled with a mournful solemnity. On the worktable, covered with a white napkin, were five or six small balls of cotton in a silver dish near a large crucifix between two lighted candles. Emma lay with her chin sunk on her breast; her eyes were unusually wide open, and her poor hands were grasping at the sheets in that terribly moving gesture of the dying that suggests that they already want to cover themselves with a winding sheet. Pale as a statue, his eyes red as coals, Charles, no longer crying, stood at the foot of the bed looking at her, while the priest, on one knee, was murmuring in a low voice.

She turned her head slowly and seemed suffused with joy at the sudden sight of the purple stole—probably rediscovering in this instant of extraordinary peace the lost ecstasy of her first flights of mysticism and beginning to have visions of eternal bliss.

The priest stood up to take hold of the crucifix. She stretched out her neck like one who is thirsty, and pressing her lips to the body of the Man-God, she placed on it, with all her fading strength, the most passionate kiss of love she had ever given. Then he recited the *Misereatur* and the *Indulgentiam,* dipped his right thumb into the oil, and began the unctions; first on the eyes, which had been so covetous of earthly splendors; then on the nostrils, avid for warm breezes and scents of love; then on the mouth, which had opened to emit lies, had groaned with pride, and had cried out in lust; then over the hands, which had reveled in sensual contacts; and finally on the soles of the feet, which had once moved so rapidly when she was hurrying to quench her desires and which now would walk no longer.

The priest wiped his fingers, threw the oil-soaked bits of cotton into the fire, and came back to sit near the dying woman, to tell her that now she must unite her sufferings to those of Jesus Christ and give herself up to Divine mercy.

As he ended his exhortations, he tried to place a consecrated candle in her hands, symbol of the celestial glories with which she would shortly be surrounded. Emma was too weak to close her fingers, and had it not been for Monsieur Bournisien, the candle would have fallen to the floor.

But she was no longer so pale, and her face wore an expression of serenity, as though the sacrament had cured her.

The priest did not fail to point this out. He even explained to Bovary that the Lord sometimes prolonged people's lives when He thought it necessary for their salvation; and Charles remembered the day when, as now, she was about to die and had received Holy Communion.

"Maybe we shouldn't give up hope," he thought.

Indeed, she was looking all around her, slowly, like someone waking from a dream. Then, in a clear voice she asked for her mirror, and she leaned over it awhile, big tears trickling from her eyes. Then she threw her head back with a sigh and fell back on the pillow.

Her breast began heaving rapidly. Her whole tongue protruded from her mouth; her rolling eyes grew pale, like two lamps about to die out. She might have been thought dead already except for the frightful pounding of her ribs, shaken by a furious breathing as though the soul were leaping to get free. Félicité knelt down before the crucifix, and even the pharmacist flexed his knees a bit, while Monsieur Canivet looked vaguely out into the square. Bournisien had begun to pray again, his face bowed over the edge of the bed, his long black cassock trailing behind him in the room. Charles was on his knees on the other side, his arms stretched out toward Emma. He had taken her hands and was holding them tightly, shuddering at each beat of her heart, as at the reverberation of a falling ruin. As the death rattle grew louder, the priest hurried his prayers. They mingled with Bovary's muffled sobs, and at times everything seemed to merge with the monotonous murmur of the Latin syllables that sounded like the tolling of a bell.

Suddenly there was a clatter of heavy clogs on the sidewalk and the tapping of a stick. Then a voice arose, singing raucously:

> *Often the warmth of a lovely day*
> *Makes a girl dream of love.*

Emma lifted herself up like a galvanized corpse, her hair undone, her eyes fixed and staring.

> *To gather up the corn*
> *That the scythe has reaped,*
> *My Nanette bends to the furrow*
> *In which it was born.*

"The blind man!" she cried. And she began to laugh—a horrible, frenzied, despairing laugh—imagining that she could see the hideous face of the beggar standing out against the eternal darkness like a nightmare.

> *There was a strong breeze that day*
> *And her short petticoat flew away!*

A convulsion pulled her back down on the mattress. They all drew near the bed. She was no more.

I X

There is always a kind of numbness after a person's death, so difficult is it to understand this new state of nonexistence and to accept the fact that it has occurred. But when he saw that she no longer moved, Charles threw himself on her and cried: "Good-bye! Good-bye!"

Homais and Canivet led him from the room. "Control yourself."

"All right," he said, trying to break free, "I'll be reasonable. I won't do anything wrong. But leave me alone. I want to see her. She's my wife." He began crying.

"Yes, cry," said the pharmacist, "let nature take its course. You'll feel better."

Weaker than a child, Charles let himself be led downstairs into the dining room. Monsieur Homais soon went home.

In the square he was accosted by the blind man who had dragged himself as far as Yonville, hoping to obtain the antiphlogistic salve, and now asked each passerby where the apothecary lived.

"Well! That's all I need! No, I can't do a thing right now. Come back later." And he hurried into his pharmacy.

He had to write two letters, prepare a sedative for Bovary, and think up a lie to conceal the poisoning for the *Rouen Beacon* obituary, as well as for the people waiting to hear the news from him. When all the people of Yonville had heard his story about Emma's mistaking arsenic for sugar while making a vanilla cream, Homais returned once more to the Bovary house.

He found Bovary alone (Monsieur Canivet had just left), seated in the armchair near the window and staring vacantly at the flagstones on the floor.

"Now you'll have to decide on the hour for the ceremony," said the pharmacist.

"Why? What ceremony?" Then, in a frightened voice, he stammered, "No, no, do I have to? I want to keep her here."

Homais, to maintain his composure, took a pitcher from the whatnot and watered the geraniums.

"Thank you," said Charles, "you are so kind." He suddenly stopped talking, overwhelmed by a flood of memories evoked by the pharmacist's gesture.

Homais thought he might distract him by talking about horticulture. "Plants need moisture," he said. Charles nodded his head in a sign of agreement. "Anyway, we'll soon have good weather."

"Ah!" said Bovary.

The apothecary, at a loss for subjects of conversation, began quietly to draw back the small curtains.

"Look, there's Monsieur Tuvache."

Charles repeated mechanically: "There's Monsieur Tuvache."

Homais did not dare mention the funeral plans again. It was the priest who finally persuaded Charles to make the arrangements.

He shut himself up in his consulting room, took a pen, sobbed for quite a while, then wrote: "I want her to be buried in her wedding dress, with white shoes and a wreath. Her hair is to be spread out over her shoulders. Three coffins—one of oak, one of mahogany, and one of lead. No one has to talk to me, I'll be strong enough. Let

328 ◆ GUSTAVE FLAUBERT

her be covered with a large piece of green velvet. These are my wishes. Carry them out."

The two men were greatly surprised at Bovary's romantic notions, and the pharmacist immediately said to him: "The velvet seems superfluous to me. Besides, the expense—"

"Is it any of your business?" shouted Charles. "Leave me alone! You didn't love her! Go away!"

The clergyman took him by the arm for a walk in the garden. He talked about the vanity of earthly things. God was great and good; we should submit to His decrees without complaining; we should even rejoice.

Charles burst out blaspheming: "I detest that God of yours!"

"The spirit of rebellion is still in you," sighed the cleric.

Bovary had walked away from him and was striding alongside the wall of trained fruit trees, grinding his teeth. He looked up to the heavens with curses in his eyes, but not a leaf stirred.

It was raining lightly. Charles, whose chest was uncovered, finally began to shiver. He went in the house and sat down in the kitchen.

At six o'clock a clanking of metal was heard in the square: The Hirondelle was arriving; and he glued his forehead to the windowpanes to watch the passengers get out of the carriage, one after the other. Félicité laid a mattress out for him in the parlor. He threw himself on it and fell asleep.

Philosopher that he was, Monsieur Homais still respected the dead. And so, without feeling bitter toward poor Charles, he came back in the evening to watch by the body, carrying with him three volumes and a writing pad for taking notes.

Monsieur Bournisien was already there. Two large candles were blazing at the head of the bed, which had been pulled out of the alcove.

The apothecary, oppressed by the silence, soon uttered a few sad remarks about "that unfortunate young woman." The priest answered that all one could do for her now was to pray.

"Yet," said Homais, "it can't be both ways. Either she died in a state of grace (as the Church puts it), in which case she doesn't need prayers; or she died unrepentant (I believe that's the ecclesiastical term), and in that case—"

Bournisien interrupted, replying in an irritable tone that one needed to pray, no matter what.

"But," the pharmacist objected, "since God knows all our needs, what's the use of prayer?"

"What do you mean?" asked the priest. "Prayer! Aren't you a Christian?"

"I beg your pardon," said Homais. "I admire Christianity. In the first place, it freed the slaves, introduced into the world a morality—"

"Never mind about that! All the texts—"

"Texts, bah! Open up the history books. We know they were falsified by the Jesuits."

Charles came in and walked toward the bed. He drew the curtains back slowly.

Emma's head was turned toward her right shoulder. The corner of her mouth (which was open) seemed like a black hole in the lower part of her face. Her two thumbs were flexed inwards toward her palms; a kind of white powder was scattered over her lashes and her eyes were beginning to disappear under a viscous pallor, as if spiders had spun a web over them. The sheet sagged between her breasts and her knees and then rose again over her toes, and it seemed to Charles that an infinite mass, an enormous weight, was pressing down on her.

The church clock struck two. They could hear the deep murmur of the river flowing past the terrace through the shadows. Monsieur Bournisien would occasionally blow his nose noisily, and Homais's pen kept scratching the paper.

"I think you should go back to bed, my good friend," he said. "The sight of her is tearing you apart."

After Charles left, the pharmacist and the curé resumed their discussion.

"Read Voltaire!" said the one. "Read D'Holbach!" said the other. "Read the encyclopedia!"

"Read the *Letters of Some Portuguese Jews*! Read *The Proof of Christianity* by Nicolas, a former judge!"

They grew heated, became red in the face, spoke simultaneously, neither listening to the other. Bournisien was shocked by such audacity, Homais amazed at such stupidity, and they were on the verge of insulting each other when Charles suddenly reappeared. He was drawn there by a relentless fascination and kept coming up the stairs.

He stationed himself opposite her to see her more clearly, and he lost himself in a contemplation so deep that it ceased to be painful.

He remembered stories he had heard about catalepsy and miracles of magnetism. He told himself that by wanting it very much he could perhaps succeed in bringing her back to life. Once he even leaned over her and cried in a very low voice: "Emma! Emma!" The force of his breath made the candleflames flicker against the wall.

His mother arrived at dawn the next day. Charles burst into fresh tears when he kissed her. She tried, as had the pharmacist, to say something to him about the funeral expenses. He became so furious that she stopped talking. He even told her to go into the city immediately to buy what was needed.

Charles remained alone all afternoon. Berthe had been taken to Madame Homais's. Félicité was upstairs in the bedroom with Madame Lefrançois.

Some visitors came in the evening. He would get up and shake hands without being able to speak, then the newcomer would sit down with the others, who had formed a large semicircle around the fireplace. They sat with their heads lowered and would dangle their crossed legs, sighing deeply now and then. They were all extremely bored, but no one wanted to be the first to go.

When Homais returned at nine (for the past two days he had been seen constantly in the square), he brought with him a supply of camphor, benzoin, and aromatic herbs. He also carried a vase filled with chlorine to purify the air.

Just then Madame Lefrançois, Félicité, and Madame Bovary senior were busy with the final stages of dressing Emma; they lowered the long stiff veil that covered her down to her satin slippers.

Félicité sobbed: "Oh! My poor mistress! My poor mistress!"

"Just look at her," sighed the landlady. "How pretty she still is. You'd swear she'd be getting up in a little while."

They leaned over to place the wreath on her head. It was necessary to lift the head slightly, and as they did this a stream of black liquid poured out of her mouth as if she were vomiting.

"Dear Lord! The dress! Take care!" shouted Madame Lefrançois. "Help us," she said to the pharmacist. "You're not afraid, are you?"

"Me afraid?" he answered, shrugging his shoulders. "Not me! I saw lots of them at the hospital when I was studying pharmacy. We would make punch in the dissecting room. Death doesn't frighten a philosopher. I even say quite often that I intend to bequeath my body to a hospital in order eventually to serve the cause of science."

When the curé arrived, he asked how Charles was and commented after the apothecary's reply: "The shock is still too fresh, you know."

Then Homais congratulated him at not being exposed, like everyone else, to the danger of losing a beloved mate. This gave rise to a discussion about celibacy of the clergy.

"It's not natural," said the pharmacist, "that a man should do without women. There have been crimes—"

"Bless me!" cried the clergyman. "How would you expect a man who was married to keep the secrets of the confessional?"

Homais attacked the confessional. Bournisien defended it; he dwelled on the acts of restitution it inspired. He cited several different instances of thieves suddenly becoming honest men. Soldiers,

Charles did not wake them when he came in. It was the last time. He had come to say farewell to her.

approaching the tribunal of penitence, had felt the scales falling from their eyes. There was a minister in Fribourg—

His companion was asleep. He himself felt a bit warm in the heavy atmosphere of the room and opened the window. This awakened the pharmacist.

"Have a pinch of snuff," he said. "Take it. It'll clear your head."

There was an incessant howling somewhere in the distance.

"Do you hear a dog barking?" asked the pharmacist.

"People say that they sense death," answered the priest. "It's the same with bees. They leave the hive when someone dies." Homais did not criticize these superstitions since he had fallen asleep again.

Monsieur Bournisien, more robust, continued to move his lips awhile longer. Then his chin dropped gradually; his thick black book slipped from his hand and he began to snore.

So they remained facing each other, paunches protruding, faces puffy and scowling, finally united in the same human frailty after so much disagreement. They budged no more than the corpse beside them, which appeared to be sleeping.

Charles did not wake them when he came in. It was the last time. He had come to say farewell to her.

The aromatic herbs were still smoking and wisps of blue vapor mingled at the window with the incoming fog. There were a few stars out. The night was mild.

The wax from the candles fell in large drops onto the bedsheets. Charles watched them burn, straining his eyes at the yellow flames.

On Emma's satin dress, as white as a ray of moonlight, the watered texture shimmered. She seemed to disappear beneath it; and it seemed to him that she was escaping from herself and had blended in a confused way with the surroundings and the silence, with the night and the passing breeze, with the damp odors that were rising.

He suddenly saw her in the garden at Tostes on the bench against the thorn hedge; or in the street in Rouen; on the doorstep of their house; in the yard at Les Bertaux. He could still hear the laughter of the boys dancing gaily beneath the apple trees. The room was filled with the scent of her hair, and her dress rustled in his arms, making a noise of crackling sparks. It was this same dress!

He stood a long time remembering his lost happiness, the way she carried herself, her gestures, the tone of her voice. After one wave of despair came another and still another, unceasingly, like the waters of an overflowing tide.

He was smitten by a terrible curiosity; slowly, with the tips of his fingers, his heart pounding, he lifted her veil. His cry of horror woke the other two men. They led him downstairs into the dining room. Then Félicité came up to say that he wanted a lock of her hair.

"Cut some off," said the apothecary. But she didn't dare, so he himself approached, the scissors in his hand. He was trembling so violently that he nicked the skin near the temples in several places. Finally, steeling himself against emotion, Homais made two or three random cuts which left white patches in the beautiful black hair.

The pharmacist and the curé resumed their occupations, not without occasional naps, of which they accused each other in turn each time they awoke. Then Monsieur Bournisien sprinkled the room with holy water and Homais threw some chlorine on the floor.

Félicité had set out for them, on the chest of drawers, a bottle of brandy, some cheese, and a large brioche. At about four in the morning the apothecary could stand it no longer.

"Lord," he sighed, "I'm really hungry."

The priest did not wait to be asked twice. He went out to say Mass and came back. Then they ate and drank, chuckling slightly without knowing why, enlivened by that vague feeling of gaiety that takes hold of us after gloomy vigils. As he drained his glass, the priest said to the pharmacist, throwing an arm over his shoulder: "We'll end up being friends!"

Downstairs in the hall they met the workers who were just arriving. For two hours Charles had to endure the torture of the hammer resounding on the wood. Then they brought her down in her oak coffin and enclosed it in the other two; but as the outer one was too large, they had to stuff the space between with the wool from a mattress. Finally, when the three lids were planed, nailed down, and soldered, they placed it in front of the door. The house was thrown open and the people of Yonville began to crowd in.

Old Rouault arrived and fainted away in the square at the sight of the black cloth.

X

He had not received the pharmacist's letter until thirty-six hours after the event; and out of consideration for his feelings, Monsieur Homais had written it in such a fashion that it was impossible for him to know what it was all about.

At first the old man collapsed as if struck down by apoplexy. Then he interpreted it to mean she *wasn't* dead. But she might be. . . . Finally he put on his smock, picked up his hat, strapped on his spurs, and went off at a gallop. All along the road he was breathless and torn by anguish. Once he even had to dismount. He could no longer see, began hearing voices around him, and felt he was going mad.

Day broke. He saw three black hens roosting in a tree and shuddered in terror at the omen. Then he promised the Blessed Virgin three chasubles for the church and vowed he would walk barefoot from the cemetery of Les Bertaux to the chapel at Vassonville.

He rode into Maromme, shouting for the innkeeper, elbowed his way through the stable door, headed for the oat sack, poured a bottle of sweet cider into the manger, and remounted his nag, whose feet struck fire as it flew off.

He told himself that they would surely save her. The doctors would certainly find a cure. He was sure of it. He reminded himself of all the miraculous cures he had heard of.

Then he had a vision of her dead—there she was before him,

336 ◆ GUSTAVE FLAUBERT

stretched out on her back in the middle of the road. He drew rein and the hallucination vanished.

At Quincampoix he drank three cups of coffee in a row to muster up his courage.

He thought that they might have made a mistake in the name. He felt for the letter in his pocket but did not dare open it.

Then he began to wonder if it were a practical joke on the part of someone who had a grudge against him. Besides, if she were dead, wouldn't he know it? But the countryside showed no unusual signs: the sky was blue, the trees swaying, a flock of sheep passed by. He caught sight of the village. They saw him rushing up on his horse, whipping it so furiously that its flanks dripped blood.

When he came to, he fell into Bovary's arms, crying: "My daughter! Emma! My child! Tell me—"

"I don't know, I don't know. It's a curse!" Charles replied, sobbing.

The apothecary separated them: "These dreadful details are useless. I'll explain things later. People are coming. Come now, be dignified! Be philosophical!"

The poor young man wanted to appear strong and he repeated several times: "Yes—courage!"

"All right then, me too," cried the old man. "I'll be brave, damn it all! I'll stay with her to the very end!"

The bell began tolling. Everything was ready. It was time to start out.

Sitting beside each other in a choir stall, they watched the three choristers constantly pass back and forth, chanting. The serpent player blew as hard as he could. Monsieur Bournisien, in full vestments, was singing in a shrill voice. He bowed before the tabernacle, lifted his hands, spread his arms. Lestiboudois moved about the church with his whalebone staff. The coffin had been placed near the lectern between four rows of candles. Charles felt like getting up and blowing them out.

He tried, however, to kindle a religious feeling in himself, to lose himself in the hope of a future life in which he would see her. He pretended that she had gone off long ago on a trip to a far-distant place. But when he remembered that she lay in that coffin there, that it was all over, that they were going to carry her off and place her in the earth, he was seized by a black, despairing, furious rage. At times he would think he no longer felt anything; and he welcomed this lessening of his misery, although reproaching himself for being heartless.

They heard a sharp, regular noise—like the tapping of a metal-tipped cane—on the flagstones. It came from the far end of the church and stopped short in the side aisle. A man in a coarse brown jacket kneeled with difficulty. It was Hippolyte, the stableboy of the Golden Lion. He had put on his new leg.

One of the choristers went around the nave to take up the collection. The heavy copper coins rang in the collection plate one after the other.

"Hurry up, please! I can't stand it!" cried Bovary, angrily throwing a five-franc piece at him.

The churchman thanked him with a low bow.

They sang, kneeled, arose. It seemed to go on and on! He remembered how, once, a long time ago, in the early days, they were seated side by side during Mass. They had been on the other side, on the right, against the wall. The bell began to toll again. There was a great scraping of chairs. The pallbearers slipped their three poles under the bier and left the church.

Just then Justin appeared on the threshold of the pharmacy. He suddenly went back in, pale and unsteady on his feet.

People were stationed at windows to watch the procession pass. Charles walked in front, holding himself erect. He tried to look brave and nodded to those who poured out of lanes and doorways to join with the crowd. The six men, three on each side, walked slowly, slightly out of breath. The priest, choristers, and the two choirboys were reciting the *De profundis*, and their voices rose and fell rhythmically over the countryside. Occasionally they would disappear as the path curved, but the great silver cross was always visible between the trees.

The women followed, wrapped in black mantles with the hoods lowered; they carried large lighted candles in their hands. Charles felt himself weakening at this constant succession of prayers and tapers beneath the cloying smell of wax and cassocks. A fresh breeze was blowing. The rye and the colza were turning green. Droplets of dew glistened on the thorn hedge by the side of the road. All sorts of joyous sounds filled the air: the clatter of a distant cart rolling over the ruts, the echoing cry of a cock, the sound of a foal scampering off beneath the apple trees. Pink clouds dotted the clear sky and a bluish haze hung over the iris-covered thatched cottages. Charles recognized the yards as he passed by. He remembered other mornings like this one when after visiting some of his patients he would return home to her.

The black pall, strewn with white teardrops like beads, would blow off at times and reveal the bier. The tired pallbearers were slowing down, and the bier advanced in a series of jerks like a boat tossing at every wave.

They arrived at the cemetery.

The men continued all the way to the far end to a place in the grass where the grave had been dug.

They gathered around it, and as the priest spoke, the red earth piled up at the edges slipped back into the corners—noiselessly and unceasingly.

Then, when the four ropes were in place, they pushed the coffin over them. He watched it go down. It went down, down. . . .

Finally a thud was heard. The ropes creaked as they came back up. Then Bournisien took the spade that Lestiboudois held out to him; with his left hand, all the while sprinkling holy water with the right, he vigorously pushed in a large spadeful of earth; and the wood of the coffin, hit by the stones, made that terrible noise that sounds like the echo of eternity.

The priest passed the sprinkler to his neighbor. This was Monsieur Homais. He shook it solemnly, then held it out to Charles, who fell to his knees on the ground, and threw handfuls of earth, crying: "Farewell!" He blew her kisses and crawled toward the grave to be swallowed up with her.

They led him away, and he soon grew calmer, sensing perhaps, like the rest of them, a vague feeling of relief that it was over.

On the way back old Rouault began quietly smoking his pipe, which Homais privately thought quite out of place. He also noticed that Binet had not shown up, that Tuvache "had slipped away" after the Mass, and that Theodore, the notary's manservant, wore a blue coat "as if he couldn't find a black one, since it's the custom, devil take it!" He went from one group to another, giving vent to his observations. They were all deploring Emma's death, especially Lheureux, who had not failed to come to the burial.

"Poor little woman! Such a tragedy for her husband!"

The apothecary said: "If it hadn't been for me, you know, he might have done something fatal to himself."

"Such a dear lady. And to think that I saw her in my shop only last Saturday."

"I didn't have the time to prepare a short speech to make over the grave," said Homais.

Charles changed his clothes when they returned home and Rouault put on his smock again. It was a new one, and as he had kept wiping his eyes with his sleeves on the road, some dye had come off on his face. Now there were traces of tears that still showed through the layer of dust covering it.

Madame Bovary senior was with them. All three were silent. Finally the old man sighed: "Do you remember, my friend, that time I came to Tostes when you lost your first wife? And I consoled you? Then I was able to find things to say; but now—" He heaved a deep sigh and groaned: "It's the end for me, you know. I saw my wife die, then my son, and today my daughter." He wanted to go right back to Les Bertaux, saying that he wouldn't be able to sleep in this house. He even refused to see his granddaughter.

"No, no, it would be too painful. But kiss her for me. Good-bye! You are a good lad. And you know, I'll never forget this," he said, smacking his thigh, "don't worry. You'll always have your turkey."

But when he reached the summit of the hill he turned back, as once before in parting from her he had turned around on the Saint-Victor road. The village windows were lit up by the oblique rays of the sun setting beyond the meadow. He shielded his eyes with his hand and looked in the distance, where he saw a walled enclosure in which the treetops showed black between white stones. Then he continued along the road at a slow trot, for his mare was limping.

Despite their weariness, Charles and his mother stayed up very late to talk. They discussed the old days and the future. She would come to live in Yonville and take care of the house. They would never part again. She was tactful and comforting, secretly rejoicing at having regained the affection that had eluded her so many years. Midnight sounded. The village, as usual, was silent. Charles, wide awake, lay thinking of her.

Rodolphe, who had been trapping in the woods all day to distract himself, slept peacefully in his château. Léon was sleeping too, in Rouen.

There was someone else who was not asleep at this hour. Between the firs, a kneeling boy was crying on her grave. His chest was shaking with sobs beneath the burden of great sorrow that was more tender than the moon and more unfathomable than the night. Suddenly the gate creaked. It was Lestiboudois, who had come to look for his spade, which he had forgotten earlier. He recognized Justin climbing the wall and then knew who the culprit was who had been stealing his potatoes.

The next day Charles sent for his daughter. She asked for Mama and was told she was away on a trip and would bring her back some toys. Berthe mentioned her mother several times again; then she gradually forgot her. Bovary felt sick at heart at the child's cheerfulness. The pharmacist's words of consolation also were hard to bear.

Money troubles soon started again, Lheureux again urging his friend Vinçart on. Charles signed notes for some exorbitant sums since he was determined not to let the least bit of furniture that had belonged to "her" be sold. His mother was furious with him. He grew angrier than she. He had changed completely. She left the house for good.

Then everyone began taking advantage of him. Mademoiselle Lempereur sent a bill for six months' worth of piano lessons, even though Emma had never taken a single one, despite the receipt she had shown him—that had been an arrangement between the two women. The lending library sent in a bill for three years of subscription. Madame Rollet, the wet nurse, asked to be paid for delivering twenty letters, and when Charles asked for an explanation, had the tact to answer: "Oh, I've no idea. Personal matters, I think."

Each time he settled a debt, Charles thought it was the last, but others continually cropped up.

He sent out bills for outstanding accounts. He was shown letters his wife had sent, and so he had to apologize.

Félicité now wore Emma's dresses; not all of them, for he had kept some and would shut himself up in her dressing room to look at them. The maid was about her height, and often, seeing her from behind, Charles would be seized by an illusion and cry out: "Oh! Stay! Please stay!"

But at Whitsuntide she ran away from Yonville with Theodore, stealing all that remained of the wardrobe.

About this time the Widow Dupuis had the honor to announce to him the "marriage of her son, Monsieur Léon Dupuis, notary in Yvetot, to Mademoiselle Léocadie Leboeuf, of Bondeville." In the congratulatory letter he sent her, Charles wrote this phrase: "How happy my poor wife would have been!"

One day as he was roaming aimlessly through the house, he climbed up to the attic. He felt a ball of thin paper beneath his slipper. He opened it and read: "Be brave, Emma. Be brave. I don't want to ruin your life." It was Rodolphe's letter. It had fallen to the floor between the trunks and had remained there until the wind coming in through the window pushed it toward the door. Charles stood there without moving, gaping at it—in the same spot where a desperate Emma, paler than he, had once wanted to die. Finally he made out a small *R* at the bottom of the second page. Who was it? He remembered Rodolphe's assiduous attentions, his sudden disappearance, and his air of constraint the two or three times they had met since. But the respectful tone of the letter fooled him.

"Maybe they loved each other platonically," he told himself.

Anyhow, Charles was not the sort of man who went right to the heart of things. He shut his eyes to the evidence, and his vague jealousy was lost in the immensity of his sorrow.

They all must have adored her, he thought. Certainly every man must have desired her. She appeared even more beautiful to him because of this; and he conceived for her a permanent, maddening desire that intensified his despair and that was limitless since it could never be satisfied.

To please her, as if she were still alive, he adopted her preferences and ideas. He bought himself patent-leather boots, began wearing white cravats. He waxed his moustache, signed promissory notes as she had done. She was corrupting him from beyond the grave.

He was obliged to sell the silverware, piece by piece, then the parlor furniture. All the rooms were stripped; but the bedroom, *her* bedroom, remained as it always had been. Charles would go up there after dinner. He would push the round table to the fire, pull up *her* armchair, and sit down facing it. A candle would burn in the gilded candlesticks. Berthe would sit near him, coloring pictures.

The poor man suffered to see her so badly dressed, her shoes without laces and the armholes of her smocks torn to the hips, for the housekeeper paid no attention to her. But she was so sweet and gentle, and her tiny head bent forward so graciously, dropping her blond hair over pink cheeks, that he was filled with infinite delight, with a pleasure laced with bitterness like badly made wines tasting of resin. He mended her toys, made cardboard puppets for her, or

He would push the round table to the fire, pull up her armchair, and sit down facing it.

sewed up the torn bodies of her dolls. If his eyes happened to light on the workbox, a dangling ribbon, or even a pin stuck in a crack of the table, he would begin to dream; and then he looked so sad that she would feel sad too.

No one came to see them now, for Justin had run off to Rouen, where he became a grocer's assistant, and the apothecary's children mingled less and less with Berthe. Monsieur Homais did not care to prolong the intimacy in view of their different social stations.

The blind man, who had not been helped at all by his salve, had returned to the Bois-Guillaume hill, where he told travelers of the pharmacist's vain attempt. It got so bad that Homais, when he went into the city, cringed behind the curtains of the Hirondelle to avoid meeting him. He hated him. For the sake of his own reputation, he sought to get rid of him by any means; so he launched a secret campaign against him, which revealed both the depth of his cunning and the viciousness of his vanity. For six months in a row paragraphs like this could be read in the *Rouen Beacon:*

> Travelers to the fertile fields of Picardy have probably noticed, on the Bois-Guillaume hill, a wretched creature afflicted with a horrible facial wound. He annoys travelers, persecutes them, imposes a veritable tax on them. Are we still in those monstrous days of the Middle Ages when vagabonds were permitted to display in our public places the leprosy and scrofula they had brought back from the Crusades?

Or:

> Despite the laws against vagrancy, the approaches to our large cities continue to be infested by bands of the poor. Among them are some who move about alone and who perhaps are not the least dangerous. What is the municipal government going to do about it?

Then Homais invented anecdotes:

Yesterday, on the Bois-Guillaume hill, a skittish horse— And then followed the story of an accident caused by the presence of the blind man.

He did such a good job that they jailed the blind man. But he was let out and began again. So did Homais. It was a battle. Homais was the victor, for his enemy was permanently committed to an asylum.

This success emboldened him. From then on there wasn't a dog run over in the district, a barn burned down, a wife beaten up that Homais did not immediately relate to the public, always guided by his love of progress and hatred of priests. He drew comparisons between public and parochial schools, to the detriment of the latter; he mentioned the Saint Bartholomew Massacre in connection with a one-hundred-franc grant to the Church; he denounced abuses and launched, to use his word, fireworks.

Homais was "undermining foundations"; he was becoming dangerous.

But he felt stifled in the narrow lines of journalism. He wanted to write a book, a "work"! So he composed his *General Statistical Survey of the Canton of Yonville,* followed by *Climatological Observations.* Statistics led him toward philosophy. He began to concentrate on major issues: social problems, morals of the poor classes, fish breeding, rubber, railroads, etc. He began to feel ashamed about being a bourgeois. He affected "the artistic approach," took up smoking, bought two chic Pompadour statuettes to decorate his parlor.

He did not give up the pharmacy. On the contrary, he kept abreast of all discoveries. He followed every stage in the development of chocolates; he was the first to introduce the chocolate foods, *Cho-ca* and *Revalentia* into the Seine-Inférieure district. He was smitten with enthusiasm for the Pulvermacher hydroelectric belts and

346 ♦ GUSTAVE FLAUBERT

wore one himself. In the evening, when he removed his flannel undershirt, Madame Homais was dazzled by the golden spiral under which he almost disappeared. She felt her passion redoubled for this man more swathed than a Scythian and as splendid as a Magian priest.

He had some elaborate notions for Emma's tombstone. First he suggested a broken column with drapery, then a pyramid, then a Vestal temple, a sort of rotunda—or even a "pile of ruins." And in all his plans he included a weeping willow, which he considered the obligatory symbol of sorrow.

Charles and he traveled to Rouen together to see some tombstones at a monument works. They were accompanied by an artist named Vaufrilard, a friend of Bridoux, who kept making puns. Finally, after examining a hundred designs, asking for an estimate, and making a second trip to Rouen, Charles decided on a mausoleum that was to bear on its two main sides "a spirit carrying an extinguished torch."

For the inscription, Homais found nothing as impressive as *Sta viator* and that was as far as he could get. He racked his brain, constantly repeating *Sta viator*. Finally he discovered *amabilem conjugem calcas*—and this was adopted.

It was strange how Bovary was forgetting Emma, even while thinking continually about her. He was in despair when he found her image fading from his memory despite all his efforts to retain it. And yet he dreamed of her each night, always the same dream: he approached her, but she would crumble into dust before he could embrace her.

For one whole week he was seen entering the church every night. Monsieur Bournisien even visited him two or three times, then gave him up. Anyhow, the old man was becoming intolerant and fanatic, said Homais; he was thundering against the spirit of the times and never failed to preach every second week about the agony of Voltaire—who died eating his own excrement, as everyone knows.

Despite the frugal way Bovary lived, he was quite unable to pay off his old debts. Lheureux refused to renew a single note. Dispossession was imminent. Then he had recourse to his mother, who consented to let him take a mortgage on her property—but not without indulging in a good many recriminations against Emma. In return for her sacrifice, she asked for a shawl that had escaped Félicité's clutches. Charles refused to give it to her. They quarreled.

She made the first overtures toward reconciliation by suggesting that she take in the child, who would be a comfort to her in the house. Charles consented. But his courage failed him at the moment of parting. This time it was a permanent and complete break.

As his other ties weakened, he devoted himself more and more to his daughter. But he was worried about her. She coughed sometimes and she had red splotches on her cheeks.

Across the square, cheerful and flourishing, the pharmacist's family grew. Everything was going well with him. Napoleon helped in the laboratory; Athalie embroidered a cap for him; Irma cut out paper tops to cover the jam jars; and Franklin could recite the multiplication table all in one breath. He was the happiest of fathers, the most fortunate of men.

But a secret ambition was gnawing at him. Homais wanted the cross of the Legion of Honor. He did not lack the proper qualifications:

1. He had displayed an unlimited devotion at the time of the cholera epidemic.
2. He had published at his own expense various works for the public welfare, such as (a) his memorandum *Cider, Its Manufacture and its Effects;* (b) his observations on the woolly aphis, sent to the Academy; (c) his volume of statistics, and even his pharmacist's thesis, not to mention his membership in "several scientific societies" (he was member of one).

"Were it only," he exclaimed, swiveling around, "my distinguished record as a volunteer fireman!"

Then Homais cultivated the powers that be. He secretly rendered important services to the prefect during the elections. In short, he sold himself; he prostituted himself. He even addressed a petition to the king in which he asked that "justice be done." He called him "Our Good King" and compared him to Henri IV.

Every morning the apothecary would tear open the newspaper to look for his nomination; it did not appear. Finally, in his impatience, he had a star of the Cross of Honor designed in his garden plot, with two small tufts of grass running off at the top to imitate the ribbon. He would walk around it with his arms crossed, pondering the ineptness of the government and the ingratitude of men.

Out of respect, or from a kind of perverse sensuality that caused him to proceed slowly in his investigations, Charles had not yet opened the secret compartment of a rosewood desk that Emma had always used. But one day he finally sat down before it, turned the key, and pushed the spring.

All of Léon's letters were there. This time, there could be no doubt! He devoured them to the very end, searched every corner, all the furniture, all the drawers, felt behind the walls, sobbed violently, screamed, crazed with rage. He found a box and kicked it open. Rodolphe's portrait stared out at him full in the face, in the midst of a jumble of love letters.

His depression astounded people. He never went out any more, received no one, even refused to call on his patients. It was assumed that he had "locked himself up to get drunk."

Sometimes, however, some curious soul would look over the hedge and gaze in amazement at this unkempt, bearded man dressed in filthy clothes, crying aloud wildly as he walked in the garden.

In the summer evenings he would take the little girl with him and go to the cemetery. They would return at nightfall when there was no more light in the square except for Binet's window.

But he could not indulge his sadness to the full since there was no one around to share it with. So he would visit Madame Lefrançois to be able to talk of *her*. The landlady heeded him with only one ear, however, having her own troubles, as he had his. For Monsieur Lheureux had finally set up *les favorites du commerce,* and Hivert, who had earned a good reputation for running errands, was demanding more money and threatening to hire himself out to her competitor.

One day when Charles had gone to the Argueil market to sell his horse, his last asset, he met Rodolphe.

They paled, seeing each other. Rodolphe, who had merely sent his card when Emma died, stammered out some excuses at first, then grew bolder, and even had the nerve (it was August and a very warm day) to invite him to take a bottle of beer in the tavern.

Facing him, with his elbows on the table, Rodolphe chewed his cigar as he spoke, and Charles lost himself in daydreams about this face that she had loved. In it, he felt as if he were seeing something of her again. It was very strange. He would have liked to be this man.

The other man continued to talk about farming, livestock, manure, stopping up with conventional phrases all the gaps into which an embarrassing allusion might have slipped. Charles was not listening. Rodolphe noticed this and studied the passage of his memories on his mobile face. It reddened after a while, the nostrils twitched, and the lips trembled. There was even an instant when Charles, filled with somber fury, fixed his eyes on Rodolphe, who stopped talking out of fear. But very soon the same mournful lassitude reappeared on his face.

"I don't blame you," he said.

Rodolphe remained mute. Charles, with his head in his hands, repeated in a muffled voice and in a resigned tone of infinite sadness: "No, I don't blame you, anymore."

He even added a rhetorical phrase, the only one he ever uttered: "Fate is to blame."

Rodolphe, who had manipulated that fate, found him much too easygoing for a man in his situation—rather comic and even a bit contemptible.

The next day Charles sat down on the bench in the arbor. Rays of light passed through the trellis; the vine leaves cast their shadows over the gravel, the jasmine scented the air, the sky was blue, beetles buzzed about the blossoming lilies. Charles was choking up like an adolescent in love in the vague flood of emotion that swelled his unhappy heart.

Berthe, who had not seen him all afternoon, came to fetch him for dinner at seven.

His head was thrown back against the wall. His eyes were closed, mouth open, and in his hand he held a long strand of black hair.

"Come, Papa," she said. Thinking he wanted to play, she pushed him gently. He fell to the ground. He was dead.

Thirty-six hours later, in response to the apothecary's request, Monsieur Canivet came. He performed an autopsy but found nothing.

When everything was sold, there remained twelve francs and seventy-five centimes—enough to pay for Mademoiselle Bovary's fare to her grandmother's. The old lady died that same year. Since old Rouault was now paralyzed, an aunt took her in. She is poor and has sent her to work in a cotton mill to earn a living.

Since Bovary's death, three doctors have succeeded one another in Yonville without being able to establish themselves, so effectively does Monsieur Homais rout them. He has an enormous clientele. The authorities cultivate him and public opinion protects him.

He has just received the Legion of Honor.

SUGGESTIONS FOR FURTHER READING

Biography

Flaubert, Gustave. *The Letters of Gustave Flaubert: 1830–1857* (vol. I), and *1857–1880* (vol. II), translated and edited by Francis Steegmuller. Cambridge: Harvard University Press, 1980–82. These incomparable letters and Steegmuller's excellent notes and commentary provide the best possible introduction to the heart and mind of Flaubert.

Flaubert, Gustave and Sand, George. *Flaubert–Sand: The Correspondence,* translated from the French by Francis Steegmuller (Flaubert) and Barbara Bray (Sand); with a Foreword by Steegmuller. New York: Alfred A. Knopf, 1993. An engrossing epistolary conversation between two of the greatest and most colorful writers of the nineteenth century.

Flaubert, Gustave and Turgenev, Ivan. *Flaubert & Turgenev: A Friendship in Letters.* New York: W. W. Norton & Company, 1985. Of these two literary giants and their intimate friendship, Guy de Maupassant wrote: "Affinities of talent, philosophy and mind, similarities in taste, life and dreams, a convergence of literary tendencies, in exalted ideals, in admiration and in erudition established between them so many points of perpetual contact."

Lottman, Herbert. *Gustave Flaubert: A Biography.* New York: Little, Brown and Company, 1989. A recent, very readable, and entertaining portrait of Flaubert.

STARKIE, ENID. *Flaubert: The Making of the Master*. New York: Atheneum, 1967.

STARKIE, ENID. *Flaubert the Master: A Critical and Biographical Study (1856–1880)*. New York: Atheneum, 1971.

CRITICISM

AUERBACH, ERICH. "In the Hôtel de la Mole," in *Mimesis: The Representation of Reality in Western Literature*. Princeton: Princeton University Press, 1953.

BAUDELAIRE, CHARLES. *"Madame Bovary* by Gustave Flaubert." First published in French in 1857. Now available in translation in Baudelaire, Charles, *Selected Writings on Art and Artists*, translated by P. E. Charvet. Harmondsworth, England: Penguin Books, 1972. A brilliant review which, not surprisingly, greatly pleased Flaubert. Of Emma, Baudelaire writes: "[T]his woman is truly great, but, above all, worthy of pity, and, despite the systematic inflexibility of the author . . . all women with intellectual pretensions will be grateful to him for having developed the feminine potential to such a degree of power, so far removed from the pure animal, so close to the ideal man, and for having made it reflect that dual character, compounded of calculation and reverie, that constitutes the perfect being."

BROMBERT, VICTOR. *The Novels of Flaubert: A Study of Themes and Techniques*. Princeton: Princeton University Press, 1968.

JAMES, HENRY. "Gustave Flaubert." Important and acute essay, written as an introduction to a 1902 translation of *Madame Bovary*, and reprinted in *Notes on Novelists* (1914). Available (with two additional essays on Flaubert) in James, Henry, *Literary Criticism*. New York: The Library of America, 1984.

KENNER, HUGH. *Flaubert, Joyce and Beckett: The Stoic Comedians*. Boston: Beacon Press, 1962.

LACAPRA, DOMINICK. *Madame Bovary on Trial*. Ithaca, N.Y.: Cornell University Press, 1982.

LLOYD, ROSEMARY. *Madame Bovary.* London; Boston: Unwin Hyman, 1990. Fresh and insightful.

NABOKOV, VLADIMIR. "Madame Bovary (1856)," in *Lectures on Literature.* New York: Harcourt Brace Jovanovich, 1980. This volume also contains brilliant and greatly enjoyable lectures on Austen, Dickens, Stevenson, Kafka, and Joyce.

PROUST, MARCEL. "To Be Added to Flaubert" (1910) and "On Flaubert's Style" (1920), both essays in *Against Sainte-Beuve, and Other Essays.* Harmondsworth, England: Penguin Books, 1988.

STEEGMULLER, FRANCIS. *Flaubert and Madame Bovary: A Double Portrait.* Chicago: University of Chicago Press, 1977 (rev. edition). A classic.

TILLET, MARGARET G. *On Reading Flaubert.* London: Oxford University Press, 1961.

VARGAS LLOSA, MARIO. *The Perpetual Orgy: Flaubert and Madame Bovary.* New York: Farrar, Straus and Giroux, 1986. For Julian Barnes, an "unconventional, shiningly intelligent and fiercely sensible homage" to Flaubert and the "best single account" of *Madame Bovary.*

WILSON, EDMUND. "Flaubert's Politics," in *The Triple Thinkers: Ten Essays on Literature.* New York: Harcourt, Brace and Company, 1938.

OF RELATED INTEREST

ALLEN, WOODY. "The Kugelmass Episode," in *Side Effects.* New York: Random House, 1980. A magician promises Kugelmass, a City College humanities professor who wants to add some romance to his life, that he will arrange for him to "meet any of the women created by the world's best writers." Kugelmass chooses Emma Bovary.

BARNES, JULIAN. *Flaubert's Parrot.* New York: McGraw-Hill, 1985. The much acclaimed novel which, according to the critic Roger Shattuck, offers the reader "the notes and fantasies of a fanatic and fetishistic amateur scholar unable to organize a book."

FLAUBERT, GUSTAVE. *The Dictionary of Accepted Ideas.* New York: New Directions, 1968. A priceless treasury assembled by Flaubert during a lifetime's obsession with the trite and the idiotic.

GRAY, FRANCINE DU PLESSIX. "PASSION IN A PASTORAL MENAGE," IN *Condé Nast Traveler*, November 1991 (volume 26, number 12). A new film by Claude Chabrol has reincarnated Emma Bovary, and the author "tracks the rich local roots of Flaubert's masterpiece."

GRAY, FRANCINE DU PLESSIX. *Rage and Fire: A Life of Louise Colet: Pioneer Feminist, Literary Star, and Flaubert's Muse.* New York: Simon & Schuster, 1994.

CHECKLIST OF
ILLUSTRATIONS

All of the illustrations in this edition are from the collections of The New York Public Library's Center for the Humanities, as specifically noted below.

Cover and title page: Portrait of Gustave Flaubert, wood-engraving, after the 1864 photograph by Felix Nadar, from "Meyers Historisch-Geographischer Kalendar" for December 12, 1908.
Miriam and Ira D. Wallach Division of Art, Prints and Photographs

Pages x, 2, 29, 51, 66, 94, 114, 160, 187, 212, 221, 244, 313, 332, 343: Etchings by C. Chessa after drawings by Alfred de Richemont from Gustave Flaubert, *Madame Bovary* (Paris: A. Ferroud, 1905).
Spencer Collection

Pages xii, xiv, xvii, xxi: Pages from the hand- and typewritten manuscript of Vladimir Nabokov's lectures on *"Madame Bovary,"* 56 sheets, heavily revised and annotated, comprising a series of lectures delivered at Cornell University, ca. 1950s.
The Henry W. & Albert A. Berg Collection of English and American Literature

Page xxiii: A page from Vladimir Nabokov's copy of Gustave Flaubert, *Madame Bovary*, translated by Francis Steegmuller (New York: Random House, 1957), with annotations in Nabokov's hand.

The Henry W. & Albert A. Berg Collection of English and American Literature

Page xxvi: Binding of dark blue crushed morocco by Gruel, 1907, for Gustave Flaubert, *Madame Bovary* (Paris: A. Ferroud, 1905). No. 72 of 200 copies on Japan or wove paper; this copy on wove paper, initialed by F. Ferroud.
Spencer Collection

Page 1: Title page with etching by C. Chessa after drawings by Alfred de Richemont from Gustave Flaubert, *Madame Bovary* (Paris: A. Ferroud, 1905).
Spencer Collection

Page 282: Etching by E. Abot et D. Mordant after drawing by Albert-Auguste Fourié from Gustave Flaubert, *Madame Bovary* (Paris: A. Quantin, 1885).
General Research Division